17/4

1 2 APR 201

Murder
in the
Rain

by

C. G. Rainsford

✳ ✳ ✳

Grosvenor House
Publishing Limited

The book cover picture is copyright to Inmagine Corp LLC

This book is published by
Grosvenor House Publishing Ltd
28-30 High Street, Guildford, Surrey, GU1 3HY.
www.grosvenorhousepublishing.co.uk

A CIP record for this book
is available from the British Library

ISBN 978-1-907211-99-7

DEDICATION

You know who you are; friend of
Oscar

* * * * * * * *

Chapter One

Sally Cooper cried out an instant before a large fist banged into her right eye, sending her staggering backwards against the dirty plates stacked on the draining board. Her eye burned in agony, and her legs threatened to collapse beneath her. She felt dizzy; her fingers grappled with the draining board to keep her upright. If she went down now he would kick her as well.

"That's what you get when you talk back to me!" her husband growled, pointing a thick, index finger at her. "I don't care if every bloody train on that line was cancelled. You make sure you leave your job in time to have my dinner ready when I come in, and no excuses; understand?"

Sally nodded, gasping from the shock.

She desperately wanted to cry, but she knew it would be the wrong thing to do. Robert hated her crying, especially when he was drunk: it made him mad.

"Well, you better understand," Robert warned. "Now, put my dinner on and hurry up about it. I'm starving."

A low sob left Sally's lips as her husband's six foot, hulking body staggered out of the kitchen.

Another sob escaped, and she quickly covered her mouth to stifle the torrent of emotions that threatened to follow it. She must pull herself together or he would come back.

Trying to ignore the burning in her eye and the dull pain that was radiating outwards from her cheekbone, Sally began the process of cooking Robert's dinner.

With trembling hands she put the potatoes in a saucepan of water, and placed it on the infra-red hob.

It would be thirty minutes before she could cook the peas and steak, so she sat at the glass-top, kitchen table to recover, and reflect on what it meant to still be married to Robert Cooper after two years. Of course she knew at the end of the first year that staying with him was going to be difficult, because that was when he began to change; to become violent. And it had turned out to be even more difficult than she expected. But she had considered her position the first time he hit her, and committed herself to a certain course of action that was beyond the tolerance of most women. She needed answers to what was wrong with her husband, and she was going to get them; one way or another. Because, as far as she was concerned, no one could change like that; not without something terrible happening to them.

In the early days of the change, she had asked many times what was wrong. And at first it seemed that he wanted to tell her, but couldn't, for some reason. She had seen the desperation in his eyes as his lips performed difficult, silent words, and her heart was saddened by his torment. But when his struggles to answer began to lead to outbursts of rage, she stopped asking.

Thirty minutes later she went to the fridge to get the large piece of rib-eye steak.

Her heart almost stopped when an empty space, where the steak should have been, greeted her.

"No. Oh no. Please, God, no!"

She straightened up, frantic for an explanation.

The fingers of her right hand ran through her blonde hair, in confusion.

Where was it?

She had definitely bought it at the supermarket on her way home: she remembered putting it in its own plastic bag to keep it away from the butter and cooked ham. It had to be somewhere.

Then a terrifying thought grabbed at her throat and squeezed, making her gasp. She must have left it behind!

She must go back for it. He was drunk, angry and hungry. He would kill her if he found out what she had done.

She turned to run from the kitchen, but spotted something white sticking out from under the table.

She flew towards it and banged her forehead on the thick glass when she bent down.

Ignoring the pain, she grabbed the bag and the lightweight object inside it sent her almost hysterical with relief.

The steak; oh thank god! It must have fallen out earlier when she put the shopping away.

"How much longer is my dinner going to be?" Robert's deep voice called out from the living-room.

"Not long now," Sally called back. "I'm just putting your steak in the frying pan."

"Make sure it's medium rare," Robert ordered. "Last time it was so overcooked you couldn't cut it with a scalpel. And it was a bloody waste of money; my money. That shitty little job of yours wouldn't bring in enough to feed a cat, if we had one."

For the first time that day, Sally felt anger. And when she retrieved the frying pan from the cupboard and put it down on the hob, she did so with force.

There was a satisfying clang.

"What the hell are you doing out there?" Robert's tone was still aggressive. "You better not have dropped my steak on the floor. Because if you have, you can go right back to the supermarket for another one. And you can eat the one you dropped. I won't see good food go to waste, especially not when it's my money that's paying for it."

Sally threw the steak into the pan and stabbed at it repeatedly with a fork. "I hope you choke on the bloody thing," she muttered.

Grumbling then came from the living-room. Sally couldn't make out what was being said, but she didn't need to: it was only more stupid threats.

In the living-room Sally watched her husband eating his dinner from his lap.

The TV was on and highlights of an earlier game of football were showing.

Robert alternated between looking at the TV and looking at his plate.

The cutlery was small in his big, fat hands.

She grimaced as she observed. Pity he didn't play the game instead of just watching it. What had happened to him? When they first met, he was slim; a little over twelve stone, which was just right for his height. Now he was tipping seventeen stone: his full head of, once Raven black, hair was now almost entirely grey, despite him being only thirty-three years of age. And his bloated face reminded her of Bernard Manning, whereas it had been his Tom Cruise looks that first attracted her to him. And why had his appetite grown so much over the last twelve months? It wasn't as if her cooking had improved, or that he started eating out; he had become far too mean for that. No, he began complaining about the size of the portions she was giving him, and as his weight grew, it seemed so did his anger. Something had brought about the awful change that turned him from a handsome, caring, witty, fun-loving young man, into a fat, violent, foul-mouth slob.

It couldn't be another woman: affairs usually made men happy. It was unlikely that he had a long-term illness: surely his weight would have reduced if he had. What on Earth could it be? If she could just find out, she might be able to do something about it. And then all she had put up with would be worth it. Above all things she wanted her loving husband back and there was nothing she wouldn't put up with to achieve that. After all, hadn't they both declared on their wedding day: a day still so fresh in her mind, to love in sickness and in health.

She jerked with fright.

Robert had stopped eating and was staring at her; his mouth half open; revealing his last mouthful of food.

She had been caught out. God, how could she have been so stupid. But it was too late to look away now. She must hold her nerve.

Robert swallowed, then his flabby face took on an awful, irritated look that was as often as not a precursor to violence. "What the hell are you staring at me like that for?" he demanded. "If you are trying to wind me up, you are doing a good job."

"I was just checking that you were enjoying the steak," she replied hurriedly. "I did my best to make sure it was done exactly how you like it. It is tender, isn't it? I only cooked it for three minutes each side, so it should be."

This explanation seemed to appease Robert. And after a single grunt, he returned to eating.

She made sure she wasn't caught staring again.

Chapter Two

The next morning at the breakfast table, Robert was reading a copy of The Guardian as he ate his toast. It was 6:45. He didn't need to leave for his job in Moorgate until 8:15, so he was in a relaxed frame of mind.

Sally, sitting opposite, was relieved that he had obviously drunk beer instead of whisky the evening before. Beer made him less prone to picking an argument the following morning and then promising to continue it when he came home from work. Arguments in the evenings were particularly dangerous affairs.

Of course, she took no pleasure these days in sharing the breakfast table with her husband, but he insisted, explaining that it was expected; traditional, and he was a great believer in tradition. But this left her sitting in silence, and that was intolerable. The lack of conversation, and the occasional rustling of Robert's newspaper always reminded her of some dismal waiting room, and so she felt a strong need to change it. Her kitchen should never be like this.

"How are things going at work?" she asked, stirring her tea.

Robert kept reading. "What was that, Sal?"

"I was wondering how things are going in the job? Any interesting discoveries?"

"No, darling."

"Really - nothing at all?" Sally replied, surprised.

Robert shrugged and scratched the back of his head. "Not a sausage, darling."

Robert's lack of annoyance at being questioned gave Sally encouragement. "But you used to find all sorts of unusual things when we were first married. Like that time a house by the Thames began to subside, and when you started work on it you discovered part of a two thousand year old ship under the foundations. It was in all the newspapers: even on the TV."

"Well, I haven't found any more ships," Robert muttered, turning a page.

5

"Surely there must have been something since?" Sally protested.

"I just told you there wasn't," Robert replied firmly.

"Perhaps you have just got used to them and don't bother to tell me?" Sally pressed on. "But I would like to hear about them. I love discoveries: it must be very exciting to be there when an important one is made?"

Robert slowly closed the paper and stared at her. His once prominent, pale blue eyes, now looking small and hooded due to being framed in fat, became hard and accusing. "What is this? Are you planning to chuck in that shitty little job of yours and become a structural engineer like me, are you? Maybe you think you could do as good a job as me. Maybe you think you could do a better job than me. Is that what this is all about, Sal?"

Sally couldn't help the annoyance that jumped into her voice. "Don't be stupid. You know very well I have no interest in engineering of any kind. I was just making conversation, and there's no need to make an argument out of it."

Robert continued to stare at Sally for a moment, deciding how to react to her defiance. Then he pulled a sour face. "If you must know, I haven't discovered a bloody thing - satisfied now - can I carry on with my breakfast in peace."

"You could have told me without being so rude about it," Sally chided.

"If I'm rude it's because you're spoiling my breakfast with your constant nattering," said Robert.

She clenched her fists. "I'm not nattering. What's wrong with a wife wanting to talk to her husband at the breakfast table?"

Anger distorted Robert's face. "If you don't bloody shut up, I'll come over and show you!"

Fear instantly replaced Sally's annoyance. "I'm sorry, I didn't mean to upset you," she said in a low voice and staring at her cup.

She could feel Robert's eyes still on her, knowing that his anger was battling to be expressed, though he never hit her in the mornings. But there was always the chance that could change.

Then she heard him opening his paper.

She gave a shuddering sigh of relief. Fool, she had nearly set him off again. She knew better than to antagonize him, so why did she do it? In some deep, subconscious level was it deliberate? Did she so badly want to see him irritated that she was willing to risk his violence?

Then she pushed the thought away. No, all she was doing was trying to engage her husband in conversation, just like women all over the country. It wasn't her fault that Robert had become unapproachable - had become a cold-hearted bully.

An hour later, Robert had left for work and Sally was in the bathroom examining her face for a second time. The injury to her forehead from her encounter with the table; an angry red patch last night, was now nothing more than a pale, soft lump. The redness beneath her eye was also hardly noticeable. Being hungry, Robert obviously hadn't intended to badly injure her. Yes the blow was powerful; nearly dropping her to the floor, but it wasn't one of his hardest - those could fracture bones and tear muscles, as she had discovered to her cost. At least she would soon be on her way to work instead of the hospital. And a bit of disfigurement-concealing makeup would help prevent any awkward questions from the staff in the insurance office where she worked three days a week: three glorious days when she could completely forget about her problems.

If her work colleagues knew the full extent of what she was going through, she probably wouldn't be able to prevent them from charging around to confront Robert, and dishing out a little violence of their own. So she made a point of never bringing up the subject or offering any information when the girls did. Of course, they knew Robert was responsible for at least some of the injuries they saw, but her denials were so fiercely emphatic, they always backed down. They probably suspected she would leave the job if they ever forced the issue.

It was a puzzle to her that Robert hadn't tried to prevent her working, but she had a suspicion that he would miss referring to it as your shitty little job if he forced her to give it up. But at least in that little game the victory was hers. She could put up with the name-calling, and a great deal more, because she took so much pleasure in getting ready to go to Chapman's Insurance - chatting to the girls in the office, and to the never-ending computer work, which the others found tedious, but she didn't. Even boredom could be a luxury under certain circumstances.

In one other important aspect she was also victorious. For despite Robert's brutality, she could still claim to be an attractive young woman.

As this thought came into her head, she stood back a little from the medicine-cabinet mirror and attempted to give a fair and balanced appraisal of what she saw.

Her blonde hair; reaching down to her shoulders and curving into nice curls, still looked fresh and healthy. Her thin, arched eyebrows; large grey/green eyes with long, curved eyelashes were still her most attractive feature, and her slim nose, high cheekbones; generous lips and pixy-like chin completed the picture.

"Not bad," she announced to the image in the mirror as her mood continued to rise, "not bad at all."

Then she leaned close to the mirror and examined the slightly thickened flesh above each eye. "But you must learn to duck more, Sal, because the signs are showing. And you don't want to be mistaken for one of those female boxers, now do you. Because, as we both know, in this house, Robert is the only expert with fists."

She laughed at herself. Wasn't it amazing how just the thought of going to work prompted her to make jokes of something so serious as being abused. And wasn't her grandmother correct when she used to proclaim that there was a soothing ointment for most ills in life. It only had to be found.

Then she remembered she hadn't weighed herself in a while. And with some expectation of weight loss, she moved towards the electronic scales. Six months previously, 4lbs of fat had crept up on her. And like stubborn squatters, refused to leave again, despite all her efforts. But now she was confident that the squatters had been evicted. After all, hadn't she removed all the skin from the chicken she cooked; cut out the chocolate; spread foul-tasting, low calorie slug-slime on her bread instead of glorious butter, and poured skimmed, see-through milk in to her hot drinks, since her last weigh in. Surely she had starved them to death by now.

Then taking a deep breath she stepped on the scales.

Like excited greyhounds chasing a track rabbit, the numbers rushed past the display window, heading for one hundred and twenty eight pounds with deadly intent.

"No!" Sally cried," don't go past twenty four."

Ignoring her pleas, the numbers continued to fly by, then quickly slowed: coming to a stop at one twenty eight.

Sally prayed, and waited for the reversal she knew would come as the machine re-adjusted itself.

And when the reading suddenly dropped back to one twenty four, her joy was unbounded.

"Success!" she shouted, punching the air with both hands. "Goodbye and good riddance. Don't come back."

The scales rocked in protest at her movements.

She was happy: five feet eight inches tall and weighing one hundred and twenty four lbs: a perfect weight for her slim build. Now she could leave for work.

Her job was far more than just a pleasant place to work and to forget her domestic problems: it was a sanctuary; a place where she could rebuild her strength; the strength needed to bring her home each time she left the house. And so long as she had that strength she would never give up on her marriage. She owed that to herself, and to the husband Robert Cooper used to be before he became what he was now.

Sally sat comfortably in her seat as the train rocked its way towards Wimbledon Station. She smiled to herself with anticipation. The previous day at work a colleague had bet her ten pounds that no song by Oasis would be played between 9 and 11:pm on a popular radio station. And only five minutes before the deadline was up, one of their hits had blasted out of the kitchen radio.

She had laughed with childish delight; even clapping her hands. She couldn't wait to get back to the office.

However, it wasn't her winnings she was looking forward to, but the fun the girls would have at the instigator of the bet's expense; one Marcia Patterson, a woman who had been known to bet on the number of times the office phone rang in a single day, and how many of the female callers would be under thirty or over sixty. And the mayhem caused as they all listened in and argued was something straight out of an Ealing Comedy.

Marcia was very popular with the rest of the staff. She didn't have a single ounce of meanness in her whole body, and she was mad; mad for bets, fun and silliness. She had many imitators, even in other departments. But no one was quite like Marcia Patterson, because no one was quite as irrepressible.

At 9:15am Sally ran up the concrete steps towards the seven story, brick building that was Cornfield House. She was late for work: she was never late for work: she detested being late for work: she even detested other people being late for work. Yet here she was, still trying to get to where she should have been fifteen minutes earlier. And was her boss Mr Henderson at this very moment staring at her empty chair, shaking his head and tutting: behaviour he reserved purely for those he was very disappointed in?

Out of breath and frantic, she finally pushed through the heavy glass, entrance doors and hurried across the marble foyer towards the lifts, barely acknowledging a greeting from the woman behind the reception desk.

To her relief the doors of one of the two lifts opened as she approached, and no one got out.

'Oh, thank you, God!' she declared in her mind, rushing inside.

She then pressed once on the button marked six.

Nothing happened.

She pressed again, harder this time.

Still nothing.

She began jabbing on the worn button, but the doors remained open, as if waiting dutifully for more passengers.

"Come on: come on!" Sally's button-pressing became close to frantic.

Then, with agonizing slowness, the doors of the fifty-year old lift finally closed.

A sudden lurch and the lift began its slow ascent; complaining about the effort by shuddering, and rattling unseen cables.

"Oh, do hurry up!" she begged, willing it to go faster. She was going to be nearly twenty minutes late, and all because of some unexplained hold-up on the train. And how she hated being late for anything. Being late usually meant explaining the reason for it, and her explanations always sounded like poor excuses. Dear God, why could she never make the truth sound convincing; surely it should happen naturally - but it never did. Now she would have to go through that particular agony once more if Mr Henderson was waiting for her.

Two minutes later she barged through the office door and ran towards her cluttered desk. She dropped her bag on the floor next to her swivel chair - dragged her jacket off and hung it across the back - then sat down and turned on her computer.

She wiped a sheen of sweat from her forehead and glanced around the large, open-plan room.

What a relief! And there was no sign of Mr Henderson - perhaps she had gotten away with it, and why shouldn't she. After all, only poor timekeepers should be tutted at, not helpless victims of an incompetent railway system.

"Winner, winner, winner!" the girls at the other desks suddenly cried in unison.

Then they gathered round Sally, and one held her right hand high. "Ladies, I give you the new Betting Queen of Chapman's Insurance Ltd. The dear old Queen is dead: long live the Queen!"

"Oi; less of the old!" Marcia Patterson chided.

A chant went up. "Pay, pay, pay, pay, pay!"

Marcia thrust a ten pound note at Sally and grinned. "This is the first bet I've lost in over a year, Sal. Well done, girl. But watch out, I'll be looking to depose you."

Sally sheepishly took the note. "It was only luck. I had nothing to do with them playing that song."

"Take a little bit of friendly advice from a deposed Monarch, Sal," Marcia replied, sounding motherly. "The best Betting Queens never make or accept excuses: they are above such weaknesses. So, what is she, girls?"

"She is the new Queen Of Bets!" came a roar from seventeen enthusiastic voices. "Her Royal Highness Queen Sal!"

Suddenly a door at the far end of the large office opened and a grey-haired, tubby little man of sixty, leaned out. "What is all the commotion, ladies?" he demanded in a not unfriendly voice.

"We have a new Queen, Mr Henderson," said a girl called Margaret, patting Sally on the shoulder.

"My congratulations, Sally," Mr Henderson replied, smiling, "And of course, my commiserations to you, Marcia. You had an exceptional reign, but nothing lasts forever. Now please, ladies, keep the noise down. I need to make a couple of long distance calls and I don't want to frighten away potential clients with sounds of rowdiness in the background."

"Will do, Mr Henderson," said Margaret as the office manager retreated back to his tiny room, once more. "Quiet as a nervous mouse creeping past a sleeping cat from now on, Mr Henderson."

The girls laughed.

Then excitement over, they went back to their desks. But Sally knew that it would return at various stages throughout the day. That was one of the best things about working in the office. Fun could break out at any time; sometimes over the most childish things, unlike at home where it had died along with many other good things in her life.

Chapter Three

Sally lay back on the pink settee with a glass of wine in her hand.

She had only just arrived home from work after a particularly exhausting day. New computers had been installed in her office, and it seemed that all nine of them had taken it turn to either crash or play up. And at one stage there was real concern that Mr Henderson might have a heart attack as he rushed, red-faced and sweating, from one machine to another like some mother hen desperate to save her chicks from a prowling fox.

Eventually the computers were working fully, and it was with great relief that everyone had put their coats on to go home. No one wanted another day of madness like that again.

Sally stretched her legs out and took a sip of the red wine from the tall, delicate glass in her hand. She savoured its combinations of tart and fruity flavours, and murmured her approval.

One of the very few things that hadn't changed about Robert was his love of good wine. And when they were first married he used to say every time he spent twenty or more pounds on a bottle 'Always remember, Sal, Backus himself never compromised on the quality of his wine and neither should we.'

Nowadays Robert said nothing about such things.

She peered over the rim of the glass as she sipped, scrutinizing every detail of the living-room. She and Robert had decorated the whole house together in the evenings and weekends during the first months of their marriage. Yes, those precious days in 2001 had been an exciting experience filled with paint fights, air-bubble squishing contests and paste-flinging mayhem, which now seemed more than a lifetime ago.

They had fallen in love with the place the instant they first stepped inside the door one autumn morning with the estate agent, and she had pestered Robert into putting in an immediate offer very close to the asking price. Being a structural engineer, Robert had been more cautious about making decisions based solely on impulse, but in those days he never could refuse her demands. And so within ten weeks they moved in to their new home.

But as the joy of their marriage faded, so did the cream, embossed wallpaper; the Magnolia-painted ceiling; the pale blue sash windows, internal, folding shutters, and double, panelled doors. No doubt Robert's sixty-a-day habit had done the damage before he decided to give up just two months ago.

Yes, this fine old house was no longer cared for, and it was waiting to be revived just as she was waiting to revive her marriage. It made her sad to think about it.

Of all the rooms in the large house, the living-room was by far Sally's favourite. She loved the extensive plaster coving that separated walls from ceiling, the white, Italian marble fireplace, the huge, Georgian gilded mirror that hung above it, which, to her absolute joy, had been included in the asking price of the house, and the wonderful plaster rose on the high ceiling that was still crying out for a sparkling, crystal chandelier. Of course all the rooms in the Victorian house were large and contained original features, but as far as Sally was concerned, the living-room was well named, for it was at the very heart of her existence.

Perhaps even now it wasn't too late to re-decorate. Perhaps Robert might even become as enthusiastic about it as he had once before.

The idea sent a shiver of excitement and anticipation through her, but then cold reality washed it instantly away. It had been a long time since Robert Cooper was enthusiastic about anything, except tormenting her.

The sound of a neighbour's car engine suddenly revving outside made her jump. Then she glanced at the clock on the mantle piece; 6:20, it was time to prepare their evening meal.

An hour later Sally and Robert were sitting opposite one another at the kitchen table.

Robert's attention was focused entirely on his plate of beef lasagne, garden peas and boiled potatoes. And at the rate he was eating, Sally guessed he was enjoying his meal.

"How's the lasagne?" she asked hopefully.

Robert swallowed but didn't look up. "Quite nice, I suppose - plenty of meat in it, and the pasta is soft too."

"I'm glad," said Sally. "That supermarket near my job does a very good range in ready meals. I don't think I could ever manage to make a lasagne as good as this."

"You could if you had more time to practice," said Robert in a firm tone.

A fork-full of potato froze half way to Sally's mouth. "How do you mean?" Her stomach immediately began doing unpleasant things that made her feel sick.

"I mean I don't see the point of you carrying on with that job of yours," said Robert, teasing a number of peas on to his fork. "I bring in enough money, and anyway, I like the house to be kept spotless. My father was fastidious about keeping his home clean, and so was my grandfather - must be something in the Cooper genes."

"I keep the place clean, don't I?" Sally protested. "I mean, you never said anything before. So I assumed you were satisfied with the work I do around here. And you always have clean shirts and underwear in the drawers. So I don't know how much more I could do even if I was here seven days a week?"

Robert put the peas in his mouth and began chewing.

He also stared at her with an unreadable expression on his face; but she suspected that he was gloating at her torment.

"Well?" she prompted.

She knew she should shut up about it, but she just couldn't give up the only good thing in her life without a fight.

Robert returned to his meal. "Granted you do a fair job. But that isn't the point. This is a big house - you need plenty of time for the cleaning. So, obviously you could do it better if you didn't have to go to that job three days a week. I've been working it out: the time taken to get ready: travelling: the job: the journey home. That's about thirty- five hours a week, and you have to be tired after it. Stands to reason the house-cleaning has to suffer."

Desperation seeped into Sally's voice though she tried to prevent it.

"I like working at Chapman's, Robert. I get on really well with the girls there. And my salary comes in handy, doesn't it?"

"Salary," Robert grunted, "paper-round money more like. I earn five times that. We don't need your money: you don't need that job: end of story."

"But I do need it!" Sally cried. "I have to get out of this house sometimes. We have no friends here; at least not since you -"

'Don't go there!' an inner voice warned, but it was too late. She had just opened a very dangerous door, and her husband's violence was waiting on the other side of it.

Robert glared at her, his eyes squinting. "Go on then; finish what you were saying: not since I what?"

"Well; not since you decided -"

"Decided what?"

"That: that the neighbours were just a load of gossips."

"They are, aren't they: bloody bunch of tittle-tattles," Robert replied scathingly. "Who needs that kind of crap. I have friends where I work; proper friends who don't go saying nasty things behind my back, or poking their noses into my business."

A shudder of relief passed through Sally. She had closed the door again. But the job; it was all she had. How could she survive without it. She must make him change his mind, for both their sakes.

"I need proper friends too, you know, and the girls at work are mine. They enjoy talking to me, and they want me to join in their fun. I feel wonderful when I'm with them, and even our boss Mr Henderson takes part sometimes. I need my friends, Robert, I really do. Surely you can understand that?"

"How can they be proper friends?" said Robert. "Not a single one has ever set foot inside this house. It's like me saying the staff behind the counter at the takeaway are friends because I see them a couple of times a week. It's bloody stupid."

Hope caused Sally's heart to race. "But that's because I thought you didn't want them here. You mean you wouldn't mind if I brought a few of them back; maybe at the weekends;

just for a couple of hours. And I promise they won't get in your way; though they might become a bit rowdy, but only in fun. And you never know, you might even find yourself joining in like Mr Henderson does. He's a bit reserved like you, but he has fun with us occasionally."

"They can damn well stay away!" Robert snapped, banging his knife and fork down hard on the table. A wild look then entered his eyes. "What's the matter with you, Sally: can't I say something without you getting the wrong end of the stick. My point is that they can't be proper friends because they have never been here. I'm not handing out bloody invitations. Now, I've made up my mind. You hand in your notice tomorrow, and give your full attention to me and this house the way you should."

Anger bordering on rage overcame Sally's caution. "I'll go crazy if I have to stay in this house the whole time, doing nothing but cooking and cleaning. Before we were married I used to work for a stockbroker, but I agreed to give it up because you asked me to. And I was happy to do so. After all, we were going to have a family eventually; that is until you changed your mind. But now I need something else in my life besides housework. I need to get away from here at least a few days a week."

"Then go to the supermarket more often like other wives of successful husbands," said Robert. "Now, let me enjoy my dinner in peace, will you, or I'll give you something to really complain about."

Sally watched him eating, her expression determined. "I don't care what you think, Robert, I'm keeping my job. You have no right to take it away from me, and I won't let you."

Robert stopped eating and glared at her. "What did you just say to me?"

Sally kept her eyes firmly on her husband. "I need my job and I'm going to keep it. You have your job and I have mine. I wouldn't dream of telling you to give up yours, because I know you love it. You should do the same for me."

An evil grin appeared on Robert's face. "You have that wrong, Sal. There are two reasons why you would never tell me to give up my job and neither of them are the one you just mentioned. One is that you would never dare tell me to do anything, and two, you know very well I would beat the crap out of you if you did."

Sally's right fist banged down on the table. "You insufferable pig!" she shouted. "I hate you."

Robert pointed his knife at her, his eyes squinting with menace. "Now you are just asking for a slap across the face."

Sally straightened her shoulders and her expression was as hard as her husband's had ever been. "Well, since I usually get a slap whether I ask for it or not, I have nothing to lose by telling you what a bore you are these days as well as a pig, Robert. And another thing, don't think you are going to get away with abusing me forever."

"Oh, and who's going to stop me?" Robert demanded.

"I am," said Sally.

Robert put his cutlery down.

Sally braced herself. There was no going back now, and she wouldn't even if she could.

"You are going to stop me!" Robert cried incredulously. "Don't make me laugh, Sal. And what are you going to do then; cry me to death? Well, don't bother. I'm immune to that sort of crap; especially since you seem to be doing nothing else these days."

Sally felt a new and terrible sensation flow through her. "I could do far more than just cry," she warned.

"You could: well, bully for you, Sal!" Robert exclaimed, spreading his hands wide. "So you have a spine after all. Wonders never cease. But now you've had your fun for one night; your five minutes of protest, and I don't want to hear any more about it. You're giving in your notice and that's final."

"I'm being serious, Robert," Sally replied. "I'm keeping it."

"No you're not."

"Yes I am, and there's nothing you can do to stop me."

"Want me to come over and prove you wrong?" said Robert.

"If you ever touch me again, I'll go straight to the police," Sally warned.

This threat seemed to catch Robert off guard and he simply stared back; searching for some indication that she really meant it. For what Sally didn't know was that her husband had a deep-seated fear of the police since childhood, and it had never left him. Even the sight of a police car could still put him on edge.

Taking his silence as a sign that she had won the argument, Sally returned to her meal. But it was already getting cold so she pushed the plate away from her.

"So, you would turn me in to the police?" said Robert in a calm voice. "You would do a thing like that to me?"

Sally nodded. "If you forced me to, I would. Because I've had enough, Robert. You won't tell me what's wrong with you, but whatever it is, you're making me pay for it. But it stop's now."

"You fucking bitch," Robert growled, "sitting there trying to give me orders! Who the hell do you think you are. I say what happens in this house; me, not you. And when I tell you to do something, you bloody well do it if you know what's good for you. Now, get out of my sight before I make you sorry for trying to ruin my dinner."

Sally remained where she was, tight-lipped and defiant.

"Did you hear what I said?" Robert snapped.

"I heard."

"So why are you still sitting there? Do as you're told."

Sally took a deep breath. "This is my kitchen too, and I have every right to stay in it for as long as I want."

Robert jumped up. "Get out of my sight, you fucking bitch!" he roared.

Holding back her fear, Sally slowly left her seat and walked out of the kitchen with no intention of hurrying. Robert would hate her apparent calmness. It would be a very small victory to frustrate him now, but a victory nonetheless.

She just as slowly made her way up the stairs to the box room at the back of the house. It was the only place of privacy she had.

And as she walked through the door, her fear turned to rage and frustration.

She flung herself face down on the single bed, her small fists pounding into it.

"Bastard: bastard: bastard!" she raged, tears staining the white duvet.

"Make sure you tell them tomorrow," Robert's voice called up from the hallway. "And I don't want to hear any excuses about having to stay on while they find a replacement: two weeks and that's it."

Sally stopped crying and listened. She had a good idea what was coming next.

She heard the front door open and then close.

The selfish pig. He was off to the pub to enjoy himself.

"But what about me?" she cried out. "What about my enjoyment?"

Her thoughts then seesawed between begging and demanding; doubt and certainty; acceptance and defiance. Oh, how she hated and despised him at times: how she wanted so desperately to strike back; to show him that she too could be violent. But no, she must never allow herself to dwell on such thoughts, no matter how desirable: they were too dangerous. For if she was to find out what it was that had changed Robert, she must do nothing to weaken the dam she had erected to hold back her negative and powerful emotions. Such thoughts could so easily turn to cracks.

Then she stood up and wiped her eyes. She was better than this. It was her choice to stay. She must compose herself. Composure was the shield that she presented to the world around her. It was all that reminded her she was not a victim.

But as she then made her way down to the kitchen to clear away the dishes, far below awareness, the very foundations of her dam were beginning to crumble.

Chapter Four

It was nearly midnight when Robert lurched through the front door in a drunken state. He lost his balance and fell against the Regency-papered wall, knocking a framed photo of his parents on the floor. But when he regained his balance and bent down to pick it up, he took a single step forward and his right foot landed on the edge of the frame.

There was a crunching sound of wood and glass breaking.

Emotion welled inside him when he realized what he had done.

"Sal: Sal!" he called out, his voice distorted by sorrow and whisky. "Look what I've done, Sal."

Sally walked out of the kitchen, her face pale and expressionless. "What's the matter?" she asked in a cold tone.

Robert didn't notice the change in her, and proceeded to point to the damaged picture. "Look, Sal, look what I've done to mom and dad's photo. The only one I've got because of that damn fire at their lovely house, and I ruined it."

"Go and sit down," Sally ordered. "I'll clear it up. It's probably only the glass and frame. The photo should be ok. I'll get them replaced tomorrow during my lunch break."

With tears in his eyes, Robert staggered along the hallway and into the living-room, knocking a valuable vase off a side-table as he went. The vase shattered on the polished wood floor of the hall, but Sally didn't care. She just felt numb, and a little strange.

She closed the front door, which Robert always left open when he came home very drunk. Then she went into the kitchen for a dustpan and brush.

Minutes later she had cleaned up, and her prediction had been correct: the photo of the elderly couple was undamaged. She stared at it and gave a shrug: two people smiling; the only smiles she had seen in her home during the past three months. How had it come to this?

She put the photo down on the hall side-table and walked into the living-room, expecting her husband to be flat out on the settee; something else he did when he had drunk far too much.

However, Robert was standing in the middle of the room, swaying gently like a tree before a strong wind. His face was blotchy and matched perfectly the colour of his blood-shot eyes.

"I'll get your coat off, and then you better go to bed," said Sally. "You have to be up early in the morning if you are going to attend that meeting."

Robert stared at her with an expression that was akin to an eagle watching a stupid and unsuspecting rabbit, as she began removing his jacket.

The strong smell of alcohol wafted from his clothes as well as his breath, but Sally took little notice. She had long ago learned to ignore the unpleasant things in life when they were minor.

"You shouldn't have gone out to the pub in your best suit," she scolded. "So you will have to wear your blue one tomorrow. I'll take this one to the cleaners at the weekend."

"I've had eighteen double whiskies, you know," said Robert with a sneering grin. "What do you think of that?"

Sally laid the black jacket on the settee armrest.

She knew full well he was trying to frighten her: whisky had a dangerous effect on his mood, and often preceded an episode of violence. But it wouldn't work; not this time.

"I think you had a good night," she replied calmly.

Robert pointed a finger at her face as she turned to him. "Now that's where you're wrong, Sal, because I didn't drink to have a good night. And do you know why I drank so much, and whisky instead of my usual beer?"

"No," said Sally.

"I drank, Sal, because I was upset. And do you know why I was upset?"

"Tell me in the morning," Sally suggested, ready to help him with the stairs.

She sighed. Those stupid questions every time: how did he manage to keep his mind so clear when his body was full of alcohol? Why couldn't he mumble unintelligently like other drunken husbands, and not notice if she was ignoring him, and right now she was desperate to do that?

"Haaaaa!" Robert cried, still swaying and pointing. "I know what you're doing, Sal. You're trying to make me go to bed so that I will forget to punish you for what you did this evening."

"Oh, and what did I do this evening?" Sally asked.

For the first time since the change, she wasn't afraid. And something told her she would never be afraid of him again. He had lost his power over her. His fists would never again control her.

Robert's eyes widened in disbelief and his normal bass voice rose in pitch. "What did you do!" he exclaimed. "You have to ask me that after the way you behaved this evening. Well, I think you fucking well know exactly what you did, Sal. You deliberately picked a fight with me. Then you ran away from the table to your box room when I was eating my dinner and needing a bit of company. All I wanted was for you to share the meal with me. What's wrong with that? But no; you had to spoil it for me, didn't you; the way you spoil so many other things. What way is that for a wife to behave; leaving her husband to eat his dinner alone. Well, not in this house, Sal. You might have your cosy little chats with those bitches at that shitty little job of yours, but you won't bring any of their suggestions home with you. I'll beat those fucking suggestions out of you if I have to. Don't you worry about that."

'So once again your sickening rage comes,' Sally thought to herself. 'Bubbling and rising until it's partnered with your violence. Well, this time I won't take it. This time I won't be afraid.'

"Are you listening to me?" Robert demanded.

"I'm listening," Sally replied. "Now let's get you upstairs to bed."

Robert yanked his right arm away when Sally tried to take it. The act nearly cost him his balance and he tottered for a moment.

"I'll go to bed when you have learned your lesson. You have been getting on my nerves lately, Sal; staring at me as if I was something brought in on your shoe, and talking about me behind my back to those so-called friends at work. Well, no more, Sal: it's time to put a stop to it: you hear me?"

"I hear you."

"Yea; well, hearing's not enough, you irritating bitch!" Robert shouted.

Experience warned Sally what was coming, and she stepped back just as a large fist came flying round towards the left side of her head.

The punch missed, but its momentum turned Robert on his unsteady feet.

He stumbled and fell into an armchair in a sitting position.

The chair tilted backwards.

Sally feared it was going over.

Her china cabinet of precious collectables was just behind it.

But when the chair tipped forwards again and its wooden, front legs banged on the floor, Robert hung on tight to the armrests.

The experience had clearly rattled him, and he looked wildly about for a moment as if expecting to be attacked.

Then he noticed Sally staring at him and he tried to lift himself up. But his muscles were too weak to cope with his bulk.

He tried a few more times, then gave up, puffing from the effort.

Sally continued to stare, contempt on her face. How could she have let a drunken wretch like that take such control of her life? It must have been her fault; her weakness that allowed it?

"What the fuck are you looking at!" Robert shouted, his head drooping. "Think you have got away with it, do you. Well, let me tell you something. Tomorrow we're going to carry on where we left off, and no amount of fancy footwork will save you. No bitch and her bitch friends at her shitty little job are going to make a fool of Robert Cooper in his own home and get away with it. You just wait until the morning. You'll be sorry you put me in this state."

"I'm going to bed," said Sally, totally unfazed by the threat. "I'll help you on to the settee if you can't face the stairs."

A fit of violent coughing and gagging took hold of Robert, and Sally thought he was going to be sick all over himself. But he quickly recovered, and his bloodshot eyes were glaring at her again.

"Never mind my sleeping arrangements. They're my business. Now go into my kitchen and get me a large glass of water, or I'll have a bad hangover in the morning. And you know what that means, don't you?"

"Yes, I know," said Sally in an even tone, "punishment for making you suffer so much."

"At least you have learnt something," said Robert. "So learn something else, like getting me a glass of water when I tell you to."

"Get it yourself!" Sally retorted. "I'm not your slave, you bloated wretch."

Robert's mouth dropped open in stunned disbelief. Then he recovered and his eyes began to bulge. "You fucking cow: when I get my hands on you I'll make you sorry; you see if I don't, you bitch!"

"Well, if I am a bitch, you made me one with your violence and your drinking," Sally shot back. "Look at you, too drunk to even get out of your chair and hit me. God, what an idiot I've been: how could I have thought for one second that there was a chance you would return to being the man I married. But that man is dead and he has been replaced by some rabid animal that should be put down."

Robert's hands twisted madly on the armrests as rage forced him to try to get to Sally, but there was no strength left in them.

Exhaustion eventually forced him to stop trying. And his next words were slow but full of menace. "Oh; you fucking bitch; you rotten, fucking bitch, I'm going to strangle the life out of you, you fucking bitch!"

"And how are you going to manage that, Robert," said Sally in a condescending tone, "when you're stuck in that chair. Now, because I wouldn't allow even a bad-tempered dog to go thirsty I will get you that glass of water before I go to bed. And if you are sick all over yourself, like you were the last time you pigged out on scotch, you can bloody well clear it up yourself. I'm done with being your skivvy."

Sally then turned and left the room, a barrage of hysterical curses and threats following her.

Once in the kitchen she removed a pint glass from the cupboard and made her way to the sink.

She turned the cold-tap full on, letting the water run to remove any build up of dissolved metals.

Anger suddenly took hold of her.

"What are you doing, you stupid cow!" she growled. "Who cares if he's poisoned!"

Her fingers turned the tap harder in response to her anger.

They began to hurt from the pressure but she couldn't stop trying to turn it: she didn't want to stop: it was defying her: she had to make it obey her.

She fought the pain, refusing to give in to the tap; hating it; wanting to destroy it.

"Turn, you bastard, turn!" The words squeezed out between her clenched teeth like a blunt knife driven through thick rubber.

She began to pull and push at the tap, but it refused to respond to her efforts.

Her anger became pure rage; a boiling fluid in her veins and arteries.

Suddenly her elbow knocked a cup into the sink where it shattered.

The jet of water rebounded from the pieces and hit her full in the face.

The shock drove her backwards, gasping for breath.

And as she then stood in the middle of the kitchen, her face dripping wet and water spraying out all over the place, something in her brain exploded.

Robert lay slumped in his armchair, snoring with vibrating lips and occasional grunts.

And when Sally walked towards him and drove the long blade of the carving knife deep into his chest, he simply stopped snoring.

Disbelief cut through Sally's rage. "No, you bastard, don't die yet!" she screamed, standing over him. "Wake up, you pig, wake up."

She yanked the knife out and glared at it. Then she glared at her husband. He can't just die; not like this; not after all the months of suffering and pain he had caused her; not after the beatings, the horrible remarks and put-downs in front of shocked friends, and the nights in bed when he forced her to do things she hated. He had to suffer for all that before he died. If there was any true justice in the world, he would pay with agony for his crimes.

She raised the knife and struck him again, just below the collarbone. Tears of rage and frustration slipped down her cheeks when he didn't react. "You pig; you dirty, rotten, filthy pig! Talk to me. Wake up."

But Robert Cooper was beyond any further acts of revenge. And as the blood spread across his white shirt, she backed away from him in disbelief. This couldn't be! She expected him to stagger to his feet at the first blow, a look of agony and horror on his fat, brutal face. She expected him to reach out to her; pleading for mercy. And she expected to gloat at his suffering and tell him why she had stabbed him. And then, as his strength finally gave out and he collapsed to the floor, she would have kicked him; oh yes, kicked him again and again in his evil face until it was as ugly as his soul. She would have taken the most sublime pleasure in hurting him as he had hurt her. And how she would have laughed at his pleading; his begging, and then she would have told him that he was going to die, right there on the horrible blue carpet he had insisted on buying, despite her protests.

But all this was not to be. For what seemed in a final act of brutality, Robert Cooper had denied her the kind of justice she craved, and she felt cheated, even though his denial of her rights were at the cost of his life. Death wasn't enough. She hadn't even made him scream.

Sally stared for a long time at her dead husband, her body shivering, and her emotions a whirlwind of rage, joy, gloating, regret and frustration. Why did nothing ever go right for her?

What had she done to deserve this refusal of her needs? She had put up with so much in an attempt to save her marriage, but Robert wouldn't have it. No, all he was interested in was his own, selfish gratification, and inflicting torment and pain on her whenever the mood took him.

Finally she consoled herself. At least he was dead. The suffering was at an end. Never again would the fists of Robert Cooper batter her body into days of pain, or the cruelty of his words batter her mind into twisted knots. It was over: she was free: she must be contented with that.

Then she realized she was still holding the knife in a tight grip.

Her clenched and bloody fingers opened slowly and painfully.

The knife slipped from them and hit the carpet with a soft thud.

She felt a splatter of wet on her right ankle and she looked down at it.

A expression of calm surprise appeared on her face at the sight of the blood. "Just look at that," she said softly as if speaking to a child. "Now you will have to change your tights and you only put them on a couple of hours ago."

Then her mood changed to casual acceptance and her mind turned to the practicalities of her situation.

She looked at Robert again.

He couldn't be left like that. But she didn't know anything about dealing with dead bodies. Someone else would have to do that; the police; yes, she must prepare herself to make the call that would bring them rushing to her home.

They would know what to do. And as for what she had done, well she only had to tell the truth when they questioned her, and they would see that she was justified in her actions. She was already a regular visitor to her GP and the local hospital. They had records of her injuries; a veritable catalogue of cuts, bruises, burns, sprains: those cracked ribs that were so bad they took three painful months to heal properly, and most serious of all the removal of her damaged spleen that had kept her in hospital for two weeks. Oh yes, her treatment at the brutal hands of Robert Cooper was certainly in the National Health computers, and would prove vital in her coming interview with the police. Robert must have been a fool not to think about that when he was beating her. Did he think she would take it forever? Yes, she had married a stupid man as well as a brutal one.

Sally walked stiffly to the phone on the small coffee table next to the TV. She pulled out a few tissues from a Kleenex box there. Then, with a steady hand, she lifted the receiver and dialled 999.

"Police please," she said when a female operator asked her which service she required.

"This is Sally Cooper," she replied in a flat, monotonous tone to the male voice who answered. "Could you send someone immediately. I think I may have just killed my husband."

Then, having given her name and address, she sat on the settee and watched the blood on her husband's shirt migrating slowly downwards; staining the leather belt around his waist that he had used on her so many times.

Five minutes later she heard loud banging on the front door. This confused her for a moment. Then she remembered. 'Of course; I didn't change those dead batteries in the bell. What will they think?'

Tutting, she stood up and made her way to answer the call.

As she walked along the hallway, flashing blue lights coming through the frosted glass panel on the door made her blink.

Four police officers and two paramedics greeted her when she opened the door. "He's in the living-room," she said as the paramedics rushed past her.

The paramedics tried for five minutes to revive Robert, but it was clear from the start he was dead.

The police cautioned and arrested Sally. And when she was then escorted by two female police officers out of the house and towards a waiting car, a small crowd of people stared at her in confusion. They would have to wait for the following day to find out what had happened in the Cooper's house to bring the authorities and ambulance crew to their quiet neighbourhood at such a late hour.

At Surbiton Police Station, once all items that could be used to do herself harm, were removed, she was placed in a holding cell.

At 1:30am a doctor examined her physical and mental state, concluding that although distraught, she was in a fit state to be interviewed by the police.

Alone in her cell, Sally sat on the side of the small bed, staring wide-eyed at the wall opposite. She didn't notice how sparse the tiny room was, or how the white paint on the plain walls and ceiling was turning a dirty yellow in places, or how a crude rhyme had been written on the back of the metal door by a previous occupant. All she was aware of was that the police must believe that she murdered her husband instead of killing him in self-defence, otherwise why did they arrest her? And if they continued to believe that and sent her for trial, the jury might think the same thing. Then she would go to prison for a long time. And didn't judges these days like to make an example of whom they considered to be violent people: show the public that the law was safe in their hands. These days wasn't it more about image than justice. And the thought of being locked up for years with real criminals was frightening.

A rattle of keys as the door was unlocked jerked her out of her haunted thoughts.

The door opened and a young WPC entered carrying a tray.

The WPC smiled. "I don't know how long it's been since you last ate, love, so I brought a sandwich and a cup of tea."

Sally ignored the tray when it was offered.

The WPC smiled again. "Not hungry; that will be the shock, I suppose. Anyway, I'll just put this beside you; in case you get hungry later."

Sally felt the young woman's closeness as she bent down to put the tray on the bed. It was a painful reminder of how lonely she was, and she turned pleading eyes on the WPC when she straightened up.

"Could you stay for a little while?" she asked in an emotion-filled voice.

"Sorry, love, I have other duties, I'm afraid," said the WPC in a sympathetic tone.

"I didn't murder him, you know," said Sally. "He was abusing me and I had to stop him, but no one seems to believe me."

"I'm not allowed to talk about it," the WPC replied. "Now, you try and eat something, or at least drink that tea before it gets cold."

Sally became desperate when the police officer turned to go. "Are you married?" she blurted out.

The WPC turned back. "Yes, I am."

Hope surged inside Sally. "And is your husband good to you?"

A stern look appeared on the young woman's face. "I wouldn't still be with him if he wasn't."

"But if he was beating you, and you couldn't leave him because you remembered his love so much, and even if you did, you knew in your heart that he would find and kill you, and maybe even kill anyone helping you? If you knew deep down that he was capable of anything, what would you do?"

The WPC began to look uncomfortable. "Sorry; I'm really not allowed to talk to you. I could get into serious trouble. Now, at least get some sleep. You look exhausted."

Please," Sally begged, "just answer me. In my position would you have done what I did?"

"I must get back to my other duties now. I'll be back later for the tray."

"No: please answer me: I need to know that what I did wasn't wrong: that I'm not an evil person?"

The WPC walked out through the door, then turned to close it.

"Please, I'm begging you?" Sally cried. "Would you?"

For just a few moments the police officer stared back at Sally. Then she nodded twice and closed the door.

Loud sobs of relief followed her as she walked back along the corridor.

Chapter Five

At 10:45am, on July 24th 2003, and having had a breakfast of toast and tea, Sally was taken to Interview Room No 1.

She felt tired and nervous. Her dreams had been terrible and she had woken frequently in tears.

Sitting beside her on an equally hard seat was her young solicitor Philip Slater, known to Sally from their mutual love of swimming. Robert had never known she went to the local baths, and would certainly have prevented her if he had. Not that she had been swimming in the past nine months: Robert discovering a damp towel in her holdall, had decided her against risking it any further.

Sally never considered Philip anything more than an occasional friend, though she suspected that his feelings towards her were stronger. But she could never have been unfaithful to her husband, no matter what the circumstances. As far as she was concerned a marriage had to be ended before a new relationship was forged. Despite the terrible violence of her husband, for some time after it started her greatest wish had been that somehow Robert would return to being the wonderful, compelling, interesting, extrovert man she had met and fallen in love with. In those days they had a great deal in common; such as their passion for long walks in the park, watching artistic French films at the cinema, fun-arguments about whether Leonardo Da Vinci or Michelangelo was the greatest Italian of the period. And the thought of abandoning those times forever was terrible indeed, so she could never risk being unfaithful. Something awful had changed Robert; surely he could have changed back. But by the time she fully realized that would never happen, it was too late. Now he was dead and so was her chance of happiness.

Also sitting at the table in the interview room were Detective Inspector Virginia Kelly, a scrawny-looking, blonde-haired, forty-seven year old career woman, and Detective Sergeant Phillip Mortimer, a dumpy, balding, fifty-two year old whose ambition had vanished on the day he reached his present rank. Both had grave expressions on their faces.

"For the purpose of the tape," said Kelly in a practiced tone, "those present in the room are Detective Inspector Kelly; Detective Sergeant Mortimer; Mr Phillip Slater Solicitor and -?"

"Sally Cooper," Sally replied in a low voice. She had seen enough crime dramas on TV to know the drill.

"Could you repeat your name a little louder, please," said Kelly.

"My name is Sally Cooper."

"Right then, Mrs Cooper," said Kelly, "would you care to tell us exactly what took place in your home at approximately 11:50 pm last night?"

A shudder passed through Sally at the request: then she felt angry. What a stupid question. It was obvious what happened; she had killed Robert: she had phoned and told them, for God's sake. Why couldn't they just let her sign a statement and go home? It was obvious Robert was a monster. No one was ever punished for killing a monster, even in these days of setting examples.

"Please answer my question, Mrs Cooper," Kelly insisted.

Sally stared at the Detective. Her anger was gone now, but self-pity replaced it. "I - I couldn't stand it any more," she croaked with a dry mouth. "He was always doing things to me; horrible things that I can't even speak about. So I had to make him stop. I mean, when someone keeps on hurting you; even someone you once loved very much, you have to do something; anything to make them stop doing it. You do see that; don't you?"

Kelly stared at an open folder. "I see that you stabbed your husband twice in the chest with a carving knife."

"Yes," said Sally, taking a sip of water from a glass on the table.

Kelly's green eyes were accusing when she looked at Sally once more. "So why did you stab him twice, Mrs Cooper? Did you believe you were still at risk from him after you stabbed him the first time?"

Sally gawked at the detective. "What do you mean?"

33

"It's a simple enough question? Were you in danger from your husband after you stabbed him the first time?"

"No; I suppose not. At least I don't think so," Sally replied, still confused.

"Then why did you stab him a second time?" said Kelly.

Sally opened her mouth to speak but nothing came out.

"You do see what I'm getting at, don't you?" Kelly continued. "You stabbed your husband twice, when, by your own admission, there was no risk to you after the first stab. And according to the preliminary medical examination, the first blow killed him, so why strike again? Was it to make sure he was dead?"

Fury sent Sally leaping out of her seat, her face twisted and ugly. "What does it matter how many times I stabbed him!" she screeched. "He was abusing me: I did what I had to do to stop him. I put up with it for a whole year; have you any idea what that's been like; afraid every time he came home; terrified I might say the wrong thing and get punched in the face, or have my ribs broken. And it wasn't as if he would allow me to learn to avoid making him angry, because what was fine one day sent him into a rage the next. I didn't know where I stood with him."

Kelly stared silently back as Sally glared down at her.

Then Sally sat in her seat once more. The outburst had drained her, and her shoulders sagged.

"How often did your husband abuse you; physically, I mean?" said Kelly, glancing at her folder.

"Too often!" Sally shot back, still seething.

"Yes, but just how often; once a week; once a month?"

"When he was in the mood to hit me, of course! What difference does it make?"

"And how often was he in the mood?"

An exasperated sigh left Sally. "I don't know. Sometimes weeks would go by without him doing anything, and he didn't always hit me very hard; just slapping me across the head. It all depended on how angry he got."

"I see," said Kelly, giving no impression of what she thought of the explanation. "Now, getting back to the incident with the knife. What interval was there between stabbing him the first time and the second time?"

"What?" said Sally, clearly taken back by the question.

"You pulled the knife out of your husband's chest and then struck him a second time. I am trying to establish how much time passed between the two blows?"

"Really, Inspector," Slater protested. "You can hardly expect my client to answer a question like that. I very much doubt Mrs Cooper had the presence of mind to time the interval. This is harassment and I refuse to allow it."

Kelly felt irritated by the interruption. 'Damn bloody solicitors!' she thought.

She managed to smile at Slater. "This is a murder investigation, Mr Slater, and even the smallest detail could have powerful implications."

Kelly then turned her attention back to Sally. "Now then, Mrs Cooper, would you like me to repeat the question?"

Sally shook her head. "I don't know; not long."

"Was it more than say, two seconds?"

"It could have been: I don't know."

"Oh, but it *was* more than two seconds, much more, wasn't it?" Kelly said firmly. "And we know that for a fact because there was almost no sign of blood from the second wound, which means that your husband was already dead when the knife went into his body the second time. Of course we will have to wait for the post-mortem, to be exact, but a doctor is of the opinion that the first blow missed your husband's heart and probably damaged the aorta. Now, the aorta is a major artery that extends from the heart, and if it is nicked by the tip of a sharp knife, the victim could perhaps survive for say twenty seconds. So, up to that time the blood would have been circulating Robert's body, and therefore if you had stabbed him any time before those twenty seconds, there would be substantial bleeding from the second wound, especially when the knife was removed immediately afterwards. But there wasn't any real bleeding, so you must have attacked him again after twenty seconds?"

"I don't know what you're getting at," said Sally. "I killed him and I admit it, so what difference does it make?"

Kelly frowned. "The difference between self-defence and murder, Mrs Cooper."

Sally gasped. "Murder?"

"If you had struck your husband in a spur-of-the-moment action, you would not have attacked him again more than twenty seconds later. Such an interval would have given you plenty of time to think about what you had done, or even regret your actions; nevertheless you did attack again; perhaps to be certain he was dead? Is that what you wanted; to be certain you succeeded in killing him?"

"I only wanted to stop him from hurting me!" Sally cried. "Why won't you believe me?"

"Oh, I think you wanted to do far more than that, Mrs Cooper. It is my belief that you made plans to kill your husband months ago, or even at the time of your marriage."

"No; I didn't! It all happened so fast. We had a row and he went out to the pub. And when he came back he was drunk and in a bad mood. He tried to punch me, but he fell into the armchair, and he couldn't get out again, so he threatened to hurt me next morning. I tried to get him upstairs to bed but he wouldn't go. He wanted to sleep in the living-room. He also wanted a glass of water and I went into the kitchen to get it for him."

"And -?" Kelly prompted when Sally stopped talking.

Sally's already pale face paled even further. "And, I remember getting the glass out of the cupboard and going to the sink. I think; I mean I did turn the cold tap on to let the water run for a few seconds. Robert said that when water in a tap isn't used for a few hours, the water dissolves metal from the pipe, and he didn't want that in his drink."

Once again Sally became silent.

"So you let the water run: go on, Mrs Cooper," said Kelly.

Sally gave a loud sigh and began picking at her nails. "I remember watching the water coming out of the tap. Then something happened; a cup fell into the sink and smashed.

Suddenly water was hitting me in the face and going all over the place. The water hitting me made me angry, and-"

Kelly leaned forwards in anticipation "And?"

"Then I found myself standing over Robert."

"Was the knife in your hand at that moment?"

"Yes."

"You brought it with you from the kitchen?"

"Yes; I suppose I must have: I don't remember exactly. It was all so confusing."

"And you brought it to kill your husband?"

"Yes; no; I don't know why I brought it. I don't know how it got in my hand. I don't remember picking it up."

"Was it a clean knife?" said Kelly, leaning back.

"What?"

"Was it a knife that had been used. Of course forensics will answer that eventually, but I'd like you to answer it now. Was the knife clean when you brought it from the kitchen?"

"I already told you; I don't remember getting it."

"A carving knife has limited uses," said Kelly. "Was it with the other cutlery waiting to be washed? Surely you must know if you had used a large carving knife earlier in the day?"

"No, I don't think I used it that day."

"Then it must have been clean. And where is it kept when it's not in use?"

"With the other knives."

"Do you mean in a set?"

Sally nodded.

"In a drawer or in one of those wooden, knife blocks?"

"A knife block."

"Which is kept?"

"At the back of the worktop."

"Which is across from the sink, and further down the kitchen from the door to the hall?"

Sally nodded.

"I see," said Kelly, clearly pleased by what she was hearing. "And that has to mean that you made a conscious decision to go and get it? You couldn't just have picked it up absentmindedly; could you?"

"I didn't make any decisions!" Sally wailed. "It just happened. How many times do I have to say it. I didn't plan anything: the knife was in my hand and I used it."

"So you keep saying. And what about the glass of water?"

Sally hesitated. "I don't know. I must have forgotten about it."

"So you went into the kitchen to get a glass of water for your husband, but you returned with a carving knife instead, and killed him. Your actions speak for themselves, wouldn't you say?"

"You make it sound so cold-blooded," Sally replied. "But it wasn't like that. He was abusing me: how many times do I have to say it. All you have to do is check with my GP and the hospital."

"What would you say your house is worth?" Kelly asked.

For a moment Sally was confused by the change of questioning. "What; oh, I don't know. Robert would never move, so I didn't bother to find out. What I wanted never came into anything."

"Would you agree that it is somewhere in the region of five hundred thousand pounds?"

Sally was thoughtful for a moment. "I suppose it could be worth that. It's a big house in a good area. But what has that to do with anything?"

"Do you and your husband have separate bank accounts?" DS Mortimer asked, speaking for the first time.

"No, we have a joint account, although Robert managed all our finances."

"How much is in the account at the moment?"

"About three thousand."

"Savings?"

"Well, there's the Building Society, which has fifty thousand. Robert's parents died in a fire a few years ago and he inherited some of the money from the sale of their house. Then there's his shares in some company. Robert had those before we met. I think they might be worth about fifteen thousand."

"Added together that's quite a sum of money," said Mortimer. "Perhaps even worth putting up with a violent husband for a year if it meant you could have it all to yourself; assuming you could get away with murdering him, of course. However, for that you would have to have very strong mitigating circumstances, wouldn't you, Mrs Cooper? And a history of physical abuse would provide them?"

Sally was outraged, but she was too exhausted to shout and scream it.

A wry laugh left her instead and she stared fixedly at Mortimer.

"You know, it's quite funny really. I get beaten by my husband for a whole year and when I finally do something to stop him, I'm accused of being a cold-blooded murderer, only out to get my hands on his money. Anyway, nearly half of that has always been mine. Why would I need to kill him just for the rest of it?"

"All of anything is better than half, Mrs Cooper," Kelly said, taking control of the interview once more.

"Is that so?" Sally felt her determination returning. "Well, let me make a suggestion, Detective Kelly, why don't you try marrying one of those serial wife-beaters you have probably put away some time in your career. Give it a go and see what it's like. But I can promise you this, after six months of his attacks on you all the money in the world wouldn't make you stay for another six."

"But you stayed; didn't you," said Kelly, accusingly. "All those beatings: all that violence and verbal abuse: terrified every time Robert came home; wondering if this was the night he was finally going to kill you."

"Yes, I did stay," Sally replied, determined not to flounder before the Inspector's aggression. "Because I wanted the old Robert back. You have no idea what he used to be like. He was the most considerate man I ever met: always putting me first: walking me to my door to make sure I was safe. And everyone who knew him said I couldn't find a better man to marry. And it was true; at least at first it was. Then he changed; almost overnight. And I believed that if he could change so quickly, he could change again. All right, so maybe I was naive and stupid. But I had to try, didn't I. What we had was wonderful. But as time passed I slowly began to realize that he might never become the old Robert again. Then it was too late to leave him. He would have found me. He had contacts."

Kelly's eyes narrowed. "What kind of contacts?"

"I don't know; just contacts. He told me once that he could even find Lord Lucan if he put his mind to it; that with the right connections anyone can be found. So I knew then that if I tried to get away from him, he would come after me."

"Why didn't you inform the police?" Kelly asked.

"I don't know; I suppose I wanted my real husband back: the one I had for a year."

"In my experience men who become violent towards their wives, rarely change," said Kelly, clearly sceptical.

"I haven't had your experience?" Sally replied. "Anyway; he did change. That's what I've been telling you. He was once a kind and gentle man. Can't you understand why I wanted him back. The monster he became wasn't the real him."

"All right," said Kelly, "let's assume for a moment I accept that you didn't want to report him while there was still a chance for your marriage. What about the shelters set up for women in your position? You could have gone to one of them to have a breathing space from your husband's violence. Perhaps it might even have given Robert time to realize what he was putting you through. You are clearly an intelligent woman, Mrs Cooper. I find it hard to believe you didn't consider such an option?"

"Of course I considered it;" Sally berated, "dozens of times, as a matter of fact. But I knew I wouldn't be safe there."

"Well, what about friends then?" said Kelly.

"The only friends I have left are the ones at work. But I couldn't put them in danger from Robert. He hated them. It wouldn't be fair."

"Surely you must have family?" Kelly protested.

"My parents are separated, and I'm an only child. My mother lives in Australia and my father in Canada. They have their own lives. Anyway, those are the first places he would look for me.

You have no idea of the violence in him. He would kill anyone to get at me; I just know he would. If my parents knew, they would only have told me to leave him. And I suppose most women would. But I have always believed that when you agree to marry someone, you should stand by them, no matter what. And if their personality starts changing, then you should try and find out why, and not just run away."

"So your defence is going to be that you had to stay behind and kill your husband?" said Kelly. "I think you are making a very big mistake, Mrs Cooper. It's clear to me that you wanted your husband out of the way in order to get everything for yourself. Why persist with this charade. Admit that you planned his death and save us all a great deal of trouble."

"I didn't plan it!" Sally cried.

"The courts are bound to be lenient," Kelly went on. "We have your medical records. No one will blame you for taking revenge on a man like that."

The DI's voice then took on an aggressive tone. "But you can't go on pretending you didn't also have a financial reason. Obviously you needed money and a place to live. After all, your husband was the one who changed and betrayed the vows he made to you when you were married. Why should you lose out because of him. And since there was no way you could force him to leave, you had to do something to get rid of him, so you took the only course open to you. Any reasonable person will understand that. In my opinion you wouldn't receive a sentence longer than five years. Also, there is the possibility that you will serve your time in an open prison. And with good behaviour you would be out in two. Then you could begin your life again with a clear conscious. However, I must warn you, if you persist in your ridiculous claim that it was purely self-defence, we will have no option but to charge you with murder. The fact that you didn't involve the police, or leave your husband, or make any attempt at all to get away from him when he was at work, will guarantee that we achieve a conviction. You must confess, Mrs Cooper; it's your only option if you don't want to go to prison for a very long time."

"Inspector Kelly!" Philip Slater declared. "You are trying to frighten my client into admitting to a crime she did not commit. Surely you can see that she is both mentally and physically exhausted. I insist that she be allowed a period of rest from your aggressive questioning."

"This interview is suspended at 12:25pm," said Kelly, looking at her watch and standing up. "Mrs Cooper, you will be taken back to your cell where you will be held until we are ready to question you again."

"Please; can't I go home!" Sally begged. "I have answered all your questions, haven't I?"

"Yes, you have," said Kelly, her expression cold. "But not to my satisfaction. For you see, Mrs Cooper, I really do believe you planned to kill your husband, and I intend to prove it. No matter what the provocation, no one has the right to administer their own personal form of justice. Justice is entirely the prerogative of the courts and the laws of this land. They were created to prevent people like you causing chaos in the community. The police were there to help you, but you decided to act alone. Now you must accept the consequences for that decision."

Chapter Six

Twice more that day, Sally was intensely questioned by the police. Sometimes she was as aggressive as DI Kelly in her replies: other times she hardly spoke at all, depression and mental fatigue numbing her mind. And if the police thought they could harass her into the kind of confession that would send her to prison, they were mistaken. For Sally had become an expert in coping with harassment: she had learned that particular skill from being married to Robert Cooper.

The following day; July 25th the police decided to try one last time to get a confession.

It was 10:30am and Sally was sitting at the table in Interview Room No I.

Philip Slater was sitting beside her, and across the table were DI Kelly, and DS Jean Mallory, a pretty, twenty-nine year old, considered by many to be a rising star in the force.

Everyone was looking very serious.

"Now, for the very last time, Mrs Cooper," Kelly declared with a sigh, "if you do not admit that you planned to kill your husband, I will have no choice but to send your case to The Crown Prosecution Services where I am confident you will be charged with murder. However, help us now and you may be charged with the lesser crime of manslaughter."

Sally met the gaze of the DI. "I did not plan to kill Robert. And no matter how many times you ask me or how many times you offer me a deal, I can't answer differently, because I am already telling you the truth. Or is it that you want me to confess to a lie just so that it will do your career some good?"

'Blast the woman!' Kelly thought to herself. 'No wonder she managed to put up with that bastard's violence. There was pure steel in her heart, and it was obvious she wasn't going to break in the time she could be held, damn her.'

"Very well, Mrs Cooper," she said aloud and standing up, "you have left me with no option."

Then terminating the interview, Kelly and her sergeant left the room.

Philip Slater put his arm around Sally. He smiled. "Don't worry. Despite what that cow says, they won't try for a murder conviction; they wouldn't get it and Kelly knows that very well. No jury would find you guilty; you would be freed. Now, as I explained in your cell, this is personal with her. She's a zealot. She doesn't care what you went through with Robert. All she cares about is that you broke the law; her law, and there's no way she want's you to go completely unpunished. You will almost certainly be charged with manslaughter; that way the prosecution at your trial will have a chance of sending you to prison."

"How long could that be for; if I am found guilty?" Sally asked, her face pale and drawn.

Slater shifted uncomfortably in his seat. "Well, technically for a number of years, but that's unlikely. Your medical record is your best defence against such an outcome."

"What do you mean a number years?"

"Up to fifteen years; technically. But as I said, it won't come to that."

"Fifteen years!" Sally exclaimed in horror. "But that's life. How could I go to prison for life when I'm only charged with manslaughter?"

An hysterical laugh then shot from her. "Listen to me; *only* manslaughter: talking about the killing of a human being as if I was discussing whether I am guilty of speeding or not!"

Slater shook her gently. "Don't go to pieces now, Sal. You can beat this thing, but only if you hold your nerve and not let the police bully you into a false confession. Your husband drove you to do what you did. And it's clear to me that you are only guilty of trying to save your marriage and stay alive. The jury will see that: I'm certain of it."

Sally gave a weak smile. She felt some small comfort from her ex-swimming partner. But how could he comfort her if she went to prison. Surely there could be none in a living nightmare.

Chapter Seven

The following day Sally was charged with manslaughter, and then transferred to Holloway Prison. And the slamming shut of the metal doors and gates behind her as she was taken to her cell were the worst sounds she had ever heard. This was a place she was sure she would never survive long-term.

The cell door was already open when she and her prison officer reached it.

She instinctively stopped in the doorway.

Inside the tiny room were two women; staring back at her with expressions of curiosity on their faces.

"This is Sally Cooper, a first timer, Veronica," said the officer. "Show her the ropes, will you."

Both women were sitting on a bunk bed either side of the room. "Come on in, girl," said a black woman in her thirties. "No need to be shy in front of me and Maggs."

Sally walked into the cell and the women stood in front of her. Both were smiling now.

"Welcome to The White House," said Veronica holding out her slim, right hand.

Sally hesitantly took it and Maggs' thicker hand when it was offered. "The White House?" she inquired.

"Both our surnames is Bush," said Veronica, who was tall, slim, and attractive.

Sally couldn't help smiling, though she had no desire to.

"Plonk your stuff on whichever bunk you like," Veronica ordered cheerfully. "But it has to be a top one: first come first served, I'm afraid. And if' you have a thing about heights then tough; you should have got yourself in here sooner, girl."

Feeling strange and lost, Sally chose the top bunk on the left. It seemed to be over Veronica's, and she had already taken a liking to the woman.

She reached up and shoved her holdall on to the narrow bed.

"Sit your bum down here next to me," said Veronica, "and then you can tell us all about yourself. That sort of information is the only thing we don't have to pay for in this dump, and we're the nosiest couple of bitches in the prison, so hold nothing back; right Maggs?"

Maggs, a chunky, forty-seven year old white girl with dark blonde, long straight hair that needed plenty of work on it, nodded. "Nosier than a cat at a mouse hole, V."

Sally sat on the bed beside Veronica.

"Does as she's told: good start," Veronica declared, obviously impressed. "Boy have we had some right bitches in here at times. Some of them would rather hold their breath and pass out, than keep on breathing just because you advised them too; correct, Maggs?"

"Yea, some right bitches," Maggs confirmed, slowly nodding her head.

"So," said Veronica, slapping her thighs, "what are you in for, girl?"

Sally stared questioningly at her. "I thought no one is ever asked that in prison?"

Veronica leaned back and fixed Sally with a surprised and humorous expression. "You, girl have been watching far too many American films. Anyway, a prison full of blokes ain't quite the same as a hen coup. We got all sorts of different rules in here such as no pissing up against walls; leaving toilet seats up; walking around bare-chested and face-shaving: you got a big, bushy beard; tough; it stays."

Sally found herself laughing. If she could forget the circumstances and the surroundings, she could be back in the office.

"Now come on, no more delays, girl; what you in for?" Veronica prompted.

Sally's humour vanished. She began picking at her fingers. "I killed my husband," she said in a low voice.

"No shit!" Veronica cried in surprise, throwing a glance at Maggs who looked equally taken back. "You don't look the type, girl."

"I don't look like a murderer, you mean?" said Sally, feeling light-headed. "And what does a murderer look like?"

"Just answer me this?" said Veronica. "Did he deserve it?"

"They usually do, don't they," Maggs offered.

"Shut up, Maggs, I'm talking here," Veronica ordered. "So, come on, girl; did he deserve what he got?"

Sally nodded.

"Glad to hear it," Veronica replied, obviously relieved. "Because me, I like men, and I don't want to be locked in a cell with no psycho bitch. So what did he do to get you going; give his fists an occasional workout on you?"

Again Sally nodded. "I had my spleen removed after one attack."

"Shit; the bastard!" Veronica spat. "I hope he was aware? You didn't do him in his sleep, did you? Most victims do, for some reason. If it was me, I'd make sure he saw it coming and bloody felt it when he got it."

"He was asleep and drunk," said Sally. "He just died."

"Ain't it always the way," said Veronica, disgusted. "But I'll bet a steak dinner he woke up with the devil smiling at him. So, you being charged with murder or what?"

"Manslaughter."

Veronica nodded slowly. "Good; good. And you got medical proof of what he did?"

"Yes."

"Then don't you worry, girl. There's usually enough women on any jury to bully reluctant men into a not guilty verdict. You won't be coming back here after your trial. Anyway, how about I make some tea to welcome you to our, bitch-free, little club. And what would madam prefer, Earl Grey or TU which is short for Tramp's Urine?"

"I've never tried Tramp's Urine before," said Sally, only too happy to change the subject.

"TU it is then," said Veronica. "Put the kettle on, will you, Maggs. And none of those used teabags you keep for unwelcome visitors, either. This girl is one of us."

The following day a guard informed Sally she had visitors.

She was made to wear an orange coat before she was allowed into the visitors room.

The room was large; containing two dozen plastic tables with chairs; most of them occupied.

Sally almost chocked with emotion when she saw Marcia and Margaret sitting at one of the tables. They stood up as she approached with the guard.

"No contacts or exchanges," the guard warned, walking away.

Sally sat down, tears filling her eyes.

"You poor thing," Marcia announced. "All the girls wanted to come, but Mr Henderson put his foot down for once, so you only have us two, I'm afraid, love."

"Thanks for coming," said Sally, wiping her eyes. "It has been a bit lonely these past few days."

"Hasn't anyone else been to see you!" Marcia exclaimed. "What about your parents?"

Determination entered Sally's voice. "I haven't told them, and I want it to stay like that."

"But you have to tell them," Marcia protested. "You can't go through this alone. They should be here supporting you."

Sally shook her head. "No, this is my problem. My parents have new lives now: I don't want to spoil that."

Marcia slid her hand across the table to touch Sally's arm.

"No contact," a stern voice said over a loudspeaker.

"God; a bit strict aren't they," said Marcia, pulling her hand back. "Anyway, how are you coping, Sal? It must be tough."

Sally shrugged. "It's not so bad; for a prison. I thought it would be worse; you know, more violent. But I'm sharing The White House with Veronica and Maggs: they're great."

The two visitors looked puzzled, and Sally explained.

They all laughed, and Margaret then made a concerned expression. "Are you sure they're not those violent types you hear about: you know; the kind that are fun, only so long as you do what they say? Because I saw this film once where this woman was locked up with these two-"

"No," Sally interrupted. "Veronica's only a compulsive shoplifter, though she probably gives the store detectives a rough time, and Maggs came up with a brilliant way of avoiding paying tax. The judge didn't think it was so brilliant though, especially when the sum involved was over twenty thousand pounds."

"At least that's something," said Margaret.

"Oh, there *are* a few violent women in here," said Sally. "In fact they were so impressed by what I did, they wanted me to request a transfer to their cell. But there's no way I'm going to do that. I find them every bit as frightening as Robert."

"Too right," said Margaret in approval. "You want to keep away from people like that. Anyway, when are you due at the Magistrate's court?"

"Next Tuesday."

"What does your solicitor think? Will you be sent to the Crown Court?"

Sally nodded, her mood suddenly subdued.

"Don't worry, Sal," said Marcia, smiling. "By the end of that trial you will be free. You should never have been charged with manslaughter in the first place. Surely the police know what that bastard did to you?"

Sally swallowed as nerves suddenly tightened her throat. "It seems that I am as much a lawbreaker as Robert was; according to the police."

"Well sod them!" Margaret snapped. "You did the right thing. And when the jury at your trial hear about Robert and his fists, I doubt they will even go into one of those rooms to discuss it. I've heard of it happening before: after a couple of minutes the jury tell's the judge that they have already made up their minds. Then we'll all go to the nearest pub to celebrate. And the drinks will be on Marcia."

"Oi," Marcia protested.

"Well, you are the one who said that the jury will take at least half an hour to decide."

Marcia grinned at Sally. "Look, love; Margaret is right. That jury is bound to make their decision straight away. And I will be delighted to lose that bet; but you keep an eye on your crown after that. I still have my eye on it."

For the next twenty minutes Sally chatted to her visitors. And when she was finally returned to her cell, she felt fortified by their confidence. After all, the jury would be ordinary, decent people, not hard-nosed police officers. All they would be concerned with was whether she was justified in killing Robert. And what decent person could say she wasn't."

At the Magistrate's court, Sally was refused bail because the police managed to convince the court that due to the severity of the charge against her, there was a strong possibility she would leave the country, and that she could also be a danger to the public, if she felt threatened.

Sally was devastated, and once back in her cell, it took hours for Veronica and Maggs to bring her out of it.

Chapter Eight

It was December 6th and Sally was sitting on a bench in her holding-cell at The Old Bailey. Sitting beside her was her barrister Andrew Murray-White, a tall, stocky, fifty-five year old with a full head of black/grey hair, a kind face and smiling eyes. Sally warmed to him at their first meeting.

"Ready?" he said.

Sally nodded.

"Here we go then," said Murray-White standing up with Sally. "And remember what I told you; try not to be frightened by what you see when you enter the courtroom. Hitler used to have foreign ambassadors walk along huge halls lined with giant statues and flags before meeting him, in order to intimidate them. But it's all show; nothing more; left over from a time when judges were treated like gods instead of what they really are; servants of the people. And an enormous courtroom doesn't mean you are going to be on trial for an enormous crime. You are innocent: keep that thought in your head. They have to prove your guilt: all you have to do is let me do the work and follow my instructions when you take the stand."

"Sir, they are waiting," said the guard at the open door.

Sally and Murray-White followed the guard along the narrow, winding corridors and up the single flight of stone steps.

Despite Murray-White's warning, Sally gasped as she emerged into the courtroom - a cavernous space, busy with, what seemed to her, hundreds of people going about some business or other.

'Oh God,' her mind protested, 'surely all these people can't be here for my trial?'

A comforting hand took hers.

She looked at Murray-White who was smiling at her.

"Remember what I told you about Hitler. It's all show; left over from an era of show. This could just as easily be done in someone's living-room, but then it wouldn't make the judges feel like emperors, and you wouldn't want to deprive them of that now would you, the poor old things."

Sally couldn't help returning the smile. And when two female guards then escorted her to the dock, she made a conscious effort to keep Murray-White's comforting words in her mind. All this wasn't really for her: she was just here to sort out a misunderstanding.

As Sally sat in the dock, she realized that her first impression of the number of people present was far less than she had perceived. Including the members of the jury, who were already seated, there were probably no more than fifty people present. Murray-White was right, the trial could indeed be carried out in someone's living-room; though it would have to be a pretty large one.

"Ladies and gentlemen of the jury!" the voice of James Peterson, Prosecutor for the Crown boomed out as he pointed an accusing finger at Sally. "The defendant, Sally Cooper, systematically planned and then carried out the murder of her husband Robert Cooper at approximately 11: 50 pm on the 23rd July 2003. The defence will try, no doubt with consummate skill, to convince you that she is a battered woman; a victim only defending herself against a violent husband. But do not let them sway you from the truth, ladies and gentlemen. Sally Cooper had options other than plunging a knife through her husband's chest when he was asleep and too drunk to defend himself. But she did not take those options, and why was that; because of greed, ladies and gentlemen of the jury: sheer, unadulterated greed!"

Sally didn't hear the rest of what was said, for at the mention of Robert's name, her mind had retreated to some deep and cold sanctuary.

And even when Murray-White countered the prosecutor's powerful words with powerful words of his own, she was unaware of their content; just a soft mumbling that was distant and meaningless.

"Mrs Cooper; are you all right?"

Sally started. Everyone was silent and looking at her.

"Are you all right, Mrs Cooper?"

Sally turned her head to stare at the judge. "Yes: I'm fine, thank you."

"Very well," said the judge. "Please continue, Mr Peterson."

James Peterson gave a curt nod of his head. "Thank you, My Lord. Now then, Mrs Cooper, you claim that your husband was both physically and mentally abusing you for the last year of your marriage?"

"I'm not claiming anything," Sally replied firmly. "Why don't you ask the doctors: they can tell you what that man did to me."

"Please answer yes or no, Mrs Cooper," said Peterson. "Now, a year of abuse is a very long time, I should imagine; surely plenty to think about your situation; to decide what you should do about the violence from your husband. Would you agree with that?"

"I - I suppose so," Sally replied, feeling she was being forced into retreat.

"And when you have a year to make up your mind, would you not agree that there is no need of spur-of-the-moment behaviour?"

A wave of dread swamped Sally's body. She shuddered. "I don't know what you mean?" she said in a weak voice.

"Could you speak a little louder for the jury, Mrs Cooper," said the judge. "They are not as close to you as I am."

Sally looked at the jury. "I said I don't know what you mean."

"Really," said Peterson in a condescending tone. "I believe my question is clear. Would you agree that a spur-of-the-moment act is brought about by a lack of time to consider that act or its possible consequences?"

"Yes; I suppose so."

"And that being the case, how then can you claim that you stabbed your husband to death in a sudden rush of violence that left you confused and bewildered? After all, you admitted your husband was asleep at the moment you drove the carving knife into his chest, and not only asleep but exceedingly intoxicated."

Sally's cold and deep sanctuary beckoned once more, and she answered the call. However, a small part of her conscious mind remained. It was the police station all over again, and even DI Kelly was there; though this time in the form of a man wearing a black gown and white wig.

"Mrs Cooper?" Peterson prompted.

"I don't know," she replied. "I was confused by what was happening to me."

"But you were clear-minded enough to murder your husband; and, by all accounts, to make certain he was dead," said Peterson. "Therefore, it seems to me that your claim of confusion must be a lie."

Sally continued to answer questions for another hour, and then a number of her neighbours were called to testify. And although a few made vicious claims about her that were untrue, most confessed to hearing Robert shouting and swearing inside the house, on many occasions.

Three hours later Sally was back in Holloway.

"How'd it go, girl?" Veronica asked, genuinely concerned.

Sally let out a long sigh as she sat on the edge of Veronica's bed. "It was awful," she replied. "They made me seem like a vengeful and greedy woman who planned the whole thing."

"What; your defence did that!" Veronica exclaimed in mock horror. "I'd ditch them sharpish if I were you, girl."

A short laugh left Sally. "No; the prosecution, you fool."

Veronica put a comforting arm around Sally's shoulders. "Look, love, it's the prosecutors job to convince the jury that's how you are. That's what they're paid to do. And even if Mother Teresa herself was in the dock, accused of beating up a professional rugby player, they would probably claim she was really a man in drag and an ex-wrestler, if it would help them get a conviction. So don't let it get to you. Anyway, that's not the least bit interesting to us: but what *is* interesting is whether your barrister is young and dishy, or a crusty old codger, hard of hearing and forgetful, like the one I had; useless old git?"

"Not so young: in his fifties, but yes, I suppose you could say he was dishy," Sally replied, her mood lifting.

"Me, I like older men," said Maggs, thoughtfully. "All that fumbling the young ones get up to, puts me right off. I like someone with experience; someone who knows exactly what to do. Anyway, I hate acne."

"Right now I'd settle for anyone with something between their legs," Veronica quipped with a sigh.

"Dirty cow!" Maggs exclaimed, laughing.

"Well, it has been two years," Veronica protested. "A girl has needs, you know. And I could always close my eyes and imagine he was Brad Pitt. It wouldn't be the first time either. In fact I've had Brad at least a dozen times: pity he doesn't know."

"If he did he'd probably give up sex," Maggs replied.

Sally listened in silence as a friendly argument about men then took place between her cell-mates. And she promised herself that she would stay in touch when she was released; if she was released.

Chapter Nine

Sally had to visit The Old Bailey three more times before the prosecution and defence finally made their closing statements. And despite the apparent confidence of her barrister, she feared the trial had gone against her.

"You are worrying again, aren't you?" Murray-White scolded as he sat next to Sally in the holding-cell. "You must have faith in British justice. The jury is made up of ordinary people, and I'm convinced that they are on your side."

"But they didn't decide straight away?" Sally protested.

Murray-White frowned. "What do you mean?"

"I mean, they retired to deliberate: that's what the judge asked them to do, and they did it."

"Of course they did," Murray-White answered. "What else did you expect them to do; stand up and declare sorry, Your Honour, but she does have a kind face and a lovely smile. And since it is perfectly clear to us that she only gave that brute of a husband what he deserved, she must be innocent, so we might as well all go home and watch TV?"

"Well; yes; something like that." Sally's voice was hesitant. "Veronica and Maggs said that if the jury was convinced I was innocent they would tell the judge that they had already made up their minds."

"That rarely happens," said Murray-White. "And when it does, the judge always tells them to retire and deliberate anyway. No one in the legal system likes snap decisions. I mean, can you imagine what would happen to the huge fees they charge for their time. The poor things would starve."

Hope glowed in Sally's eyes. "You think that was the reason: do you really think so?"

"I do," said Murray-White, smiling. "And another thing, when your medical records were read out, I saw two jury women wipe their eyes."

Sally shrugged. "Maybe they had a cold."

Murray-White chuckled and took her hands in his. "You *are* a cynic this morning; aren't you."

"Just being practical. After all, I could go to prison for a long time; couldn't I?"

The humour left Murray-White. "I suppose that is a possibility." Then his mood became earnest. "However, I have all the confidence in the world that even if you are found guilty, which I doubt, the judge will be lenient. I know him well. He's one of the kindest men in the legal system."

"The jury has returned, sir," said a male guard who appeared in the doorway.

"Only an hour," said Murray-White, glancing at his watch. "That sounds good to me."

"I hope it is," said Sally, not feeling convinced.

"Chin up," said Murray-White. "You are going to be all right, Sally Cooper. Trust me."

Once more Sally was sitting in the dock.

The courtroom looked more crowded than ever.

Her fears returned. Who were all these extra people? The Visitors Gallery was crammed. She could just make out a few people waving at her, and she waved back, assuming they were the girls from work. But the rest; she didn't know them. Had they turned up to gloat as the judge sent her to prison for fifteen years? The bastards: that's probably why the majority of them were there! And if it was allowed they would probably throw rotten fruit and eggs at her, the bastards. How she hated them all.

She felt odd now. Her emotions were all over the place. She could feel them battling for supremacy; fighting for control of her mind, just the way Robert used to. Except he didn't have to battle: what sort of fight did she put up. But he had the same effect on her as her emotions had now, sending fear, confusion, hatred and desperation clawing around inside her body like wild cats trying to get out of a cage. And this was her punishment for losing control and killing Robert. Perhaps DI Kelly was right:

perhaps anyone taking the law into their own hands in such a brutal fashion deserved to be locked up.

She looked at the jury members. They were sitting absolutely still. She didn't like the expressions on their faces; they were all exactly the same: cold: hard: emotionless. They didn't look like twelve ordinary people having to decide an ordinary woman's fate. They looked like judges; ready to judge; ready to do their duty, no matter what their personal feelings might be. They were marble statues devoid of pity and they were going to lock her away for a long time.

"All please rise," a voice that sounded like God to Sally, boomed out.

Everyone, including Sally stood up, though in her case it was at the prompting of one of the guards next to her.

The judge, dressed in a red gown and a white wig made his way to his throne. Then he bowed once and sat down.

"Please be seated," God ordered.

Sally dropped into her seat. Why was she so weak: why did her legs feel like they only had the strength of soft rubber?

"Members of the jury," said the judge in a far less impressive voice than God's, "have you chosen a spokesperson?"

A middle-aged woman at the end of the row of jurors, stood up. "Yes, Your Honour."

"And have you reached a verdict?"

"We have, Your Honour."

Immediately the clerk of the court made his way to the woman.

She handed him a piece of paper.

The clerk took it. Then he walked towards the Bench and handed the paper up to the judge.

The judge unfolded it; read for a moment, then re-folded the paper and stared at the jury. His expression was grave. "And is this the decision of you all?"

"Yes, Your Honour," said the spokesperson.

The judge turned to Sally. "Will the defendant please stand."

Sally felt her mind detach itself and float freely. Why was it so hard to think? Why was everything so foggy? She knew she had been spoken to, but she couldn't understand the words.

Both of her arms were gripped and she felt herself being lifted. Her rubber-like legs tried to help but it wasn't much.

"Members of the jury," said the judge, "on the charge of Manslaughter, how do you find the defendant Sally Cooper; guilty or not guilty?"

The spokeswoman braced herself. "We find the defendant; not guilty."

A roar went up that assaulted Sally's eardrums like battering-rams. She closed her eyes but the roar continued. What was going on? Why were these people making such a noise? What were they cheering about? Were they glad Robert was dead? How could Robert have made so many people hate him? Was he beating them as well?

Then a loud banging cut through the roar. "Silence in court!" shouted the judge. "Silence in court!"

The roar trailed away and Sally sighed with relief.

"Sally Cooper, you have been found not guilty of the charge against you," the judge announced. "This trial has concluded. You are free to go."

The roar was back; more intense than ever.

Again she closed her eyes.

But this time she could make out individual voices, shouting her name; shouting 'Murderer; murderer!'

Robert didn't have any family: why were they so angry?

Then the din faded, to be replaced by the shuffling sounds of people leaving the court.

One of the guards smiled at her. "Would you like me to escort you out. There may be a bit of a crush?"

"No thanks," said Sally, sitting back down. "I'll stay here for just a few moments, if that's all right?"

"You take your time," said the guard, and both of them left.

Sally stared around the fast-emptying courtroom. She was already feeling better; stronger. But she didn't feel free. She didn't believe the nightmare was over.

A little while later Murray-White approached. He had a huge grin on his handsome face. "I though I would give you a few moments to collect your thoughts. So, how are you feeling?"

"Finding it difficult to believe that I don't have to come back here again," she replied.

Murray-White sat down beside her. "That's only natural. This sort of thing is like getting a serious dose of flu. It can come on frighteningly quick sometimes, but it always goes away slowly, almost reluctantly. Give it a few weeks and you will begin to think about the future."

"Doesn't feel like it," Sally replied with a sigh.

"It will: give it time. Now, how about a drink to celebrate? I know a nice little pub not far from here. They keep a snug just for the very best barristers to unwind in. I'm a frequent customer there, you know."

Sally smiled at the humour.

Then a door, thirty feet to Sally's left, opened, and a head appeared.

Next thing Sally knew, a crowd of women were quickly tiptoeing towards her like students sneaking to a late night drinking session.

Murray-White stood up. "I think you are going to be far too busy to sit in a snug with me."

Sally stood up also. A wave of emotion put a tremble in her voice. "Thank you: thank you very much for all you did."

"I'm not sure you will think that when you receive my bill," quipped Murray-White. "We exceptional barristers have to support a high standard of living."

Then Marcia and the rest of Sally's work colleagues were surrounding her.

"Take care of yourself, Sally," said Murray-White retreating towards a different door. "And have a good life."

Sally gave a small wave, and there was sadness in her smile.

Chapter Ten

It was December 29th 2003; the day after Sally's acquittal at the Old Bailey, and the sun was shining from a blue sky on to a chilly morning.

She put down her holdall and bag of groceries, and then opened the door of her house.

The silence within felt like it reached out and slapped her across the face.

She gasped for breath.

Anxiety spiked every cell in her body. What was she doing back here? This was a house of death; not a home. She must be mad!

Then she forced the doubt and the anxiety away. Why shouldn't she return to the place she had help choose, decorate and maintain; to the place she had loved; at least for the first year of her marriage. The house had been hers every bit as much as Robert's, even if he had treated it as if it was nothing more than a place for him to torture his wife in privacy. And maybe that was her fault. After all she had let him do those terrible things to her - she had let him drive her love to a deep and empty place, where it had all but ceased to exist.

But Robert was gone now: the house was still here and so was she.

Of course, it could never again be what it was for her during the first year of her marriage - a place of fun, warmth and tenderness. But it could be a means to a new life somewhere else. And there was no way she was going to allow Robert's ghost, or memory, or whatever she sensed might be lingering within its four walls, to get in the way of that. Robert owed her a decent life, and she was going to see that, *that particular* debt to her, at least, was paid.

Suddenly aware that she must look suspicious standing before an open door for so long, she picked up the bags. Then having stepped inside and closed the door behind her, she put the bags down once more, and slowly walked towards the living-room.

Her heart thumped inside her chest when she walked through the doorway.

Her eyes instinctively darted towards Robert's armchair, half expecting to see him slumped in it with the front of his shirt stained with blood.

She let out a loud sigh when she saw that the chair was empty, and then scolded herself for being silly.

She looked around the large room.

The cleaners had done an excellent job, and nothing valuable had been stolen, as far as she could see.

The Georgian mirror was still hanging above the fireplace. The mantelpiece still had its collection of early Blue and White figurines, and in the corner of the room, next to the bay window, the Victorian, mahogany display cabinet was full of the little crystal animals she had bought during her childhood in Devon.

These little animals were priceless to her by their association with a time when she was gloriously happy. For, although she was an only child, she had many friends. And when one day her mother told her that they would be moving to London, without her father, she was heartbroken.

Suddenly weary, she walked to the settee and sat down. It cushioned her wonderfully. How long had it been since she had sat in something designed for comfort; five months, five very long months that tested her mental strength almost to breaking-point.

She leaned down and ran her fingers through the dark blue, shagpile carpet. How on Earth did Robert think it went with the pink, three-piece suite. It was the most awful, dull colour, and clashed horribly with just about everything; a big dark, ugly stain in an otherwise perfect room.

It had to go! There was no way she was going to invite prospective buyers in to walk on such a monstrosity. They were bound to snigger behind her back.

She then smiled and lay back, enjoying the soft pressure against her. What was she doing worrying about what people might think; it was the least of her problems?

A few minutes later she got up and collected the carrier bag from the hall.

Then she made her way into the kitchen.

It was as spotless as the living-room, and far cleaner than it had ever been when she lived there with Robert. Yes, the cleaning company had done a first class job. She would have to phone and thank them.

She walked over to the stainless steel sink and turned on the cold tap, letting the water run for a few moments.

She then filled the electric kettle and switched it on. The resulting click sounded unusually loud; the way many sounds do in the early hours.

She held her breath as she opened the fridge door: good, it was empty and as clean as everything else: no stink of sour milk or bad food. She was *definitely* going to phone the cleaning company.

A minute later the fridge had acquired a packet of extra mature farmhouse cheddar: a packet of butter: a carton of skimmed milk: two packets of sliced ham and a small jar of English mustard.

The empty bread bin was treated to a white-sliced loaf, and a lime-washed cupboard a jar of coffee and a packet of tea bags.

She savoured every single moment of putting those groceries away. It was amazing what was missed when all you did was what you were told by someone else for five months.

Ten minutes passed and she was sitting at the kitchen table, enjoying a cheese sandwich and a cup of tea. Just the experience of being able to eat alone was exquisite. Veronica and Maggs were great company, and she owed them more than she could ever repay. But there had been many times when she would have cheerfully shinned up the Great Dome of St Paul's, in the pouring rain, just to get away from them.

The next thing she would have to do is contact the bank and rearrange her finances. The cost of her defence was going to be around sixty thousand pounds, but she wasn't worried. There was enough cash in different accounts to pay for it. However, she would have to return to work soon. Fortunately Mr Henderson decided to keep her job open; a decision he didn't have much choice in; the girls had seen to that.

At first she decided to sell the house immediately and move away, but she didn't feel up to it. She would give it a year; then she would be off.

No doubt she would have to put up with people staring at her. A few might even be actively hostile: some people seemed to seek out conflict for the sake of it. But what did she care. A six foot, seventeen stone monster failed to drive her away, so what chance did they have.

"Do you hear me, Robert, you pig?" she called out to the empty house. "I don't know where you are, but it certainly isn't here and that's the only thing that matters. I have my life back now and neither you nor anyone else is going to force me to leave until I'm good and ready."

Sally leaned over one of the huge chillers in her local supermarket for a bag of organic peas. She liked the fresh flavour of frozen vegetables best, and didn't mind the extra cost involved.

"Excuse me," said a harsh-sounding female voice from behind.

Sally straightened up without the peas. She turned to see a short, middle-aged woman with dark brown hair glaring at her.

"I just wanted you to know that I think it's disgraceful how you got away with killing Robert the way you did," the woman went on. "You should be in prison, not shopping in this supermarket as if you had never even been on trial for murder."

Sally's heart began to race, but she forced her rising anger down. This wasn't the first time someone had accosted her with their grievances, and it wouldn't be the last.

"I wasn't charged with murder," she corrected in an even tone. "I was charged, and acquitted of manslaughter."

"You killed him, didn't you!" the woman snapped. "It makes no difference what you call it."

"Did you know him?" Sally asked. "You called him Robert?"

The woman hesitated. "Yes; in a way I did. But that has nothing to do with it. And for your information, I run a refuge for women who suffer domestic violence. Clearly you have no interest in such places. You would much rather become a brutal person like your tormentor, and commit the most terrible act of savagery on another human being. Your husband must have had mental problems; many violent men do, and you should have seen to it that he received medical attention instead of attacking him in his sleep. And let me ask you this, did you even once try and find out what was wrong with him: I suppose you didn't: much easier to bide your time and do him in at your leisure."

Despite Sally's resolve, her anger began to get the better of her. "Look, I am trying to put all that behind me, and I don't need someone like you venting your frustrations on me because you don't like the decision the jury made. You may run a refuge, but that doesn't mean you know what it was like for me. And even if you were in a violent relationship yourself, it wasn't with Robert Cooper. So you really don't know what you are talking about, do you. There are many forms of violence both physical and mental, and if you are really that fascinated with the subject, maybe we could go and have a coffee somewhere, and I can fill you in on all the sordid details of what he did to me in the bedroom. I'm sure you will enjoy hearing it; people like you usually do."

The woman's mouth had dropped open in outrage as Sally's words stung like a sand-storm. She tried to speak, but only gurgling sounds came out.

"No: oh what a shame," Sally cooed. "Well, it was nice talking to you, but if you don't mind, I have more shopping to do."

Then picking up the bag of peas and placing them in her trolley, Sally moved off, her head held high and a smile on her face.

Chapter Eleven

Exactly twelve months had passed since Sally shouted her defiance to an empty home.

Her house was sold now, and she was walking down a street in Highgate towards her new purchase.

Her heart quickened in anticipation when she reached the four storey, late eighteenth century, red-brick building.

She had purchased the ground floor maisonette for exactly the same price that she sold her previous house for. But she had enough money still in her account to decorate and keep her going for a while.

Suddenly her excitement was replaced by an attack of nerves.

With a slight tremble of her hand she inserted the key into the lock of the security door and let herself into the shared entrance hall.

An attractive winding stairs on the right allowed her neighbours access to the maisonette above, and the floor was covered in black and white tiles.

Her panelled, varnished, oak front door was on the left, and she approached it with even more trepidation.

Why was she feeling like this?

Was it because once inside her new home, her old life would be gone forever; the good as well as the bad?

Again her hand trembled when she used her key.

Inside, the hall was large and finely decorated with cream wall paper and a beautiful oatmeal carpet.

Sally liked these colours; they would certainly escape the blitz she was going to carry out on the rest of the maisonette with it's dark red-painted walls in the living-room; the intense blue walls in the three bedrooms; the avocado bathroom and the Formica kitchen.

"God; some people's taste!" she declared aloud.

Clearly she had purchased the maisonette just in time to save the hall from the ravages of its previous owner.

Her nerves settled and some of the excitement returned.

Yes, she had lots to do in her new home and the best thing about it was that Robert Cooper had never set foot inside its door. Ghosts only haunted the places where they were created, and that was far away.

The following week, Sally saw an advert in the local paper which was of some interest to her. A large supermarket store in nearby Finchley was looking for checkout staff. She had no wish to begin her new life working in that particular kind of job, but it would at least provide her with an income until she found something better. She had only started redecorating her home so she hadn't spent very much money, but that would soon change. Also, the supermarket was only two stops on the train so fares wouldn't be a problem.

"Have you had any previous experience in checkout, Miss Bain?" asked Mrs Tobin, Staff Supervisor of the Finchley branch of Mulville's Supermarket Ltd.

Sally had returned to her family name after her trial, and it still sounded odd to her. "No; sorry, I haven't, I'm afraid."

Mrs Tobin pulled a disapproving face. "I see. That is most unfortunate. But you must understand, Miss Bain, that Mulville's Supermarket Ltd, only employ qualified staff. Our customers expect the very best service. Many of them are elderly and remember the days when good service and good manners were a byword of all decent establishments. We at Mulville's consider ourselves to be a beacon of propriety in an ocean of insolence and indifference."

Sally knew she would have to act quickly if she wanted a chance of being taken on. "Oh, I understand exactly what you mean," she declared. "My mother is always saying that good manners cost nothing but enriches all our lives."

"Your mother is quite correct," Mrs Tobin replied with the same firmness. "And since it is clearly evident that you have been brought up to understand such things, I feel that I can dispense with the usual requirements, on this occasion. I have decided to take you on a month's trial. And if all goes well, I am sure you will enjoy being a permanent member of staff. Our manager Mr Harris likes to think that we are all one large family here. Now, how soon can you start?"

"Will Monday be all right?" said Sally, greatly relieved.

Mrs Tobin smiled and stood up. "Until 8am on Monday, then, and welcome to Mulville's, Miss Bain."

Sally stood also. "Thank you, Mrs Tobin. I won't let you down."

A month later Sally was offered the job permanently, and she quickly settled into the rather staid routine of life on the checkout. She often found the work boring, but there was usually an interesting or amusing customer to lift her mood. And the other members of staff were nice.

However, one particular member of staff stood out above all the rest as far as Sally was concerned. His name was Jimmy Mason, Assistant Manager.

Jimmy was tall; just over six feet two inches, with a slim but strong frame. His hair was brown and cut in the style of what was called 'Short, Back and Sides.' His features were thin, and his eyes an attractive blue. All the girls thought he looked a bit like Justin Timberlake, but Sally disagreed: to her he looked definitely more like Brad Pitt, though not quite so handsome.

Sally knew that Jimmy played squash twice a week at a nearby club, and she considered becoming a member. But she refrained from doing so. The women fancied the socks of him, but she feigned disinterest. And taking up squash would certainly reveal her true feelings. Then she would be teased unmercifully.

However, her attraction towards Jimmy demanded that she make at least some attempt to get to know him on a personal level. She must have a plan; but one that wouldn't expose her to rejection. She was feeling far too fragile still to cope with something harsh like that.

A couple of days later, Sally discovered, in the colourfully decorated staff canteen, that she didn't need a plan after all.

"Mind if I sit here?" a familiar voice inquired.

Sally jerked in shock, and then became flustered when Jimmy placed his lunch tray on the table and eased his long frame into a yellow, moulded-plastic seat next to hers.

"Yes; I mean no, of course not."

Margaret Brown, another checkout girl and friend of Sally, who was sitting opposite, put her plate of Shepherd's Pie and baked beans, back on her tray and stood up. "Sorry, Sal, but I need to discuss something with Tracy over there. You don't mind, do you?"

"What; oh, no; that's ok," said Sally, pink-faced with embarrassment.

Margaret gave a sly wink and walked off.

Out of the corner of her eye, Sally watched as Jimmy put his plate of Dover Sole, boiled potatoes and carrots on the table. Then having put his knife and fork in the correct position, shoved the tray away from him.

"How's the roast beef today?" he asked, cutting into the fish. "Sometimes it can taste like a tramp's old leather shoe."

Sally gave a small laugh which was born out of a combination of humour and nerves. "It's quite nice actually."

"Aaaa, but don't be fooled," said Jimmy, knowingly. "They probably won't serve you the real nasty stuff until you have been here too long to tell the difference. Their plan usually is to reduce the quality gradually; let the nasty stuff creep up on you. And do you know, there is an ex-Michelin chef working in our accounts dept: two stars would you believe. And when he first came here, he could tell by smell alone, and from another room, how many hours earlier a bunch of carrots had been picked. After four years eating in this canteen, he can't even tell the difference between a carrot and an onion unless he can see them; poor devil."

Sally began laughing, then coughing as a trickle of her gravy went down the wrong way.

Jimmy slapped her gently on the back. "Steady on!" he cried. "I sat here to chat you up, not choke you to death with my bad jokes."

Eventually Sally recovered, and they both continued eating in silence.

Although Sally stared at her plate the whole time she ate, her mind was entirely on the person sitting next to her. How wonderful it felt to be so close to a man's body; a man she longed for after being so alone.

The sudden clatter of Jimmy's cutlery being dropped on his plate made her jump.

"Boy; that was good!" said Jimmy. "But then how would I know; I've been here nearly six years."

Laughter burst out of Sally.

"Hey, you're not going to choke on me again, are you?" Jimmy cried.

Sally turned to look at him. There were tears in her eyes. "No, Mr Mason. I'm fine."

Jimmy began looking wildly about him, an expression of shock on his attractive face. "What's going on here?" he shouted. "I thought this was the canteen where everyone is called by their first name. This woman has just called me Mr Mason! Where's the complaint office?"

"Sorry; Jimmy. And no, I'm not going to choke on you again," said Sally, embarrassed once more since every head was turned towards her table.

Jimmy then stared firmly at her, his large blue eyes taking in every detail of her face. "I'm very glad to hear it, Sally, because it's taken me ages to pluck up the courage to do this, and I wouldn't want to ruin it. So, how about a coffee, and don't worry, they keep the good stuff for the management behind the chips. I won't tell them that one cup is for the most attractive checkout girl this sad old store has ever employed or you'll get the gravy-blend like the rest of the poor sods."

"Yes, I would like some coffee please," Sally replied.

A couple of minutes later Jimmy was back with a tray containing sachets of sugar, a small jug of milk and two cups of dark liquid that smelt wonderful to Sally.

"Milk?" Jimmy offered, holding the jug over her cup.

"Just a little, please."

Jimmy grinned as he poured. "And I bet you don't take sugar?"

Sally was puzzled. "How do you know that?"

"Someone who looks like you rarely has a sweet tooth," Jimmy replied.

"As a matter of fact I do have a sweet tooth," Sally corrected, "but I weaned myself off sugar when I gained a few unwanted pounds."

Jimmy gawked at her. "You; fat; never! I've seen more fat on a stick of celery."

"Yes, well I lost it again when I cut out the sugar."

"So, tell me about yourself?" said Jimmy, pouring sugar into his coffee. "Where does Sally Bain hail from?"

All sense of joy instantly drained from Sally.

She suddenly felt empty and defensive.

Jimmy noticed the change in her. "Look; I'm sorry," he said with genuine regret. "I can see from your reaction that I'm prying now. I'll leave you to enjoy your coffee in peace."

"No!" Sally's hand shot out and grabbed Jimmy's arm as he made to stand.

He felt her desperation in the grip, and smiled warmly. "Never let it be said that Jimmy Mason; 'Mrs Mason's Pride and Joy' refused an invitation from a beautiful woman. And furthermore, Mrs Mason's 'Pride and Joy' knows when he has put his size elevens in it. So, no more questions; agreed?"

Warmth began to return and Sally nodded. The directness of the question had shaken her. She must learn not to react so badly every time she was reminded of her past. This problem had become more acute as the months had gone by since her trial. And it was one of the main reasons she left everything behind, including her friends at Chapman's.

"Now then," Jimmy went on, "I hear there's a great film out at the cinema. And if a certain young lady would care to accompany Mr Jimmy 'Always Putting His foot In It' Mason to said great film, he promises to provide that certain young lady with the very largest tub of popcorn money can buy. And if that certain young lady discovers even a single un-popped popcorn lurking in her tub of popcorn, Mr Jimmy 'Always Putting His Foot In It' Mason promises to take the un-popped popcorn right back to the popcorn seller and demand that the un-popped popcorn be popped the way proper popcorn should be popped."

Sally laughed so much she began coughing again.

Jimmy gave her a silly look of surprise. "God, I hope something hasn't popped."

Chapter Twelve

After the film Jimmy took Sally to a Thai restaurant in Newbury Street. She took great delight in the exciting new tastes she discovered, much to Jimmy's satisfaction. And they stayed on, drinking wine and chatting for nearly two hours after the meal was eaten.

They had much in common, particularly in their love of jazz, and somehow it never seemed the right time to break the spell they had cast upon one another.

Eventually an awkward-sounding restaurant manager politely asked them to leave.

For a time they walked arm in arm through the surrounding streets, pointing out shops of particular interest, and architecture that left them awed by the skills of past stonemasons, or simply laughing at Jimmy's jokes which were humorous and varied, but never crude.

Sally loved his good manners, and suspected that beneath all the rather corny chat-up lines and humour, was a reserved and gentle spirit. And these were qualities she needed in any man she might want to have a long-term relationship with.

All too soon for Sally the evening came to an end.

Jimmy dropped her off outside her maisonette.

He held the passenger door of his Ford Mondao open for her to get out. Then he escorted her to the security door.

She turned to face him, her eyes bright with happiness. "Would you like to come in for a coffee?"

Jimmy smiled down at her. "I'd rather not, if you don't mind." Then he added hurriedly when he saw disappointment on her face. "I know you're probably going to think I'm some sort of throwback, but I prefer to date a girl the old fashion way; flowers, chocolates and all that stuff. I know it's not the way things are done these days, and to be perfectly honest I have been dumped a couple of times because of it. So if you want to end this now, I'll understand. Of course I'll have you seeing to the most foul and smelliest customers for the next six months, but I *will* understand."

Sally's happiness returned. "Well," she replied thoughtfully, "I wouldn't want to have to wear a clothes peg on my nose for six months, so I better agree to let you take me out again."

Jimmy's face lit up. "Great!" he cried.

Then he gave her a quick kiss on her left cheek and ran towards the car. And as he finally pulled away he gave two loud beeps on his horn, and waved through the window.

Sally stood where she was for a full two minutes after he had gone, savouring the memory. She was already eager for their next date.

She slept gloriously well that Friday night, and awoke the following morning, feeling as if she had been reborn into the human race where happiness only had to be reached for and held tight.

At work she was pestered mercilessly for the gritty details of her date, by her female colleagues, but she refused to divulge any information at all. She simply smiled in a way that suggested everything and told nothing. This, of course drove her colleagues into frantic conjectures, which in turn only added to Sally's desire to repeat the experience with Jimmy at the first opportunity.

On their second date a week later, Jimmy accepted an invitation for coffee and he stayed long enough to watch a midnight film with Sally.

Four more dates followed before Jimmy finally made love to her. And at that moment Sally was certain that she had found the man she wanted to spend the rest of her life with.

Six months later Jimmy was sprawled on the settee with Sally in her living-room.

"Hmmm, pink settee, pink armchairs and pink curtains," he said thoughtfully as he cast his eyes around. "I'll feel I'm living in a flamingo colony when I move in here. Something pink will definitely have to go!"

"Who said you're going to move in here?" Sally corrected, putting her arms around his neck and smiling.

Jimmy pulled a shocked expression. "Are you mad, woman. Of course your husband is going to live here. Where else do you think he will live; in that run down Haven For Giant Spiders-shed at the bottom of your garden; *I think not!*"

Sally's heart began galloping with joy and excitement, but she managed to present a calm exterior. "And who said I'm going to marry you?"

Jimmy stroked her hair. "Oh, make no mistake about it, Miss Sally Bain. When Jimmy Mason decides to marry a beautiful young woman, she'd better accept his proposal. Because she will never get a better one; that's as sure as this room is: what is it now: oh yes; pink!"

"Then it's decided, is it?" said Sally.

Jimmy's voice took on a firm tone. "It is.; so get rid of the pink. Black is my colour."

For a few moments Sally and Jimmy stared silently at one another, then they burst out laughing.

"Black, in my beautiful home!" Sally cried suddenly. "Oh, all right; but so long as it can go in the drawers I won't mind too much; I suppose."

"Does that mean the concert-size grand piano I was planning on buying is out?" said Jimmy, pulling a disgusted face.

"It certainly is; unless it can fit in the drawers," Sally quipped.

"Hmmm, but you didn't specify what size drawers it had to fit in; did you," said Jimmy, "and I've seen some right whoppers hanging on your neighbour's line. Think Mrs Harper would let me borrow one if I was nice to her?"

Sally laughed and poked Jimmy in the belly. "I'll let you have my fist if I catch you looking at other women's underwear; even if they do belong to Mrs Harper who is eighty-five if she's a day."

One day, when Sally popped out from work during her lunch break to look for a new blouse, she noticed a woman staring at her.

As she browsed through the store, the woman seemed to follow, but always keeping her distance.

Finally Sally decided to ignore the woman, who always busied herself with whatever was to hand, when she stared directly at her.

She was probably a store detective, and it made Sally wonder what it was about her that aroused the woman's suspicions.

Then, as Sally moved towards the exit, deciding that the store had nothing to tempt her, she felt her right arm touched.

"You're Sally Cooper, aren't you, Chuck?" said a female voice.

Sally froze, and a wave of nausea savaged her body. She staggered as the room began to spin.

"Oh; I'm sorry, Chuck!" the woman's voice declared. "I think you better sit down."

Then strong arms slowly escorted Sally towards a pair of seats.

"How stupid of me to pounce on you like that," the voice went on. "You just sit here, Chuck, and rest yourself."

Still in shock, Sally allowed herself to be guided into one of the padded seats in front of a rail holding various styles of dressing gowns. She was only dimly aware of the presence that sat next to her.

"Would you like me to get you some water?" the voice asked.

Sally shook her head. "No; thank you. I'm fine."

"Me and my big mouth," the woman berated herself. "What was I thinking; coming up behind you like that. It's just that I recognized you from the newspapers, and I wanted to tell you that you did the right thing when you knifed that bastard: me, I'd have done him in the first time he used his fists. Men like that never change: they do it once they go on doing it."

Tears ran from Sally's eyes.

"God, I'm doing it again!" the woman exclaimed. "Look, Chuck, take no notice of me. I'm always putting my foot in it - subtle as a hippo but with a bigger mouth, my mother used to say."

A memory of Jimmy having lunch with her in the canteen suddenly drove the torment from Sally, and she looked at the woman sitting beside her. She even managed a smile. "I'm sorry," she said in a weak voice, "I didn't mean to go to pieces like that. It was just hearing that name again. You see, I don't use it now. I use my maiden name of Bain."

The woman, in her forties and dowdy-looking, smiled also. "No need to apologize, Chuck. My name's Sarah: how do you do."

Sally gave a little laugh as she shook the offered hand.

"Now then," said Sarah, "I think I owe you an explanation after the shock I gave you. So, where do I begin - silly me, at the beginning of course. Anyway, I followed your trial; every detail of it. And I promise you, Chuck, if you had spent a single day in prison for killing that monster, us women would have got you out of there even if we had to dismantle that building one brick at a time, and to hell with our nails. And boy was I glad when you were acquitted."

"Do you live around here?" Sally asked, desperately needing to change the subject.

"Just visiting my aunt," said Sarah. "I was in here trying to find a cardigan for her. But seeing you put it clear out of my head. No; I'm originally from Manchester, but I moved to Perth two years ago - I must like the cold or something. And what about you, Chuck, where are you living now?"

"I moved to Highgate a year after -" Sally's voice failed her.

Sarah frowned. "Had to get away, eh: don't blame you. So, have you managed to make a new life for yourself?"

Sally nodded.

"That's good," said Sarah. "And how's it going?"

A big smile lit up Sally's face. "Fantastic."

"Fantastic, eh," said Sarah with a knowing look. "That can only mean there's a fella in your life?"

"Yes, I have met someone, as a matter of fact," said Sally.

"Serious, is it?"

"I think so."

"Then good for you, Chuck," said Sarah. "Out with the old and in with the new; that's my motto."

Suddenly her eye's widened in horror. "Oh my twisted knickers: I didn't mean it like that, Chuck!"

Sally was still smiling. "That's all right. I know what you meant."

"And he's good to you, is he?" Sarah's tone was almost threatening.

"We're very happy together, Sarah. He's the most wonderful man I have ever met."

"Going places, I hope?"

"He's the Assistant Manager Of Mulville's Supermarket: the one in Henshaw Street."

Sarah pursed her lips. "Not bad; not bad; not great, mind you, but not bad. Me, I'm saving myself for a man with a garage full of cash and another one with a Ferrari in it. Can't understand why he's taking so long to find me."

"I have to be getting back: I'm only on my lunch break," said Sally standing up.

Sarah jumped out of her seat and began fiddling around in her handbag. "Look, Chuck, I have a feeling that you and I are going to be best friends. A chance meeting like this usually has a purpose behind it; destiny if you like. So, I'm going to give you my telephone number; when I can find a blasted pen, that is, and you call me when you want a good old chinwag."

Sally laughed, delighted at the prospect of meeting this bubbly stranger again. Somehow Sarah seemed a tonic for her negative emotions, and she could do with lots more of it.

Once Sarah had given Sally her telephone number, Sally walked towards the exit.

"Hey, Chuck," Sarah called out after her.

Sally stopped and turned.

Sarah's expression was serious. "If he lifts just one finger to you, give me a ring; ok?"

Sally nodded and left the store.

Chapter Thirteen

"You look happy," said Jimmy as he and Sally ate their dinner in the kitchen that evening.

He was still living in his own home and enjoyed his visits to Sally very much indeed. Soon he would arrive and never leave.

"Don't I always look happy?" said Sally, who was sitting opposite him at the small, circular, pine table."

"Course you do: after all, you're engaged to me, aren't you," Jimmy quipped. "But I mean happier than usual; as if another dimension has been added to your life?"

"You're very perceptive at times, darling," Sally replied evenly.

"Aha; I knew there was something!" Jimmy declared with a laugh. "Give woman, give."

"I met someone today; in that clothes store in Houlton street."

Jimmy dropped his knife and fork. "Aha; an usurper! Then I shall have fisticuffs with him at dawn. No bounder nicks my girl without a fight."

Sally laughed. "You are an idiot at times, darling. If you must know she's a woman: her name is Sarah, and I think we're going to be very good friends."

Jimmy picked up his knife and fork and began cutting into his pork chop. "So how did you come to meet this new friend of yours?"

Sally hesitated. "Oh, we were after the same blouse, and she offered to let me have it."

"Hope it fits you better than the last one," said Jimmy.

"Actually, I didn't buy it in the end," said Sally. "But we started talking, and it's obvious we like one another; so -"

"Oi," Jimmy interrupted, "I'm not above fisticuffs with the ladies, you know. They have their equal rights now, so they can expect the same sort of treatment when they go trespassing on a bloke's territory."

Sally threw a pea, which sailed over his head.

"Up the drawbridge and man the battlements!" Jimmy cried. "The English are coming."

"You're every bit as English as I am," Sally laughed.

Jimmy fixed her with a steely glare. "I'll have you know that Hamish Mc Something Or Other was my great, great, great, grandfather's uncle's, nephew's, cousin. And once a Scot always a Scot. So none of your missiles, wench. For centuries you English have been firing things at us, and we have had enough of it - though I have to admit it's a sad state of affairs and a downright insult when it's peas you are throwing."

"I shall remember to throw something more substantial at you next time, darling," Sally promised. "After all, I wouldn't want to hurt your feelings, even if I put a lump on your head."

"So you and this other woman are destined to become friends?" said Jimmy, more serious now.

"Funny you should say that," Sally replied. "Sarah mentioned destiny as well."

"She's not one of those religious fanatics, is she?" Jimmy cried. "I don't want to lose you to some cult. They have God on their side and its not fair."

"No, darling. She's just someone who knew me before."

"You mean like a neighbour?" said Jimmy. Sally always refused to talk about her past, but it didn't stop him from being curious.

Sally paled slightly. "No, not a neighbour."

"Oh, you mean someone from where you used to work?" Jimmy pressed, not noticing the change in her.

"I don't feel like talking about it now, darling," said Sally concentrating on her dinner. "How are things in the captain's office these days."

"Oh, exciting as usual," said Jimmy. "We might even be getting a new range in flavoured spring water if we play our cards right."

Chapter Fourteen

Four months later Sally and Jimmy were married in a register office. Sally's mother flew over for the event and instantly took a liking to her new son-in-law.

But within hours she was flying back to Australia, much to Sally's disappointment. Her father phoned to say that the company he worked for were involved in the takeover of another company, and he couldn't get away. However, Jimmy's parents, two sisters; Sarah and a dozen employees of Mulville's also attended, and they were determined that Sally didn't brood. They provided all the distractions she needed and she enjoyed herself immensely.

She and Jimmy decided not to go on a honeymoon; settling for two weeks off work in order to concentrate on redecorating the maisonette into a home they could both appreciate. The only rule was that they could each have up to three items in their favourite colours, and they could be no larger than a TV. They found the silly arguments over it great fun, and they sometimes laughed for hours.

Sally finally decided on three pink cushions and Jimmy went for a black, slate clock for the mantelpiece and two black leather armchairs for his new study upstairs. Sally protested about the size of the armchairs but Jimmy tickled her into submission.

Sally was happier that she had been in a very long time. She prayed to God that it would last.

As their marital bliss continued, a small worry began to form in Sally's mind. They had been married five months without any financial problems, but it was becoming apparent to her that her husband was living beyond their means.

In recent weeks he had exchanged his four year old Ford Mondao for a new BMW. And when she asked about it he just said that they could afford it. But shortly afterwards she noticed a Rolex watch on his wrist. He assured her it was only a cheap fake he had bought from some man in the local pub.

At first she accepted this explanation, but when he began wearing designer clothes and playing golf at an expensive club, she decided it was time to have the truth from him.

However, Jimmy was dismissive, and completely ignored her protests, but this only served to make her more determined: he was obviously hiding something and she had no intention of allowing secrets during such an early stage in their marriage. In the distant future, trust may allow a certain degree of privacy, but it was far too soon for that. It had to be sorted out.

It was 6:30 on a rainy, Monday morning. Sally sat at the breakfast table opposite Jimmy who was eating toast and browsing through a Thompson holiday brochure.

"I think we need to talk about this," she said over her cup of coffee.

Jimmy kept on browsing. "What's that, darling?"

"About your spending."

"Oh, not more of that rubbish," Jimmy sighed.

"It's not rubbish!" Sally cried. "Can't you see I'm worried about all this spending. I don't want us to end up in debt when we're just beginning our lives together."

Jimmy looked up from the brochure. There was an impatient look on his face. "I told you, Sal, we can afford it. After all, we both have full-time jobs so why shouldn't we have a few luxuries while we can. I mean, when the kids finally come along, we'll be paying buckets of cash for them; what with ninety pound trainers, computers, video games and such like. Now, don't get me wrong, I'm going to love spoiling them, but until then, what harm is there in indulging ourselves a little. And as I said, we can afford it. And another thing, I keep telling you to spend more on yourself, but all I get is moaning from you. Why can't you just accept that we can afford to splash out occasionally."

"You keep saying that, but how can we afford it?" Sally demanded. "Of course I don't have any objections in you spending money on yourself: you deserve it. Everyone at the store says that you are the most hard-working person there. But you earn five hundred pounds a week and I earn two. How does that translate into new cars, Rolex watches, designer cloths, and expensive clubs? Have you got a credit card I don't know about; is that it?"

"We've had this argument a dozen times already, Sal," Jimmy protested, "and I keep telling you. I don't have a card, and I pay cash for everything. Now, can we please drop the subject once and for all before I start thinking I've married a nag."

Sally fell silent, and Jimmy returned to his browsing.

She stared into her coffee cup.

She was never going to find out the truth so long as Jimmy stuck to his argument. But she just couldn't let it go. She was worried, worried for their future happiness. How many times had it said in the papers recently that most marriages fail, and the main reason was financial problems. She couldn't help feeling that Jimmy was storing up serious trouble for their future together. She had to try again, even if it ended in a row.

"Another cup of coffee?" she inquired, getting up from her chair.

"Mmmm," said Jimmy, turning a page.

Sally picked up the jug from the percolator that was a wedding present from the girls in the store.

She filled Jimmy's cup to overflowing. And since he had his hand on the handle of his cup, the hot liquid burnt his fingers.

"Watch it!" he cried, quickly putting his fingers in his mouth.

"I'm surprised you felt anything with your nose stuck in that holiday brochure," Sally replied casually, taking her seat once more.

Jimmy glared at her. "What the hell's the matter with you lately, Sal? You seem to be fretting all the time."

She turned away from him and began fiddling with one of the buttons on her dressing gown.

Jimmy let out a loud sigh. "Look, Sal, I wish you would stop going on about money. Is it your job on the checkout that's bothering you? Do you think I should be using my influence to get you a higher position? Well, I'm sorry, I just can't do that, much as I'd like to. Harris told me that he doesn't tolerate any kind of nepotism amongst his employees. I've told you that he expects everyone to climb the ladder under their own steam. That's how things are. There is nothing I can do about it. And if you can't accept that, maybe you should put in for a transfer to another branch where you could work your way up to management. You are a good worker. I'm sure Mrs Tobin would give you a excellent reference."

Sally turned her attention back to her husband. "It isn't the job," she said evenly. "And for your information I'm quite capable of, 'climbing the ladder,' as you put it, on my own. I've told you what's wrong and you keep fobbing me off with excuses. I've always had to be careful about money because I've never had very much of it. And to see you spending it the way you do is making me nervous."

"You're talking about your previous marriage; aren't you?" said Jimmy sympathetically, placing the brochure on the table. "Oh look, darling, why won't you ever discuss it? You know it makes no difference to me that you were married before, so why keep quiet about it?"

Sally felt the blood drain from her as if a major artery in her body had suddenly split open, and the kitchen began to spin.

Jimmy noticed that something was wrong and moved quickly to her side. He leaned over and then hugged her.

"See what I mean, darling," he said with sadness and concern in his voice. "You get yourself all worked up about nothing. Now, I think you should go and lie down. Take the day off. I'll square it with Mrs Tobin."

Sally didn't resist her husband's instructions: she was just too tired. An image of Robert Cooper with a knife in his chest had flashed in her mind and driven the energy from her body as effectively as the knife had driven the life from her first husband. She hadn't thought about that terrible day for months. Now it had returned to haunt her new life.

Chapter Fifteen

When Jimmy returned from work that evening, his dinner was waiting, and so was Sally.

After a brief welcome-home kiss, she placed the food on the table, and they both sat down without saying anything.

Then Sally launched her attack.

An idea had come to her earlier in the day and it had been buzzing around in her mind with all the irritation of having to listen to the sound of a wasp trapped in a light shade.

She could wait no longer; not even until the meal was finished.

"Are you and some of the others at the store helping yourselves to the stock?" she asked.

A fork-full of mashed potato was half way to Jimmy's mouth when the words hit. He lowered the fork and glared at his wife.

"What the hell are you going on about now?"

Sally picked up a piece of meat with her fork, American style, and put it in her mouth before answering. "It's the most logical explanation to me," she said casually. "I mean, where could you lay your hands on a lot of cash, except from where you work?"

Anger twisted Jimmy's features. "I told you to stop going on about money!" he retorted. "And since you haven't bothered to ask, I've had one hell of a bad day. That stupid fool Andy forgot to order the spring water, and Harris was wittering on at me all afternoon about 'If our customers have to go to another store for their water, Jimmy, they might forget to come back. And where would that leave us.' And that bitch Mrs Tobin had a go at me about it not being the Assistant Manager's job to convey messages from the checkout staff. So do me a huge favour will you, Sal, and let me eat my dinner in peace."

"I will, when you start telling me the truth," said Sally.

"Fuck this!" Jimmy shouted, jumping up from the table and storming out of the kitchen.

Sally rushed after him. "Where are you going?" she cried in alarm.

"To find some peace and quiet, and to get away from you and your bloody non-stop nagging about money!" Jimmy shot back. Then he grabbed his coat and left.

The next morning at work, Mrs Tobin had something to say to Sally about not turning up the previous day.

She told Sally to close the door of her office and take a seat.

The severe expression on the Staff Supervisor's sixty year old face as she stared at an open folder on her desk warned Sally that she was in for a serious reprimand at the very least.

"I see from your file that your attendance has been good up to now," said Mrs Tobin. "But failing to turn up for work and not phoning in is totally unacceptable behaviour."

"But I told my husband to tell you," Sally protested.

The supervisor gave Sally a steely glare. "You must understand something if you are to continue working here, Mrs Mason. There are no husbands, wives, brothers, sisters, uncles or aunts in this store: there are only staff. And since I am your supervisor, you should have telephoned me at your earliest convenience. Now, you may feel privileged being married to a rising star in the company such as Mr Mason. But let me assure you that you are no different than any of those girls out there on the checkouts. Do I make myself clear?"

'As clear as the bags under your eyes, you old bitch,' Sally said to herself, and a tiny smirk showed on her lips.

"Well - ?" Mrs Tobin prompted.

"You have made yourself perfectly clear, Mrs Tobin," said Sally. "I can assure you it won't happen again."

"I am glad to hear it," said Mrs Tobin nodding her head in a condescending manner. "Then I trust we shall not have a repeat performance, or matters will certainly become far more serious."

Sally stood up and left the office without waiting to be dismissed.

During a tea break at 11:30am Sally asked Margaret Brown about shoplifters. Margaret explained that during the seven years she worked at the store, she had seen the problem go from strength to strength. Then Sally carefully brought up the subject of missing stock from the huge storeroom at the back of the store.

"Funny you should mention that, love," said Margaret. "When Paula took tea and biscuits into Mr Harris's office during a visit from the Area Manager yesterday morning, she heard them discussing the possibility of installing cameras there in order to curb the huge losses. Why, have you heard more?"

"Nothing much," said Sally. "Just that the management are unhappy with the situation."

"I'll say they are," Margaret laughed. "Tim Redding in accounts reckons they've lost a good few thousand in the last nine months."

"That much!" Sally replied in shock. "So why haven't they called in the police?"

"Tim thinks that head office is reluctant to do that, in case the papers get hold of it. You know; bad publicity and all that. And it could even be a computer error: they haven't ruled that out yet."

"I see," said Sally, dropping the subject. She had what she wanted. A large share of the missing money might just provide enough to put a deposit on a BMW and pay for a few luxuries. And she must do something about it before Mr Harris found out who was involved. Perhaps she could even find a way to pay back the money, though it would probably take a long time.

Armed with this new information, Sally was determined to have it out with Jimmy that night.

Jimmy hadn't returned to the flat the previous night until well after 2:am, and he was gone before breakfast. She only caught the odd glimpse of him at work and decided that he must still be angry with her.

It was 9:15 in the evening. Jimmy and Sally had eaten their meal in silence, and now they were sitting in separate armchairs in the living-room watching a programme about wildlife on TV.

Sally got up and made two mugs of coffee.

Jimmy didn't say anything when she handed him his.

She sat back down and sipped the hot liquid. She was finding the atmosphere in the room unsettling, and she knew it was the wrong time to bring up such a volatile subject as money, but she couldn't help it. It had been festering away inside her all day, and she couldn't keep it in any longer.

"I know what you're getting all that extra money from," she said in a flat tone, staring at her husband.

The shocked expression that suddenly appeared on Jimmy's face told her she was on to something. However, he didn't say anything, but just sipped his coffee and stared at the television.

Sally pressed on. "I was talking to one of the girls today, and she told me that they're considering installing cameras in the storeroom."

"So what?" Jimmy replied casually.

"So we will have to try and find a way to pay it back without anyone noticing," said Sally. "Now, I have been working it out. If we pay a hundred pounds a week for the time being, and increase it to two when you become manager, it shouldn't take us any longer than about two years. Whether the others are willing to pay their share back is up to them. Maybe you could speak to them about it. Oh, I know it will be difficult to do without being found out, but surely you can come up with something. Mr Harris trusts you, and you have access to the store's computer. I've seen lots of films where people manipulate the transfers of cash, on line."

Jimmy was now staring fixedly at her. There was a blank expression on his face. "What are you going on about, Sal?"

Sally shrugged. "I don't want you to get caught; that's all. If we pay the money back, you will be in the clear."

Jimmy's eyes showed his sudden irritation. "Caught; doing *what* for Christ sakes?"

"Stealing from the storeroom, of course," Sally countered.

"You don't know what you're talking about," Jimmy scoffed.

"Yes I do. Margaret Brown told me that they have lost thousands of pounds in the last nine months. So if you could tell me exactly how much your share was, I could work out the time we need to pay it back more accurately."

"You're talking rubbish," said Jimmy.

"No I'm not," said Sally. "Mr Harris and the Area Manager were overheard discussing it.

"So what! As if I give a damn what happens in that over- size garden shed!" Jimmy snapped. "I've got more important things to worry about, such as making sure we have enough bloody spring water and keeping our precious customers happy."

Sally was confused. Her husband seemed angry but certainly not worried or defensive. Could she be wrong?

"But you're the Assistant Manager?" she protested. "You're supposed to be concerned. The store is your future."

"Like hell it is," Jimmy laughed. "If you think I'm going to spend the rest of my life slaving in that place, then you're crazy."

Sally's confusion grew. "I thought you wanted to stay there; to move into higher management? It's what you always said you wanted to do."

Jimmy shrugged and a look of contempt appeared on his face. "Yea, well when I was six I wanted to be an astronaut: so what; people change. They come to their senses as they get older and realize that most of their dreams are just plain stupid, or stay just dreams unless they do something to make them come true. I've got other plans now and they certainly don't include Mulville's Supermarket Ltd."

"And you didn't think to include me in these new plans?" said Sally in a quiet voice.

Jimmy climbed to his feet and glared at her. "Look, Sal, I'm fed up of being interrogated every time I come home. I'm going out for a while to give you a chance to have a rethink about the way you've been treating me lately."

Sally flew out of her chair, suddenly angry and determined. She stood square-shouldered before her husband, blocking his way. "You're going nowhere until you tell me where you're getting the extra money from."

Caught off guard by his wife's actions, Jimmy simply stared for a moment. Then he reached out and grabbed her shoulders to move her aside.

"No!" she cried, knocking his hands away with surprising strength.

"Don't make me angry, Sal," Jimmy warned.

Defiance hardened Sally's expression. "Why? What are you going to do; hit me? I'd like to see you try."

Jimmy hesitated, then he sat back down in his seat and ran his fingers through his hair. He looked distraught. "This is crazy, Sal. What the hell's wrong with you lately? I don't know you any more."

Sally sat on the arm rest of Jimmy's chair. She felt sorry for him and put her arms around his shoulders. "Look, darling, I know you're getting the money from somewhere, and it's driving me around the bend with worry. Please, can't you just tell me where you're getting it; if nothing else, to put my mind at rest."

Jimmy's left arm snaked around Sally's waist. Then he looked up at her and she saw the vulnerability she always knew to be there. "I've got involved with some people, Sal."

Sally frowned. "From work?"

"No: I mean a couple of the guys from work are involved too, but the people running everything have nothing to do with the store."

"What kind of people? Who are they?"

"Some pretty nasty ones, Sal. I met one of them in a pub a while back. He made me a proposition, and because the money was good, I accepted it."

"What kind of proposition?"

Jimmy let his breath out in a long sigh. "All I had to do was hold on to a few small packets for a couple of days; hide them in my office at work until they wanted them."

Sweat broke out on his face and he began pulling at his fingernails. "I mean what was the harm. It was only a couple of small packets. I didn't even bother to open them. They could have been just a few diamonds for all I knew. Maybe it was someone trying to avoid paying tax, or something. At least that's what I thought at the time."

Sally felt something cold clutch at her heart. "But they weren't diamonds; were they?"

Jimmy slowly shook his head.

Sally had to force the next word out of her. "Drugs?"

Jimmy nodded. "At first it was simple. I kept the packets in a locked drawer in my desk until someone posing as a dissatisfied customer or a rep called for them. They paid me two hundred pounds a time for doing it."

Sally did a quick mental calculation. "But that wouldn't pay for the new car? So where did you get the rest from?"

"After a month the money went up to twelve hundred a week," said Jimmy.

"For keeping a few packet of drugs!" Sally exclaimed. "That doesn't make any sense?"

Jimmy shifted uncomfortably in his seat. "No, Sal," he replied in a soft tone, "not just for a few packets."

Sally's foreboding grew. "You mean something bigger?"

"A lot bigger, Sal. The last seven batches they told me to look after contained over a hundred kilos of cocaine, each."

"Oh my God!" Sally gasped. "But how could you hide that much in your office?"

"I use the storeroom. You could hide a Double-Decker Bus in that place. I involved a couple of the guys in it as well. One is the Storeroom Manager, and the other one is his assistant, so I'm well covered."

"How did you know you could trust them?" Sally managed to ask.

"I was told they had financial problems, so I dropped a few hints. And when they responded, well, I took a chance and told them everything. Eight hundred a week for the manager, and six for his assistant, tax free, was quite an incentive to go along with it. The drugs arrive packed in crates either marked tinned peaches or tinned apricots. It helps reduce the risk of their being a mistake when it's time for them to be collected. And they have a special mark on the outside, of course: it's a small circle inside a larger one."

"So that's how you could pay a cash deposit for the car. But you didn't seemed bothered when I told you about them installing the cameras?"

Jimmy grunted. "That's because I knew about them already, and it's being sorted. None of the cameras will be directed anywhere near those crates."

Sally left her husband's side and went back to her own chair in a daze. She slowly sat down. She needed to think. This was far worse than she expected.

"Are you ok, Sal?" Jimmy asked.

"Just trying to get my head around it," she replied with a vague expression on her face. "My husband the drug dealer; it's a lot to take in."

Jimmy rushed over to kneel before her. "Don't say that, Sal!" he pleaded. "I'm not one of them. I just hold on to it for a while. I don't sell it to anyone."

Sally stared deep into her husband's troubled eyes. "You're part of the whole, rotten system, darling. You're part of the buying and the selling: part of children taking tablets and injecting themselves so that they end up dead in some alley. You store the drugs for these evil people. You make it possible for them to avoid the police so that they can go on selling their death to children and vulnerable adults. So how can you say you're not one of them, when you're obviously an important part of their business? Without people like you they couldn't flourish as well as they do?"

"It's too late to do anything about it now!" Jimmy declared. "Even if I wanted to get out of it, I couldn't. These people don't trust anyone that tries to pull out. They get rid of them."

"You mean they would kill you?" Sally whispered, her voice trembling.

"After torturing me first. You read about it in the papers all the time: some bloke found in the river with his hands and his head missing. I don't want to end up like that, Sal. I have to go along with them. I'm in too deep. Oh, I know now that they were probably after me all along. And to draw me in and to make sure they could trust me, they got me to handle tiny amounts of drugs. So that if I went to the police the charges against them would probably be minor and they could try again with someone else. Maybe I should have done that; at the beginning. But once the big stuff arrived, I knew there was no going back. If I crossed them, I would be dead in a week. So, you see, Sal, I have no choice now: I'm in too deep."

After talking for another half an hour, Sally finally gave up.

They didn't say very much more to one another that evening; each lost in their own thoughts. Sally had been shocked by her husband's confession, and realized that he was in far more trouble than she could ever have imagined. But what could she do to get him out of it? He obviously enjoyed the money and promised that from now on he would spend half of it on her. But she didn't want it. That money was made from selling people their own deaths. She told Jimmy how she felt, but he said she should remember that money, like guns, wasn't evil. He said that money had the Queen's head on it, and it was printed by the government for the people. But she couldn't see it that way and she never would. No, she would have to find a way to extract her foolish husband from the clutches of these people, and soon, before the police found out what was going on in the supermarket.

Chapter Sixteen

"I want to meet those men in the storeroom," Sally said at breakfast the following morning.

Jimmy's mouth dropped open in disbelief. "Don't talk stupid, Sal!"

"I'm not talking stupid. I'm going to get you out of the mess you're in, and I'm going to start by meeting those men."

"No way," Jimmy protested. "That's just crazy talk."

Sally stared across the table at him. "I'm meeting them whether you like it or not. You've already told me they're the Storeroom Manager and his assistant."

"Now look, Sal!" Jimmy snapped. "This isn't a game. The people we work for won't put up with anyone interfering in their business. If you go poking your nose in, the both of us will end up dead."

"Not if we're careful," Sally replied. "Anyway, if you don't introduce me to them, I'm going to do it myself; today, during my lunch break."

For half an hour Jimmy tried desperately to change his wife's mind, but to no avail. Finally he agreed, but on the condition that he was present every second of their meeting.

At one 1pm Jimmy took Sally to the storeroom for the prearranged meeting. The Storeroom Manager and his assistant were furious that Jimmy had revealed their involvement to his wife, and at first refused to meet her. But when Jimmy explained that Sally was adamant, they agreed.

Jimmy led Sally along a corridor formed by six meter high stacks of electrical goods. Her heart was racing and she felt a strange anticipation growing inside her.

Jimmy then turned left and headed for a small office.

Sally could see two men inside through the window. One was in his early fifties, about five feet nine inches tall, with a stocky

94

build and a full head of grey hair. The other was in his thirties, over six feet tall, with a muscular build and curly brown hair. He had a mean and nasty look about him, she thought.

Jimmy opened the office door, and Sally followed him in.

Jimmy then closed the door and turned to face the men. "This is my wife Sally."

"Hello," said the older man in a cold voice. "I'm Jeff. This is George."

George simply glared at her and she managed to glare back.

"So," said Jeff, "what exactly is it that you want?"

"I want my husband out of this nasty little business you're involved in," she replied firmly.

"Fair enough," said Jeff, showing no emotion. "If that's what you want. But why are you talking to us about it?"

"Because you're his partners," Sally replied.

"No we're not," said Jeff. "If anything Jimmy's our boss. He's the one who recruited us."

"Jimmy didn't recruit anyone!" Sally snapped. "He was told what to do and he did it."

"Whatever," said Jeff. "But there's no point talking about it to me and George. If Jimmy wants out, then he knows who to go to."

Sally looked at Jimmy. "Who's he talking about?"

Jimmy sighed. "Billy Bennifield. If there's a problem we give him a ring."

"You could have told me that before," Sally replied testily, feeling more than a little foolish.

"You didn't ask," said Jimmy.

Sally turned her attention back to the two men. "I don't care who's in charge of your drug dealing or who isn't, but I want you to be clear about one thing. From now on my husband is no longer involved in anything going on in this storeroom; do you understand?"

"As I've already told you," said Jeff, "he knows who to talk to about it. It's none of our business."

"Then leave him alone!" Sally snapped, trying to force strength and authority into her voice. "Keep away from him, or I'll make it your business."

Jeff's expression hardened. "Now you listen carefully to me, Mrs Mason. Don't go stirring things up. I'm sure Jimmy's told you the kind of people we're dealing with, and they won't like anyone getting in their way. In my opinion you're wasting your time, so why don't you go home and keep your nose out of what doesn't concern you. Jimmy came into this with his eyes wide open just like the rest of us. That's the way things are and that's the way they are going to stay. Anyone stupid enough to cause trouble will end up getting a lot more than they cause, believe me."

"We'll see about that," said Sally, turning quickly and opening the door.

"You better sort her out, Jimmy, or she could drop us all in the shit," Sally heard Jeff say to her husband as she left the office.

"She's just worried about me," Jimmy replied. "I'll talk to her."

"She'll have cause to worry if you don't keep her quiet," Jeff warned. "Just sort her out before Billy Bennifield gets to hear about it. He's got a reputation for violence and we don't need any of that. Me and George have a sweet deal going on here and we want to keep it going. Unlike you, I wasn't stupid enough to tell my wife what I'm up to. And if she finds out, things could get complicated for me at home; so sort it, or someone else will have to."

"I said I'll talk to her!" Jimmy growled, feeling sudden resentment towards the man.

"You better, " Jeff growled back.

"What the hell are you playing at?" Jimmy demanded as he followed Sally back along the corridor. "If they report this to Bennifield, I'll really be in trouble."

"You already are in trouble," said Sally. "That's why I'm trying to do something about it."

"Why did you have to talk to them like that?" said Jimmy. "It's probably made things worse."

"Plain speaking is the only way to get anything from those people," said Sally unrepentant.

"Oh, you got something from them all right, Sal; hostility. George looked as if he wanted to strangle the life out of you there and then."

"So what; I'm used to that sort of thing."

The reply took Jimmy by surprise. "How do you mean?"

"I mean George doesn't frighten me," said Sally. "Now let's get out of here before I change my mind and go straight to the police."

At home that evening Sally made a demand that Jimmy was expecting, but hoped desperately she wouldn't.

"It's out of the question, Sal!" he exclaimed. "That number is private."

"I don't care," Sally shot back. "I'm going to talk to Billy Bennifield. Obviously he's the one that can give you permission to leave."

"Give me permission," Jimmy laughed. "What do you think this is; some gentlemen's club. These people are dangerous, Sal. The only permission you ever get from them is to keep on living. And when they take that permission away, you're dead - understand - they kill you and dump your body. And they don't care whether you're found or not. No; on second thoughts scrap that. They do want you found, but as a lesson to others who might be thinking of doing the stupid thing you want me to do. No, I'm sorry, Sal but I'm in with them now and there's nothing you or anyone else can do about it. We can have a very good life if we just do as we're told; at least for the time being."

"You sound just like that Jeff," said Sally. "Well, I didn't listen to him and I'm not listening to you. I want you clear of that horrible business and I don't care what I have to do to make it happen. Now Billy Bennifield is the one to talk to, and if you don't give me his number, or at least phone him for me, then I'm going back to the storeroom and cause all the trouble I can."

"You know, you can be a right bitch at times," said Jimmy, realizing that he had no choice but to give in.

"I'm doing this for us, darling," said Sally, her voice softening. "And if that makes me a bitch, then I'm happy to be one until this is over. So, how about that number?"

Chapter Seventeen

Billy Bennifield was a ponderous, brutish-minded and brutish-looking man with a full head of coal-black hair, a thick neck and hands as big as paws on a Grizzly Bear. He had spent most of his working life on building sites, and considered educated and cultured people parasites living off the backs of working people. As far as he was concerned, the only real work was done with the hands and with the fists. And when he first became involved with drug-dealing, as an enforcer, he embraced the job with a passion; cheerfully beating into submission anyone foolish enough to displease his employers. However, he soon rose to his present position as Controller, which he was equally passionate about. For although the job no longer left him much of an opportunity to beat transgressors half to death, it did provide him with different kinds of pleasure. For as well as earning far more than he ever did on the building sites, it also gave him the chance to get back at those on a higher social level. It gave him a deep, inner satisfaction that he was supplying many of them with the means to rot their brains and eventually to end up in the gutter where, with luck, they would die. Yes, the drug trade was good to him, and he saw a great future for himself and his family.

But at this particular moment, Billy Bennifield wasn't working; he was stretched out on his eight foot long settee reading the morning paper.

His three children were racing around the lavishly furnished living-room, screaming and shouting in a game of Catch.

Billy continued to read undisturbed. He had long ago conditioned himself to blot out such mayhem, which was not true of his wife Shelly, who was in their bespoke kitchen trying to make packed lunches for her six year old son, and seven year old twin daughters.

"For heaven's sake, Billy!" she called out. "Will you please do something about those kids. I've got a terrible headache."

"Cut it out, kids, will you," said Billy in a vague tone as he concentrated his attention on an article about a drug's bust.

But the children continued to chase each other, and Billy continued to read.

Then the phone, sitting on a small, mahogany table next to the settee, rang with a soft purr.

Billy reached behind his head; picked up the receiver and put it to his right ear. "Yea?"

"Hello, Mr Bennifield."

"Oh it's you, Jimmy," Billy replied with a touch of concern. "What's up?"

"I'm sorry to bother you, Mr Bennifield," said Jimmy who was phoning from home, "but there's someone who wants to talk to you."

Billy's mood geared up from concern to anger. "What the bloody hell do you mean someone wants to talk to me? You haven't told them about me have you? Because if you have, Jimmy, I'll break your bloody legs, and that's only for starters."

"No, Mr Bennifield, of course I haven't!" Jimmy replied earnestly. "It's my wife, Sally. She insists on having a word with you."

Billy sat up and slapped the paper down on his lap. He couldn't believe what he was hearing. His home number was only for emergencies.

"Are you out of your fucking mind!" he roared down the phone. "How can your wife want to have a word with me when she doesn't even know I exist. Are you telling me that you not only told her my name, but that you know how to contact me. You fucking idiot, Mason. When I get my hands on you I'll break every bone in your fucking body."

"Please, Mr Bennifield," Jimmy pleaded. "Talk to her. She'll explain everything. Please."

Billy shook his head. "All right, put her on. But it better be good."

"Hello, is that Mr Bennifield?" said Sally a moment later. "My name is Sally Mason: I'm Jimmy's wife."

"What can I do for you, Mrs Mason?" Billy replied trying to control the anger in his voice. To him women were irrational: he had to be careful.

"Well," said Sally, "Jimmy has very good prospects at Mulville's, and I don't want him jeopardising them by doing anything illegal. So I'm just phoning to let you know that he won't be involved with your organization from now on. Please leave him alone. That's all I wanted to say."

Stunned disbelief froze Billy's vocal cords for a few moments. Then he found his voice.

"Are you taking the bloody piss or something!" he roared down the phone. "Get off this line and put that idiot husband of yours back on."

"No I won't," said Sally firmly. "You will only try and bully him. Now, Jimmy has nothing to say to you and you certainly have nothing to say to him; not anymore. And I want to be very clear about this, Mr Bennifield. I would strongly advise you not to send any more of your drugs to Mulville's, or I shall be forced to do something about it. Oh, and before you waste time threatening me, I already know you could probably send someone to hurt me and Jimmy, but I wouldn't do that if I were you. And let me ask you something; do you have connections; I mean people good at finding other people for you?"

"You bet I have, you bitch," Billy warned. "So you better not get in my way. Now put your -"

"Do these connections of yours know my friend?" Sally cut in, totally unfazed by Billy's hostility towards her. "Oh, I don't mean one of my local friends but the one I am discussing with you?"

"What the fuck are you prattling on about now?" Billy retorted.

"Because if they don't," said Sally, "then there isn't much chance of them ever finding that friend, or the package I'm sending them. Because you see, Mr Bennifield, five minutes after I put this phone down, a parcel containing everything I know about your drug dealing, and a tape of this conversation, will be posted to that friend for safe keeping. And I don't need to tell you what will happen if my friend doesn't hear from me on a regular basis. Oh, and just in case you are thinking of forcing the truth out of me, well, that won't work either, because my friend will be expecting something like that. And if I or any strangers suddenly turn up on their doorstep, or I phone them with new instructions, they won't carry them out, but will immediately inform the police. So keep your filthy drugs away from Mulville's if you want to stay out of prison, Mr Bennifield; I mean it!"

When the phone then went dead, Billy flung the receiver from him and jumped to his feet in a rage.

The children, used to such outbursts from their father, simply carried their game upstairs.

"Who was that on the phone, dear: you sounded terribly cross with them?" Shelly called out from the kitchen.

The only answer she received was the harsh sound of the front door slamming.

Jimmy rested on the settee, his head in his hands. Sally sat at the dining table putting the last piece of sticky tape on the large, brown envelope in front of her with a smile of satisfaction. She would nip out in a few minutes and post it to her friend Sarah Kenford in Perth.

Sally then looked at her husband. "There's no need to worry, darling. They won't dare touch us now, and you can concentrate on your career."

"I told you, Sal, I have no intention of working at that bloody store for the rest of my life," Jimmy replied in exasperation.

"And you don't have to," said Sally. "I'm sure one of the other major supermarkets would be glad to employ you. That Mrs Tobin might be a right, pompous cow, but she did say that you were a rising star. You obviously have a talent for management, and I wouldn't be surprised if you didn't eventually end up as Chief Executive of Tesco."

Jimmy's fingers clawed through his hair. "How many fucking times, Sal," he snapped. "I don't want that kind of job."

"Then what do you want," Sally snapped back, "to go on selling drugs to children: destroying their lives: buying expensive cars with blood money: terrified any time someone rings the doorbell because it might be the police, or some other gang trying to get rid of the competition?"

"Now you're going over the top," Jimmy replied, calming down. "It's nothing like that with us. We leave each other alone. Nobody wants trouble."

"It *could* happen, couldn't it?" said Sally. "You hear about it all the time. And sometimes it isn't even another gang doing the killing. As far as I can tell, a gang of drug dealers is like a pack of wolves. The only way to get to the top is by inflicting injury or death on whoever's higher up than you are."

"I told you, it's nothing like that," said Jimmy. "We all have a job to do and we do it. And since everyone gets well paid, they're all satisfied. There's no need for the kind of nonsense you're going on about. You watch too many films."

"So everyone is satisfied," said Sally, incredulously. "I suppose George is perfectly happy earning less than Jeff, and Jeff is perfectly happy earning less than you, even though all three of you take the same risks?"

"I'm telling you that you have it all wrong," said Jimmy. "There hasn't been any trouble up to now, and there won't be; unless you start it."

"Oh I see," Sally declared in a condescending tone. "So there's no such thing as ambition among drug dealers. How silly of me to think so badly of them."

Jimmy glared at his wife. "I'll tell you what's silly; what's fucking stupid as a matter of fact, and that's you giving Billy Bennifield orders. Have you any idea what you've done, Sal? At this very minute he's probably phoning his boss. And do you know what he's going to say to him, Sal; no; well I'll tell you. He's going to say that Jimmy Mason and his wife have become a serious problem: a danger to every one of them. That's what he's going to say, Sal, because it's true. Just by you insisting I make that stupid call, we have become a threat to a gang of brutal people, and they're not going to sit back and do nothing about it."

"They will have to if I can get this posted," Sally replied casually, and she jumped up and put her coat on.

Jimmy watched in despair as she left for the Post Office in Crompton Road. What was he going to do? Of course Sally hadn't managed to actually tape her conversation with Bennifield, but the Controller couldn't be certain of that. As far as he was concerned the possibility was there, and that would be enough to make the entire organization behave like a hornet's nest that had been given a good whack with a stick.

"God almighty Sal," Jimmy cried, clawing his hair again, "what have you done to us!"

Chapter Eighteen

Billy Bennifield waited in the small office of a tool-making firm called Saunders. Billy found the noise of the machines working irritating. Somehow it reminded him of home on a bad day.

Suddenly the office door opened, and a thin-featured man, with combed-back blonde hair walked in.

"What are you doing here, Billy?" the man inquired, sitting at his small desk. "You know the rules: no visits?"

"We've got a problem," said Billy, placing both hands on the desk and leaning on it.

"Then get it sorted," said the man. "That's your job, isn't it; smoothing out the wrinkles in our little enterprise."

"It's no wrinkle, Andy," Billy replied. "Someone's black-mailing us."

Andy Saunders looked up from the file he was about to read. "What are you talking about?"

"Jimmy Mason," said Billy. "He's the Assistant Manager at the branch of Mulville's, and his -"

"I know who he is," Andy interrupted. "So why is he blackmailing us? Looking for more money I suppose. Well, you know our policy. Have him taken down some alley and given a good reminder that we decide how much he gets paid, no matter how important to us he is."

"It's not him, Andy, it's his wife," said Billy.

"His wife?" Andy was clearly surprised.

"A right bitch too," said Billy, pulling a sour face. "She wants her husband out of the organization: say's he's got good prospects at the supermarket and she doesn't want him doing anything illegal."

"So change her mind!" Andy snapped. "And don't bother me with rubbish like this in future. Talk to Malcolm or Charlie or one of the others. I've got too much on my plate running this place as well as the organization. I can't do everything."

"Talking won't do any good," Billy replied, and a few beads of sweat popped out on his forehead. "She's sent details of our business at Mulville's, and a tape to some friend of hers for safe keeping."

Andy's eyes narrowed. "A tape of what?"

Billy straightened and rubbed his forehead. "The bitch recorded our conversation."

"How the hell does she know about you?" Andy demanded. "And what was this conversation about? You weren't stupid enough to say anything incriminating, were you?"

Billy began to rub the side of his face. "Christ, Andy, she caught me off guard. I was at home having a rest. I didn't expect a call like that. One second the husband was talking to me, then it was his wife; making all kinds of threats."

"You didn't mention my name did you?" Andy's expression was a mixture of fear and anger.

Billy laughed nervously. "Course not! What do you take me for. She just mentioned drugs, and I didn't deny it; that's all."

"It's enough, you stupid fool!" Andy snapped. "So, what details does she have?"

"Well, she knows that we store the stuff at the supermarket, and that the Storeroom Manager and his assistant are involved."

"Christ, this is a fucking disaster!" Andy declared. "I know the Storeroom Manager at that supermarket, but more importantly, he knows me. If the police pull him in he'll probably bring up my name. I don't need that kind of shit."

"I'm in this too you know," Billy protested.

"You deserve to be locked up, " Andy growled.

"It's not my fault!" Billy wailed. "How was I to know Mason would tell his wife about me?"

Andy glared fiercely at him. "You recruited Mason, didn't you. That makes it your fault. Now get out of my sight and let me think of a way to get us out of the mess you just dropped us into. And another thing, don't think for one minute that this won't reflect in what we pay you over the next three months, *if* we bother to pay you at all."

The possible loss of one hundred and fifty thousand pounds nearly drove Billy into a panic. "It's not my fault, Andy!" he pleaded. "It could have happened to any of us; even you."

"Get out!" Andy roared.

Billy left, cursing Sally's name.

It was 8:25 on a Thursday morning, just two days after Sally had presented her ultimatum to Billy Bennifield. She was standing on her platform at Highgate Station, waiting for the Northern Line train that would take her to work. The rush hour was in full swing and so the platform was crowded. Sally had a fear of being too close to the platform edge, so she always stood a couple of steps back. And as she waited for the train, she was aware that there was a man standing directly behind her, reading a paper.

She was feeling a bit lonely, and wished Jimmy didn't have to start work an hour before her, or finish an hour and a half later. But Jimmy always quoted Mr Harris whenever she complained about his hours. 'Always remember, Jimmy, (her husband did an excellent mimic of his boss's Scottish accent) having a career is like climbing a mountain. You must work very hard, and have tremendous endurance in order to reach that summit. But when you finally get there, then you can occasionally sit back; make yourself comfortable, and look down with great pride at what you have achieved. But until then, you must climb, lad, you must climb.'

Sally smiled to herself as she recalled Mr Harris's words. She liked the old chap. He was retiring next year and he was going to recommend Jimmy as his replacement. And with over ninety branches around the country, there was plenty of scope for a keen young man to make his mark.

Suddenly there was a rush of warm wind and a distant roar. The train was coming and everyone prepared for the dash for any empty seats that might be available.

The roar of the approaching train grew louder, and then it was hurtling out of the tunnel like some enraged, prehistoric beast from its cave.

A man moved in front of Sally and took a single step forward.

She tutted in annoyance at the man's rudeness, but instinctively followed without comment.

An announcement from the platform speaker was lost in the sound of the approaching train.

Suddenly something slammed into her back.

She was pushed violently forwards.

She felt a powerful impact against her chest: the man in front of her cried out and disappeared.

Then she was falling.

She caught sight of something huge coming at her.

Her arms flayed wildly; desperately reaching for a hold.

The fingers of her right hand touched, then grasped something.

She heard screaming; the screech of brakes. Everything around her was spinning.

Her arm was grabbed, and she was pulled. There was pain. She felt sick. Her legs gave way and she slid to the floor; strong hands slowing her progress. There were distorted faces; more screaming; someone was shouting 'get back - get back!'

She lay on the platform, her back raw with pain. Her right shoulder throbbed, and a dozen blurred faces stared down at her.

"She's the one!" a woman's trembling voice exclaimed. "She pushed that poor man under the train: I saw her."

"It was an accident," said a calmer male voice. "She tripped and fell against him. He shouldn't have been standing so close to the edge. It was just a terrible accident."

Sally's swirling mind suddenly became still, and full clarity returned.

She tried to rise.

"Don't get up, love," said a man wearing a London Underground coat. "You've had a bit of a shock."

"I'm all right," said Sally. "I just want to go home."

"Sorry, love," said the man, "but someone's been killed. The police are on their way and you'll have to wait, I'm afraid."

"Please help me up," Sally begged. "Please!"

"If you're sure," the man replied. Then he helped her to her feet.

People were getting off the train under loud instructions from station staff.

A few moments later the transport police arrived, and after taking statements they asked Sally to go with them to the local police station. A police doctor confirmed that she had indeed received a recent and powerful blow to her lower back.

Fortunately the blow had been a few inches to the left of her spine, or the damage could have been more serious.

She was allowed home on police bail, and informed that she would have to return to the police station in two weeks. Meanwhile they would be interviewing any witnesses to the incident.

"Sal; Sal; it's me!" Jimmy shouted, rattling his key in the Yale lock of the front door. "Why's the door locked? Let me in."

A few moments later the door opened.

"What's happened?" Jimmy demanded as he stepped passed his wife.

Sally slowly closed the door behind him without comment.

She was in her dressing gown.

Her hair was unkempt and she had a deathly pallor.

She returned to the settee she had left and sat wearily on it.

Jimmy followed and sat next to her.

When she looked at him, Jimmy saw the shock that was still in her eyes. "Someone tried to kill me," she whispered.

"What!" Jimmy jumped out of his seat. "When: how? All Mrs Tobin would say is that you phoned in to say you had an accident, and would I come home straight away."

"At the Underground station," said Sally, trying to keep a tremble of fear out of her voice. "Someone behind, pushed me or kicked me or something, and I knocked some poor man under the train. Oh, the police believe it was probably an accident on my part, but they only let me come home on police bail. They say they have to interview witnesses. But I know someone tried to push me under that train. And I think I saw the man: he was standing just behind me reading a newspaper. Of course I can't be positive, but it had to be him."

Jimmy sat back down. He became agitated and began clawing at his hands.

"Did you see his face?" he asked.

"No," said Sally. "But I do know he was tall, and -"

"I told you, didn't I!" Jimmy cut in furiously. "These people won't stand for anyone messing them about. And now they're going to kill the both of us. I should never have told you where the money was coming from. You thought it was a credit card and I should have let you go on thinking that. I must have been crazy."

Sally didn't seem to hear her husband. "Anyway, the doctor examined my back," she went on in an even tone. "He said the marks confirms my story that it was someone behind me that was responsible for what happened. Of course I couldn't tell them someone was trying to kill me, or the whole thing would have come out."

"I need a drink!" Jimmy got up and went to a cupboard next to the fireplace. He reached inside and pulled out a bottle of scotch. He filled a whisky glass to the top and took four long swallows of the fiery liquid.

He gasped and coughed when some of the whisky went down the wrong way.

"This is a right bloody mess," he went on, taking another swallow. "Now what are we going to do. And how can I go to work tomorrow. They might arrange an accident; maybe have me run over with a forklift truck or something. You hear about it all the time; some poor sod being crushed by machinery at work and we put it down to carelessness or a case of being in the wrong place at the wrong time. But what do we really know about it. How do we know it wasn't a case of someone shooting their mouth off about the wrong people, or worse still, trying to blackmail them."

"Oh shut up for, God's sake!" Sally screamed, now on her feet. "Is that all you can talk about; those bloody drug dealers. I was nearly pushed under a train a couple of hours ago, and I killed someone. Don't you care about how that makes me feel?"

Jimmy put down the glass and rushed over to her. His arms wrapped around her shoulders in a tight embrace. "Of course I care, Sal. It's just that I know you're safe at the moment, and I'm worried about what will happen next. I don't know what to do, Sal. I can't think of a way out for us."

Sally hugged him back and fought the tears that were filling her eyes. She would not lose control, because Jimmy wasn't strong enough to cope if she did. No matter how badly she was affected Jimmy would always rely on her to show the way. Emotionally he was still a kid, just a big, wonderful, but stupid and greedy child, and he needed her protection. And she would give it: come what may she would protect her husband, and God help anyone who tried to hurt him.

Her grip on Jimmy tightened as her resolve grew. She tilted her head back to look up into his worried face.

"Now listen to me, darling," she said in a firm tone. "We're not going to stay cooped up in in here; too scared to go out. So you put the kettle on and make us both a cup of tea. I have something important to do."

"What's that, Sal?" said Jimmy, his face looking older, but calmer.

Sally smiled fondly. "You'll see soon enough, darling. Now go on and put that kettle on."

As Jimmy went into the kitchen to make the tea, Sally sat in an armchair, the phone on her lap and the receiver pressed hard against her right ear. She waited as the ringing purr continued. Then a voice answered. "Yea; who is it?"

"Hello, Mr Bennifield," said Sally in a light, casual tone, "this is Jimmy's wife again."

There was silence, followed by a muffled curse.

"What the hell do you want now, Mrs Mason?"

"Just letting you know that your attempt to kill me didn't work, but you did manage to kill some poor man instead. So when I put this phone down I'm going to make another call; a call that will send some very determined police officers with their guns and their dogs and their big white vans along to knock on your door. And when they send you to prison for twenty years, you can reflect on the huge mistake you made in trying to push me under a train."

"Now wait a minute!" Billy cried, suddenly in a panic. "What the fuck are you talking about? I didn't try and push you under no train."

"So you sent someone else; same difference," said Sally a little more firmly. "Anyway, I'd just like you to know what your future will be. So goodbye, Mr Bennifield. I can't promise I'll visit, but do watch out for prisoners with families. I hear they just love to get their hands on people who sell drugs to their children."

"Wait. Wait, Sally, please!" Billy begged. "I swear on my mother's life I didn't try and kill you: on the life of my kids I didn't. Please; let's talk about it. Why would I want to kill you before I got that tape back? Be reasonable. Why would I do a stupid thing like that?"

"Goodbye, Mr Bennifield," said Sally.

"No: don't hang up!" Billy shouted in terror.

Sally lowered the receiver, then hesitated. Was she hearing the cries of a desperate man who had been found out, or one that was being falsely accused and was about to be severely punished? She put the receiver to her ear once more. "If you didn't try to kill me, Mr Bennifield, then who did?"

"Christ; I don't know, Mrs Mason," Billy replied, hope removing the panic from his tone. "Maybe it was an accident. Did you think of that? Maybe someone fell against you: it happens, you know."

"If it was King Kong, then that would explain the state of my back," said Sally scathingly. "But I'm afraid it was a completely different kind of ape that did this to me, Mr Bennifield. You know the ones, don't you. They sell death to children and destroy thousands of innocent lives. And when someone tries to do something about it, they get shoved under trains."

"Look, Sally," said Billy in a calmer voice. "Think about it. We wouldn't kill you without getting that tape back first, now would we? Be sensible?"

"Oh, I see," said Sally. "So, even if I did hand over the tape to you, you would still kill me?"

"That's not what I meant!" Billy protested, the panic in his voice returning. "I'm only saying what's logical. That tape could cause trouble for us, and we don't want any trouble. Now, I think you should put down what happened to you as an accident, and we can go back to our original agreement."

"All right, Mr Bennifield," said Sally, allowing menace to enter her voice. "But if anyone so much as sneezes in my direction, that package will be handed to the police."

Sally hung up when Billy began expressing his gratitude.

Jimmy came into the room with two mugs of tea. "How did he take it?"

"A little bit of denial, a bit of begging, and I'm number one on his Christmas list," said Sally.

After handing her a mug, Jimmy sat opposite. "What happens now? Do we go back to work tomorrow?"

Sally pulled a thoughtful face. "I suppose so. At least that business with the drugs is finished, and that's the main thing."

The muscles of Jimmy's jaw tightened.

Sally noticed. "What?"

"I didn't say anything," Jimmy replied defensively.

"Oh My God; you want to keep on with it, don't you?" Sally exclaimed in anger. "You want to keep dealing with that filthy stuff so that you can have money to spend on clothes and new cars?"

"No I don't!" Jimmy retorted. Then he sighed. "It's just that -"

Sally's eyes were bright with anger. "It's just what?"

"If you must know I've booked us a fantastic holiday in Florida next month, and I've already put a sixteen hundred pounds deposit down. The balance is just over five thousand, and we can't afford it without the extra money I was bringing in. I've already sorted out the time off with Mr Harris."

Sally's anger evaporated. She put her mug on the carpet and joined her husband on the settee. She put her arms around him and kissed him on the cheek. "Look, darling, I know that holiday sounds just brilliant, but don't you see, I could never enjoy myself there knowing where the money to pay for it came from. All that horrible business is over with, so let's forget it ever happened. And when you're manager of Mulville's, we will have enough money to holiday in America the way most people do - with a clear conscience and a feeling that we deserve having the time of our lives."

"I suppose so," said Jimmy, sounding resigned. "I sure was looking forward to it though."

Sally gave him a kiss on the forehead. "Course you were, darling. But I promise you, it will be far more enjoyable knowing you earned it: it definitely will be for me."

Jimmy slipped his hand inside Sally's dressing gown. And when it snaked around her lower back she winced. "Oops; forgot about your poor back," Jimmy chuckled. "Guess it's you on top for the next few weeks then.

Chapter Nineteen

Ten days had passed since the incident at the station. The bruising on Sally's back was fierce looking, but her GP had confirmed the police doctor's diagnosis that there was only muscle damage and it was not too serious. Most of the pain was gone, and she and Jimmy were settling into routine work at the supermarket.

Jimmy promised Sally that he would keep well away from the storeroom when possible, and only ever talk to the Storeroom Manager about stock business. And when Sally inquired about Jeff and George's attitude towards him, he said they were cold and barely acknowledged his presence, but that was to be expected since their income had been reduced by two thirds.

It was 10;30 on a Sunday night. Jimmy and Sally had just finished making love in their usual fashion since Sally's back had completely recovered.

"How's your back, Sal?" Jimmy asked as he sat propped up by a pillow.

Sally, also propped up, turned her head to look at her husband. "You don't have any complaints do you?" she said with a smile.

"Oh, none worth mentioning," came the casual reply.

Sally sat up straight with a 'just you dare!' look on her face. "Oh; you mean you do have some complaints?"

"Just the one, now that you mention it," said Jimmy.

"Well come on then; out with it?" Sally demanded, poking him in the chest with an index finger.

"Ok then," said Jimmy. "But don't forget, darling, you did ask."

"Just get on with it," Sally ordered giving him another poke on the chest.

"Right. Well, I must admit it was better when you were on top; you know; when your back was bad."

Sally jerked her head in surprise. "Really?"

"Mmm," said Jimmy.

"Is it something I'm doing differently?" said Sally, real curiosity overcoming her mild annoyance.

"As a matter of fact, yes, Sal it is."

"What; with my hands?"

"Amongst other things."

"With my thighs, then?"

"Amongst other things, Sal."

"You mean my whole body?"

"Got it in one, darling."

"I'm intrigued," said Sally. "So, what exactly was I doing when I was on top that you liked that I'm not doing now that I'm not?"

Jimmy stared stone-faced at his wife. "All the work, of course. Because you see, Sally darling, when I was lying on my back I could see the TV, which was good because you have an unfortunate habit of getting randy just when they're showing highlights of the day's football matches. But now that I'm back on top; well, you can understand my dilemma. I can't see a thing when -"

Suddenly Jimmy was covering his head as he was attacked by a pillow, wielded by a laughing, outraged wife.

At 5:30 on the following afternoon, Sally left Mulville's with two of the other women who worked on the checkouts. The sky was overcast, but it hadn't rained so the pavement was dry. Ballards Lane was busy with rush hour traffic and the three women had to speak in raised voices in order to be heard.

"See you tomorrow, girls," said Sally, laughing at a particularly saucy joke just told to her.

Then she started walking towards Finchley Central Station.

A few drops of rain began to fall, and as if by magic, numerous umbrellas were produced: though in her case, she had left hers at home that morning.

She grumbled to herself about the weather, as she walked.

She couldn't remember a day that it didn't rain. She also grumbled about the fact that Ballards Lane was misnamed. Far from being just a lane, it was a main road nearly a mile in length, and meant she had a long walk each day to and from the station.

Despite this, she rarely opted for the buses that were available, having a particular dislike for the swaying and the sudden stops and starts she experienced whenever seats on them weren't available.

She put this down to a possible poor sense of balance.

But she also had hated the rain ever since she was caught out in a thunderstorm when she was five years old. This was a phobia she suspected she would never get over.

Her thoughts then turned to her love-making with her husband the previous night, and she couldn't help smiling.

She had never met anyone with such a fantastic sense of humour, and she had a wonderful feeling that she was going to spend the rest of her life with Jimmy Mason, laughing at his jokes, though they were sometimes downright silly. For wasn't that what she needed in her life; to find each day a source of amusement.

She cheerfully skipped around a puddle outside a newsagent and walked on.

Then she made to cross Hervey Close, and a sudden explosion of pain in her head sent her plummeting down into a dark, spinning place.

The voice she couldn't understand seemed very far away.

There was darkness and pain.

The voice became louder and the pain grew.

A light; strong like a car headlight, blinded her from the darkness.

She tried to turn away from it, but she couldn't move.

Panic began to take hold. Why couldn't she move?

"Mrs Mason?" said the voice, clear now and close by. "Try and open your eyes."

She made an attempt to follow the order, but nothing happened.

She tried again and soft light greeted her.

She saw a blurred face for a moment, then her vision cleared.

"Now I don't want you to worry about anything," said the elderly man who was leaning over her. "You're in hospital. You've had an injury to your head, but you'll be all right in a few days."

"What happened?" Sally asked weakly. Her mouth felt as if it had a thick wad of toilet paper stuffed inside it.

Then a nurse was holding a glass of water in front of her.

A hand gently lifted her head and she sipped the water through the straw.

The toilet paper dissolved away.

"You're in St Clare's Hospital," said the doctor, as her head was lowered back on the pillow." And as I said, you've had an injury to your head, but I don't believe any lasting damage was done. The x-ray didn't show any fractures. Obviously you have a thick skull, which probably saved your life. From the size of that lump I would say that you were hit very hard indeed; possibly with a hammer."

Sally managed a smile. "I thought I was only thick-skinned."

The doctor smiled too. "I want you to keep your head straight for me, but follow my finger with your eyes."

"Good: excellent," said the doctor, when Sally performed the task perfectly. "And any dizziness?"

"No, but I have an awful headache," Sally replied.

"Only to be expected," said the doctor. "I'll have the nurse give you something for that. And it would be best if you stay here for a couple of days. You may have survived the assault surprisingly well, but I don't want to take any chances."

"How long have I been here?" she asked.

"You were brought in earlier this evening," said the doctor.

"What about my husband?" said Sally, the panic returning.

The doctor smiled. "He's just popped out for a coffee. I'll send someone to get him."

"Yes please," said Sally. "And may I have some more water."

A few minutes later Jimmy came charging along the ward. "Thank God you're ok, Sal!" he cried, frantically kissing her repeatedly on both cheeks.

A nurse brought a chair and he sat on it.

"What happened to me?" Sally asked, realizing for the first time that there was a large bandage stuck to the back of her head.

The joy left Jimmy's face. "It seems you were mugged, Sal. A witness said that a man hit you from behind and then took off along Hervey Close. Obviously he was going to rob you, but something must have scared him."

Sally ran her fingers over the bandage. "Did they catch him?"

Jimmy shook his head. "By the time the police showed up he was long gone."

Then his expression became a scowl. "If I ever catch the bastard I'll beat him to death with my bare hands!"

"But if he was trying to mug me, why didn't he just push me over and take my bag?" said Sally. "That's what muggers usually do to women, isn't it?"

Jimmy frowned. "I told you, Sal, he must have been scared off."

"Yes, but why hit me?" Sally persisted. "The doctor thinks a hammer was used. Muggers don't usually hit women on the head with hammers. They just knock them down and take their bags?"

"What are you saying, Sal?" Jimmy asked giving his wife a strange look.

"I'm saying it was another attempt on my life!" Sally snapped, her anger rising. "That horrible Billy Bennifield is still trying to kill me. Just wait until I get out of here. I'll make him sorry."

"For Christ's sake, keep you voice down!" Jimmy hissed, glancing fearfully around the ward. "And when the police call, don't forget, as far as you're concerned it was a robbery attempt."

"Is that all you care about," said Sally accusingly, "what the police might think?"

"No; of course not, Sal. But they have to be considered. You know what I was involved in. If the police find out, they won't think I'm a victim like you do. I'll go to prison for years. So, please; for my sake, don't involve them."

"Oh don't you worry, darling," said Sally in a firm tone. "I won't involve the police: I won't need to. Because Billy Bennifield is going to get another phone call from me that he won't like one little bit."

Within an hour Sally was questioned by the police at her bedside. They were very interested in the fact that she was involved in another violent incident, but without proof or her corporation, they couldn't make much out of it.

Two days later, Billy Bennifield swore under his breath when he heard Sally's voice on the other end of the line. "What is it this time, Mrs Mason?" he sighed.

"I'm through playing games with you!" Sally snapped. "I've just come out of hospital after being attacked, and unless you admit it was you, I'm phoning my friend."

"We've been through all this before!" Billy cried. "I'm not trying to kill you. In fact I'm scared shitless that something might happen to you."

"Well I don't believe you," said Sally. "And if you think I'm going to sit back and let you go on trying to kill me until you eventually succeed, then you're obviously a very stupid man."

"Please, Sally," Billy pleaded, "can't you look at this thing from another angle. Maybe someone *is* trying to kill you, but what if it isn't us?"

Sally grunted with contempt. "What are you talking about: of course it's you?"

"But what if it isn't? Maybe someone else wants you dead."

"That's crazy," said Sally, in disbelief. "Why would anyone outside your organization want to kill me?"

"We all have enemies, you know," said Billy in a calm voice, "sometimes even from the time we take our first breath. It's just that most people don't know it. Sometimes we upset people intentionally, but other times we do it unintentionally and unknowingly, and these are the worst enemies of all, because you never see them coming. And don't give me any rubbish about never seriously upsetting anyone; unless you think you're a saint."

There was a long silence at the other end of Billy's phone. And when Sally eventually spoke, her words were slow and soft. "You mean it could be someone close to me?"

"Only you can answer that," said Billy in an equally soft voice. "Just do me a favour, Sally, will you. Try never to be alone until this is sorted out. Because believe it or not I want to find out who's trying to hurt you as much as you do. Give it some serious thought. Who might you have upset recently: maybe someone at Mulville's, or even at -"

"At where?" said Sally when Billy's voice trailed off.

"Well, at home, if you know what I mean?" Billy replied.

Billy heard a sharp intake of breath. "Are you all right, Sally?" he inquired.

"I'll get back to you, Mr Bennifield," Sally replied, and then she hung up.

She was sitting in one of the armchairs in the living-room.

Jimmy was on the settee, looking at her with some concern. "So?" he asked in an even tone. "What did he have to say this time?"

"He denied it of course, and somehow I believe him," Sally answered, frowning. "But you know something, darling, you're never around when I'm being attacked."

"Of course I'm not," said Jimmy. "I mean, it stands to reason that no man is going to assault a woman when her husband is with her, now is he?"

"I suppose not," said Sally thoughtfully. "Can I ask you something?"

"Fire away, Poirot," said Jimmy with a grin.

The humour was lost on Sally. "All that money I made you give up?"

The grin faded from Jimmy's lips. "What about it?"

"You don't miss it, do you?"

"Of course I bloody miss it!" Jimmy retorted. "What a stupid question."

"All right, I suppose it was a stupid thing to say," said Sally keeping calm. "But you don't resent me for it? I mean, you do realize it was for the best?"

"Your best, Sal, not mine," Jimmy replied, now tense with anger and disappointment.

"What do you mean?" Sally was shocked by his reaction to her questions.

"I mean that you decided what was best for me. I was doing very well until you poked your nose in. All right, so I was doing something illegal, but so what. Everyone has some sort of scheme going to make money; even MP'S. You read about it in the papers all the time. And they get away with it, so I don't see why I should have to lose out on twelve hundred pounds a week just so that you can enjoy being moral."

"But drugs?" Sally exclaimed. "How can you sit there and tell me that you are willing to-?"

"So what if it is drugs?" Jimmy interrupted. "What the hell do you think tobacco and alcohol are: one rots your lungs and the other rots your liver, and I don't see anyone giving up twelve hundred a week to do anything about them. And before you go spouting on about children, the smoking age in this country is sixteen. Why is it moral for the government to allow shops to sell tobacco to children? Why can they make money and not me; tell me that?"

Sally remained silent for a few moments.

She had no idea Jimmy was so upset by what she had done, and it was clear that he would go back to working for Billy Bennifield at the first opportunity if she would let him. But there was no way that was going to happen. Drugs were being sold to children in schools, and she just couldn't be a part of that no matter how badly Jimmy felt.

Then her conversation with Billy Bennifield came back to her, and how he said it was possible to make enemies without knowing it. But was Jimmy angry enough to want to harm her; surely not. He loved her as much as she loved him, didn't he? He certainly did when they got married, but that was before she took twelve hundred pounds a week from him.

Sally watched Jimmy as he tried to compose himself, and it was clear that he was having great difficulty doing so. Then an awful thought came to her. If Jimmy was planning to go back to working for Bennifield, then the details she posted to her friend were a threat to that plan.

She struggled to remember if he had seen her friend's surname, and address. She hoped to God he hadn't, and it suddenly hit her; she didn't trust her own husband.

"Coffee?" Jimmy asked, suddenly heading for the kitchen.

"No, thanks," Sally replied instinctively before realizing she was thirsty. But something stopped her from changing her answer to yes.

Chapter Twenty

Four days later Sally reported to her local police station, where she was informed that no charges, concerning the death of the man in the underground station, would be placed against her. As far as they were concerned she was also a victim of a person or persons unknown, and that investigations would continue.

Sally left the police station, relieved, but not taking very much comfort from the decision. After all, someone was still trying to kill her, and since she had no idea who it was, there was little she could do to prevent them trying again.

A week later she noticed something about her husband to give her further concern.

She saw a change in him that she didn't fully understand.

It wasn't anything obvious: his sense of humour was still intact, but it had lost some of its richness and spontaneity. He smiled more or less in the same boyish way that had charmed her from the day she first met him, and he certainly continued to make awful sexists jokes in bed. However, there was something slightly strained about them and it made her worry that the first, faint cracks in their marriage were appearing in response to all the stress that had lately invaded their home. But could there be something other than stress.

At first she considered asking him about it, but soon decided against the idea. She was well aware that anyone feeling stressed often considered even the most gentle questioning a form of attack, and would only respond with anger. And she didn't need any more anger in her life.

No, maybe silence and time was the best way to deal with certain situations, difficult though it may be not to speak to the man she loved more than life itself.

It was just after 6:30 in the evening, and Sally was walking through her hallway with a cup of tea in her right hand.

The door bell rang.

She transferred the cup to her left hand and opened the door. "Oh God!"

The hot cup of tea fell from her grasp and shattered on the floor.

A tall figure, his face covered by a balaclava, reached for her.

He grabbed her hair as she turned to run.

She screamed; pulled free and flew towards the stairs.

She bounded up the steps; terror giving her speed.

The intruder followed.

She could hear his heavy footsteps pounding behind her.

She screamed again when something clutched at her back.

Then she was at the top of the stairs and running towards her bedroom.

She shot through the open door and slammed it shut.

She threw her weight against it, holding the handle rigid with both hands.

A tremendous force threw the door open and she was thrown across the room where she lost her balance and fell to the floor.

The intruder charged in, roaring with rage.

Sally jumped to her feet.

She made for the bed, but was grabbed by the hair and yanked backwards.

The force nearly snapped her neck.

Then she was spun around to face her attacker.

The man smashed her across the mouth with the back of his hand; a stunning blow that loosened two of her teeth.

She cried out with pain and her legs gave way.

Powerful hands dragged her to her feet and she was hit again and again; smack; smack, blows that sent shockwaves tearing up into her brain.

Blood seeped out between her battered lips: bubbling as it flowed down her chin.

A battering-ram of a fist drove deep into her stomach.

She doubled up in agony and dropped to her knees.

Gasping for air she tried to crawl towards the door, but the man took hold of her long hair and dragged her backwards around the room.

Piercing needles of fire drove deep into her scalp.

She screamed her suffering at the top of her voice, but a powerful blow on the top of her head stunned her into silence and unconsciousness.

The man sat on the bed waiting for his victim to recover.

He swung his legs rhythmically back and forth like a child; a child revelling in his torment of another living being. And he had to be patient if he wanted to extract every last vestige of agony his victim's tormented body was capable of giving, because, 'she had to pay!' he told himself, 'she had to pay.'

Sally was racked by a fit of coughing when she came round.

The man jumped from the bed and dragged her to her feet.

"Let me go!" she cried, trying to break the powerful grip on her arms. "Please; let me go."

He jerked her face close to his.

There was a strong smell of alcohol on the breath that came through the material covering his mouth.

She could see the insane, hate-filled eyes staring back at her through the holes in the balaclava, and she knew there would be no mercy. She was going to die.

Strong fingers slid round her throat and suddenly she couldn't breathe.

Her body stiffened in response.

He shook her as he squeezed.

She slammed her clenched fist repeatedly against his face and chest.

He squeezed her throat tighter.

Agony robbed her of strength, and she began to pass out.

"Oh no; not that easy, you bitch!"

The man lessened his grip on her throat, and when the renewed flow of oxygen began to clear her mind, he guided her slowly backwards towards the bed.

The firm edge of the mattress bent her knees and she was forced down on it.

The man climbed astride her, and lowered his face down close to hers.

"Oh God, he's going to rape me!' The thought increased her terror.

"You're going to die, you fucking slag!" the man hissed in a muffled voice.

She clawed at his hands with her fingernails when he tightened his grip on her throat again.

She felt the leather of gloves.

She dug her fingers into his sides.

"That's it, bitch," he growled, shaking her. "Fight me. Fight and die."

A fierce and terrible pain grew inside her chest.

Her lungs burned, furnace hot.

A sneering laugh shot from the man. "You're out of luck, slag. I'm going to make your eyes bulge out of their sockets, and your tongue turn black. And won't you look a pretty sight for the police photographer."

A roaring sound in her ears began to drown out his voice as he told her of his pleasure in killing her.

His covered face began to blur and through her agony her body felt light and detached.

Death was drawing her away from life. Somewhere it was calling to her, and she was responding.

Then she heard the distant bleep of her bedside phone.

The pressure around her neck lessened.

A wild hope surged up inside her, and placing the palms of her hands on the bed either side of her, she pushed herself up with all the strength she had left.

She heard the man cry out in surprise, and then his weight was gone.

There was a thump and a grunt.

Coughing and retching she staggered from the bed and made for the door.

Behind her the man jumped to his feet and ran after her.

"Get back here, bitch!" he roared. "I'm not finished with you yet."

Renewed strength and a desire to live sent Sally flying out on to the landing.

She shot towards the top of the stairs.

Her left shoulder was grabbed.

She pulled away and lost her balance.

Suddenly it was the train station nightmare all over again. She was falling through space - her hands searching madly for something to hold on to.

"Get back! Get back." a voice shouted.

She could hear the sound of a train approaching; women screaming; brakes screeching. Then something crashed against the side of her face. Pain exploded out of the top of her skull. Strong hands lifted her up.

"I'd like to go home now, please," she whispered as her brain reeled under a barrage of confusing thoughts and images.

"So you want to go home, do you," a voice laughed. "Well your home is a grave, and that's where I'm going to send you right now."

Panic returned when she thought that someone was dragging her towards the edge of the platform. "No; no!" she screamed, hitting out with hands and feet. "I won't go; I won't."

"Hold still, you filthy whore," the voice snapped.

She continued to kick and punch at what she couldn't see.

There was a sickening lurch; then a hard thump against her back, and a shout, followed by a number of thuds; then silence.

For a few moments she was still - confusion in complete control of her thoughts.

Then her vision and mind cleared.

She was half way down the stairs, lying in an upside-down position.

Slowly and painfully she turned herself the right way up.

At the bottom of the stairs was the intruder, sprawled on the carpet; unmoving.

"Please God let him be dead!" she begged.

Then to her horror the man struggled to his feet.

He stood swaying for a few seconds, before staggering towards the front door. And as he left the house, slamming the door behind him, a huge sob burst out from her, carrying all the emotions of despair and injustices that had been building inside her for weeks.

For what seemed an age, she sat on the stairs crying.

Then she began to pull herself together.

Her whole face throbbed and pulsed with hot pain.

Her exploring fingers discovered the beginnings of a large lump high up on her forehead. Obviously she had banged her head as she fell down the stairs. And although the top of her head, where her attacker had struck her, was tender, there was little indication of swelling.

Then she realized that the phone was still ringing.

She slowly made her way to the living-room, begging the ringing not to stop.

She picked up the receiver.

The voice on the end of the line sounded the most wonderful she had ever heard. Self-pity welled up inside her. "Oh, Sarah!" she cried with swollen lips. "Thank God it's you."

"Well, it's me or someone doing a pretty good job of impersonating me, Chuck," Sarah's friendly voice replied. "But if I ask you for money or your bank details just tell me to piss off. Anyway, what's up; you sound terrible? You're not coming down with a dose of flu, are you? I know just the thing for it - have you better in four months, or your money back."

Sally wiped tears from her eyes and laughed. "Oh, nothing as serious as flu, Sarah, only a few minutes ago some man chased me up the stairs. And after punching me a dozen times and dragging me around the bedroom by my hair, he tried to strangle me on the bed, and then you phoned and it must have distracted him so I managed to push him off me and he chased me along the landing and I fell half way down the stairs and ended upside-down, but I banged my head and I think I knocked him down the stairs and he ran off. So as you can imagine, Sarah, it's been a pretty dull day as usual."

"Christ almighty, Chuck!" Sarah gasped. "What the bloody hell have you got yourself into? I knew that envelope you sent me was trouble the minute it arrived. I should have ignored your instructions not to open it. So; out with it; what's going on?"

"You tell me," said Sally still laughing. "But thank God you phoned when you did. A couple of seconds later and I wouldn't be talking to you now."

"I only called because you didn't phone me last night like we agreed," said Sarah. "Anyway, look, Chuck, you better come and stay with me for a while if you're not going to call the police, and you're not, are you?"

Sally pushed back the laughter which was desperately trying to become hysterical. "I told you, Sarah, I can't involve the police. Jimmy would get into serious trouble, and probably end up in prison. He's not a criminal, but he's not strong enough not to become one if he was locked up in one of those terrible places for any length of time. Anyway, these drug people probably have friends there. God knows what they might do to him in revenge."

"Jesus, Chuck!" Sarah cried. "Drugs: I knew you had problems but you never said anything about that filthy stuff."

"I'm sorry, but I couldn't tell you the full story," said Sally. "I thought if you knew about the drugs; well; I didn't know what to think."

"You just come and stay with me, Chuck - both of you," Sarah ordered.

"I'd like nothing better, Sarah. But this thing is not going to go away. I have to stay here and sort it out."

"That's crazy. You can't sort anything out if you're dead," said Sarah. "And you think it's the drug dealers doing this to you?"

"It must be. But I think Billy Bennifield isn't involved in it. There was something in his voice when I spoke to him."

"Who's Billy Bennifield?" Sarah asked.

"He's one of the drugs gang," Sally replied. "But I don't think it's him."

"Then it's probably another member of the gang," said Sarah. "A bit like the IRA were. When some of them didn't agree with the decisions made by their superiors, they took matters into their own hands. Maybe Billy Bennifield has been told by his boss to leave you alone, but some other gang member feels that you should be killed. I suppose you didn't get a look at the man that just attacked you?"

"He was wearing a balaclava," Sally replied. "His voice was muffled so that I couldn't recognize it. I don't know if it was intentional, or just the balaclava covering his mouth."

"You mean you might know him personally?" Sarah declared, clearly shocked at the idea.

Sally hesitated before answering. "Bennifield hinted that it could be Jimmy."

"Jimmy: that's crazy talk!" Sarah retorted. "You're not seriously thinking it might be him, are you?"

"No. But he's really upset with me, Sarah, and I mean *really* upset. I forced him to give up twelve hundred pounds a week, and he had all sorts of plans. But you should have heard him going on about it the other day: swearing and getting red in the face. It isn't like him to behave like that, Sarah. I'm terrified he might have changed."

"Now come on, Chuck," said Sarah with a laugh, "he's hardly going to murder you for a lousy sum like that. And don't take this the wrong way but I don't think he has the bottle to kill anyone: at least not the man I talked to at your wedding. It's obvious he worships every hair on your head - even the grey ones."

"You think so?"

"Course. Now if it was two thousand a week, that would be a different matter. I might even be tempted myself. You should see the rags hanging in my wardrobe these days."

Sally laughed. "Thanks again for phoning, Sarah."

"I didn't have anything more important to do, so it was worth it," Sarah quipped. "Now if you have any more trouble, you pack your bags and come and stay with me. You'll love it here in Perth, and the Scots are nice enough, but I warn you now, Chuck, their accent can be a right bugger to understand at times."

"I will. And thanks, Sarah. I'll phone you at the usual times in future."

"You do that, Chuck. Now get yourself to the doctor for a check up. And another thing, have Jimmy put a bloody great chain on your front door. See ya."

"Bye, Sarah."

Sally put the receiver down and quickly made her way to the kitchen. She wanted to do all she could to reduce the swelling on her face, and hoped she had enough ice cubes in the fridge.

Chapter Twenty One

When Jimmy came home from work a short time later, he reacted as he always did after hearing bad news: a prolonged outburst about the trouble they were in, then a drink followed by an apology for not considering her first. And as usual it ended with Sally consoling him, though he did occasionally interrupt her words of comfort to remind her to see her GP first thing in the morning.

Later, as they watched TV, Sally found herself staring at her husband at every opportunity, searching for signs that he wasn't as worried as he appeared to be. She tried to remember how he was when he came home: was he his usual self or was he edgy? Was his shock as she told him about the intruder genuine, or did it look forced? She wished bitterly that she had managed to inflict some obvious injury on her attacker's face.

Then she remembered that she had dug her fingers into his sides. She couldn't have hurt him much because he had laughed at her efforts, but there must at least be marks. She decided she could check Jimmy that night when they were in bed.

Then a shudder passed through her. What if she found them: it would mean that he wanted her dead; just over money. No, that couldn't be! There was no way he would kill her just to improve his living standards; he loved her too much, didn't he?

"You all right, Sal?" Jimmy asked.

Shecame back to reality. "Course I am, darling."

"It's just that you were staring at me with an odd look on your face. You're not angry because I wasn't here when you were attacked, are you?"

"Course not," said Sally with a false laugh. "You were at work. You couldn't know that someone would attack me here."

Jimmy smiled. "That's ok then. I'll make us a drink and we can have an early night. Oh, and another thing, I'm going into that hardware store across the road from work and buy the strongest door chain they have. Make sure you keep it on when you're alone here."

"Don't you worry, darling, I will," Sally promised.

That night as Jimmy lay sleeping, Sally gently pulled the duvet back and examined his right side. There seemed to be a faint mark on the skin just above his hip, but she couldn't be certain. She had sat up reading, so the bedroom light was on. But it was only a sixty watt bulb and not quite bright enough for her to see properly.

She peered closer, trying to remember what pattern her fingers had taken when she dug them into her attacker.

"What the hell are you doing, Sal?"

Sally jumped, then sat up straight. "Nothing. Go back to sleep, darling."

"Not until you tell me what you're up to," said Jimmy.

"I told you, I wasn't doing anything, so go back to sleep."

Jimmy sat up. "Why were you staring at my side like that?"

Sally became defensive. "I don't know. I must have been dreaming."

"You were looking for something; weren't you?" Jimmy's eyes were hard in the soft light of the bedroom.

"No," said Sally, feeling trapped by her husband's aggressive questioning, "unless I was looking in my dream. Anyway, I can't remember, ok, so can we please forget it and go back to sleep now. I'm exhausted."

Jimmy wasn't satisfied by the explanation. "You didn't look like you were dreaming to me, Sal. It's something to do with whoever attacked you this evening, isn't it?"

"Don't be ridiculous!" Sally shot back. "How could it be?"

"Did you actually fight back?" Jimmy demanded.

"What?"

"When the intruder attacked you, did you fight back?"

"Of course I did! What did you expect me to do."

"Did you hurt him?"

"I already told you, I knocked him down the stairs."

"I mean did you inflict a particular injury on his body?" Jimmy pressed.

"I don't know. I wasn't thinking about particular injuries. I was fighting for my life."

"You're lying, Sal, I can tell you are."

"No, I'm not. It's just that -"

"You think it was me," Jimmy interrupted. "You think I'm the one trying to kill you."

Sally turned away from her husband and threw herself flat on the pillow.

"Well, come on!" Jimmy snapped. "Admit it. You think I'm the one who tried to push you under the train, and attacked you in the street. And you think I left work early this evening to come here and try and kill you."

"That's just stupid talk," Sally muttered. "Now will you please go back to sleep. I don't feel well enough for a silly argument at this time of night."

"That's what you meant when you said that I was never around when you were attacked," Jimmy went on. "I thought you were blaming me for not protecting you, which I thought was unfair, but I understood. But no, you meant that I wasn't there as your husband because I was standing behind you as your attacker on the station, and waiting for you at Hervey Close. What a bloody fool I was not to see what you were getting at."

Angry at being questioned, Sally sat up and glared at Jimmy. "All right then, where were you tonight?"

"At work as usual; overseeing a large delivery, if you must know," Jimmy declared.

"In the warehouse, I suppose?" Sally's tone was condescending.

"That's where all the deliveries go, isn't it," Jimmy replied in the same tone. "Or am I guilty for that too, according to your twisted logic."

Sally ignored the remark." So, you're alibi is that you were with Jeff and George; how convenient."

"Alibi; who the bloody hell do you think you are, Sal. I'm your husband, and if you think that I have to explain my whereabouts every time something happens to you, then maybe I shouldn't come home at all."

Sally's determination faded suddenly. "Well, you would say that, wouldn't you," she muttered.

"Ask them!" Jimmy demanded. "When you go in to work on Monday, ask anyone you like if I left work early this evening."

"If I do that they will only get suspicious," Sally replied, "and I don't want to draw attention to us. Now, I'm going to sleep, even if you're not."

"All right then," said Jimmy. "Say it is me. What's to stop me killing you now. Have you thought of that?"

A cold wave chilled Sally's body, and she tensed.

"Not very bright are you, Sal," Jimmy carried on in a sneering tone. "I mean, you wait until you are alone with a man to tell him that you believe he is trying to kill you."

Sally still remained silent.

"Oh: wait a minute: I get it!" Jimmy exclaimed. "You're not stupid after all. You figure that I would never kill you at home during the evening because then I wouldn't have an alibi. That's why you can accuse me like this. Well, you're wrong, Sal, because it's not me trying to kill you. I warned you what would happen if you threatened Billy Bennifield. And now that it is happening, you're accusing me."

Sally felt herself bounce a few times when Jimmy threw himself back on his pillow.

Then he sat up and punched it half a dozen times.

Each blow made Sally flinch.

And the last thought she had before she finally fell asleep was a question; was her husband's outrage genuine, or just a show to divert her from his real intentions towards her?

Chapter Twenty Two

Sally didn't get up until 9:30 the following morning. Jimmy had already left for work, and it was clear from the tidiness of the kitchen that he hadn't made himself any breakfast.

Being a Saturday, she didn't have to go into work, but Jimmy did. She always felt deprived on days like this.

Remembering the argument from the previous night, she flopped on to one of the kitchen chairs, feeling weary, depressed and guilty.

Could she be completely wrong about her husband? Or was he being clever? Of course he would have an alibi; someone to cover for him if he was trying to kill her because of the drugs money, so there was no point asking at work. And being in management it would be easy to just disappear for an hour or so without anyone noticing, if it was planned right. But then again, was she taking too much notice of what Billy Bennifield said. After all, he had to be clever as well as ruthless to reach the position he had in the organization. Maybe he decided to gamble that she didn't have a tape of their conversation. Maybe he was willing to risk doing away with her, since a letter didn't have quite the damaging evidence of a live witness. Maybe she was underestimating the man all along.

Suddenly fresh determination powered through her. She went to the living-room and sat by the phone. She stared at it for a moment, then she lifted the receiver and pressed the buttons.

A female voice answered.

Sally introduced herself and asked to speak to Billy.

"For the love of God, Mrs Mason," Billy sighed a few moments later. "You'll have my wife getting the wrong idea about us. What is it you want now?"

"I've been attacked again: this time in my home, Mr Bennifield, and I'm tired of being fobbed off by you!" Sally declared.

"I'm not fobbing you off," Billy pleaded. "What else can I do but deny what I'm not responsible for?"

"I don't care about that. Now I want to talk to your boss right away."

"I am the boss," said Billy.

Sally managed to laugh despite the pain it caused her bruised face. "You may be the boss in your own home, Mr Bennifield, but you certainly don't strike me as having the brains to run a major drug's ring."

"You fucking bitch!" Billy roared. "I don't have to take that kind of crap from you."

"A package and an unknown friend says you do," Sally replied firmly. "Now shall we try again. I want to speak to your boss."

There was a short silence before Billy answered in a calm voice. "I'm afraid that's out of the question, Mrs Mason. He doesn't speak to anyone outside the organization. It's a matter of security."

"I'm not concerned with his security," said Sally. "What I *am* concerned with is getting my husband away from filthy people like you and your boss, without either of us ending up under a rush-hour train. And to do that it seems I must speak to the person in charge, and that's what I'm determined to do."

"It's not possible!" Billy wailed, almost panic-stricken.

"Then you better make it possible, Mr Bennifield or you know what the consequences will be. I'm warning you now, being nearly murdered three times is making me desperate."

"Jesus, you don't know what you're asking," Billy replied, trying to divert Sally from her course. Saunders was already furious with him, and it wouldn't take much more going wrong before he decided to replace him. And there would certainly be no finances involved in the redundancy package he received, only a bullet through the head.

"I'm well aware what I'm asking," said Sally. "So do I get what I want or shall I let the police do it for me?"

"There are rules you know nothing about," said Billy. "If I break them, then there's a very good chance I'll be killed. And what good will that do you or Jimmy?"

"I'm not listening to any more of your arguments!" Sally snapped. "Do I talk to your boss or the police; decide now?"

There was another silence, but Sally thought she could hear faint curses.

"Well?" she said, her impatience growing.

"All right, you win," said Billy with a sigh. "I'll give him your number and ask him to get in touch."

"Not good enough," said Sally. "You could get anyone to call me, so I want to talk to him face to face, and believe me I *will* know if he's the one."

More faint curses.

"I'll see what I can do, Mrs Mason. I'll call you back in half an hour."

"You do that," said Sally, and she put the receiver back in its resting position.

Exactly thirty minutes later Billy phoned.

"You win, Mrs Mason," he said in a strained voice. "He'll meet you in his office at Saunders Ltd; a tool-making factory in Grafton Street at exactly 1:30pm on Friday. Don't be late. Oh, and his name is Andy Saunders: but for Christ sakes, don't say anything to anyone else but him. His firm and staff are legit. No one else there knows anything about the drugs."

Sally was pleased that she had six days before her meeting with the drug boss. Although most of the damage to her face was inside her mouth, the bruising on the outside was noticeable. But she hoped that with a great deal of luck and even more makeup it would reduce considerably by Friday.

Despite Jimmy's instance that she see her GP, she decided against it. There was no serious damage, except for two slightly loose molars, and she certainly had more important things to do.

On Thursday evening Sally phoned her supervisor at Mulville's to say that she was unwell. And although Mrs Tobin expressed some surprise since she seemed perfectly fine when she left work only hours earlier, she could do little about it but wish her better and a swift return to work. Perhaps even with Mrs Tobin, nepotism was something to fear after all.

Sally knocked on the office door at Saunders at 1:30pm on the Friday. The office was situated at the top of a long flight of steep stairs. And down below, a huge, open plan workplace was filled with all kinds of heavy duty, tool-making equipment. The noise from these machines was deafening, and grated on her nerves.

She was relieved when the door opened.

"Come in, Mrs Mason," said a man with a friendly smile. "I'm Andy Saunders."

Sally stepped inside, and when the man closed the solid-looking door behind her, the racket turned into a faint, background hum.

Then he made his way to his desk and sat down.

He pressed a button on the intercom system on his desk and leaned towards it. "Please come up now, Barbara," he said.

Sally was just about to sit in the chair on her side of the desk when Andy stretched out his right hand to stop her.

"Please don't sit just yet, Mrs Mason. Before you do, I must take certain precautions."

Sally felt her heart miss a beat. "What kind of precautions?"

Andy smiled. "Nothing to worry about, I assure you."

"That's easy for you to say," Sally replied, her nerves starting to play up. What was she doing here alone with this man? She must be crazy.

Suddenly the door opened and the racket from outside assaulted her ears once more.

A young woman walked into the office carrying something Sally remembered seeing at airport security checks.

"I hope you don't mind," Andy went on, "but I can't risk our conversation being recorded. I'm sure you understand."

The young woman took Sally's bag out of her hand and put it on the desk. Then she proceeded to slide the circular disk of the metal detector over her body. A minute later the job was done, and the young woman left the office taking Sally's bag with her.

Andy smiled. "Handy little gadgets those metal detectors. Some of the tools we make cost thousands of pounds even though they may be no bigger than a packet of cigarettes. Of course, we trust our staff, nevertheless it doesn't do any harm to keep a tight check on things. And don't worry about your bag. It will be returned when you leave. Now please; take a seat."

Sally sat down without comment.

For a few moments she stared at Andy, and was surprised to find that she liked the look of him. He was about forty five years old: good looking, with a full head of blonde hair, and well-defined features. But most surprising of all to her, he had a kind face. He also had an intelligent, educated air about him and she had to push away an instinctive and favourable comparison with her husband. How could people who sold death look so normal?

Mentally she scolded herself. For if she was going to achieve her goal, she would have to stop being so naive. For however attractive this man sitting before her appeared to be, he nevertheless represented a foul and evil organization. And hadn't the American Serial Killer Ted Bundy, beguiled his many victims with his good looks and charm.

"Now then?" said Andy, leaning back in his leather, executive chair and interlocking his manicured fingers under his chin. "Billy said you insisted on meeting me."

"I'm sure he's kept you up to date on what's been happening to me?" said Sally.

Andy frowned. "Yes he has. I must say it has caused me a great deal of concern. And have you discovered any clues as to the identity of this attacker?"

Sally's expression was cold. "Not yet," she said in a flat voice. "But I intend to put a stop to him; one way or another."

"Pity," said Andy. Then his mouth opened in apparent embarrassment and he said hurriedly. "Forgive me, I don't mean that it is a pity that you intend to stop him, of course: just that it would have made things much simpler for our organization if you did know his identity."

"It would have done more than that for me," Sally replied caustically.

"Of course it would," said Andy spreading his hands. Then he smiled. "Sorry, thinking too much like a businessman with a problem, I'm afraid. But you see, Mrs Mason, our little enterprise has been moving along quite nicely for some time now, and we don't like it when things start going wrong."

"Then put a stop to it," Sally replied instantly.

"Ah yes," said Andy with a sigh. "Billy did explain that you think we are responsible for the attacks."

"Stands to reason that you are," said Sally. "I mean, how do the police handle cases like this. I believe the first questions they ask themselves is, who has the motive and the opportunity. And your organization, Mr Saunders, is very much in the frame."

"But it ain't a fair cop, guv!" Andy exclaimed in a cockney accent. Then he laughed. "I do beg your pardon, What you just said reminded me of an episode of The Bill I once saw."

"I don't see anything to laugh about," said Sally. "So can we get on with it."

"Very well. But do we have to be so formal. As I said my name is Andy. And I'm sure you won't mind if I call you Sally."

Sally's defences went up. "Why should I. Billy Bennifield sometimes calls me Sally and I don't like him one little bit."

"Ouch," Andy winced. "The lady has claws. But I must tell you that Billy is correct in what he says. We are not responsible for the attacks."

"Of course being an honourable man, you would tell me if you were," Sally replied scathingly.

A hard expression took the kindness from Andy's face. "No, Sally. If it was us you would already be dead, and certainly not here now accusing me of something I have played no part in. The person who attacked you three times and failed to kill you is clearly a bungling idiot, and I would certainly not employ someone like that - even at the very lowest level of our organization. The police just love talking to fools, and they are inclined to talk back."

"Perhaps I should keep a letter of recommendation for him in case he succeeds next time," said Sally. "Then you can employ him."

"Aaaa; those claws again." Andy smiled. "Can't we discuss this problem like sensible adults?"

"I'll discuss it with your boss," Sally replied.

Andy frowned. "What makes you think that I'm not the boss? Of course it's no surprise to me that a clever girl like you twigged that Billy wasn't. However, I can assure you that I am of a much higher calibre than that ham-fisted, bullish individual."

"You referred to our little enterprise, not my little enterprise," said Sally. "And to be perfectly honest; I just don't get the impression that you're at the very top and running things - close to it yes, but not quite there."

A laugh burst from Andy. "You *are* a clever girl, aren't you."

Then Andy's expression became grave. "Look, Sally, I like you: I like you a lot as a matter of fact. You have more tungsten in you than most people I know; even the so-called hard men. I've had more than a few of those in here, but always tooled up to the eyebrows - if you will pardon the pun. Yet believing that we are responsible for three attacks on you, you walk into my office armed with nothing but your determination, and you have no idea how much I admire that. And because of that admiration I'm going to give you a piece of advice. There is only one man I answer to, but don't have anything to do with him. You would get more understanding from a rabid dog."

Sally shrugged. "I'll take my chances."

"With him there are no chances," said Andy. "For your information, he doesn't know about your threats against us, or that we have lost Mulville's. And believe you me, if he finds out, your life and that of your husband's wouldn't be worth the price of a phone call."

"I have my friend?" Sally protested with a degree of anxiety.

Andy sighed. "Your friend wouldn't do you one bit of good, because the man we work for is called The Sailor. And do you know why we call him that?"

Sally shook her head.

"Because," said Andy, leaning forwards and resting his arms on the desk, "when sailors in the days of sailing ships found themselves encumbered with a damaged sail during a storm, they used to cut it loose from the ship, often taking some good sail with it. In other words, Sally, if it came to it, my boss would have you, your husband, Billy, the Storeroom Manager at Mulville's, his assistant, and me killed to protect him and the organization. So as you can imagine, I don't want him to find out about our little problem. As it is he will find out soon enough that we aren't using the supermarket, because we haven't been able to find a suitable alternative yet. However, I am hoping to eventually convince him it was no longer safe to use Mulville's because of the police snooping around. And if we do have a replacement chain when we tell him, I'm sure he will accept my explanation without question."

"And if you do find another chain of stores, does that mean my husband won't be involved any more," Sally asked hopefully.

"Aaaa -" Andy sat back in his seat again. "Unfortunately, my boss keeps a detailed file on everyone who works for him. And when he discovers that your husband's branch is no longer suitable, he will expect Jimmy to transfer to management in the new chain, and of course, recruit people there."

"You must be joking!" Sally snapped. "If you think I'm going to let Jimmy get involved all over again, then you don't know me."

"But I'd like to," said Andy.

Sally was thrown off guard by the answer. "What?"

"I said I'd like to get to know you. What's wrong with that?"

"I'm happily married; that's what's wrong with it," said Sally.

"An old fashion girl I see: very nice."

Sally felt her cheeks flush as Andy's eyes transfixed her.

"A blusher too," said Andy. "Things just keep getting better."

Sally jumped out of her seat, her lips tight with anger. "Listen, Mr Saunders, I want you and your organization to leave my husband alone from now on. And if there are any more attacks on me, I'm sending that parcel to the police. And The Sailor can do all the cutting he likes. It won't keep him or you, out of prison."

"I understand," said Andy gravely. "However, before you go, Sally, may I ask you just one question?"

"What sort of question?" Sally replied.

"How far would you go to break your husband free of this problem?"

"I told you. I'm willing to send -"

"Not the right answer at all, I'm afraid," Andy interrupted. "Seems to me the reason you are willing to send the parcel is because you have it, and it's the only thing you can think of."

"What else is there?"

"That's answering a question with a question."

"Then the answer is I don't know."

Andy's eyes were piercing as they stared at Sally. "That's because you haven't heard my proposition. However, before I offer it, I need to know one thing. Would you kill, Sally? Would you take a life to protect yours and your husband's?"

Sally felt her legs weaken and she began to feel faint.

She slowly sat down again.

An awful dread had come over her, and she wondered if Andy had discovered her past.

"Are you all right?" Andy asked, showing concern. "You look pale."

"I think I must be coming down with something," she replied, her voice trembling.

"Then I suggest you go home, and we can discuss this some other time."

Sally began to pull herself together. "No; I'm all right. Go on with what you were saying."

Andy visibly relaxed. "Very well, Sally, I'll get straight to the point. You see, you want your husband free of the organization and for the two of you to live the rest of your lives without fear of reprisals. But that won't happen. And at any time my boss could find out what is really going on, and then you will be in serious trouble."

"You've already told me that," Sally replied.

"But what I haven't told you is that there is a way for you and I to get what we want."

Sally fixed her eyes on Andy's face. "And what do you want, Mr Saunders? I take it, it involves me in some personal way?"

Andy sat up straight in his seat and his shoulders were squared. "Depends what you mean by that remark. However what I want, Sally, is to take over the whole shebang. You know, I run the entire organization from this office. I arrange distribution of the product; keep an eye on over eight hundred people across the country, with the help of a few select people like Billy Bennifield, of course, and sort problems out on a daily basis. And yet my share of the profits is only twenty percent. I deserve more; a great deal more and I intend to get it."

"What a sad story!" Sally sneered, her anger returning. "What an injustice, you poor man. You only get what; a few million a year, for selling death to children."

Rage showed in Andy's eyes. "If you weren't useful to me, Mrs Mason," he growled, "I would have you thrown from the roof of a very high building, for talking to me like that."

Then he took a deep breath to calm himself. "However, you are clearly under a great deal of stress, so I shall let it pass. And if you must know I make damn sure as little as possible of our product goes to children. Furthermore, should I manage to accomplish my plan to gain full control of the business, not a single gram will go anywhere near young people. I have kids of my own, you know. And the way I see it, as with most things, it's up to adults whether or not they indulge themselves in our products. After all, are we not considered grown up when we are old enough to make our own decisions in life."

"I've heard that ridiculous argument before, and quite recently, as a matter of fact." said Sally with a touch of resignation in her voice.

"But true nevertheless," said Andy.

"Perhaps. So, why are you telling me all this?"

"Because you have had someone try and kill you three times in the last few weeks, and instead of falling apart, you're here in my office laying down the law to what you believe to be a gang of evil drug sellers. You have guts, Sally Mason, and I think you can help me get us both what we desperately want."

"Go on," said Sally, now interested despite her resentment towards the speaker.

Andy opened a drawer and pulled out a packet of cigarettes. He offered one to Sally. She declined. She gave up smoking the previous year.

Andy lit up and deeply inhaled. And when he blew out the smoke, a small , white ring drifted across the office.

He watched the ring of smoke for a moment, then he looked at Sally. "There is only one obstacle standing between me and what I want, and that is the loyalty a handful of top people in the organization have for the boss. If anything happened to him and I took over, I wouldn't last five minutes. I would be blamed. And even if I had an alibi, it wouldn't make any difference. They would still think I was behind it. And that's where you come in."

"I don't understand," said Sally. "What can I do about a power struggle inside a drug organization?"

"Oh, it's very simple really," said Andy. "All I want you to do is kill The Sailor for me, and when I'm in charge, you and your husband can live your lives any way you want."

"That's ridiculous!" Sally retorted incredulously. "I'm not going to kill someone for you: it's crazy."

"It's practical," Andy replied, clearly becoming excited. "I mean, what better way to get rid of him without suspicion falling on me, than by some crazy woman turning killer. Think about it. The Store Manager and his assistant are really angry with you already and probably think you are unstable. I know for a fact Billy Bennifield regards you as one vindictive bitch. So if you suddenly went off your head and killed the boss, they would back up my story. Of course, you would have to move well away from here; abroad probably. But that wouldn't be a problem with plenty of cash to fund your new lifestyle, and I would see to it that you had plenty."

"You seem to have it all worked out," said Sally, recovering from the shock of such a proposition.

Andy nodded. "It has been on my mind now for quite some time. And with the boss dead, and the support of Bennifield and a few others, I should be able to convince the rest that his passing is no bad thing for them. I have no intention of getting between a dog and his dinner, so once I take over I intend to substantially increase their earnings. In this business, loyalty is finally judged by the size of the pay cheque."

"I can believe that," Sally quipped. "So, who are these people who are loyal to your boss?"

Andy hesitated before answering. "Phil Mansted, Pete Bradshaw and Terry Wilson."

"What kind of men are they?"

"You have to ask?" said Andy in surprise. "Don't worry, you will never run into any of them if everything goes to plan."

"So you already have a plan of how to kill him?" said Sally.

Andy grinned. "To be honest, I began working on the means the first time Billy phoned me about you."

"You're asking an awful a lot from me," said Sally.

"You have an awful lot to gain, and lose," said Andy. "Anyway, it won't be so bad. I'll supply the gun. All you have to do is point it and pull the trigger."

"A gun!" Sally couldn't disguise her shock.

"Why?" said Andy. "What did you intend to use?"

"I didn't intend to use anything," Sally replied, feeling strange.

"Naturally I thought a woman would prefer to use a gun, rather then get up close and personal with a knife," said Andy, ignoring her negative reply. "And a gun is easier too: it should be all over in seconds. Then we can part as friends, and I'll even throw in a million pounds to give you and your husband a good start somewhere else."

Sally stiffened with outrage. "Let's get one thing absolutely clear from the start, Mr Saunders. Whatever I do to help you, it will not be for money. I don't want a penny of the filthy stuff; is that understood?"

Andy spread his hands. "Fine by me. And does that mean you're on board?"

Sally took a deep breath and rose to her feet. "I'll need time to think about it, obviously. It's a lot to take in."

Andy stood up also. "Then I look forward to hearing from you very soon, Sally."

"Look forward to what you like," said Sally, "but don't hold your breath doing it."

Chapter Twenty Three

At home that evening, Sally found that Jimmy was still upset about the night he discovered her examining his side. The Jimmy, Sally knew, couldn't stay angry for such a long period of time, unless the anger had turned into a sulk; a childish sulk, but fuelled by the resolve and energy of an adult mind. And no matter how hard she tried he couldn't be placated.

Jimmy was eating his dinner on his lap; silently watching the TV while Sally ate hers in the kitchen. And as she looked at him through the serving hatch, she realized that there was a gulf forming between them. But she couldn't do anything about it until she could trust him again. And how could she trust him when she was still trying to recall the dimensions of the intruder. Was he taller; shorter or a similar height to Jimmy? Was he fatter or thinner, or the same build? She tried to imagine what Jimmy's voice would be like if it was muffled by a balaclava. But most of all she wondered if it was possible that her apparently loving husband could really hate her that much. These were the uncertainties that powered the widening gulf between them, and she was left to wonder if they could ever be truly happy again.

Jimmy dropped his knife and fork on to his empty plate with a clatter.

It made Sally jump, and this reminded her that she was still on edge from her visit to Andy Saunders.

Then Jimmy climbed to his feet and carried his plate into the kitchen.

Sally tensed. "Was it all right, darling?" she asked stiffly.

"Edible," said Jimmy putting the plate in the washing-up bowl.

"About that night," said Sally, "I wasn't really thinking that you -"

"I know damn well what you were thinking!" Jimmy snapped.

Sally sighed. "I'm sorry, I was a bit shaken up after what happened, and -"

Jimmy suddenly sitting down opposite her and fixing her with a cold stare froze the words in her throat.

"If you're really sorry, then make it up to me," said Jimmy.

"That's what I'm trying to do!" Sally exclaimed. "How many more times do you want me to apologize?"

"Not with words, Sal; with deeds."

"How?"

"By allowing Billy Bennifield to use Mulville's again: not for long: just until -"

Sally leaped to her feet. "No!"

"Damn it!" Jimmy's fist slammed down on the table.

"Don't you see?" Sally pleaded. "Sooner or later those people will get caught and end up in prison. Do you want to go with them; do you?"

"I'll get out long before that happens," said Jimmy. Then his voice took on a begging tone. "Please, Sal, give me three years; just three years and we'll have enough money to buy a proper house with a double garage and a garden big enough to take a swimming pool, without having a twenty year mortgage hanging around our necks."

"How many times do I have to say it," Sally protested. "I don't want any of that kind of money. We both have good jobs. And what's wrong with a mortgage. Most people have them; even rich people. Why can't we just work hard for what we want like ordinary, decent people?"

"And end up in debt for the best part of our lives: no thanks; I'd rather risk going to prison."

"Well, working for it is the only way we're ever going to get the kind of house you want," said Sally, "because I'm not letting Bennifield into Mulville's again."

"And how are you going to stop him!" Jimmy barked. "If you think he's really that bothered by that fucking parcel of yours, then you're an idiot. They know you won't inform on them to the police, because you will be informing on me as well. They're not stupid, you know."

"That won't stop me," Sally replied.

Disbelief showed suddenly on Jimmy's face. "What: you would actually contact the police; even though I'd go to prison as well?"

"I would say that calling them was your idea," said Sally. "You would probably only get about five years, and be out in two; maybe even less."

"You stupid cow!" Jimmy roared. "I'd be found dead in my cell within a week."

"Then they would have to place us on a witness protection programme," Sally argued, ignoring her husband's swearing. "I'm sure the information you could give the police would be worth them doing that for us."

Jimmy shot to his feet, his eyes staring in anger. "Where the hell did you get all this shit from; a fucking police drama. Did it ever cross your mind that they probably have corrupt police officers working for them. They would find out where we were and blow our brains out, you stupid bitch!"

Sally felt something terrible rise up inside her that she hadn't felt since the night she killed Robert Cooper. It was hot; scalding hot, and it burned in her brain like lava.

"Don't talk to me like that," she warned in a harsh voice. "Don't you *ever* talk like that to me again."

Jimmy detected something in his wife's words and backed down immediately. "All right, Sal, I didn't mean to swear at you. I was only saying that what you're proposing wouldn't work."

"Then I'll find something that will work," said Sally.

Jimmy frowned. "How?"

"I have something in mind. But for now I don't want you having anything to do with Billy Bennifield. Just keep away from him until I sort it out."

"I don't usually have very much to do with him anyway," Jimmy muttered, looking dejected.

Sally couldn't help smiling. "When this is all over, darling, I think we should have that honeymoon we never had. Maybe it was a mistake not going away. I'm sure it will do us the world of good."

Jimmy smiled back, but said nothing.

Chapter Twenty Four

Sally sat alone on the settee, her hands wrapped around a half-drunk mug of coffee. She was in her dressing gown, and she had her bare legs tucked beneath her. Jimmy was in bed, and she was glad. She had a great deal to think about, and an irate husband was certainly not conducive to clear thinking, especially when his irritation was fuelled by simple greed.

She took another sip of coffee, allowing the warm liquid to trickle down her throat.

In her mind she went over Andy Saunders' incredible offer. But could she accept it, even though it was the perfect solution to her problems? She would have to kill another human being; a person she had never even met. And she would have to kill him on the say-so of someone who was relatively a stranger to her. It was all so surreal and frightening. She clearly remembered how she felt at the moment she killed her first husband; the desire for vengeance and justice; the hatred; the fierce joy as she plunged the carving knife into his chest. But when she killed Andy Saunders' boss, she would feel none of these things. How could she when she didn't even know his name.

But as she continued to run these perplexing thoughts through her mind, there was one inescapable conclusion she knew she would come to in the end, no matter what her emotional state. That it was as necessary to kill the Drug Baron as it was to kill her ex-husband, because in the end it was all about survival. Robert had threatened hers, and this man was doing the very same. Why kill one and not the other.

Suddenly she smiled. For the first time she remembered her ex-husband without going to pieces. Maybe she was becoming stronger: she would certainly need to be strong to kill again.

"You coming to bed, Sal?" Jimmy called out from upstairs.

"I'm coming up now, darling," she shouted back. Then she put down the coffee mug: turned out the lights and slowly made her way to the stairs.

Sally sat at a small, square table in the staff canteen at Mulville's, having her lunch. She was alone until Margaret Brown joined her.

"Are you sure Jimmy's not gay?" Margaret said with a laugh as she stirred her cup of tea with a plastic spoon.

Sally thought she had misheard. "What did you say?"

Margaret leaned closer, a mischievous smile on her face. "Your Jimmy; are you sure he's not gay? I mean, is everything all right in the bedroom?"

Sally wasn't in the mood for Margaret Brown's sense of humour. "Don't talk stupid!" she snapped.

Margaret pulled back, a look of indignation on her face. "Well, pardon me for only trying to help. I just thought that if you were having problems at home, I might be able to explain why; if you didn't already know, of course."

"For your information, Margaret," Sally declared, "we're not having any problems at home. And even if we were, how would they be any of your business?"

"I can see I really touched a nerve there," Margaret replied evenly. "But as you say, it's none of my business."

"Look," said Sally, "what's this all about?"

Margaret turned her face away in a huff. "What your husband gets up to is none of my business, and I certainly have no intention of telling you again after you just bit my head off."

Sally took a few deep breaths to blow the anger away. Then she stared at her friend. "I'm sorry about being so snappy just now. We're going through a difficult patch at the moment, and it's been playing on my mind. Sorry."

A genuine smile of affection appeared on Margaret's chubby, forty-seven year old face. "That's ok, love. Me and my big mouth. Sometimes I think I could put a Jumbo Jet inside it; airport and all."

Sally managed to smile in return. "So, can you tell me what this is all about?"

"Sure I can; if you want. It's just that Jimmy and Jeff have been spending a lot of time together in the storeroom lately, and people are beginning to notice."

Sally turned pale as fear rushed through her.

"Oh, I'm sorry, love," said Margaret, putting her hand on Sally's and giving it a squeeze. "I can see that you know about Jeff already."

"Know what?" Sally whispered through a dry throat.

"That he's gay, of course."

Sally's mind reeled with confusion. "What are you saying?"

"Well, let's put it this way, love," said Margaret, "if my bloke spent half as much time with me as Jimmy does with Jeff, by now I'd be demanding an engagement ring at the very least."

"Jimmy's not gay!" Sally retorted, pulling her hand away. "You don't know what you're talking about."

"Look, love," Margaret protested, "don't blame me for what's going on between the two of them. I'm only telling you what everyone here knows, so don't go taking it out on me."

Sally glared at Margaret, then she grabbed her bag and quickly left the canteen. And instead of returning to work, she went home. As far as she was concerned, Mrs Tobin could go and hang herself; Margaret Brown too for all she cared.

When Jimmy came home at eight-o-clock, he was in a good mood; but not for long.

Sally had been pacing up and down for nearly three hours; clock-watching and drinking an expensive bottle of wine.

"What's the matter, Sal?" Jimmy asked as he took off his coat.

"I'll tell you what the matter is!" Sally cried. "All the staff at Mulville's think you're gay."

"What?" Jimmy declared with a surprised laugh.

"That's right. Margaret Brown told me during our lunch break that everyone knows about your affair with Jeff, the Storeroom Manager. She even assumed that we were having problems in bed. And as far as the staff are concerned, you two are doing a lot more than discussing deliveries behind those stack's of tinned tomatoes."

"That's bloody ridiculous!" Jimmy shot back, all humour gone now. "I've never heard such a load of crap in all my life."

"Of course it's crap," Sally shouted, pointing a finger at Jimmy. "Because what they don't know is that you and Jeff are back working for Billy Bennifield; drug dealer and destroyer of children. And don't bother to deny it. What other reason would you be seen together so often, unless Margaret is right."

"Oh, don't be so bloody stupid," Jimmy retorted. "Anyway, I need a drink."

Sally sipped the last of her wine as Jimmy poured himself a glass of whisky. She was devastated. Although she knew the truth, deep down she was hoping that he would convince her she was wrong. Now there was no doubt in her mind at all that her only option was to go along with Andy Saunders' plan.

"So when's the next drug delivery: I take it there is one?" she asked, breaking the uneasy silence that had settled between them.

"Tomorrow morning," said Jimmy, taking a large mouthful of whisky. He screwed up his face when the liquid went down his throat.

"And who approached whom this time?"

Jimmy shrugged and poured himself another drink. "Jeff mentioned that he'd spoken to Billy Bennifield, and he told him to sort it out with me."

"And you agreed; just like that; after all you promised me?"

Jimmy crossed the room and dropped onto the settee. "My cut has gone up to two thousand a week, Sal. What could I do except say yes."

Sally sat down beside him. She was suddenly calm. "You could have said no."

"Well I didn't: I couldn't. Jeff and George are in debt and need the money even more than me. They started dropping hints; making veiled threats. George was becoming more and more desperate, trying to pick fights with me over the smallest things. I was worried Harris would start asking questions, so I agreed to allow the drugs back, if for no other reason than shutting George up."

"And I suppose you think that's the end of the matter?"

Jimmy looked at his wife. "There's no way I can back out again, Sal. They wouldn't stand for it."

"And you think I will?"

Jimmy frowned. "What does that mean?"

Sally laughed, but it was totally lacking in humour. "It means that you have the nerve to think that because you have willingly allowed yourself to fall into that drugs trap for a second time, I can't do anything to get you out of it."

"I don't think that business with the tape will work," said Jimmy. "They know you won't involve me with the police. I already told you that."

"No; I guess not," Sally replied matter-of-fact.

Jimmy looked surprised, then relieved. "Really? You mean that; even after what you just said?"

"Of course. How can I after you telling me you wouldn't last a week in prison."

"That's great!" Jimmy cried with excitement. "And don't worry, Sal, after three or four years we'll have enough to sell up and start a fantastic new life for ourselves well away from here."

Sally smiled. "Oh we'll do that all right, darling."

"Sure?" said Jimmy.

Sally stared fixedly at him. "I'm absolutely positive that we will start fresh somewhere else, and we won't have to worry about anyone looking for us."

Jimmy let out a wild cry and hugged her. "I just knew you would come round to my way of seeing things when you had a chance to think about it, Sal! And just imagine, a six bedroom house in the country, with a full size swimming pool, a tennis court, and stables to provide horses for our kids to ride across the acres of land that belongs to us, and all in a couple of years. Fantastic. I thought I would have to work for twenty or thirty years to get half that. Now I can almost smell the stables and the horses. It's going to be great, Sal; just great!"

"I'm happy for you, darling," Sally offered in an even tone.

Jimmy kissed her on the forehead. "I fancy another scotch: want one?"

"Make mine large, will you, darling," said Sally. "I think I'm going to need it."

Chapter Twenty Five

It was just after 6 :15pm, and it was raining.

A man stood on the pavement opposite Sally's maisonette.

He had been there for nearly thirty minutes, and the curtains of nearby houses were occasionally pulled back by concerned occupants. It was a quiet street and strangers standing about for no apparent reason was something very much out of place.

But the man didn't care what people thought, because he was completely preoccupied by a searing hatred for the female occupant of the maisonette across the street. How he ached with a desire to get his hands around her throat once more; to slowly squeeze the life out of her until nothing remained but an empty image in flesh; a shell without substance. But the bitch led a charmed life, there could be no doubting it. Three times he had attempted to kill her and three times he had failed. But he would not fail a fourth time, he promised himself that. And when he next had her in his grasp, it would be face-to-face; he would not be wearing his mask, so that she could look into his eyes, knowing that they were the last things she would ever see.

Some of his rage turned suddenly towards himself. What a fool he had been. Had any of his previous attempts succeeded, the bitch would have gone to her death not knowing who it was that was killing her or why. And wouldn't her knowing be the icing on the cake? Of course it would, and his recklessness had almost deprived him of it. No, he must be patient. He must plan more carefully. And then when the time was right, and only then, would he strike against the bitch that was causing him so much torment. She had deprived him of his dreams and she must pay.

The man smiled, even as the rain ran down his face. He felt much better now. And next time it would be all so different.

"Excuse me?" said a thin, female voice.

The man turned to stare at the elderly woman standing in the doorway behind him.

"I couldn't help noticing that you have been there for rather a long time," said the old woman. "Are you looking for someone? Perhaps I can help. I'm afraid I don't know any of the people living in this street anymore, but I do know all the house numbers."

"That's ok, love," said the man with a grin. "Just sorting out a few problems in my head."

"In the rain?" said the old woman in surprise. "You want to be careful, young man, or you'll catch your death."

The man's grin broadened. "Not me, love. I won't be the one to catch my death; don't you worry. Anyway, the rain has cleared my thoughts so I'll be off. You take care now."

The woman watched as the man strolled away, whistling something from the pop charts.

"Who is it, Hilda?" a gruff, male voice called out from the house. "Who are you talking to out there?"

"A young man was standing out in the rain, dear," the old woman answered; still watching as the whistling stranger receded into the night.

"Not those Jehovah Witnesses again?" her husband complained.

"No, dear, just a nice young man doing some serious thinking."

"Well close the bloody door before my arthritis starts up again. And where's that tea I asked for?"

"I'm just getting it, dear."

"Then get a move on," the man growled. "And don't forget the sugar this time. You know very well I hate tea without sugar, unless I'm having biscuits with it. And you left the tea bag in the mug too long the last time, so take it out sooner. And another thing, how many times have I told you I want my coffee in the plain mug and my tea in the flower mug. I'm sick of thinking I'm drinking one when I'm drinking the other."

"Yes, dear," said the old lady with a sigh, "the plain mug for coffee and the flower mug for tea. I'll remember in future. But you'll have to wait a bit, dear. I'm just going out into the street for a few minutes."

"What for?"

"To do some very serious thinking, dear."

"But you just told me it's raining, you stupid cow?"

The old woman gave another sigh. "That's right, dear, it is."

Sally sat down as Andy Saunders' secretary left his office with the metal detector and her bag.

"Right then," said Andy. "I take it you have decided to accept my offer?"

"Yes I have," said Sally. "And of course you must know about the drugs delivered to Mulville's this morning?"

"Yes. I apologize for that. But once Billy phoned me to say that the lads at Mulville's had convinced your husband to allow it, I couldn't very well turn around and prevent it. Billy would have become suspicious, and sooner or later it would have got back to Steve Wilson."

Sally looked puzzled. "Steve Wilson?"

"He's the man you have to kill," said Andy.

Sally suddenly became preoccupied with her hair, dabbing at it with the fingers of her right hand.

"You're still ok with that, aren't you?" said Andy, suspiciously. "I mean, it's what you're here for, isn't it?"

"Of course. It's just when you say it like that."

"Yes: go on," Andy prompted.

"Look!" said Sally, suddenly agitated. "To kill someone you've never even met before; well; it's not easy."

"Of course it isn't, Sally," Andy replied sympathetically. "But then, some of the most important decisions in our lives are difficult: whether to leave a comfortable, well paid job for something less financially sound but more exciting: whether or not to marry the person you are engaged to: deciding if now is the right time to have children: all of them full of uncertainties. And look at it like this. Steve Wilson has never met you or your husband and yet he has no problems with keeping the two of you in prison, and make no mistake about it, you are in prison. For a start, he will never allow Jimmy to work anywhere else but within the Mulville's chain, and you'll probably find that you can't leave either. Furthermore, if you decide to move house, it

156

will have to be somewhere near the job. So you may be in the biggest open prison you can imagine, but it's still a prison. And there's only two ways out of it: either when you and Jimmy are dead, or Steve Wilson is: it's your choice, Sally."

"So how do we go about it?" Sally replied instantly.

"Good girl," said Andy with a smile. "Now, I've arranged for you to pay him a visit tomorrow night at his house. And when you - ."

"So soon!" Sally interrupted in shock.

"He who hesitates is lost and all that malarkey," said Andy. "Anyway, as I was saying, you are to visit him at home tomorrow night at eight. I told him about you, that you and Jimmy want to go abroad and start a new life, and that you insist on seeing him."

"What if he just sends someone to kill us?" said Sally.

"Don't worry, he won't. I made you sound very interesting, and if there's one thing Steve Wilson loves, it's interesting women. He's not married and he thinks he's God's gift. And since you are very much his type, he's sure to try it on with you."

"What do you mean; his type?" Sally asked suspiciously.

Andy smiled. "Attractive; confident; a woman determined to get her own way, and not afraid of upsetting powerful men. Oh, don't you worry, Sally, I have it on very good authority that Steve will be as attracted to you as politicians are to call girls. Now, I know this may seem a bit over the top, but I want you to dress up a bit for the occasion."

"I don't have much at home," said Sally. "But I suppose I could do a bit of shopping."

"Yes, but I wasn't talking about clothes. The first thing you need to get is a wig; the short curly ones; a dark colour would be best. And I notice you wear very little makeup. I want you to plaster it on thick; red lipstick and plenty of blusher. Then there's those breasts of yours. Now, perfect though they are, I want you to pump them up with a bit of padding, so that they seem much fuller."

"Is that the sort of women he likes?" Sally asked indignantly.

"Not quite. But Steve will see beyond the makeup so it won't put him off. In fact he will be thinking how much he could improve your appearance. Also, since you can't turn up wearing a balaclava, there's always the possibility you might be seen, and we don't want the police getting an accurate description of you, now do we. Oh, and of course you'll need this."

Andy opened a drawer in his desk, and reaching inside, pulled out a shoe box. He took off the lid to reveal a small automatic pistol; a Walter PPK.

"You ever seen a gun before?" he asked.

Sally stared at the weapon, her lips firm with tension. "No."

"Well, don't worry about it. This one is very reliable and accurate. All you have to do is make sure you're close to him when you use it; no further away than three feet, to be on the safe side. And don't take any chances. Aim for the centre of his chest and keep pulling the trigger until the gun is empty. And don't forget to take it with you. You'd be surprised what people do under stress: clear?"

Sally nodded.

"Good. Now keep it in your pocket, and make sure you don't have anything else in there. I don't think Steve's going to hang around while you try and extract a bundle of used tissues jammed between the trigger and the guard. And see that little leaver; that's the safety and it's on at the moment. Keep it that way until tomorrow night, but for Christ's sake, don't forget to slide it to off before you go into his house, because you sure as hell won't remember to do it after."

"What about staff?" Sally asked.

"Shouldn't be a problem," Andy replied. "I'm reliably informed that when he's entertaining a female guest for the first time, he gives his staff the evening off."

"Isn't it dangerous to assume that all assassins are men?" said Sally.

"Maybe he likes to live dangerously," Andy answered. "Anyway, as I said, it shouldn't be a problem."

"But what if he isn't alone?"

Andy frowned. "Then save a couple of bullets and shoot anyone who tries to stop you."

Sally stared fixedly back at Andy for a moment, then she reached inside the box and took the gun. She was surprised by its weight. It felt heavy, unnatural and alien in her hand. She was relieved to put it in her pocket.

"How do I get away afterwards?" she asked.

"I've got a car you can use. It has false number plates. After you've done the job, drive away in it and dump it before you get home. And keep your head down if you're walking. These days there are more cameras than people on the streets. Any more questions?"

"Only to be clear on one thing," said Sally. "Once I have done this thing for you, Jimmy and I are free to leave?"

"That's the deal," said Andy. "But of course I expect you to hand over that tape you have."

"Sorry," said Sally. "You might suffer from a bout of amnesia."

Andy frowned. "Amnesia?"

"Yes," said Sally. "You might forget once Steve Wilson is dead that you agreed to let me and Jimmy leave. The tape will be a reminder of our deal."

Andy smiled and nodded his head.

Sally smiled too. "I may have to trust you for the moment, Mr Saunders, but I'm not stupid. That tape is insurance that we will be left alone, and allowed to have nothing whatsoever to do with your filthy business."

The smile left Andy's lips, and for a moment Sally saw anger in his eyes. Then it was gone. He shrugged. "I suppose it doesn't do any harm to have some insurance in this life, even if you don't need it."

"None at all," Sally replied. "And I suppose you are going to be in a very public place tomorrow night?"

"Absolutely. However, it won't be the big row with the waiter about my food being cold. The restaurant I plan to be in at the time of the killing has a number of security cameras. After all Steve Wilson is an important man and his death will draw a lot of police attention. I don't want to rely on people. God knows what they might come out with. No, when it comes to alibi's you can't beat the cameras; bless their little microchips."

"And the men you were worried about?"

"As a matter of fact, they will be with me. Oh, and by the way, they already regard you as a threat so watch yourself. Now, here's Steve Wilson's address. And as I already told you, he has a couple of staff working there, but they should be gone by the time you arrive."

"And if they're not?" Sally inquired again, not convinced she could shoot her way out.

Andy grinned. "You're a clever girl. Remember what's at stake and improvise. If Steve Wilson gets wind of this we'll all be sharing the same concrete grave."

Sally passed through two huge, ornate gates and along a four-hundred metre, winding, gravel drive before she reached Steve Wilson's home in Chelsea.

The large house was in a Georgian style and had to contain at least thirty bedrooms, Sally decided. She couldn't help feeling impressed.

And as she finally climbed from the car, the front door opened.

"Mrs Mason?" a large, powerful-looking man in his late twenties, inquired.

Sally nodded, and managed to keep a casual look on her face as she approached the man. But inside she was cursing Andy Saunders. She hadn't even managed to get inside the house and there was already a problem. The Walter PPK felt a ton weight as it bounced against her right thigh; as if reminding her of the task she had accepted.

"Good evening, Mrs Mason. My name is Terry," the man continued. "Mr Wilson is expecting you. Please come in."

Sally moved past the man and into a massive hall that had a floor of chequered tiles and an impressive staircase that spiralled upwards through an exquisitely ornate plaster ceiling. A large, eighteenth century crystal chandelier hung from a plaster rose embossed with gilt, summer flowers. On one wall hung a Georgian gilded mirror, and on another a painting of riders on horseback by George Stubbs.

For a few moments Sally was lost in the beauty of her surroundings. Then a voice brought her back to reality and the precariousness of her situation.

"May I take your jacket and bag?" Terry asked, holding out his hands.

"No thank you," said Sally, noticing that two other large men were standing in the hallway, watching her.

"I'm afraid I must insist, Mrs Mason."

"And I said no thank you," Sally replied, trying to force down the panic rising up inside her.

Terry frowned with annoyance. "And I said I must insist."

Sally allowed annoyance of her own to show on her face. "Insist all you like, but I'm keeping them with me."

"We'll see about that," said Terry firmly.

Sally watched as Terry then walked quickly across the hall to a panelled door. He knocked once, opened it and spoke to someone on the other side.

A tall and extremely handsome man of thirty-five years of age dressed in a dark blue jumper; black slacks and dark, leather shoes then accompanied Terry back to where Sally was standing. His blonde, curly hair was striking against his tanned, chiselled features. Sally felt something stir inside her at the sight of him, but she ignored it.

The man's smile revealed perfect white teeth. "Welcome to my home, Mrs Mason. My name is Steve Wilson. I understand from Terry that you are unhappy with our security procedures?"

"I just want to hang on to my coat and bag," Sally replied with a forced smile. "I don't think that's too much to ask."

"Look around you, Mrs Mason," said Steve with a sweeping gesture of his right hand. "I have no need to rob my guests. Your property will be quite safe in the care of my staff."

"Nevertheless I wish to keep them with me," Sally answered.

"Oh dear," said Steve, still smiling. "Then we appear to have a problem. You see, Terry here is part of a security team I have hired for a couple of weeks, and their remit is to never, under any circumstances, admit anyone carrying a coat or a bag, in case they contain weapons. Now, even if I ordered him to make an exception in your case, he would refuse to comply, because if he let you in he would be instantly dismissed by his employers for such a serious breach of security. And since you wouldn't wish a nice man like Terry to lose his job, I'm sure you will be gracious enough to waver your quite understandable right to hold on to your property during your visit. And please don't worry, they will be as safe as if they were in the Bank Of England itself."

After a few moments hesitation, Sally handed her jacket and bag to Terry, revealing the pale blue blouse and navy skirt she was wearing.

Steve looked her up and down with obvious approval. "Excellent!" he declared, then he gestured towards the door he had come through. "Now, if you will please join me in the drawing room."

Sally led the way, her heart thumping in her chest with fear. If her coat was searched, she would be in very serious trouble. She cursed herself for creating such a fuss. It may have given the impression that she had something to hide.

As she walked into the drawing room, she gasped in amazement; her fear forgotten. She had only ever seen such a room in magazines that specialized in the lifestyles of the very rich, and it took her breath away. Everywhere she looked she saw early furniture of the finest quality, in the rococo style. A few pieces were clearly Japanese due to the black lacquer and mother-of-pearl inlay. Others appeared to be French since they were finely carved and covered in gold leaf. On the walls were large paintings of men in wigs, and over a huge, marble fireplace hung a Titian-like nude. A frequent visitor to the major art galleries in London, she wondered if the painting was indeed by the Italian master himself.

"So, what do you think of my home, Mrs Mason?" Steve asked, having invited Sally to sit on a pink settee. The colour brought back bad memories.

"You have a beautiful place, Mr Wilson," she said. "It must have cost you a fortune."

Steve smiled from another pink settee opposite. "I like beautiful things, Sally. May I call you Sally? I just hate being formal in this room. I feel it promotes congeniality and a sense of well-being."

"I can see why," said Sally, staring up at the very high ceiling that contained the most beautiful and decorative plasterwork she had ever seen in her whole life. Large squares made up of various flowers and twisting vines lay in regimented rows against a plain background, and at the exact centre was a huge circular rose from which was suspended an early twentieth century chandelier. Sally knew little about chandeliers, but she was in no doubt that this one must be very special to occupy such a prominent position in such a room.

"May I offer you tea, coffee or something stronger?" said Steve.

"Tea would be fine, thank you," Sally replied, focusing her attention on her host.

As he rang a small silver bell on the coffee table in front of him, Sally took in every detail of this compelling man who looked like a member of the aristocracy. She noticed his fine eyebrows and beautiful green eyes that any woman would die for; his nose was slender and refined; his mouth thin but sensuous nevertheless. She liked tall men, and Steve Wilson was certainly tall; edging over six feet two, and his build was on the slender side. But for all that he seemed strong, agile and very fit. And despite her reasons for being there, which had been removed along with her coat, she was attracted to this Drug Baron in a way she would have never dreamed possible. And she was left to wonder how it was that such a refined man could bring himself to deal in death.

"Please bring us some tea, Francis, will you," Steve said to the elderly man who answered the bell. "Oh, and tell Philip to have the Bentley checked in the morning. That clicking sound is back again, and the dashboard could do with a polish."

"Yes, sir," said the old man, and he left the room.

Steve smiled and something inside Sally responded. "Francis used to be a butler to the Royal Family at one time. Oh, I know I may seem rather ostentatious, but it gives me a buzz to think that the Queen herself used to ask him to bring her tea as well."

"He goes with a house like this," said Sally.

"Yes he does," said Steve. "That's just what I thought when I hired him. Now, to more serious business, Sally. I understand from Andy that you and your husband wish to leave my employment?"

Sally's expression hardened. "My husband and I work for Mulville's, Mr Wilson; no one else."

"I see," said Steve, the smile now gone. "And does your combined salaries from Mulville's allow you to purchase brand new BMW's and Rolex watches? For if they do, Mulville's must think very highly of you both."

"You know very well where the money to buy those things came from!" Sally snapped. "I didn't come here to play games."

"And I didn't invite you here to play games, Sally," Steve replied. "But the facts speak for themselves. We approached your husband with an offer. He didn't have to accept it, but he did. And before you start claiming that we pressured him into accepting, you should know that we consider a reluctant employee to be more trouble than they are worth. Your husband not only accepted our offer, he went so far as to recruit others at the store."

"Because he was told to!" Sally retorted.

"Asked to, Sally. Even at that stage he could have said no."

"Well, I don't care what Jimmy did in the past, Mr Wilson. It's the future that I want to sort out. If you will just allow Jimmy to leave, you need never hear from us again, and that's a promise."

Steve spread his hands. "But you are assuming that I don't want to hear from you again, and that certainly is not the case. You husband is very useful to us, Sally. Branches of Mulville's are spread right across the country, and in very favourable locations. Why, the locations couldn't be better if we'd picked them ourselves. And when your husband eventually climbs to the top of the Mulville's ladder, he will become an extremely valuable investment, second only to our product. And as for you."

Steve smiled and leaned forward in his seat.

"Well, all I can say is that I like you, Sally. Andy told me you were special, but he failed to convey just how special."

"May I remind you that I'm married, Mr Wilson," Sally replied coldly. "And I'm also faithful."

Steve settled back in his seat. "Faithful: now that is a concept I believe has had its day, wouldn't you say?"

"No I wouldn't."

Before Steve could reply, the door opened and the old man entered carrying a silver tray containing a silver teapot; two early, decorative Minton cups and saucers; a silver milk jug and sugar bowl, and a plate of various Fortnum and Mason biscuits.

"Just leave it on the table, Francis, thank you," said Steve.

When Francis left the room, Steve turned his attention to the tray and began to pour the tea.

"This may surprise you, but I wasn't born rich. In fact my parents lived in a Council house for most of their lives. And when I was a child I used to watch those TV programmes about the olden days - especially the ones where there were servants living in a big house. My friends thought I was a bit funny in the head, but it was just that I had a passion for that sort of thing. I used to think that the tea in those silver teapots must taste like magic, and the cakes; well, as far as I was concerned they must have been made by the angels. So, when I found myself in a position to have these beautiful things, naturally I indulged my passion. Sugar?"

"Just milk," said Sally in a flat tone. The mention of wealth had suddenly soured her mood and reminded her what she must now do.

Steve carried the tea to Sally.

Sally took the cup and saucer; thanked him politely, and then took a few sips of the hot liquid. It tasted excellent.

"Now then," said Steve, holding his cup close to his mouth, "enough of the days when I was poor and dreamt of better things. So, where were we; oh yes, we were discussing certain outdated values."

"They're not outdated to me," said Sally. "Can we please drop the subject."

"For now," said Steve. "But please don't expect me to stop trying to win you over, Sally. I find you attractive, and I make it a point never to allow a desirable woman to slip easily through my fingers. It just isn't done in polite circles."

A frown creased Sally's forehead. "You have a quaint and old fashioned way of speaking, Mr Wilson, but it doesn't alter the fact that all this is the proceeds from other people's misery."

Steve put his cup down slowly. Then he leaned back and stared at Sally. There was a look of disappointment on his face. "And here was I thinking that we were going to get along. So may I ask how you have acquired such a low opinion of me?"

Sally laughed. "You're a drug dealer. That hardly puts you in line for a knighthood."

"No, I suppose not," Steve replied, again sounding disappointed. "Although the tobacco and alcohol industries produce the occasional Lord, I believe."

"I've heard that weak argument too many times in the past," Sally scoffed. "How it's up to each person to decide for themselves whether they take drugs or not. Well, let me tell you something, Mr Wilson, some people are weaker than others, and they shouldn't have to make that choice."

"Do you have children?" Steve inquired.

"I doubt very much that you have to ask that question," said Sally, "seeing as you have a file on all those working for you. But no I don't have children; if it's any of your business."

"You are correct, it is none of my business," said Steve. "But please indulge me for a moment. Say you had a daughter of sixteen. Would you allow her to smoke?"

"I would certainly try and convince her not to smoke."

"Try and convince her, but not stop her, even though there was a strong likelihood that she would suffer terrible health problems later in life. And would you despise the tobacco industry as much as you appear to despise me?"

"It's not just the drugs," Sally replied defensively.

"Oh?"

"I've heard about your methods. I know that people call you The Sailor."

Sally was startled by the laughter that shot from her host, and it was a few moments before he stopped.

"I don't see what's so funny about it," said Sally. "It's a terrible way to behave."

166

"What's so terrible about it?" Steve replied, trying to control his amusement.

"If you don't know the answer to that, then you're even worse than I thought."

"As a matter of fact I don't," said Steve. "Sailing ships are just another of my passions, and I happen to own two of them. And in case you're wondering, I don't flog my crew, or keelhaul them for insubordination. They are all sailing enthusiasts; having the time of their lives and eating only the finest foods, cooked by a Michelin Star chef in two rather excellent kitchens."

Sally was astounded. "You mean, you really are a sailor?"

"For my sins. And you should join us on one of our trips. People who go on cruises in those floating cities have no idea what they are missing."

"I see." Sally took a large gulp of her tea.

"You look surprised," said Steve. "I haven't heard the name used to describe me, but I suppose it's apt. What did you think it meant; clearly something derogative?"

Sally stared back at the very handsome man sitting opposite her. "I must have misheard. And I suppose you don't sell drugs to children?"

The humour left Steve's face. "Everyone who works for me knows that if they are caught selling children drugs, they won't be in a position to sell anything to anyone ever again."

Sally suddenly stood up and put her cup on the coffee table. "I have to get back. My husband will be wondering where I am."

"Of course," said Steve standing also. "Perhaps you will have dinner with me sometime. Oh, and by the way, my interest in antiques over the past few years has given me a very good eye for fine detail. So, when you do decide to join me for dinner, I trust you will leave that rather unflattering wig behind. And I just can't believe that a beautiful face like yours is used to all that makeup."

Sally hid her unease quite well, and said nothing as they left the room.

But her heart began to pound in her chest when Terry held out her coat and bag to her.

She tried to read his expression as she took them, but his face was blank.

The weight of her coat told her the gun was still there.

Steve then escorted her to her car. "Thank you for coming, Sally," he said, opening the car door for her.

Sally sat in the driving seat and pulled the door shut.

She opened her window and smiled at Steve. "Thank you for seeing me."

Steve smiled back. "It was my pleasure. And we must have another chat about your husband's future during your next visit."

Sally closed the window without replying.

Then she started the engine, and moved slowly down the drive.

In her rear-view mirror she could see Steve and Terry talking to one another. She wondered what about.

And when she drove Andy's car towards the maisonette, she parked it just around the corner. All she wanted to do was to get home as quickly as possible. She had a great deal of thinking to do, and she needed to be on her own to do it. It was already 11:15 and Jimmy would be in bed; at least she hoped he would be.

Two hours of sitting on her settee, drinking coffee and thinking passed before she finally retired herself. And before she left the living-room she took the phone off the hook. She didn't want calls from anyone.

Chapter Twenty Six

The phone ringing woke Sally the following morning.

She turned over in the bed and looked at the clock. It was 7:45. Jimmy would be at work by now, and had obviously reset the receiver on the downstairs phone.

Sally leaned over and lifted the receiver and put it to her right ear. "Hello?"

"What the hell are you playing at?" an irate, male voice shouted down the line. "I've been ringing you all bloody night. What's happened? Is it over?"

Sally took a very deep breath. "No, Mr Saunders, it isn't over."

"What do you mean no?" Andy cried. "Stop pissing about will you and tell me what happened?"

"Don't speak to me like that," Sally warned.

"Ok; sorry," Andy replied in a calmer voice. "It's just that I was worried sick that something had gone wrong. I expected you to be waiting for a call from me when you got in last night, but your phone must have been off the hook. Now, can you please tell me what happened?"

"I went to his house like you said," Sally replied. "And, for your information, it was full of security guards."

"Damn!" Andy exclaimed. "So what did you do?"

"Exactly as I was told. I handed over my coat and bag, and I had tea with Steve Wilson."

"And they didn't find the gun?"

"If they did, they didn't mention it," said Sally. "And another thing, that idea of yours that I should wear a wig and extra makeup. He saw through those probably the instant he saw me. And I don't mean he thought I was made up like I was due to bad dress sense. He knows I wore that wig and makeup as a disguise."

"Damn," Andy repeated. "But you don't think he suspects anything at the moment; about our plan, I mean?"

"If he knows about the gun, then of course he will be suspicious. Mind you, he was very nice to me, so you can come to your own conclusions. Oh, and he's invited me to dinner sometime."

"At least that's something," said Andy sounding relieved. "When he takes you to dinner you can do it then. Perhaps you could follow him to the bathroom. And -"

"Hold on a second!" Sally cut in angrily. "I've just had one of the luckiest escapes of my life, and all you can say is, do it when he takes you to dinner."

"You want him dead, don't you," Andy replied firmly. "How else are you going to get Jimmy away from him?"

"You're the one that wants him dead," Sally snapped. "But you expect me to kill him; to take all the risks. And I'll bet anything you have a second plan to cover yourself, just in case I make a mess of it. Why don't you do it if you want him out of the way."

An exasperated sigh shot from Andy. "I've already told you why. I wouldn't get away with it."

"And another thing," said Sally. "You told me he was called The Sailor because he cuts people loose when they become trouble for him. But when I asked him about it, he said -"

"You did what!" Andy exclaimed. "You stupid cow. What the hell did you do that for? Now he knows you've been talking to someone in the organization about him?"

"I didn't say who told me," said Sally.

"He can probably work it out for himself. Only three of us know that nickname, and you haven't spoken to the other two yet. The man's paranoid. If he even suspects that I'm up to something, I'm dead."

"It's all right," said Sally. "He just laughed about it."

"What do you mean, laughed?"

"I mean he found it funny. I think you're wrong about him. He told me about his passion for sailing ships; about the couple he owns; how he goes off with his crew of volunteers on trips around the world."

"That's a load of nonsense!" Andy cried. "He doesn't own any ships. What the hell did he do to you in that place?"

"You're wrong, Mr Saunders," said Sally. "You should see his house, and how passionate he is about it. And that's how he was when he talked about sailing his ships."

"I'm telling you he doesn't own any bloody ships. And I know for a fact that he flies everywhere because he gets seasick. He's just trying to impress you; make you think he's really a nice person. He will tell you anything to get you into bed. You can't trust him."

"And I suppose you wouldn't say anything to get me to kill him, and I can trust you," Sally countered, sarcastically.

"I'm telling you he's stringing you along," Andy replied after a short pause.

"How many times have you been to his house?" Sally asked.

"I haven't. But what's that got to do with it?"

"If you haven't even been invited to his house, how can you say whether he has ships or not. I bet he has lots of things you don't know about."

"We're getting away from the point," said Andy. "Now we both want him dead so we'll just have to come up with another plan."

"I'll have to think about it," said Sally.

"What's there to think about?"

"I'll call you later, Mr Saunders."

"Wait a minute, Sally! Don't hang up."

"Later, Mr Saunders. Bye."

"How was the film last night, Sal?" Jimmy inquired at the dinner table that evening.

"Nothing special," Sally replied, ignoring the guilt about lying to her husband. "Too much sex, swearing and violence for me, darling."

"Sounds a great film to me," Jimmy grinned.

Sally threw a pea at him, which bounced off his forehead.

"You didn't get in till late," Jimmy added.

"I felt like a walk after the film."

Jimmy grew concerned. "You shouldn't really go out on your own, especially with some lunatic after you."

"I was all right. I kept close to other people."

"Ok," said Jimmy with a frown. "But next time I'm coming with you whether you want me there or not. Oh, I forgot to tell you, Mr Harris called me into his office this afternoon and told me I will be having a sixty pound a week raise from next month."

"That's great!" Sally cried, genuinely delighted.

"Mind you, you should have seen his face," said Jimmy with a laugh. "I think he got a real kick out of telling me. And you know something, Sal, I nearly blurted out what's a crappy sixty pounds a week compared to two thousand."

The remark hit Sally like a bucket of cold water. "It's good money and it's honest money. And we can get all the things we want by working for them without resorting to drug dealing."

"Maybe, but when we're too old to enjoy them," said Jimmy pulling a sour face. "No thanks, Sal, give me a few more years and we're on our way. Anyway, after telling me about the increase Mr Harris went on about the rich fruits of hard labour. I'm sure he has a secret desire to be a reform warden in one of those tough prisons where he could convert all the inmates into model citizens: what an old dreamer."

"Well, whatever you think, for heaven's sake don't ever let on that you aren't absolutely delighted with your position as Assistant Manager," Sally warned. "He might become suspicious."

"Course I won't, Sal. And look."

He reached into his back pocket and put a thick, folded wad of fifty pound notes on the table. "Billy Bennifield sent this around for me. There's three thousand pounds there. It's a welcome-back bonus. I'll tell you something, Sal, I can make some real money over the next five years. And who knows, maybe they'll make me one of the bosses. Jeff told me he heard Billy Bennifield is on twelve thousand a week; imagine, twelve thousand pounds a week tax free. So you can take a very good guess at how much his boss must be making; eighty thousand at least."

"You said we would leave here in three years?" Sally replied in a cold voice.

"I know I did, Sal." Jimmy's tone became pleading. "But I'm important to them, and that means I will probably earn very big money later on. And if we did stay on for say five years, we could even make enough to buy a mansion with hundreds of acres of land. I mean, who needs a house when you can have a mansion."

Sally stood and picked up her dinner plate. "Put that money away will you, darling. The sight of it makes me feel sick."

Jimmy followed as Sally carried her plate to the sink. "But I thought you were coming round to my way of thinking?" he protested.

"I am," she replied, turning on the hot water tap.

"So what was that about just now?"

"I don't want to look at it; that's all."

"But you're willing to spend it?"

Sally turned to her husband. "I'm willing to let you spend it; there's a difference."

Anger flared in Jimmy's eyes. "Oh is there now. Then let me ask you something, Sal, will you drive the car I buy with this money that makes you feel sick? Will you wear the nice things I buy you, and live in the mansion I plan to get?"

"Yes, I will," said Sally in a low voice.

Jimmy spread his arms in total exasperation. "But you won't look at the money that buys them. You women are all crazy."

"I've agreed to you accepting delivery of the drugs again and doing so for three years," said Sally, turning back to attend to the dishes. "What more do you want?"

"A little bit of enthusiasm!" Jimmy cried. "For God's sake, Sal, is it asking so much. You know, I feel really proud that I'm doing as well as I am. I'm bringing in twenty five hundred pounds a week; that's at least five times more than other men my age. But all I get from you is that the sight of the money makes you sick. Well, for your information, Sal, I love the look of that money; the feel of it; and the smell of it. And most of all I love having it bulging in my back pocket, as a reminder of my success. Money on tap; it's great."

"I'm pleased for you," said Sally. "But I don't feel the same way, so can we drop the subject."

Jimmy sighed and stomped into the living-room. And having thrown himself down on the settee, turned on the TV by remote control. The sound of football fans cheering blared through the serving hatch and into the kitchen where it made Sally wince.

Chapter Twenty Seven

It was six days later that Sally received the call that she was half expecting.

The caller was Steve Wilson.

"Hello, Sally. I hope you don't mind me calling you at home, but I'd like to ask if you've decided to accept my invitation to have dinner with me? Surely I have given you enough time to make up your mind about it."

"To be perfectly honest, Mr Wilson," said Sally, "I don't see any point. As I've already told you, I'm happily married, and I don't think my husband would like it."

"Then don't tell him. And can't you please call me Steve?"

Sally couldn't help smiling, "No to both suggestions, Mr Wilson. I'm sorry."

"Oh come on!" Steve pleaded. "What harm can it do? It won't be a date or anything like that; just two people having a business dinner?"

Sally frowned. "But it won't be a business dinner, will it?"

"It could be."

"What kind of business?"

"The kind that covers employees wishing to leave their employer."

"You mean you've changed your mind?" Sally exclaimed in excitement.

"Hey; not so fast," Steve laughed. "At least allow me to indulge my fantasies about us for a little bit longer. Anyway I believe the idea is that the subject of your husband will be discussed over dinner, and it would hardly be right for either of us to expect a final decision to be made even before serious negotiations have begun. So come and have dinner here with me at my home and see what transpires?"

Sally was silent for a few moments. She couldn't tell Jimmy that she was having dinner with the boss of the organization; he wouldn't understand and would probably do something stupid.

"Are you still there, Sally?" Steve asked.

"Just deciding what to do," said Sally. "Ok, I'll have dinner with you; but nothing else."

"Sally!" Steven exclaimed in mock horror. "I'll have you know that I'm a gentleman and would never even dream of trying to take advantage of a guest; no matter how great the temptation. Now, how about Wednesday; eight-o-clock at my place? You will be as safe as my ninety year old aunt, I assure you."

"And do you have a ninety year old aunt?" Sally inquired.

"No, but I would have if she hadn't died twenty years ago at the age of seventy," Steve quipped.

"I'll be there," said Sally with a laugh, and she put down the phone.

She felt a tingle of excitement, even though she knew it was wrong.

Sally arrived at Steve Wilson's house at exactly eight pm.

This time she came in the BMW.

"Good evening, Terry," she said, handing the bodyguard her coat and bag in the hall.

"Please go on through to the drawing room, Mrs Mason," Terry replied formally. "Mr Wilson is expecting you."

Sally crossed the hall and went through the door into the drawing room.

"Sally!" Steven cried with obvious pleasure, coming towards her. "I'm glad you've come."

Sally instinctively flinched as her host kissed her on the left cheek, but quickly felt at ease for some reason.

"Have a seat," said Steve. "And something to drink before dinner?"

"Any chance of a dry Martini and lemonade?" Sally asked, sitting on one of the settees.

Steve picked up the silver bell and shook it a few times.

Francis entered the room and Steve asked him to bring Sally's request and a Teachers whisky for him.

"You know something," said Steve, "I must confess that I've thought about you every day since you were last here."

Sally smiled. "That's flattering, but I don't see why you should. Surely you have plenty of female friends?"

"Of course I do. But I'm not one for close relationships; unless the lady is very special, of course."

"I would never be unfaithful to my husband," said Sally.

"I understand that," Steve replied. "But haven't you ever been curious?"

"About what?"

"About other men, of course? When you're out with your husband and an attractive man walks by, don't you ever wonder what it would be like to spend just one night in his arms?"

Sally pursed her lips thoughtfully. "I suppose I do, Steve. But wondering is something we all do at some time or other, and there's no harm in it. For instance, when we're short of money and we find someone's wallet with cash in it. It's natural to wonder what we would spend the money on, but most of us look for an address and give the wallet back to the owner."

"Yes, you're right," said Steve, "and thanks."

"For what?"

"For calling me Steve."

Sally wondered if she blushed. "I didn't realize that I had," she said.

"Well, the main thing is that you must be feeling a little more comfortable and relaxed with me, and that's what counts."

Sally concentrated her attention on her nails. And she was relieved when Francis entered with their drinks.

"So, does Jimmy know you're here?" Steve asked when the butler left.

"No, of course not."

Steve pulled a face. "Oh I see, this is a clandestine meeting. And would that be because your husband is the jealous type?"

"I wouldn't call disapproving about your wife having dinner alone with another man in his house being jealous," said Sally.

"What would you call it?"

"Being justifiably concerned."

"And why would his concern be justified; if he knew?"

A look of annoyance entered Sally's eyes. "Can we stop this silly game please. I agreed to have dinner with you on the understanding we would discuss my husband leaving your organization."

"So we did," Steve replied instantly. "My apologies. But there is plenty of time for that. So, just for a little while, lets discuss our growing relationship."

Just then the door opened. "Dinner is served, sir."

"Thank you, Francis."

"I'd better go," Sally announced, suddenly standing up.

"Hey, what about our dinner?" Steve protested.

"I'm sorry," said Sally. "I shouldn't have agreed to any of this."

"Is it the fact that we're going to have dinner? Is that what's bothering you?" Steve asked anxiously.

Sally nodded, though it wasn't entirely true."

"Then don't have dinner; have a sandwich instead?" Steve pleaded.

Sally was caught off guard. "What?"

"Have a sandwich. I mean, what harm can there be in it? Surely a sandwich doesn't have the same connotations as dinner?"

Sally was undecided. "I don't know."

Steve called Francis back. "Make up some sandwiches with the roast beef, will you."

Then he turned back to Sally. "Tea, coffee, or wine?"

"Tea," Sally answered automatically.

Relief showed on Steve's face. "We'll have it in here on our laps, Francis. Oh, and bring some of that cinnamon cake as well."

"Yes, sir," said Francis, and he withdrew with a disapproving expression on his face.

"Oh, come on!" Steve laughed when Sally remained standing; looking as if she might rush from the room at any moment. "Please sit down. I've been so looking forward to you being here. And I promise not to play any more silly games. This is purely business, and I accept that."

Reluctantly Sally sat back in her seat. Inwardly she was fighting a battle; a battle between her love and loyalty to her husband, and her growing attraction to this cultured man who was turning out to be far from what she expected.

Steve was obviously pleased and rubbed his hands in anticipation. "Right then, what shall we talk about while we're waiting for our sandwiches?"

"What I came here for," said Sally, "my husband."

"Fair enough: let's talk about Mr Jimmy Mason," said Steve undaunted. "Now why should I just relinquish what promises to be a very valuable asset? After all, what can you offer me in return?"

"Well, for a start," Sally replied in a formal tone, "we'll be out of your hair for good, because there's no way I'm going to stand by and watch my husband ruin our lives. And secondly, I have a tape and written details about some of your employees that I can hand over to you."

Steve slowly nodded his head. "Yes, I suppose most people would consider those a fair trade, but you see, Sally, I'm rather different than most people, and so I'm saying to you that what you have to trade with is not enough. Jimmy will be worth millions eventually, whereas that tape and the written details cannot be linked to me in any way, I assure you. True enough, if you went to the police, there would be some loss to me, but nothing personal. Furthermore, I have one of the finest legal teams in the country on my books, and your so-called written details would be seen as nothing more than the ranting of a jilted woman."

"Jilted woman!" Sally cried in shock.

"Of course. This is your second visit to my home. How could you prove that you haven't been calling here for an illicit liaison?"

Sally knew that she should be on her feet and storming out of the room, but to her surprise she found that she wanted to continue sitting where she was; talking to Steve about Jimmy; about anything at all.

There was a smile of satisfaction on Steve's lips. "You're an intelligent woman, Sally. You know what you want, and you understand that to get it, it is sometimes necessary to make sacrifices."

"In other words, if I sleep with you, you'll let Jimmy go!" Sally declared stiffly.

"Crude; but more or less accurate," said Steve. "However, I'm not just looking for a one night stand; I could have as many of those as I wanted, but they are as shallow as the women who agree to them. No, what I would like from you, Sally is some form of relationship."

"I thought relationships weren't your thing," said Sally.

Steve shrugged. "There is always the exception that proves the rule; as I'm sure you know. Anyway, that was before I met you. And since you have dispensed with that ridiculous wig and makeup, I can see that you have an unique beauty. Oh, I don't mean the conventional beauty of say Jennifer Lopez. She has the look very much loved by the camera. But your beauty must be seen directly by the eye of the beholder. It cannot be reproduced or copied in any way. You see, the camera is only the eye of the people, but the eye is the camera of the soul."

Sally couldn't help smiling. "I think you need to work on your prose skills for a little bit longer."

Steve laughed. "I suppose you're right. But I do mean what I say. I find you extremely attractive, and I hate having to use your husband to keep you here, but I can't think of anything else."

A moment later Francis arrived with two silver trays containing sandwiches, tea, and cake.

Sally was surprised at how hungry she was and she had eaten two of the sandwiches before she realized that Steve was watching her with a bemused expression on his face.

"Sorry," she said, quickly putting a third sandwich back on the plate in embarrassment. "I didn't get a chance to have lunch today at work."

"You tuck in," said Steve. "All I want you to do is enjoy yourself."

The rest of the meal was eaten in silence, and finally they both settled back in their seats. Steve called for Francis who cleared everything away, but returned later with a decanter of brandy and two glasses. Sally had a fondness for brandy but limited herself to having it only on special occasions.

Was this a special occasion? she asked herself as she watched Steve pouring out the golden liquid into the balloon glasses.

"This is thirty-five year old brandy," he said as he handed her a glass. "I hope you find it as special as I do."

Sally sniffed then took a sip. Her host was right, she had never tasted such excellent brandy before. It was a delight.

Steve sat back down. "I can tell that you enjoy the finer things in life, Sally. I can't understand what you're doing married to someone like Jimmy Mason."

"You probably don't even know what he looks like," Sally countered.

"You would be surprised what I know about the people who work for me," said Steve. "And I can tell you here and now that he isn't good enough for you."

"I don't know if I should be flattered, or outraged on behalf of my husband," said Sally with some levity.

"What does your heart tell you to be?"

"My heart, Steve, tells me to tell you that it's none of your business how it's feeling."

"And that's me put firmly in my place," Steve laughed. "But strangely enough I like you putting me in my place, Sally. So why do you think that is?"

"Because you're either stupid, or a masochist," Sally replied with an edge to her voice. She suddenly felt that she was being manipulated and needed to hit back.

Steve nodded slowly, refusing to be baited. "Probably both of those things when it comes to women. However, joking aside, I'm going to be honest with you, Sally. I haven't made up my mind about your husband yet, and I won't; at least not tonight. So, I'm asking you to go out on a proper date with me; no strings, just dinner and a show in the West End. And when the time is right, I'll give you my decision concerning Jimmy's future. Who knows, perhaps we'll all go our own way amicably."

"All right," said Sally. "But I want your decision soon."

"Excellent," said Steve. "And don't worry, I'm too much of a gentleman to keep a lady waiting; too long."

Chapter Twenty Eight

"Where the hell have you been?" Jimmy called out from the kitchen as soon as Sally entered the maisonette. "It's nearly midnight?"

"You know where I've been; to see a film," Sally replied calmly as she took her coat off.

"Like hell you have!" Jimmy came storming into the hall, his face white with rage. "I stood outside that bloody cinema tonight and you certainly didn't go in there."

Sally frowned. "I thought you were working late tonight?"

"That's what I told you, because I suspected you were up to something, so I got to the cinema early," said Jimmy.

"And what if I had shown up, what excuse would you have had?"

"I'd have told you I finished early and decided to join you: but what's that got to do with it? You didn't turn up, that's the whole point. Where were you?"

"I went to another cinema," said Sally, cursing her decision to sit in a Tesco car park for a couple of hours to think. "That local one tends to get loads of kids in there lately; shouting and screaming every few minutes."

"There's no point lying to me," Jimmy snapped. "Because all I have to do is ask you about the film."

"Do what you like!" Sally retorted, pushing past her husband. "I'm going to bed."

Jimmy glared after her. "You're seeing someone, aren't you? I know you are because you're acting as guilty as hell."

Jimmy then followed Sally up the stairs.

"I'm going to the bathroom, unless you want to follow me in there as well," said Sally.

Jimmy forced himself to wait in the hall when the bathroom door slammed shut in his face. It was all he could do to restrain himself from barging in and continuing the row.

Sally came out of the bathroom a few minutes later and walked quickly past him, and into the bedroom.

He rushed after her. "Sal; please! We have to talk about this."

Sally sat on the edge of the bed.

She stared fixedly at her husband. "Look, darling, you want to know if I'm having an affair with another man, and the answer is no: happy now."

"Swear on our unborn children," Jimmy shot back.

"Oh for God's sake!" Sally declared, pulling off her shoes. "I've told you the truth, and if you don't believe me, then that's your problem. Obviously you don't know me as well as you should."

"All right, I believe you're not seeing another man," said Jimmy in a calmer tone. "But what about - ?"

Sally's eyes widened in disbelief. "Another woman? Are you saying you think I'm a lesbian?"

"No; not a lesbian as such," said Jimmy, obviously embarrassed by the subject. "But you read about it a lot lately; couples married for years sometimes, then one of them leaves to set up home with someone of the same sex. And there's nothing wrong with that, but all I'm saying is if that's what's happening with you then can't we at least talk about it. It might be a phase you're going through, but if it isn't then all I'm saying is that we could come to some sort of arrangement; maybe you could see this Sar - this person two or three times a week. I mean we don't have any kids yet so there wouldn't be a problem on that score; at least not for the time being. And then when we do eventually have kids, well I'm sure the situation could be explained to them in a way that wouldn't cause them too many problems."

"Are you finished now?" Sally asked, having listened to her distraught husband's outpourings in utter astonishment.

Jimmy nodded.

"Then listen carefully. I - am - not - a - lesbian. I wouldn't mind if I was, but I'm not. Now do you believe me, or do you think I'm lying to you?"

"No, of course not," Jimmy exclaimed. "It's just that when you didn't show up, and you have this new friend: what I mean is: oh I don't know what I mean."

"Just come to bed, darling," Sally replied, yawning. "I'm too tired to talk about this now. We'll sort it out in the morning; unless I decide to creep away during the night."

Jimmy didn't sleep at all that night, and he noticed that Sally dropped off as soon as her head touched the pillow. His frantic mind spent hours trying to figure out if that meant something good or bad for his plans.

Chapter Twenty Nine

The following morning at breakfast, Sally lied to Jimmy, telling him that she needed to spend a few hours that evening with Sarah who had a personal problem. She assured him it wasn't anything medical, and there was nothing for him to be concerned about. But it was just too personal to even tell him what it was.

Reluctantly Jimmy accepted this explanation, and decided to try to put it from his mind, even when Sally said it would be necessary to be with her friend on more than one occasion.

He knew that Sarah was important to Sally, and hoped nothing would ever happen to their friendship.

During a short tea break at Mulville's, Margaret Brown joined Sally at her table.

"Guess what I've just heard!" she said excitedly. "The police called here before opening time this morning."

Solid fear ballooned in Sally's stomach. "What did they want?"

"No idea," said Margaret. "But I do know they spent nearly an hour talking to Mr Harris about something."

"How do you know they were here?" Sally asked, trying to recover.

"One of the cleaners told me. And who'd ever have thought there would be any excitement in this drab old store."

"How did Mr Harris seem afterwards?" said Sally.

Margaret frowned. "What do you mean?"

"Was he shocked; or angry - ?"

"She didn't say. Why should he be angry: do you know something I don't?"

Sally's defences shot up. "No; of course not. I was just wondering if it might have been about the storeroom shortages or something."

"That wouldn't anger Mr Harris," said Margaret. "He's known about the shortages for ages. Anyway, I've heard him say lots of times that where there is plenty there is greed in plenty."

"You're right," said Sally. "I've heard him say that too. I wasn't thinking."

"You sure you're ok?" said Margaret. "You look a bit pale to me."

Then her eyes lit up. "You're not pregnant, are you? You must be so excited, love."

"No I'm not!" Sally retorted. "So don't go spreading that story around."

"As if I would," Margaret laughed. "What would be the point if it isn't true. Anyway, how are you and Jimmy getting on? I've noticed that he hasn't been seeing so much of Jeff the last few days. Did you have a word with him?"

"I told you; Jimmy's not gay," Sally replied.

"Bisexual then," Margaret prompted. "Did you make him choose, because if you did, he made the right choice in you. That Jeff is a creep if you ask me: they would never be happy together."

Suddenly Sally was too tired to argue. "That's right, Margaret. He chose me, so can we stop talking about it."

Margaret took a drink of her tea. "Men; they must have invented trouble, because they cause it wherever they go. And would you credit it, next month we're going to have a new manager and of course it's going to be another man."

Sally's mind began to spin. "What are you talking about? What new manager?"

"Good God, love!" Margaret cried. "You're not up to much when it comes to gossip are you. Didn't you know, Old Harris is retiring next month, and guess who's taking his place?"

"You've got that wrong," Sally replied. "Mr Harris doesn't retire until next year."

"That was the original plan. But you know that back trouble he's been suffering from for years, well, it's got worse lately, and the doctors told him that if he didn't have an operation soon, he could end up paralysed. So he's decided to have it and take early retirement. And that means Jimmy is going to be boss of this store."

And of even greater value to the organization: Steve Wilson's probable words when he found out, entered Sally's mind like an intruder.

"What's the matter?" Margaret inquired. "You don't look too happy about his promotion?"

"It's just a bit of a shock," said Sally.

Margaret laughed. "What's there to be shocked about; more authority and more money: Jimmy will be over the moon. Ok, I must admit I would like the new manager to have been a woman, but we think Jimmy's a nice bloke so what the hell. We can always gaze into those gorgeous blue eyes of his when he's giving us a telling off. I'll bet they're real sexy when he's angry. Mind you, will he feel the same way about us; you know, with him being in two camps. Thing is, I've always wondered about BySexs: do they have only half the attraction towards women as normal blokes, or is it full on, depending who they are with. Funny the tricks nature plays on some people."

Sally tried to share Margaret's humour, but she couldn't manage it. Why had Mr Harris not told Jimmy about his early retirement? And when Steve Wilson found out about Jimmy's promotion, he may well call off that date they had planned.

"You know, you worry me lately, Sally," said Margaret frowning. "Nothing seems to put a smile on your face these days. When you first came to work here, you were a good laugh. Remember the time that moaning old biddy of a customer Mrs Watkins was going on as usual about the prices the store was charging, and then you deliberately charged her seven hundred pounds for a tin of cat food, and she nearly choked on her false teeth. And remember how it took Mr Harris over an hour to calm her down. I mean, we all laughed for days about that. So what's happened to our fun-loving Sally, lately?"

Sally shrugged. "I suppose I've found more to worry about than Mrs Watkins."

Margaret reached out and touched Sally's right arm. "Whatever's bothering you, love, don't forget I'm your friend. Oh, I know I come across as Margaret The Mouth at times, but I really don't mean anyone any harm. I have my own problems and the only way I can get through life without living on prescriptions is to laugh at them and every one else's. But I want you to know, if you need a shoulder to cry on, then you won't find a softer one than mine."

A smile touched Sally's lips. "Thanks, Margaret, I'll remember that. It's a comforting feeling to know I have a friend who cares."

"You just holler when you need me, love, and I'll come charging to help," Margaret declared with a grin. "And God help any bastard who tries to stop me. Now, how about a bit of gossip to lighten the mood, and I have a real juicy one. You know that new checkout girl, Rachel. Well, it seems that she's dropped her latest boyfriend because she only caught -"

Sally didn't really hear the rest of it. She simply nodded in the right places and thanked God for Margaret Brown.

Chapter Thirty

Andy Saunders was a worried man. His perfect plan to take over the drugs organization; set in motion the second Sally Mason entered his office for the first time, was in trouble. But the worst thing was he didn't really know exactly what kind of trouble. He had sent Sally to kill his boss Steve Wilson, and she had failed. She visited Steve at his home once more and again she left without doing the job. What the hell was going on? At best, she was still trying to find the courage to kill another human being. At worst she had changed her mind; but if so, why did she go back to his home a second time?

Andy had an awful feeling in the pit of his stomach that the situation might deteriorate even further, to a point where he himself was in deadly danger. Sally Mason was an attractive woman; Steve Wilson was a handsome man with power and wealth. He didn't have the ties of a married man, and he was well known for his fondness of married women, if his sources were to be believed. If Sally was falling for him, she would want to protect his life, and there were two ways she could achieve this; come back and tell him to call it off, or tell Steve Wilson what he was doing. So far Sally had refused to return his calls; most of which were made to her home when he knew Jimmy wouldn't be there. This couldn't continue. He had to do something, and soon, before he lost all control of the situation.

He tapped in a number on the telephone on his desk.

Billy Bennifield answered.

"It's me," said Andy. "Did you sort out that problem with Peter Harrison?"

"All done," said Billy. "I paid him a visit myself: put the fear of God into him. He'll behave from now on; trust me."

"And what about Heston's?"

"I took Alex and Mick with me yesterday. Gave that manager a painful reminder of who's calling the shots. You won't have any more problems with delivery. Anyway, why the questions all of a sudden? I do my job, you know. If this has anything to do with that bitch Mason is married to, I -"

"No," Andy interrupted. "Just checking, that's all. But since you mention Sally Mason, has she been in touch with you lately?"

"Not a word from the bitch in days!" Billy growled. "I hope I never hear her voice again. You know, my wife grilled me for over an hour the last time she called. Something should be done about her."

"Never mind that," said Andy. "If she phones you about anything at all, let me know immediately."

"Don't I always," Billy replied.

Andy then dropped the receiver back in its resting position, his expression a mixture of anger, confusion and worry. "What are you up to Mason?" he muttered. "Well, whatever it is, I promise you this: one way or another you're going to pay for what you've done to me."

Jimmy sat in his small office at Mulville's, pouring over figures on the computer. The store was doing well, despite a local newspaper stating that all food retailers in the area were suffering from diminishing profits. Jimmy smiled to himself. It was good that the store was bucking the trend, because Mr Harris just told him yesterday that he would be the new manager in exactly five weeks time. His pay would go up by one hundred and fifty pounds a week, and of course there were many other benefits that would be his.

"Can you come into my office for a minute, Jimmy," said a voice from the doorway.

Jimmy jumped. He didn't realize he had been daydreaming. "Of course, Mr Harris," he said, following his boss to his office.

"Take a seat," Mr Harris offered, sitting behind his desk.

Jimmy sat down in a padded, chrome chair and crossed his legs.

The office was small, and reminded Jimmy of a furnished storeroom.

"The police were here early this morning," said Mr Harris, a grave expression on his face.

Jimmy felt a lump of fear lodge in his throat. "Oh; what about?" he asked in a stiff voice.

"Well," said his boss, "incredible as it seems, they have had a tip-off that our storeroom is being used as a holding area for drugs."

"That's ridiculous!" Jimmy exclaimed as the lump in his throat doubled in size. He tried to swallow it, but it remained.

"That's what I told them," Mr Harris replied. "Nevertheless they are taking the tip-off very seriously, although I can't think why. Mulville's has had a reputation for honest and decent trading second to none since the year of its conception in 1896. God knows what Head Office will make of it. And to think such a thing has happened just weeks from my retirement. And do you know, Jimmy, I first came to work at Mulville's as a delivery boy, and at this very store, exactly fifty years ago, and through hard work and determination I worked my way up to my present position. And now my exemplary record has been tarnished by this nonsense. No doubt some disgruntled ex-employee has chosen his moment very carefully to seek his misguided revenge, I should imagine."

"Probably," said Jimmy. "So, what happens now?"

"I shall send a report to Head Office, of course," said Mr Harris, his heavily-jowled face hard with concern. "And as for the police, I fear they are sending a team to search the storeroom this afternoon, and no one is to know about it in advance except for the two of us. I want you to make sure that none of the shop staff has any contact with the storeroom staff until the search is completed. I shall make sure no one in the storeroom leaves it. You may tell the shop staff that we are expecting a very important visitor and they must dispense with their lunch breaks just for today and stay at their posts. I do hate lying to them, but it is unavoidable under the circumstances. Of course their cooperation will be generously reflected in their salaries at the end of the month."

Mr Harris managed a weak smile. "Never let it be said that Mulville's do not appreciate its employees, for they are the bedrock of its foundations. Oh, and please see to it that they are provided with free sandwiches and cakes from the chiller. I'm sure they will keep their hunger pangs at bay until their evening meal."

Jimmy began to sweat under his clothes. "Perhaps I should see to the storeroom myself, Mr Harris? I usually see to any problems there?"

"Aaaa; I was afraid you were going to suggest that," said his boss, suddenly looking awkward.

Jimmy's mind seemed to become detached from the rest of him. "What do you mean?" he croaked.

Mr Harris stared at his assistant. "I'm afraid the police have requested that you do not enter the storeroom for the rest of the day."

"But why? I'm the assistant manager; it's part of my job?" Jimmy protested.

"It's probably nothing personal," Mr Harris replied. "I'm sure it's just a precaution; you know, in case they find anything."

"This is complete nonsense, Mr Harris!" Jimmy barked. "All this hassle because of some tip-off."

"I agree entirely, Jimmy. But the police were insistent."

Jimmy stared at his boss for a few moments, desperately trying to find a solution to the chasm that seemed to be opening beneath his feet. Sweat was now beading on his brow.

"Are you all right?" Mr Harris inquired with some concern. "You don't look very well at all?"

Jimmy wiped his forehead. "When I woke up this morning, I felt a bit under the weather. But it passed. Now it's back again, I'm afraid. So if you don't mind, Mr Harris, I'd like to take the rest of the day off."

"I'm sorry, Jimmy, that won't be possible."

"But I don't feel well," Jimmy protested.

"It's the police again, I'm afraid," said Harris. "No one is to leave the store, or even phone out. Incoming calls are all right, but none out."

Desperation turned Jimmy's fear to anger. "So, if I fall down dead from a heart attack, you'll ask one of the girls to get a packet of aspirins from the pharmacy, will you!" he retorted.

"Oh, come now, Jimmy," Mr Harris smiled. "Emergencies are a different matter. And if you are that ill, then you will require a police officer to escort you home. However, I must say that I'm rather puzzled by your attitude. I would have thought that as the manager-to-be, you would understand that sometimes problems arise that have to be dealt with in a calm and rational manner. Panic won't help the situation."

"I'm not panicking!" Jimmy snapped. "I don't feel well. Don't you understand that, you stupid old sod. I need to go home and get some rest."

Mr Harris paled with shock. "Yes, of course, Jimmy," he stammered. "I had no idea you were feeling so unwell. By all means go home immediately. I shall phone for a taxi. And I believe we shall dispense with the police escort on this occasion. I'm sure they will understand, given the circumstances."

Within fifty-five minutes, Jimmy was at home.

Frantically he phoned Billy Bennifield.

"Jesus Christ, Jimmy," said Billy, "if it isn't your bloody wife phoning me, it's you. This line is only to be used in emergencies. What is it now?"

"The police are going to raid Mulville's!" Jimmy shouted. "You've got to get that shipment out straight away."

"Calm down will you," Billy replied. "If you give yourself a heart attack, what good will you be to us."

"Didn't you hear what I said!" Jimmy screamed. "The police are going to search the storeroom this afternoon. You've got to get the stuff out or we'll all end up in prison."

"You know you're problem, Jimmy," said Billy in a calm voice. "You worry too much. Relax: pour yourself a drink."

Jimmy's voice broke with emotion. "Jesus, I'm talking to an idiot," he sobbed.

"Hey, watch the language!" Billy snapped. "And for your information, we know about the raid. We've known about it since yesterday, as a matter of fact. Now they won't find anything in that crate but tins of peaches, so get a grip."

Jimmy fought to control his emotions. "Then why didn't you warn me, you bastards; you dirty, rotten, fucking bastards!"

"There's that language again," Billy warned. "But don't feel too bad about us not telling you."

"Like fuck I won't!" Jimmy shot back. "So who was it that told you about the raid?"

"We didn't need anyone to tell us, because we knew exactly when the police received the tip-off."

"How?" Jimmy asked, at last beginning to calm down.

Billy laughed. "We knew because I was the one who phoned them. You see, Jimmy, it was a test. We have big plans for you, but before we could trust you as much as we will need to trust you, we decided to see what you would do when you found yourself really in the shit. And I'm glad to say that I was wrong about you, Jimmy. I would have given ten-to-one odds that you would confess to the police; spill your guts and make a deal."

"And what if I had?" Jimmy managed to ask despite the confusion still in his mind.

"Don't you worry about that," said Billy. "The police wouldn't have found a single shred of evidence to confirm your story, but plenty to convince them that you were dealing drugs on your own. Take a look behind your bath panel, and behind the tray of ice cubes in your fridge, if you don't believe me. Now, all I have to do is to phone up the police again, trying to implicate each of the major food retailers in the country. The police will soon come to believe they are dealing with a crank. You see, we're not amateurs, Jimmy, but we have to take risks occasionally when someone who has the potential to be very valuable to us is being undermined by a third party."

"Third party?" Jimmy asked.

"That bitch you call your wife," Billy growled. "She is very unhappy about your situation, and we needed to know how much of an influence she has on you."

"That's all finished with now," Jimmy replied. "We've talked about it and she's come round to my way of thinking. You won't have any more trouble from her."

"We'll see. But I'm telling you now. If she starts making things difficult for us again, we will have to do something about it."

"What do you mean?" Jimmy demanded, becoming defensive.

"Oh for fuck's sake, man, use your bloody imagination!" came the harsh reply.

The line went dead before Jimmy could respond.

Jimmy decided to report back to work that day. And when he entered Mr Harris's office, two men were just leaving.

"Oh, Jimmy," said Mr Harris, "this is Detective Inspector Adamson, and Detective Sergeant Wolbon. You will be pleased to hear that nothing has been found anywhere on the premises. Probably just a hoax call, wouldn't you say, Inspector Adamson?"

Adamson stared fixedly at Jimmy. "You're the Assistant Manager, aren't you?"

"That's right," said Jimmy.

"I understand from Mr Harris you were taken ill earlier?"

"Just a bit of a chill," said Jimmy. "Sorry I wasn't here when you arrived."

A hard look appeared in Adamson's eyes. "Ordinarily Mr Harris would be in very serious trouble for allowing a member of staff to leave the premises without a police escort; against our express orders. But fortunately he had the presence of mind to contact us immediately, and since we had a unit in the area at the time, we are satisfied that your absence played no part in our investigation."

"I didn't mean to ignore police instructions," said Jimmy. "It's just that I was desperate to get some rest, and Mr Harris was only being kind."

"I appreciate that," said Adamson. Then he turned to Harris. "As you say, sir, that was probably just a hoax call. Could be a disgruntled customer or maybe even an ex- employee. And perhaps you will give us a call if you hear from the man. We take a very dim view of people deliberately wasting police time."

"Yes, of course," said Harris. "And I'm sorry you have been put to all this trouble, Inspector."

"That's all right, sir," said Adamson. "You'd be surprised where some members of the public send us."

As the two police officers left, Jimmy followed Mr Harris into his office.

"Thank goodness that's all over with," said his boss with a sigh. "There must have been at least two dozen policemen with dogs here. And a few of them even had guns. Most unsettling. Anyway, I see that you have made a swift recovery from your illness."

"I'm really sorry for the way I spoke to you, Mr Harris," said Jimmy. "I don't know what was wrong with me. I began to feel extremely hot and tired, and all I could think about was getting home to bed. I'm sure I would have gone to bed even if the house was on fire when I got there; I was feeling that terrible."

Harris smiled. "Think no more about it, Jimmy. I have known you for six years and that was the first time you were ever rude to me. And do you know what I think? I believe that the police coming here to search was your first crisis, and combined with your illness, it brought on some form of panic attack. And would I be right in assuming you received the fright of your life today?"

"Oh, I did!" Jimmy exclaimed in a half laugh. "It was terrible, Mr Harris, just terrible."

"Of course it was. Mind you, the police were rather angry with me when they discovered that I had allowed you to go home unescorted, but they quickly calmed down when a call came through that they had just received another tip-off from the same person about a different supermarket chain. Anyway, I want you to put this unpleasant incident from your mind. And believe me, my boy, no other crisis will seem so bad after this one."

"I suppose they won't," said Jimmy. "So, do you mind if I return to my office. There are a few calculations to complete on the computer?"

"You go ahead. And take it easy for the next couple of days."

"Thank you, Mr Harris." said Jimmy, and he left the office.

Jimmy hadn't progressed very far with his calculations on the computer when there was a knock on his office door.

"Come in," said Jimmy.

The door slowly opened, and a young man of about eighteen years of age with close cropped black hair and a gold stud in his right ear came into the room.

Jimmy was surprised to see him. "Hello, Dennis. What can I do for you?"

Dennis Smith closed the door and approached Jimmy's desk. He seemed agitated about something and kept clenching and unclenching his fingers.

"Have a seat," Jimmy offered.

Dennis dropped into a chair and began nervously looking around the office.

"Right then?" said Jimmy. "What's up?"

"I'm not sure," said Dennis, turning his attention to Jimmy. "I mean, I think you're the person to talk to, Mr Mason. But I can't decide if I'm doing the right thing or not."

"I see," said Jimmy, smiling to put the youngster at ease. "Is it something to do with working in the storeroom? Is someone picking on you?"

"Oh nothing like that, Mr Mason," said Dennis, a smile switching on and off rapidly on his lips as he fought his obvious nerves. "In fact everyone treats me ok over there. It's just that; oh, I don't know if I should say anything."

"Look, Dennis," said Jimmy in a calming tone and leaning forwards on his desk, "I can see that something's bothering you. And it's been my experience that the best way to broach a difficult subject is to just come right out and say it without thinking too much beforehand, and then see what happens. Also, you don't have to worry. Whatever you say to me in this office is confidential, and even if it's to complain about someone, I can promise you that you won't be punished in any way; unless it's about me of course, and then I'll have you cut into little pieces and sold at fifty pence a pound in our fresh meat section."

Dennis stared at Jimmy with a very serious expression on his face. Then he gave a nervous laugh.

"That's better," said Jimmy. "Now; out with it."

Dennis took a deep, shuddering breath. "It's something that's going on in the storeroom, Mr Mason."

The humour left Jimmy in an instant. "What sort of thing?"

"I'm not sure, Mr Mason," said Dennis going back to finger clenching. "It started about five weeks ago. I was told to move a crate from one part of the storeroom to another, and because I wasn't used to the new forklift, I knocked against the crate next to the one I was supposed to move. George saw what happened and he had a go at me. I mean he really had a go, Mr Mason - cursing and swearing - telling me that he had a good mind to sack me on the spot. The thing is, Mr Mason, I don't know why he reacted like that. I mean, we break up the crates anyway once they've been opened. And I didn't damage any of the stuff inside the crate. It was full of tins of peaches and they would have leaked. So why go on like that just because I scraped one of the corners with the fork?"

Jimmy relaxed and leaned back in his seat. "I wouldn't take any notice of that, Dennis. George is a miserable git at the best of times. Maybe you caught him at a particularly bad time."

"I did think of that, Mr Mason," Dennis replied. "But then I noticed that the crate I bashed was sent to one of the other stores."

"What's so unusual about that?" said Jimmy. "The storeroom is one of three emergency distribution areas for the whole Mulville's chain? When one of the branches runs short of something and the supplier is having a problem with their supplies, the branch asks us for it? After all, our storeroom is always very well stocked."

"I know all that, Mr Mason," said Dennis, his finger clenching becoming frantic. "But it doesn't happen all the time, so I found it a bit odd that the next week another crate was sent out, and another the week after that, and always on a Thursday."

"A bit like buses," Jimmy managed to say with a smile. "Nothing for ages, then they come along three or four at a time."

There was a strange look in Dennis's eyes that Jimmy didn't like. "No, Mr Mason, it's not like that at all."

Jimmy began to feel like he was being interrogated by the young man sitting before him, and he felt a sudden and desperate need to get him out of the office. He leaned forwards on his desk once more. "Look, Dennis, you're a good kid for being so conscientious – most lads your age wouldn't give a fig about what happens around them. But I'm really rather busy at the moment;

what with hoax phone calls to the police and Mr Harris taking early retirement. So I'm afraid I don't have time to listen to you going on about you finding our other branches demands for stock, strange."

"But I don't, Mr Mason," Dennis protested. "At least not on their own. But I do think it's odd that they always ask for a crate of goods from the same place in the storeroom. And I mean the exact same place every time. That's strange isn't it?"

Jimmy could no longer look into Dennis's eyes, and began fiddling with papers on his desk. "I don't see anything strange in that at all," he replied stiffly. "It's obvious that the call comes in from a branch the day before and the crate of goods asked for is placed there for the purpose."

"No, that can't be it," said Dennis, leaning on the desk as his confidence grew and his nervousness was replaced by excitement. "Because I know for a fact that the crates in that particular space in the storeroom are put there when they first arrive with the others. And they're always tins of peaches too. It could happen by coincidence once or twice, but not five times in a row, Mr Mason. It's as if they know someone is going to want them."

"Perhaps Jeff and George can predict the future," Jimmy said with a strained laugh.

"Do you know what I think, Mr Mason," said Dennis in a slow voice. "I think those crates are not going out to other branches."

Jimmy stared hard at the youngster. "And where would they be going?"

"I think George and Jeff are selling stuff to line their own pocket; that's what I think."

"That's rubbish!" Jimmy snapped. "Those crates are collected in a Mulville's truck aren't they. It's not as if they're being loaded into someone's van in the middle of the night."

Excitement continued to grow in Dennis's voice. "I've been trying to work that out, Mr Mason. And I think I have the answer. Some of the drivers are in on it."

"Well, you certainly seem to have given this a great deal of thought," said Jimmy realizing that nothing he could say would alleviate the young man's suspicions.

199

"Yea; I'm good at things like that, Mr Mason," Dennis declared with a proud smile. "I know I'm not management, but that don't mean I don't have a brain. I watch every TV programme about what crooks get up to, and you wouldn't believe some of the things they come out with: really clever, some of them. On one programme this gang managed to hide twenty million pounds inside -"

"So, you've noticed funny business going on and you decided to come directly to me about it?" Jimmy interrupted, playing for time. He had to come up with a plan and quick.

Dennis suddenly became embarrassed. "Everyone likes you, Mr Mason. And they're always saying that when you take over as manager, you'll make sure everyone is treated fairly. And like just now when I came into your office. You told me to sit down and relax. And you told me that anything I said about the others would be kept confidential. So you see, Mr Mason, they're right about you. You'll make a great manager."

"Thanks, Dennis, that's nice to hear," said Jimmy. "But, as you can imagine, I'm going to need time to look into this matter, so I want you to go back to the storeroom and say absolutely nothing to anyone: understand?"

"Right you are, Mr Mason," said Dennis, standing up. "And if I discover anything else going on, I'll come straight to you. I've even got a good reason for seeing you now. I'm going to tell Jeff that I wanted to talk to you about a pay rise."

Jimmy frowned. "But won't he be annoyed that you didn't discuss it with him? After all, he is your boss in the storeroom?"

Dennis pulled a sour face. "I already did, but he told me there was more chance of David Beckham becoming Prime Minister than me getting a pay increase this year."

"Don't worry about that raise," said Jimmy. "I'll see what can be done. Now you get back to the storeroom before someone comes looking for you."

"Thanks, Mr Mason," said Dennis.

Then he was gone.

Jimmy reached inside his pocket and pulled out his mobile phone.

He tapped in a number.

"Jeff, it's me. You better get in here straight away. We've got a serious problem."

Three minutes later, Jeff was in Jimmy's office. "So what's this problem?" he asked.

"Someone's on to what we're doing."

"Fuck!" Jeff retorted. "Who?"

"Dennis."

"Dennis!" Jeff scoffed. "He's just a bloody kid. Don't take any notice of him."

"Well, we better take notice," said Jimmy. "Because he has it all worked out; the drivers; you and George; the crates. The only thing he's wrong about is that he thinks you are stealing the stock."

"Christ almighty," said Jeff. "What are we going to do? Has he talked to anyone else about it?"

"No. But he expects me to do something."

"How long can you stall him?"

"A week, maybe longer."

"That's something at least," Jeff replied. "But we can't leave it that long to sort it out. What if he starts talking to the others in the storeroom, or even that checkout girl, Allison. He's keen on her. He might want to boast about it."

"Maybe I should talk to Billy," Jimmy suggested.

"Good idea," said Jeff. "I'll go and keep an eye on Dennis. Give me a call when you've spoken to Billy."

A minute later Jeff had gone back to the storeroom and Jimmy was on the phone to Billy. And when he finished explaining about Dennis, it was clear Billy wasn't very happy about the situation.

"Jesus Christ!" he exclaimed. "If it isn't one thing with you, Jimmy it's another. How the hell did he find out so much?"

"He worked it out for himself," said Jimmy. "He's an addict for those crime programmes on TV."

"Is he now," Billy growled. "Well then it should come as no surprise to him what happens to people who go poking their nose in where it doesn't belong."

Jimmy was startled. "What do you mean?"

"You know, you ask more bloody questions than a three year old," said Billy scathingly. "Work it out: you have to get rid of him, of course"

"You mean; kill him?"

"Got it in one, Einstein. And do it soon. I don't want Andy finding out about it. He might think you lot in that store are getting sloppy - which you fucking are, I might add."

Jimmy put his mobile down on the desk in slow motion when Billy hung up. His mind was in a spin. All he wanted to do was to make a bit of extra money. Now he was being told to kill someone. What the hell was he going to do?

He picked up the phone and called Jeff back to his office.

"Bloody hell!" said Jeff. "I never thought we'd have to do something like that. A good pasting maybe: but murder."

"You'll have to take care of it," said Jimmy.

"Don't you mean we'll have to take care of it?" Jeff corrected.

"Don't be so bloody stupid!" Jimmy retorted. "I'm the Assistant Manager here, and I'll be manager by next month. You can't expect me to get involved."

"Like fuck I can," Jeff shot back. "When it comes to murder, mate, you can't bloody well hide behind your position in management. This isn't a meeting about company policy, you know – it's about killing some nosey kid. Now we're all in this together and any dirty work has to be carried out together. So how soon do we have to do it?"

"Billy wants it done soon," Jimmy said quietly.

"Right. Then we better get on with it."

Jimmy's eyes widened in alarm. "What: now?"

"You give me ten minutes to set something up, then come over," said Jeff ignoring the question. "I'll send Tim out to get me a pair of pliers from that hardware store at the bottom of the high street. You know how slow he is. It'll take him about three quarters of an hour. That should give us plenty of time to see to Dennis."

"God almighty!" Jimmy began to rake his head with his fingers. "I don't believe we're doing this."

"Pull yourself together!" Jeff snapped. "I don't want to kill the little fuck any more than you do, but he could send us all to prison."

"Maybe if I had him transferred to another branch, or offered him money to keep quiet?" Jimmy pleaded desperately.

"And have him shooting off his mouth when he gets bored or pissed," said Jeff. "No, Billy's right, we have to get rid of him as soon as possible. So don't forget; ten minutes, ok?"

Jimmy nodded, then watched in a daze as Jeff left his office and crossed the yard to the storeroom. And for a single moment he considered going home and never coming back. But he knew that if he did, Billy would see to it that he was blamed for Dennis's death. For when he had finished talking to Billy from home just prior to the police raid, he had looked behind the bath panel and in the freezer compartment of the fridge. He found two pounds of cocaine. And if Billy could get into his home without leaving any signs of a break-in, then what else could he do?

Jimmy stared at his watch. Three minutes had passed; seven minutes to go; to murder! It wasn't happening: it couldn't be happening! He just wanted to make a bit of money!

His hands began to sweat.

His breathing became shallow. He felt sick. His tie was chocking him. He pulled it off and unbuttoned his collar. He looked at his watch again. Just five minutes to him becoming a murderer. Please God, don't let this be happening!

He clawed at his face with his hands, trying to drive his terrible predicament away. But it wouldn't go. It clung to him; burrowing inside him; right down to his soul which cried out in protest: murderer - murderer - murderer!'

"Good heavens, Jimmy!" a voice declared through the haze. "Are you all right? You look absolutely dreadful?"

Jimmy's head shot up. "Mr Harris! I didn't see you there."

"I didn't mean to startle you," Harris replied. "I only called to ask if you have finished those calculations you were doing, but I see now that you are obviously not up to it. I really think you should have a few days off."

Jimmy pulled himself together; tidied his hair and put his tie back on. "Thanks, Mr Harris. I do feel a bit rough. I'll just lock up here and go home, if you don't mind."

Harris smiled. "A couple of days rest will have you back on your feet again. You look after yourself now. I wouldn't want anything to happen to my successor."

"Thanks, Mr Harris," Jimmy called out as his boss returned to his office down the corridor. Then he looked at his watch. The ten minutes Jeff had given him were up. The torment returned, and then his mobile rang and he answered it.

"I'm coming over now," he whispered down the line.

Chapter Thirty One

When Jimmy walked through the huge doors of the storeroom, Jeff and George were waiting for him. They were both grim-faced.

"I've sent Tim out, so we better get on with it before he comes back," said Jeff.

"Where's Dennis?" Jimmy asked with a dry mouth.

"In the back; behind the office. I spilt some rice there and I told him to sweep it up."

Jimmy was still looking for a way out. "Do we have to do it here? Couldn't we arrange something like a hit-and-run or an accident in his home?"

"Too complicated and too risky," said Jeff. "Who knows when he'll start telling what he knows. I only hope to God he hasn't told anyone already."

"What are you going to do to him?" Jimmy asked; just to keep talking - anything was better than doing.

"What are we going to do, you mean," said Jeff. "Show him, George."

George reached into his right pocket and pulled out an eight inch butcher's knife with a riveted, black handle. Jimmy had seen them in some of the major stores for about forty pounds.

"Right," said Jeff. "This is how it goes. George will stab him in the chest. Then I'll stab him, and then you, Jimmy. That way we won't know which of us actually killed him. Everyone happy with that?"

"Fine by me," said George, clearly feeling some excitement at the prospect of killing another human being.

"Jimmy - ?" said Jeff.

"God!" Jimmy shook his head and took a step back.

"Get a fucking grip will you!" Jeff snapped. "There's no other way, so come on, let's get it over with."

Jimmy followed automatically as Jeff led the way along a corridor of six metre high stacks of wooden crates. His legs felt stiff and weak, and he could feel a tremor starting up somewhere inside him.

Soon they had passed the office, and then Dennis came into view. He had swept the spilt rice into a large pile and was in the process of shovelling it into a black plastic bag.

He heard them coming and looked in their direction. But from the expression on his face it was clear that he was disturbed at seeing his three bosses together.

Jeff noticed and stopped. Jimmy and George followed suit.

"Hello, Mr Mason?" said Dennis.

Jimmy didn't answer because his tongue seemed to be glued to the inside of his mouth.

"Let's have a chat in my office, Dennis," said Jeff.

"What about?" Dennis asked.

"About that pay rise you wanted. Mr Mason has been telling me that he feels you should have it, but I'd like to discuss it before I agree."

Dennis was fifty feet from a fire exit behind him, and he turned his head to look at it.

"Well come on then," Jeff said cheerfully. "What are you waiting for?"

"We can talk about it here, can't we?" Dennis replied, looking at his bosses once more.

"Don't be silly, son," said Jeff. "Who ever heard of anyone discussing a pay rise between crates of Long Grain Rice. Come into my office and we can have a chat about it in a professional way."

"Is that right, Mr Mason?" said Dennis, his voice beginning to tremble. "Do you think I should go into Jeff's office to talk about my pay rise?"

"Of course he does," said Jeff. "Now, what I'm asking you to do is reasonable, isn't it?"

"Mr Mason?" Dennis tightened his grip on the full length coal-shovel he was holding.

"Answer him, will you," Jeff ordered.

"Jeff's right, Dennis," said Jimmy in a flat tone. "We should discuss this matter in his office."

Dennis was undecided for a moment. Then he began walking slowly towards the three men. But when he saw George reaching into the right hand pocket of his trousers, he stopped.

"What's he doing?" he demanded.

Jeff frowned. "Who?"

Dennis pointed at George. "He's got something in his pocket?"

George quickly pulled his hand out.

"Aaaa, take no notice of him," said Jeff, grinning. "He's probably playing with himself. Now are you coming into my office, or do we forget the whole thing? It's up to you, son."

"I've changed my mind," Dennis replied. "I don't want a rise after all."

Anger entered Jeff's voice. "Now don't be stupid, Dennis. You made it perfectly clear that you want more money, so let's stop fucking about and come into my office so that we can discuss it."

"Time's getting on, Jeff," George said in a low voice, looking at his watch.

"What's he mean by that?" Dennis cried. "And why did you send Tim out, Jeff? You never send him out for anything. You're always saying he would take a week to boil a three minute egg. So if you needed pliers why didn't you send me like you always do?"

Jeff didn't reply.

Suddenly a look of horror appeared on Dennis's face and his mouth dropped open. "Oh Christ! You're going to kill me!"

"Get him!" Jeff snapped, and George shot along the corridor towards Dennis.

Dennis took a couple of faltering steps backwards before turning on his heels and running towards the fire exit.

"Help me someone!" Dennis screamed at the top of his voice as he ran for his life.

George, a keen jogger, quickly caught up with Dennis and slammed into him just as he reached the door.

Dennis crashed to the ground with George on top of him.

George then climbed to his feet, dragging the youngster with him. But as he began to manhandle Dennis back towards Jeff and

Jimmy, the youngster stabbed the edge of the shovel into George's left shin.

George screamed and staggered backwards; blood trickling from the tear in his trousers.

Dennis then swung the shovel at head height, catching George on the side of the face.

George's legs buckled and he went down hard.

Jeff shot towards Dennis when he turned towards the fire exit again.

Dennis heard him coming and turned back - raising the shovel in a threatening manner.

Jeff came to a skidding halt.

"Keep back: keep back!" Dennis roared with tears pouring down his face. "I swear to God I'll use this if you come near me, Jeff. I swear to God I will."

"Now look here, Dennis," Jeff replied trying to smile. "This is getting out of hand. All right, I admit the plan was for George to give you a good hiding in my office to make sure you kept your mouth shut. But we weren't going to kill you, you plonker. What gave you a crazy idea like that?"

"I don't believe you!" Dennis shot back. "I'll bet George has a knife in his pocket. I'm not stupid you know."

"A knife; that's rubbish," said Jeff still trying to smile. "All he's got is a knuckle duster. But he wouldn't have used it on you; honest he wouldn't: would he, Jimmy?"

No one could hear Jimmy's muttered reply.

"Get down here, Jimmy, for God's sake, and tell him!" Jeff ordered.

Jimmy slowly made his way towards Jeff.

"Go on: tell him!" Jeff barked.

Jimmy looked at Dennis with glazed eyes. "Jeff's right, Dennis. George was only going to frighten you with the knuckle duster."

"I don't believe you, Mr Mason!" Dennis cried. "You're in with Jeff. I trusted you, and you told me that anything I told you would be confidential. But you're just a rotten crook like him, and you're here to kill me."

"I told you that's all rubbish," said Jeff. "Now it's obvious to me that you have been watching far too many of those crime series on television. And I'll bet The Bill is one of your favourites; isn't it? Course it is because The Bill is the best, and most people watch it. But it's fiction, son. I mean think about it for a moment. Sun Hill Police Station has to be the most dangerous place in the world for anyone to work. I mean, all those explosions; fires; murders. Now tell me honestly, son, have you ever even heard of a police station like that in real life; course you haven't, because it's fiction; great fiction, but just fiction nevertheless. And once you understand that, I'm sure you'll realize that you've just got yourself a little bit mixed up. Now there's nothing wrong with fiction, but you have to keep it separate in your mind from reality. So, look, Dennis, tell you what we'll do. You put that shovel down and we'll go into my office without George. Then we can discuss sharing the money we're making with you. And just think of all the things you can buy for Allison; things she can only dream about at the moment. So how about it, son?"

Dennis stood undecided and wiped sweat from his forehead with a forearm. Then he raised the shovel a little higher. "No! You just want to get me into your office so that you can kill me."

"No I don't!" Jeff exclaimed in frustration. "Oh come on, Dennis, we can't stand here all day looking as daft as we probably do. I mean, if Mr Harris decided to pay a visit right this minute, what would he make of you standing there ready to bash my head in with a shovel, and poor old George unconscious on the floor? At the very least he'd want another of his bloody meetings, and you remember the last one we had, what did he call it; Staff Satisfaction. And all it meant was that we had to sit in his office for nearly two hours listening to him rabbiting on about how we should feel part of a very special Mulville's family. Now, surely you wouldn't want another of those, would you?"

"I'm not going anywhere with you," said Dennis.

"Ok then," said Jeff, trying to control the rage that was growing inside him. "What if I prove to you that George only has a knuckle duster in his pocket? Will you put the shovel down then? And don't forget, two witnesses saw you attack poor old George. They'll lock you up for ten years for that. So why don't you accept my offer, and I'll make sure George doesn't press charges when he comes round? Anyway, he can't complain: he's always sleeping on the job; right?"

Dennis squeezed his eyes shut for a second in concentration. "Ok; but if it's a knife, then I'm getting out of here and I swear I'll use this if you try and stop me."

Jeff nodded and was clearly relieved to be getting somewhere with the frightened Dennis. "Fair enough, son. Right then, Jimmy, have a look in George's right pocket, will you."

As if in a trance, Jimmy moved towards George's motionless form.

The Assistant Storeroom Manager was lying face down on the concrete floor. He was still breathing.

Jimmy dropped down next to him and reached into his pocket with his right hand. His fingers touched the handle of the knife and instantly pulled back.

He looked up and was uncomfortably aware that Dennis was towering almost directly above him with the shovel. He was too close to that shovel and he wanted to move away.

Dennis stared down at him. "What are you waiting for, Mr Mason? I want to see that knuckle duster."

Jimmy's fingers touched the knife handle again, but he dared not pull the knife out. Dennis would probably bash his skull in the instant he saw it.

"Well show him, Jimmy!" Jeff snapped.

Jimmy hesitated, then slowly withdrew his hand. And as the knife was revealed, a gasp of horror came from Dennis. Jimmy then placed the knife on the ground and stood up. "I'm sorry, Dennis, I didn't know it was a knife; honest I didn't."

"You fucking liar!" Dennis screamed; just as Jeff lunged at him, grabbing for the shovel.

Dennis cried out and tried to pull away, but Jeff had obtained a good grip on the wooden handle.

For a few moments the two of them struggled for control.

Then Dennis skidded on a small patch of blood.

He lost his balance and toppled backwards.

Jeff fell on top of him when he landed on his back

Dennis took his right hand from the shovel and punched Jeff in the face.

Jeff ignored the blow and head-butted Dennis.

Dennis grunted in pain and lost his grip on the shovel.

Jeff grabbed it and flung it aside where it clattered noisily on the concrete floor.

"Got you now, you little shit!" Jeff declared, grabbing Dennis by the collar of his shirt. "You should have minded your own business."

Dennis lashed out again and his fist caught Jeff in the mouth.

The punch was powerful.

Blood spurted from Jeff's split lips and he rolled away from Dennis.

"Get him, Jimmy!" Jeff spluttered as Dennis shot to his feet.

Jimmy stood where he was, unable to respond.

Dennis made to run towards the fire exit, but Jeff, still on the ground, reached out with his right hand and gripped his ankle.

Dennis went down again.

Then Jeff was on him.

The two of them struggled to their feet, but Dennis found himself in a half nelson - Jeff's arms going under Dennis's armpits and his fingers locking behind the youngster's neck. The hold was a wrestling technique designed to immobilize an opponent and it was effective. Jeff then spun around so that he and his captive were facing Jimmy.

"Get the fucking knife!" Jeff shouted at him.

With both his arms held above his head, Dennis could do little to fight back, except by pushing with his feet; trying to upset Jeff's balance.

But Jeff was bigger, stronger and very determined that his captive would not get away.

"Jimmy, get the fucking knife!" Jeff repeated as Jimmy just stared back at him with a strange expression on his face.

"Let me go!" Dennis begged. "I won't tell anyone. I promise I won't."

"You fucking arsehole, Jimmy!" Jeff roared. "Will you get that fucking knife. Tim will be back in a few minutes. Do you want to have to kill him as well."

Slowly, Jimmy bent down and picked up the knife.

He stared at it. Somehow he couldn't feel it properly in his hand: it seemed detached as if it wasn't really there: just part of some terrible nightmare that he couldn't wake up from.

"Don't stand there admiring the fucking thing," Jeff barked. "Stab him in the chest with it."

"No; no!" Dennis cried, struggling like mad to break free.

"Stick it in him," Jeff repeated. "I don't know how much longer I can hold him."

Jimmy moved closer until he was standing directly in front of Dennis. The butcher's knife was gripped tight in his right hand; held at waist height.

"Mr Mason; please!" Dennis begged, staring at the blade. "I didn't mean to cause any trouble, honest I didn't. Please don't kill me, please."

"Do it for Christ sakes," Jeff ordered.

"But you like me, Mr Mason!" Dennis wailed, his face wet from tears and sweat. "I know you do because Margaret Brown said you did. And I like you too, so please don't kill me, Mr Mason. I don't want to die."

"Jimmy!" Jeff roared. "Stick that fucking knife in or when I'm finished with this little shit I'm going to do the same to you."

"But you said George would do it first," Jimmy protested, "then you, then me? I don't want to go first: I can't."

"Don't be so fucking stupid," Jeff retorted. "George isn't in a state to do anything, and I'm holding this little bastard. Stick him first, then I'll do the same. Now, get a bloody move on, will you. Tim could come back any second."

Jimmy tightened his grip on the knife and drew his arm back.

"That's it!" Jeff laughed with relief. "Drive it into his chest as hard as you can: right through the heart."

"No; no!" Dennis cried, his eyes staring in absolute terror.

Then his body sagged, and Jeff grunted as he adjusted his grip. "Thank God for that. He's passed out. Do it now while he's unconscious."

Jimmy held his breath and drove the knife forwards.

But the instant the blade entered Dennis's body; just below the breastbone, the youngster came round with a terrible scream of pain.

Jimmy jumped back in fright; the bloodied knife still in his hand.

"Higher up in his chest, you stupid idiot!" Jeff retorted as Dennis fought to get free.

Jimmy stared in horror at a bright red stain that was quickly spreading across Dennis's pale blue shirt.

"I don't want to die! I don't want to die!" Dennis screamed. "Mum. Mum. Don't let me die."

"Do it; do it!" Jeff shouted through clenched teeth.

Jimmy stepped forward again and shoved the knife deep into Dennis's body, this time nearer the middle of his chest.

Dennis shuddered and stopped struggling.

His head lolled for a few moments. Then he focused his wide, staring eyes on Jimmy, and there was a look of utter disbelief on his tortured face. "Mr Mason?" he said in a weak voice. "Mr Mason?"

"I'm sorry," Jimmy whispered, his voice hoarse with emotion.

And then as Dennis's head dropped forward for the last time, a sob of regret left Jimmy's lips.

Jeff allowed the lifeless body to slide to the floor, and he rushed to his Assistant Manager's side. He slapped his face hard a few times. "Wake up, George you careless bastard; wake up, damn you!"

George moaned and opened his eyes.

"Come on, get to your feet," Jeff ordered, trying to lift his assistant.

George's feet began to slide on the concrete floor as he struggled to stand.

"That's it, mate," said Jeff. "Come on; you can do it."

With great effort Jeff helped George to his feet and held him steady.

"What happened?" George asked, touching the side of his red and swollen face with his right hand.

"That little bastard Dennis gave you a bash with the shovel," said Jeff. "Now we have to clear up before Tim gets back. Can you stand on your own?"

George took a few faltering steps. He moaned when pain from his injured leg increased, but he stayed upright. He then nodded.

"Good man," said Jeff. "Jimmy, you get round the front and watch out for Tim. If he comes back tell him to move those crates of cat food that came in this morning to that empty space near the old freezers. And tell him not to stop until the job is done or I'll come down on him like a ton of bricks."

When Jimmy moved away, Jeff ran to his office and returned with a heavy duty dust sheet. He lay it on the floor and rolled Dennis's body in it. Then he folded over the ends and ordered George to help him carry the body to a nearby empty crate. And having placed the body inside, he put the lid back on and banged a few nails through it.

Jeff then used a crowbar to smash a crate of catering size plastic bottles of tomato ketchup. He drove a sharp end of the crowbar through several bottles, and a torrent of red liquid gushed out all over the floor; covering George and Dennis's blood.

"What the hell did you do that for?" George managed to ask even though one side of his face was swollen badly. "You've made an even bigger mess to clean up."

Jeff watched the ketchup spreading into a huge pool. "The colour of that stuff is perfect, and I'm betting that the acid in it should bugger up any forensic tests that might be carried out. Now leave it like that for the rest of the day. Then we can clear it up tomorrow using plenty of strong bleach. I'll tell Mr Harris I had an accident with the fork lift."

Jeff suddenly heard distant voices arguing. "What the fuck is happening now?" he growled.

"Want me to see?" said George.

"In that state, you stupid git," Jeff snapped. "You better get home and stay there for a few days. Say you had a bad fall if anyone asks. And leave by the fire exit."

George hobbled out of the storeroom, and Jeff went to see who was arguing. He found Jimmy standing on his own, repeatedly running the fingers of his right hand through his hair.

"What the hell's going on?" Jeff demanded.

"It's Tim," Jimmy replied with obvious irritation. "He's complaining that he hasn't had his lunch break yet, and it will be three-o-clock by the time he finishes moving those crates."

Jeff scowled. "I'll give him lunch breaks; the lazy little shit. Kids these days don't know they're born."

"Tim," Jeff then shouted at the top of his voice as he heard the fork lift start up.

"What?" came a faint reply.

"If you set one foot out of that fork lift before you've finished that fucking job, I'll have you scrubbing this floor every day for a month - get me?"

There was another faint reply.

"What was that?" said Jeff.

"I said I got you, Jeff."

"You better."

Jeff then looked at Jimmy. "I'll bring my estate around to the fire exit, and you see where Harris is."

"You're not going to move him now, are you?" said Jimmy incredulously.

"I want him out of here as quickly as possible," Jeff replied. "The wall opposite the fire exit should prevent anyone seeing us. And you know Harris stay's very late sometimes. If he walked in on me when I was moving Dennis, I'd have to kill him as well. So you go and check on him, then get back here."

Still deeply troubled, Jimmy made his way back to the offices situated at the back of the store. Then he noticed that he had small traces of blood on his right hand. He ran for the gent's toilet and washed them off.

After washing his face as well, Jimmy returned to his office and slumped into his chair. He was desperate for a drink, and couldn't rid himself of the feeling he felt in his right hand as the knife forced its way through Dennis's resisting flesh. And that expression on the youngster's face; the shock and disbelief as he realized that it was the man he respected and admired who was killing him. Worse still, did he have to say his name like that, Mr Mason! Mr Mason!

Jimmy suddenly flew into a rage and slammed his fist down on the desk. "Damn you, Dennis! Damn you for calling my name like that. Damn you for poking your nose into other people's business. Damn you for being too young to trust. And damn you for turning me into your murderer."

Jimmy than lay his head on the desk as powerful emotions ran their course. But when he heard voices, he quickly pulled himself together and left his office.

Mr Harris was standing in the corridor talking to Veronica Harley, his secretary.

"Ahhh, Jimmy, still here I see," said Harris as his secretary walked away. "You are certainly full of surprises."

"I'm sorry about that, Mr Harris," said Jimmy. "But one minute I'm feeling terrible; the next I'm feeling fine. I don't know what's the matter with me."

"A clear case of nerves," said Harris. "And perhaps work is the best therapy for you at the moment and that is why you are still here, despite your resolve to go home?"

"I think you're right," said Jimmy. "I do feel reluctant to stay at home at the moment."

"Very well then," said Harris, "if you are feeling better perhaps we could have a quick discussion about some new products that head office are sending over. I'm sure that won't put you under very much pressure."

"That will be fine. But could you give me about half an hour, Mr Harris?" said Jimmy. "I need to sort out a small problem with Jeff in the storeroom?"

"Of course, Jimmy. You go ahead. I shall be in my office when you have finished."

Jimmy waited to see that his boss did in fact go into his office, then he rushed back to the storeroom. Jeff was slowly backing his car up to the fire exit, and soon they were both standing by the crate containing Dennis's body. The sound of the fork lift could be heard at the front end of the storeroom, and Jeff estimated that Tim would be busy for at least another hour.

Jeff and Jimmy found the crate extremely heavy as they lifted it into the back of the estate, and there was so little room that they had to repeatedly slide the crate back out as it caught on some obstruction.

Eventually the crate was safely inside the estate and Jeff drove it back to the car park. Jimmy meanwhile was worried that someone had seen them, despite the fact that the back of the storeroom wasn't overlooked or visible from the store. And when Jeff arrived back on foot, Jimmy let out a sigh of relief.

"Right," said Jeff, "you get back to your office and I'll give Billy a ring."

"What about Dennis?" Jimmy asked.

"I'll dump his body tonight when it's dark. I know a good place, and with a bit of luck it'll never be found."

"His family will miss him?"

"We probably have until tomorrow before we have to worry about them, so we should get our story straight. You haven't seen him since yesterday, and as far as I'm concerned, he went to lunch early today and never came back. I'll phone his parents in the morning and complain about his behaviour."

Chapter Thirty Two

Sally looked at herself in the mirror with a sense of satisfaction. Her long hair perfectly framed her still-pretty face, and she was pleased to see that she had as yet not acquired any frown lines. 'Never frown at the world,' her mother used to say, 'because your skin keeps a record of such things and will send you a permanent reminder later on in life.' Well, she had a great deal to frown about lately, but not for much longer. Steve Wilson was expecting her that evening, and if all went as well as she hoped it would, she and Jimmy would soon be on their way to a new life far away from a world of drugs.

Very much a slacks-and-top girl, she was determined to make an effort for what she felt was the most important date of her life. Steve Wilson was clearly impressed by the fashions of past times and so she had decided to wear a black, low cut slim-line dress; black, flat-heeled shoes, and carry a black Lamé evening bag. She found the overall effect stunning, and it came as a shock to her to realize that she was beginning to experience a delicious anticipation at the thought of what Steve Wilson's reaction might be when he saw her, and not just because she was hoping to convince him to release Jimmy.

Convincing herself that there was no harm in trying to impress another man when it was in a good cause, she left the maisonette and made her way to the garage where Jimmy's BMW was sitting. He had phoned to say that he was staying very late at the store in order to make his transition to manager a little easier the following month. And although he sounded tired and a little strange, she was pleased that she wouldn't have to bother with excuses for her absence. With a bit of luck she would be home before him.

Within the hour she was pulling up outside Steve Wilson's home. Terry was waiting at the door. He invited her inside just as Steve, dressed in a dark grey, Savile Row suit, and black shoes, came into the hall. He stopped in his tracks; spread his hands and smiled.

"Exquisite; truly exquisite!" he declared.

"Thanks," said Sally, doing her best not to blush. It had been a very long time since someone had complimented her in such a flattering manner, and she liked it very much indeed. She also liked the man who said the words.

"Now, I have booked a restaurant in Leicester Square called The Stilton," said Steve. "Mark can drive us there in the Bentley."

When Sally and Steve arrived at The Stilton, Sally was delighted by its old world charm; with it's Victorian décor and subdued lighting. They were shown to their table, and they began the meal with a bottle of Chateau Cos d Estournel 1999, followed by a Stilton and Red Onion Salad with Peppered Beef Fillets, followed by a main course of Chicken Fillet Steaks with Chestnut, Mushroom, Sage, and Lime Sauce. And desert consisted of Gateau Opera, with White Chocolate and Coffee Ice Cream. Sally admitted that she had never eaten such delicious food in her whole life, which obviously pleased Steve very much.

They both then opted for one of the very fine coffees the restaurant was well known for. Sally found the flavour exquisite.

"So," said Steve, looking across the table at Sally as she sipped her coffee from a delicate china cup. "I take it that Jimmy has told you about his promotion?"

"Yes," said Sally, having a very good idea what was coming next.

"He must be very pleased," said Steve. "But of course this early rise through the ranks has increased his value to us enormously. I'm sure that within the next three or four years he will make area manager, and won't that be a bonus for my organization."

The taste of the coffee suddenly turned sour in Sally's mouth. "Not necessarily," she answered in a flat tone. "After all, there must be other capable branch managers wanting the job. Jimmy might have to wait many years before he's offered the position. And I happen to know that the current area manager and the previous two were in their fifties when they were promoted to the position."

"Times have changed, Sally," said Steve casually. "The world of business has become a young man's game. Nowadays a man in his fifties is coming to the end of his career, not beginning it. And your point that Jimmy might have competition, well normally that would be true. However since I'm quite determined to see Jimmy's career at Mulville's proceed forwards with the speed of a Ferrari, I have no intention of allowing any competition to impede that progress."

Sally frowned. "And I suppose you mean by that an unfortunate accident happening to anyone likely to get the job before Jimmy," she said scathingly.

Steve laughed. "Nothing so crude, I assure you. As a matter of fact they would find themselves head hunted by another company. Because you see, Sally, I have a very long reach."

"I'll bet you have." Sally took another sip of coffee. It had definitely lost its taste.

"Look, I know what's troubling you," said Steve. "You think now that Jimmy is about to be promoted, I will find him too valuable to let him go. Well, you're wrong. I said that if you went out on a date with me, I would consider releasing him, and I will; in time."

Sally arched her eyebrows. "What's that suppose to mean? I thought you were going to make your final decision tonight?"

"And I shall; assuming that you present me with a favourable answer to my next question, that is."

"What question?" said Sally, and her heart began to beat faster, but she wasn't sure why.

Steve leaned forwards and placed his elbows on the table. There was an expression on his face that Sally couldn't fathom. "I will let your husband go; if you spend just one weekend with me."

Sally tried desperately to feel shocked and outraged, but the most she could manage was an incredulous shake of her head. "You must be joking!" she declared.

Steve shrugged his shoulders. "Entirely up to you, of course. But consider this. You are asking me to give up one of my greatest assets, and in return for what; for a smile of gratitude from that beautiful face of yours. Tempting I grant you, but I'm a business man; I weigh up the pros and cons of every deal I make, and in this particular case I would be losing out if I released your husband. However, should you agree to spend a weekend with me, then I shall feel we both have had value for money?"

"I'm not a prostitute!" Sally snapped, suddenly angry.

"Of course you're not," Steve said with some sincerity. "But surely you're willing to make sacrifices for you and your husband's future together? And the way I see it, Sally, you have a choice to make. Jimmy Mason is mine. How much do you want him back? Now, shall we go. There is a very good play on at Drury Lane I would like you to see."

The drive to Drury Lane was brief, but an ordeal for Sally. Her emotions were all over the place. Yes, she was angry with Steve, but only because of the manner in which he had asked her to spend the weekend with him. Which meant, if he had asked her in a kinder, more gentle and respectful fashion, she might well have said yes immediately. She had known for days she would probably accept almost any offer if it meant she would get Jimmy free, but she couldn't understand why deep down, a part of her was excited by the idea. Could she really be unfaithful to Jimmy with this devastatingly handsome and charming man sitting beside her? She didn't want to answer that question; not there; not then.

The show wasn't really to Sally's liking. She was very much a TV soap addict, and didn't care for the cast shouting and tearing around the stage.

She was glad when it finished.

Steve took her back to his house, and insisted she join him for a coffee.

"So, what have you decided?" Steve asked in a firm tone as they sat in the drawing room.

"What will happen if I don't accept your offer?" said Sally.

"Nothing; except Jimmy will fulfil his role in my organization. Make no mistake, you both will have a very good life - within the framework I allow, of course. And I think most people would envy you. But if you want a different life, then to put it bluntly, you must pay for it."

"All right, I'll do it!" Sally blurted out suddenly.

"You make it sound like you're accepting some sort of dare," Steve replied disapprovingly.

"What do you expect?" Sally shot back. "You're blackmailing me and you expect me to be happy about it."

"Not true," said Steve. "A blackmailer always approaches his victim. You came to me, Sally; remember? So the truth is that you have asked me for a favour, and I have agreed on the understanding that you do me one in return."

"You can twist it around all you like," said Sally, "but it ends up as blackmail."

Steve put down his cup of coffee; left his seat and sat next to Sally on the settee.

A momentary shiver ran through her at his closeness.

"Look, can we please stop all this arguing?" Steve said in a soft tone. "After all, we did have a wonderful evening; at least I did, and it would be a very great shame to conclude that wonderful evening with bad feelings between us. Now, to be perfectly honest, Sally, I like you a great deal more than I can remember liking any other woman. And if I've been clumsy in my attempts to convince you to spend some time with me, then I apologize. I haven't had a great deal of practice lately. I suppose I spend so much time surrounded by men; ordering them about and such like that I seem to have forgotten how to woo a beautiful woman."

Sally couldn't help smiling. "Woo: you really do live in the past, don't you. I suppose my dad wooed my mother, but everyone just 'go out' with each other these days."

Steve grinned. "Obviously I was born too late. But I like to woo, and I suspect every girl likes to be wooed; even the modern, trendy ones."

"Maybe," said Sally. Then she turned her body so that she could look directly into his eyes. "Jimmy won't find out about it, will he?" she asked with some concern. "I don't know how he would take it. Emotionally he's not very stable."

"Well, I certainly have no intention of telling him," said Steve with a shrug. "So, you accept my invitation?"

Sally nodded.

"Wonderful. This weekend ok by you?" Steve prompted.

Sally's breath caught in her throat. "Of course not! Do you think I can vanish for two days just like that. I'll have to arrange something that won't make Jimmy suspicious."

"When then?" Steve asked, reaching out with his right hand and stroking Sally's bare arm.

She flinched. "Not for a couple of weeks at the very least."

Steve stood up suddenly and crossed the room to an ornate, eighteenth century desk. He opened a drawer and took something out. Then he came back and sat next to her again. He handed her a brown leather, rectangular box.

Sally was suspicious. "What is it?" she asked.

"There's only one way to find out," Steve answered, smiling.

Sally slowly took the box and opened it. Inside, resting on cream velvet, was a large, oval sapphire mounted in a platinum setting, attached to a platinum and gold chain. The gem sparkled - responding with a pale blue light to the soft glow from the magnificent chandelier suspended directly above them.

"Like it?" said Steve.

"It's beautiful!" Sally whispered, touching the blue stone with her finger tips.

"And just like you it's flawless," said Steve. "Why don't you try it on."

Sally closed the lid and held out the box. "I can't accept this. How could I ever wear it? It must have cost a fortune? Jimmy would get suspicious straight away?"

"Just say an aunt left it to you in her will," said Steve.

"Jimmy knows I don't have an aunt that rich. How much did it cost you?"

Steve looked surprised. "Surely you don't expect a true gentleman to answer a question like that? A lady must have faith that the cost of such a gift would bring the bailiffs to the gentleman's door at the very least."

"How much?" Sally demanded.

Steve sighed. "Ninety thousand pounds, if you must know."

"Drug money I suppose?" said Sally with obvious distaste.

"No," said Steve firmly. "And there you go again; thinking the worst of me. Well, for your information, Sally Mason, I made a lot of honest money before I became involved in the drugs business. And with some of that money I bought this for someone who obviously didn't feel the same way about me as I did about her. So you see, you can accept this gift without sacrificing your morals. And if you don't want to wear it, then keep it tucked away somewhere as something to remember me by."

Sally's lips tightened with renewed determination. "I apologize for what I just said, but I really don't think you will ever come into my thoughts again once this business is done with."

"And why is that?" said Steve, tilting his head and smiling. "Don't you find me even the least bit attractive?"

"That has nothing to do with it," said Sally defensively.

"At least you didn't say no," said Steve. "That's something, I suppose."

"I didn't say yes either. Now, I better be getting back."

"Of course you must," said Steve, still smiling.

When Sally opened the door to her home an hour later, she found Jimmy standing in the hall.

"It's bloody one-o-clock in the morning!" he snapped. "Where the hell have you been this time?"

Sally walked past him and went into the living-room.

She dropped on to the settee, and sighed with relief as she removed her tight shoes.

"Well?" said Jimmy when she didn't answer.

"We went to a show and for a drink afterwards," Sally said through a loud yawn, leaning back in the settee. "We didn't realize how late it was. Sorry, darling."

"We? Who the hell is we?" Jimmy stormed across the room and poured himself a drink. Sally could smell that it wasn't her husband's first.

"Just Sarah," she replied. "I told you I would have to spend some time with her

Jimmy sat down in an armchair and took a few moments to calm down. Then he stared at Sally. "Look, Sal, don't you think it's time for the truth? I trust you so I don't think you've met someone else, but I don't believe either that you are spending time with Sarah. Something's going on and I want to know what it is?"

"All right, darling, I'll tell you the truth," said Sally. "I have been seeing someone as a matter of fact, but we're not having a relationship."

Jimmy was shocked. "Who?" he whispered.

"Steve Wilson."

Jimmy's brow furrowed in puzzlement. "Who the hell is he? Can't be anyone from work?"

Now it was Sally's turn to be puzzled. "I thought you might know him, or at least have heard of him?"

"Why should I? He's not a rep is he?"

"He's your boss in the organisation."

"That's Billy Bennifield," said Jimmy. "And his boss is Andy Saunders: that's it. So who the hell are you talking about?"

"I mean the boss of the whole organization," Sally answered. "His name is Steve Wilson and he runs everything."

"I don't believe you!" Jimmy snapped. "I thought you were going to tell me the truth?"

"I am telling you the truth, darling. I knew if I was going to stand any real chance of getting us out of this mess, I would have to go right to the top. So I made Andy Saunders arrange a meeting with Steve Wilson."

"So that's where you've been going?"

"Yes."

"I can't believe this is happening!"

Jimmy left his seat and poured himself another drink. "All this time I thought you had come round to my way of thinking and instead you were going behind my back, making plans with a boss so high up I never even knew he existed."

"I'm sorry, darling," said Sally, " but I had no choice. You were determined to stay at Mulville's, taking delivery of those horrible drugs. So the only thing I could do was find my own way of putting a stop to it."

"There is no stopping it; not now!" Jimmy retorted, his hands shaking as he poured more whisky into his glass.

Sally went over to him. "Of course there is, darling. I think Steve Wilson will agree to let you go. All I need is a little more time."

"No: it's too late for that, Sal! I'm in too deep."

"No you're not. All right, so you were in charge of the storage of drugs for a while. That doesn't make you a criminal; at least not a serious one. All I'm saying is that we should get out now before things become worse."

Jimmy stared into his wife's eyes. Sweat had formed a sheen on his face, and his eyes had a haunted look about them.

The look frightened Sally. "What is it, darling? Has something happened?"

"Yes." Jimmy whispered, lowering his head. Then he began to cry.

Sally put her arms around him. "What's the matter, darling? Tell me; please. Has someone been threatening you? Is that it? Has someone been making you do things you didn't want to do?"

Jimmy nodded through the sobs.

"Well they won't anymore!" Sally declared with fierce determination. "When I've finished with Billy Bennifield, he will be down on his knees apologizing to you."

"It's too late for that, Sal," Jimmy said, wiping his eyes. "No one can do anything for me now. I killed someone."

Sally stepped away from her husband in horror. "What?"

"That's right, Sal. I killed someone. So how are you going to talk me out of that?"

Sally went back to her seat and slumped into it. She couldn't get her head around what Jimmy had just said.

Jimmy sat next to her.

He held his glass of whisky between his hands, rolling the glass back and forth. "You know Dennis, don't you. He works part time in the storeroom. Well, he came into my office this morning telling me how he knew Jeff, George and some of the drivers were involved in stealing stock from the storeroom. I phoned Billy Bennifield and he ordered me to get rid of him."

"And you just followed an order like that without any questions," Sally whispered.

"I had no choice, Sal. And when I told Jeff, well, he sort of took over. Next thing I knew, me Jeff and George were in the storeroom getting ready to murder just some nosey kid. I tried to convince Jeff to kill him somewhere else, but he wouldn't have it."

"And that would have made it all right, would it?" Sally replied.

"No; of course not. I was hoping that if a bit of time was allowed to pass, everyone would calm down and maybe some other way could be found to make Dennis keep his mouth shut."

Sally stared at him. "So Jeff killed him; in the storeroom?"

Jimmy nodded.

"How; with the fork lift I suppose?"

"A butcher's knife."

"Oh my God; that poor child!" Sally gasped.

"I know!" Jimmy cried, suddenly overcome with remorse. "How do you think I feel."

"But just because you were there, doesn't mean you killed him," Sally said, desperately trying to find a way out of the nightmare. "I mean, you didn't hold him, did you?"

"No, Sal, I didn't hold him," Jimmy replied, the haunted look returning to his eyes.

"Well then. You were a witness to a killing; that's all."

"I didn't hold him, Sal. Jeff did."

An angry expression appeared on Sally's face. "So it was that horrible George who killed that poor child! I should have known. I thought there was something cruel about him when I met him in the storeroom that time. He gave me the creeps."

"George was unconscious, Sal," said Jimmy. "Dennis managed to hit him with a shovel before we grabbed him."

Sally stared uncomprehendingly at her husband as her thoughts struggled in quicksand, trying to bring clarity to what he was telling her. Then the answer came to her like a physical blow that was devastating in its power. "Oh my God, no!" she cried.

Tears suddenly flowed from Jimmy's eyes. "I didn't want to do it, Sal! Honest to God I didn't. But Jeff was holding Dennis, and Dennis was struggling, and then the knife was in my hand and Jeff was screaming at me, and Dennis was begging for his life and calling for his mother. I didn't know what to do. I didn't want to kill him, but I was afraid to go to prison, and Jeff was threatening to kill me as well, and I knew if I didn't -"

"So you stabbed an innocent child to death with a butcher's knife," said Sally as Jimmy's voice trailed off. And when he then broke down once more, she did nothing to comfort him.

Jimmy went to bed on his own that night. Sally explained that she wasn't tired and needed some time to think. She spent hours sitting on the settee and drinking coffee. There were important questions she had to ask herself; the most important being could she spend the rest of her life with a murderer; a child-murderer? However much Jimmy explained how he didn't want to kill Dennis, he still plunged the knife into his body, and therefore he was a murderer whichever way it was looked at. Perhaps she should just pack her bags and leave. After all, was there really anything to keep here there, besides her love for her foolish husband? The answer to that was no. And this problem was so much of Jimmy's own making she could strangle him. Maybe she should just go and leave him to his fate. But, no sooner had she asked herself that question, than she knew she couldn't abandon him, because there had to be a difference between a determined killer like Jeff, and a weak puppet like Jimmy, and it was this difference she was in love with. Jimmy was a kind man at heart. It wasn't in his nature to hurt anyone, but he was also weak; easily falling for the trappings of success the drugs provided. She knew in her own mind that Jimmy would never have even contemplated killing Dennis no matter how much a threat he was. As he said, Jeff just took over the situation; leading him into murder as if he had no will of his own. She could imagine Jimmy's state of mind as events in the storeroom unfolded; the fear, the disbelief and the horror of it all. And because she knew Jimmy suffered for what he did, she decided he was worth her love. Obviously Dennis would have been killed by Jeff and George anyway, so why should she punish only Jimmy.

When Jimmy wandered slowly into the living-room at 6am, Sally was still on the settee, but she was fast asleep. He got a spare blanket from the bedroom and covered her. And by the time she woke up, he had already left for work.

She looked at the clock; it was 6:45am. And just as she was about to have a shower, the phone rang.

"Sally, is that you?" said the urgent voice on the other end of the line.

"You're not supposed to phone me here, Mr Saunders," Sally replied.

"Why the hell haven't you returned my calls? What's going on: it's been over a week? I tried to give you as much time as possible, but you have to decide now. I'm not going to wait any longer."

"I'm sorry, but I can't go through with it," said Sally.

"Why the hell not? You're not falling for him are you?"

"Don't be stupid. Of course I'm not. But I don't need to commit murder to get what I want from him."

"So what *do* you need to do?" Andy's tone was accusing.

"We're discussing the matter at the moment, and I think he'll agree to let Jimmy go."

"Not without payment of some kind he won't," Andy shot back. "I know him, Sally. He wouldn't give his mother the price of a meal if she was starving unless she promised him something in return."

"Think what you like, Mr Saunders," said Sally in a calm and firm tone, "but I'm not going to kill him, so you'll have to do it yourself if you want to take over the organization."

"And you wouldn't care if I did, I suppose?"

"Why should I. With him dead, Jimmy and I are free to leave."

"That was the deal only if you helped me," said Andy. "If I have to do the job myself, then all deals are off."

Sally's voice turned cold. "You mean you would hang on to Jimmy?"

"Like the goose that was about to lay the golden eggs, love. You better believe I would."

"Then maybe I should make a deal with Steve Wilson; a deal you wouldn't like one little bit."

"Listen you, bitch!" Andy growled. "Don't you fucking threaten me. I might not be the top boss of this organization, but I have enough power to deal with the likes of you. All I have to do is snap my fingers and you and that husband of yours will be floating face-down in the river by tonight. You might inform on me to Wilson, but I guarantee that you won't live long enough to see what happens to me."

Sally realized that the situation was getting out of hand, and she had to do something to calm things down a little. "Listen, Andy," she said in a softer voice. "Obviously you're upset because I haven't been in touch, and I understand that. And I admit I thought I had another way out besides killing Steve Wilson. But now that you've explained that I haven't, I want to go back to the original plan. But you have to give me a bit longer."

"All right," said Andy, calming down. "You have a week. But don't try and set me up with Wilson or you'll regret it, I promise you that."

Sally put the receiver back and sat down in the armchair. Then she lifted the receiver again and dialled a number.

"Hello, this is Sally Mason. May I speak to Mr Wilson, please."

A few moments later a male voice answered.

Sally took a deep breath. "Hello, Steve. About that matter we discussed last time we met. I've decided to accept your offer, but it will have to be this coming weekend."

"I'm delighted of course," said Steve. "But why the sudden rush?"

"I just want to get it over with," Sally replied.

"You make it sound like some horrible chore," said Steve.

"What do you expect. You're forcing me to be unfaithful to my husband. I'm hardly going to thank you for that, am I?"

"No - I suppose not. Ok; I'll see you here on Friday at nine pm. Don't be late."

Then he hung up.

Just six days to go, Sally said to herself. Just six more days and she and Jimmy could start a new life somewhere far away from Steve Wilson and his terrible organization.

She made herself another coffee.

Of course Jimmy, the stupid idiot, would create one hell of a fuss about leaving behind his new position as manager and all that money, but she knew he would come with her when it came to a choice. But if he didn't, then she would leave without him.

Chapter Thirty Three

Sally invited Margaret to join her in the canteen for lunch the following day. Sally noted with satisfaction that there were plenty of empty tables around them as she didn't want to be overheard.

"So," said Margaret, munching away on her salad, "what's the big mystery? You don't usually invite me. I always have to invite myself; you stand-off cow."

Sally toyed with her plate of lasagne and chips. Then she looked across the table at her friend. "Before I tell you anything, Margaret, can I say how sorry I am that I haven't been a very good friend to you in the past."

"That's all right, love," Margaret said with a smile. "I knew you had your problems, and that sooner or later you would get round to it as long as I kept reminding you that I would always be here for you."

"Thanks for being so patient," said Sally, smiling back. "So, what do you think of Jeff and George?"

Margaret pulled a sour face. "They're obviously a couple of creeps." Then she frowned. "Why, has someone been saying something about me and them, because if they have, I couldn't care a fig. Those two know I don't like them and I'm glad they know; especially that George."

"No, I didn't mean that at all," Sally protested. "It's just that I was wondering if there was any history between you and them?"

"I'm not that desperate thank you very much!" Margaret laughed. "When I first came here they both asked me out, but I'd seen more good manners in a randy dog so I turned them down. Jeff is the kind of bloke you dread turning up on a blind date, and George is someone you wouldn't want to run into in the dark. Anyway, why are you asking?"

"Just to be sure about something," said Sally.

"Sure about what, love?"

"That it's safe to tell you about them."

Margaret's lips twisted with distaste. "I don't think you can tell me anything about those two mongrels, love."

"I think I can," Sally replied.

Margaret's eyes lit up. "Don't say you have finally got hold of a juicy piece of gossip?"

Sally's expression became very serious. "Can I ask you something first, Margaret?"

"Jesus, it must be juicy!" Margaret cried. "But I can be patient. Ok, ask away."

Sally hesitated. "Oh God, I hope I'm doing the right thing."

"You are, you are," Margaret prompted excitedly. "Ask, ask, ask!"

Sally stared fixedly at her friend for a few moments, then she took a deep breath. "If someone told you something about some people; something dangerous for you to know, would you rather they hadn't told you?"

Margaret arched her eyebrows and put a finger thoughtfully to her lips "Now let me see. Would the people involved; I mean the dangerous ones, know that I know?"

"No. But if they found out, and they might, your life would be in danger?"

The excitement returned to Margaret's eyes and she shivered. "This sound's really exciting, love. What the Dickens is it?"

"I'm being deadly serious, Margaret," said Sally. fearing that her friend was being far too frivolous.

"I know you are, love," said Margaret, doing her best to sound focused. "Now spit it out before I faint from antici-pation."

"Here goes then," said Sally. "This branch is being used to store huge quantities of drugs. Jimmy, George, Jeff, and some of the drivers are involved, and Dennis, the youngster who works over in the storeroom, found out about it and Jeff killed him with a butcher's knife."

Margaret stared at Sally with her mouth open. "Really. Now that is a juicy piece of gossip, love."

"I'm telling you the truth," said Sally.

"I don't know what to say to that, love," Margaret replied in a quiet voice. "I mean, you look like you're being serious, but of course you can't be. I mean, what you've just told me sounds like something from one of those crime novels."

"It isn't a crime story!" Sally snapped. "If it was, then Dennis wouldn't be missing, would he?"

"Is he missing?" said Margaret, surprised. "I mean, how would I know if he is or if he isn't? I don't work with him?"

"Then ask someone," Sally ordered. "Jimmy told me Dennis fancies one of the girls here."

"You mean Allison?" said Margaret. "I did hear she was seeing a young lad who works out back, but I don't know his name."

Margaret then looked around the canteen. "Hold on a sec, love; won't be long."

Then she stood up and went to another table at the other end of the canteen, where a couple of young girls were eating. Margaret spoke to one of them for a few minutes, then she came back.

"I've just had a word with Allison," she said, her expression grave. "It seems Dennis went out to lunch the other day and didn't come back. They had a date that evening so she phoned his house when he didn't call for her. His mother said that he hasn't been home either."

"Don't you think that's suspicious?" said Sally.

"I suppose so," Margaret replied, "considering what a stunner Allison is. But that doesn't mean he's dead, love. You know what youngsters are like these days; won't commit themselves to anything. He could have found another girl and didn't have the bottle to tell Allison. Mind you, she does have a bit of a temper."

"But you said yourself that Jeff and George were a couple of creeps?" Sally protested.

Margaret gave a half laugh. "Creeps yes, but not murderers. Look, love, I'm afraid you've got the wrong end of the stick there somewhere."

"No I haven't," said Sally with an edge to her voice. "And I need you to take me seriously, Margaret. I'm going to spend the weekend with Steve Wilson: he's the boss of the whole drugs business, and I would feel much better knowing that I'm leaving someone to do the right thing if anything goes wrong."

"You mean you're actually going to sleep with this man?" Margaret exclaimed, her excitement returning.

"I have no choice. Jimmy got himself dragged into this drugs thing and now he can't get himself out of it. But Steve Wilson's agreed to let Jimmy go if I spend a couple of days with him. I think it's worth it."

"And does Jimmy know what you're up to?"

Sally sighed. "No, and that's the way I want it to stay."

"So what is it exactly you want me to do, love."

"Got a pen and paper on you?"

Margaret searched her bag and produced a pen and a used envelope.

"I want you to write all this down," said Sally. "And if you don't hear from me by next Monday afternoon, I want you to go to the police. And for God's sake don't tell anyone here what you know."

"Ok," said Margaret, "fire away. Although I'm not sure yet whether to believe you or not, I can tell you one thing, love. If what you say is true, come Monday and there's no sign of you, this dusty old place will certainly see some action."

Margaret spent the next few minutes writing down what Sally told her. Then she folded the envelope and put it back in her bag.

"What are you going to do between now and Friday?" she asked Sally.

Sally smiled. "Worry a great deal, I suppose."

Margaret frowned. "Look, love, why don't you let me come with you to this Steve Wilson's place? Us girls should stick together, you know."

"I appreciate the offer," said Sally. "But I'd rather you were out of it until something goes wrong."

"Ok, if you insist," Margaret agreed reluctantly. "But watch yourself. And if you need any help, you just scream down the phone and I'll come running. I'll give you my home number."

In the storeroom at Mulville's, Jeff was checking the stock when Tim approached. Tim was a seventeen year old student, working part time to raise cash for a new motorbike.

"I've finished checking those crates of bottled water for leaks, Jeff," he said casually.

"Then how about giving the floor a sweep," said Jeff.

"Right," said Tim, turning away. Then he stopped. "Any idea when Dennis is coming back?" he asked.

"No," said Jeff, writing something on his clipboard.

"Only it's a bit funny him going off like that," said Tim.

"What's odd about it?" Jeff replied. "You kids these days are just bloody minded, lazy and good-for-nothing too. Now get sweeping if you want to keep your job."

"Only the thing is," Tim went on, "Dennis told me he had a secret, and he was going to tell me what it was after lunch, on the day he disappeared."

"What secret?" said Jeff, still writing, although his expression had hardened.

"Something about this place," Tim replied. "He said he was going to report it to Mr Mason."

Jeff shrugged. "He was probably having you on."

"I don't think so," said Tim, "because I saw him going in to Mr Mason's office."

Jeff stopped writing and stared at the youngster. "If you must know, he was after a pay rise, and I wouldn't let him have it, so he went over my head."

"I think it was more than that," said Tim, scratching his head of cropped, blue-tinted hair. "He was really excited about his secret: I mean really excited. He said that this place would be on TV, and that I should find a way to come in every day for the next week to make sure I didn't miss it. Do you think him going missing has anything to do with his secret?"

"How the hell should I know!" Jeff snapped. "Now do you want this job or not. If you do, get that broom and do as you're told."

Jeff watched as a disgruntled Tim walked away, then he cursed under his breath.

Five minutes later he was in Jimmy's office.

"Oh God; not again!" Jimmy moaned, when Jeff finished telling him about Tim.

"We'll have to get rid of him as well," said Jeff.

"No; no!" Jimmy retorted, and raising his hands defensively. "I'm never going through an experience like that again. You do it without me. I don't want any part of it. You tricked me last time into killing Dennis by myself. You can do it alone this time."

Jeff leaned forwards, both hands resting on the desk. He glared down at Jimmy who was looking back at him with desperation in his eyes. "I told you before Mr Assistant Manager, you're in this right up to your white collar. And when it comes to murder the blood is going to stain your hands every bit as much as mine. But if you're too gutless to use the knife again, you can hold Tim while I do it. Either way you're helping."

"I can't; I can't!" Jimmy shook his head. "You do it all and I'll accept equal responsibility, but please don't ask me to kill someone again."

"Don't worry," said Jeff. "I'm not asking; I'm telling."

"But I can't, Jeff. I'm sorry, but I won't go through that again."

Anger blazed in Jeff's eyes. "You listen to me, you snivelling piece of shit! That fucking kid is a threat to all of us, so, you're going to help me get rid of him whether you like it or not."

Jimmy was still shaking his head. "No, I won't do it: I won't."

"You fucking well will!" Jeff snapped.

"Is there a problem, gentlemen?" a soft voice behind Jeff asked.

Jimmy shot to his feet when he saw Harris standing in the doorway with a concerned expression on his face.

"No problem at all, Mr Harris," Jeff said with a forced smile.

"I could hear the both of you shouting from my office," Harris replied. "And when I find the Assistant Manager of this store and the Storeroom Manager at loggerheads with one another, I am left to wonder if there is a matter that concerns me."

"Oh nothing like that, Mr Harris," Jimmy replied hurriedly. "Just a small difference of opinion."

"Oh; and what might that be?"

Jimmy glanced at Jeff. "One of the part-time storeroom staff requested a pay rise. Jeff refused to give him one and so he came to me instead."

"Surely you know how our system works by now?" Harris replied somewhat sternly. "If one of the part-time staff in the storeroom wishes to have a pay increase, they must first approach the Assistant Storeroom Manager and then the Manager who makes the final decision. And you, Jeff, instead of arguing with Jimmy, you should sort the matter out with the young man who made the request in the first place. Surely you can see that it is most unprofessional for the both of you to be heard arguing like this. I hope there will be no more of it."

"No, Mr Harris," said Jeff. "And I'm sorry you were disturbed."

"Then we shall say no more about it," said Harris. "Now, I suspect you have work to do in the storeroom."

Jeff left the office without further discussion.

"I have to say that I'm very disappointed in you, Jimmy," said Harris. "This is no way for the Assistant Manager to behave. Arguing solves nothing. If there is a disagreement between you and Jeff that cannot be resolved without resorting to shouting, then you should have brought the matter to me."

"Of course, Mr Harris," Jimmy replied. "I'm very sorry. It won't happen again."

Harris smiled. "I suppose it is all part of the learning process, Jimmy. Within a few weeks you will take over the responsibility of this store. And remember, a good captain of any ship always listens to his officers. He may not always take their advice, but he always listens."

When Harris then left the office, Jimmy dropped back into his seat. And for the second time in a week a terrible nightmare was unfolding around him; sucking him into its deadly embrace.

For the rest of the day Jimmy couldn't concentrate on his work. An image of Dennis's anguished face refused to leave his memory and the thought of doing the same to Tim was more then he could bear. He just had to find a way out.

It was 4:20 pm and Jimmy's mobile phone rang.

It was Jeff.

"I'll be over in a minute," Jimmy replied to the order he was waiting for. And it was an order, because when it came to murder, Jeff was certainly in charge.

When Jimmy walked into the storeroom, he could feel the silence like a held breath.

Jeff stepped out from behind a crate and gestured with a jerk of his head for Jimmy to follow him.

Jeff didn't stop until he came to his office, and checking that there was no one else about, closed the door.

Jimmy felt an almost overpowering desire to run out again.

"Right," said Jeff, pacing up and down and wringing his hands in agitation. "I've been thinking about it. We have to get rid of Tim straight away, before he mentions his suspicions to Dennis's parents. I was hoping to put it off until tomorrow; you know, give us a bit more time to plan it properly, but we can't risk it."

"You can't murder two people within a week and hope to get away with it," Jimmy protested. "The police will be all over this place if Tim goes missing as well."

"I realize that, but what choice do we have," Jeff replied. "We can't have some kid wandering around wondering if Dennis' disappearance has anything to do with his visit to your office. The police can be as suspicious as they like when he goes missing, but without any evidence to back up their suspicions, they won't be able to do fuck all. I've already spoken to Billy and there won't be any more deliveries for a few months, so the police won't find anything here when they search the place. And of course once things calm down we can get back to earning some real money again. And as for Tim, I have no intention of making the same cock-up we did with Dennis. All we have to do is get him in here for a chat about overtime. He's not as bright as Dennis so he won't suspect anything. I'll have a plastic dust sheet down so there won't be any blood on the floor this time."

"I'm not using that knife on anyone ever again!" Jimmy declared.

"Haven't we discussed this crap already," Jeff growled. "Anyway, you would only balls it up like you did last time. So you hold him and I'll do the rest. And another thing, don't fall apart again or you'll end up buried with Tim. Nobody wants a fucking liability in our organization, and those were Billy's exact words when I spoke to him, so take heed."

"But why do we have to use a knife?" Jimmy protested. "Couldn't we hit him over the head with something; or poison him?"

"Maybe we should just bore him to death with your stupid suggestions!" Jeff growled. "A knife is more certain. People have been known to recover from blows to the head, you know."

Jimmy stared at Jeff for a moment; then he nodded, and some part of his awareness began to detach itself.

All of a sudden he felt light-headed and had to tense his legs to stay upright.

"Right then," Jeff went on, not noticing the change in Jimmy, "you return to your office, but be back here in half an hour. I'll have a word with Tim."

Thirty minutes later, Jimmy, Jeff and Tim were in the small storeroom office. Tim was standing between the two men, facing Jeff, and he was clearly tense about being there.

"What's going on?" he asked with a nervous laugh. "I'm not getting the push am I because I got on your nerves about Dennis? I was only asking about him; honest I was, Jeff. What Dennis gets up to has nothing to do with me. We're not really good mates. I mean we don't hang out together or anything like that."

"It's ok, son," said Jeff with a grin, "you're not getting the sack. In fact quite the opposite. Now Dennis told you to find some reason to be here every day, and since you're a good worker I have decided that you can have as much overtime as you want for the next couple of months. And if you do a good job, who knows; George needs an assistant himself, and that would at least double the money you're getting now. You up for it?"

Tim visibly relaxed, and a big smile revealed small, perfect teeth. "That's great, Jeff! Thanks a lot."

Then Tim noticed he was standing on a thick polyethylene cover. "What gives with the dustsheet?" he said.

"I'm glad you asked that," said Jeff. "I need this office painted, and I want you to it for me. And I'll even throw in an extra fifty quid on top of the overtime if I'm satisfied with the results."

"Great," Tim beamed. "I'm really good at painting. When my big sister and Rick got married last year I painted nearly every room in their new house and they paid me a hundred quid extra because I did such a good job."

"I'm sure I will be just as pleased as your sister," said Jeff. "But fifty pounds is all the extra you're getting for painting this place, you cheeky sod."

"Thanks, Jeff," said Tim, still smiling. "I suppose I better get back to moving those crates of peas before you change your mind and give me the push after all."

"Hang on a second, son," said Jeff. Then he gave Jimmy a hard stare. "Don't you have something to do right away, Mr Mason."

Sweat popped out on Jimmy's forehead, but he didn't answer.

The expression on Jeff's face showed suppressed fury. "You did say it was urgent, didn't you? And now would be a good time, don't you think."

Jimmy continued to stare back unmoving, though his mind was in a violent state of flux.

"Of course if you don't do it," Jeff went on, "there's a very good chance that you will be in very serious trouble, so if I were you I would get on with it straight away."

Tim was obviously puzzled by what was going on and he turned his head to look back at Jimmy. "Are you all right, Mr Mason?" he asked. "You don't look very good?"

"Mr Mason is fine, Tim," said Jeff. "He has a lot on his mind. That's what happens when you move into management; sometimes having to make very unpleasant decisions because not making those decisions could have terrible consequences for certain people. Isn't that right, Mr Mason?"

Jimmy wiped the sweat from his face and nodded.

"Good," said Jeff. "Now then, Tim, about decorating this office."

Jimmy quickly stepped forwards as Tim turned back to Jeff, and wrapped his arms around him in a bear hug.

A startled cry of confusion shot from Tim, "Mr Mason; what are you doing?"

And when Jimmy didn't answer, Tim began to struggle.

Jimmy was surprised at the strength of his captive, since he was of a small and slight stature.

"Let me go!" Tim cried. "What's going on? Stop pissing around, Mr Mason."

Jeff quickly reached into a drawer in his desk and produced the butcher's knife Jimmy had used on Dennis.

Tim's eyes went wide with shock. "Jeff; stop messing about; it's not funny!"

"For Christ sakes hold him still!" Jeff barked as Tim's struggles grew in intensity.

Jimmy tightened his grip.

Jeff approached with the knife held ready.

Tim began to scream and throw himself from side to side.

"Hold him!" Jeff shouted.

Then he drove the blade towards Tim's chest; just above Jimmy's encircling arms.

Tim saw it coming and shoved backwards; upsetting Jimmy's balance.

Jimmy gasped when the blade skewered his left forearm.

"Shit!" Jeff exclaimed, pulling the knife out.

"My arm; my arm!" Jimmy moaned, releasing his hold and leaning back against the closed door.

Blood oozed from the wound.

Tim saw his chance and kicked Jeff between the legs.

Jeff grunted and doubled up in pain, but didn't go down.

Tim spun around and frantically tried to get out of the office, but Jimmy was blocking his escape.

He grabbed the lapels of Jimmy's coat and tried to drag him out of the way, but Jimmy managed to resist whilst cradling his injured arm.

Panic drove Tim on and he began punching Jimmy in the face and body in an effort to make him move.

"Fight back, Jimmy you fucking bastard!" Jeff shouted through racking coughs. "If he gets away we're finished."

Jimmy made no effort to resist his attacker, instead trying to present his back to him.

Jeff suddenly lunged at Tim.

Tim grunted when he felt Jeff's powerful right arm going around his neck.

"Got you, you little fuck!" Jeff growled.

Tim began screaming again.

But Jeff cursed when he realized he had dropped the knife when he was kicked.

The weapon was only a metre away but he couldn't reach it without releasing his captive.

Jeff's hesitation as he sought a solution gave Tim his chance.

The youngster suddenly kicked backwards with his right foot.

Jeff lost his hold when the heel of a boot smacked into his right leg with painful force.

Tim turned and his small fist caught Jeff on the jaw.

"That won't save you, you little shit," said Jeff grabbing at him.

Tim fell back and Jimmy gripped him around the neck with his good arm.

"Hold him properly this time!" Jeff ordered, bending down to pick up the knife.

Tim threw his weight up; back, and simultaneously both of his feet lifted and shot out; smashing Jeff on the side of the face.

Jeff was sent crashing against his desk and fell to the floor.

Tim drove his right elbow into Jimmy's belly.

Jimmy sank to his knees in agony.

Tim spun around: grabbed Jimmy by the hair and toppled him away from the door.

Then it was open and he was through it and running for the exit.

"You fucking, useless bastard!" Jeff screamed, picking himself up. "You've finished the lot of us."

Jimmy, in a state of shock, stared up from the floor to see Jeff standing over him with the knife in his right hand. There was blood and pure hatred on the face of the Storeroom Manager.

"On your feet!" Jeff roared, reaching down with his left hand and pulling at Jimmy.

With Jeff's help, Jimmy managed to stand up. Then his eyes went wide with shock and he stared down with disbelieving eyes at the knife handle that was sticking out of his stomach.

"You fucking useless lump of shit, Jimmy," said Jeff. "I should have done that to you when you fucked up with Dennis. Now get back down on the floor and die like a dog."

Jimmy's strength drained instantly from him as Jeff pushed him down on the polyethylene sheet.

Jeff wiped the blood on his face with his sleeve; glaring at his victim with contempt.

"Seems you won't be making manager after all, Mr Jimmy 'Rising Star' Mason. But look on the bright side, you won't have to suffer the humiliation of being sacked for being the biggest prat in the country."

Jeff then went to his desk, and having unlocked a couple of drawers, put a dozen very large, brown envelopes into a carrier bag. The handles stretched under the weight.

Jimmy watched from his position on the floor; fighting to stave off the darkness that was approaching.

He cursed himself for allowing his existence to end in his own murder at the hands of a scumbag like Jeff. And what would Sally do when she heard about his death? If she had any sense she would pack her bags and find a better life somewhere else. But he knew her better than that. She would stay and seek justice for him at the risk of her life. And at this thought something inside him changed. Despite the pain: the dizziness: the despair and the approaching oblivion, a new energy began to grow: an energy of pure rage towards the Storeroom Manager. And as the energy increased, a determination, like none he had ever experienced in his entire life, took control of him: tearing away the despair and other negative emotions: becoming a power that burned in its intensity until it was furnace-hot.

Jeff put on his coat; tided his hair, and stepped over Jimmy.

Then he stopped and looked down at his victim. "You know something, Mason, what I have in these envelopes will be worth over five hundred thousand pounds when I have finished cutting. I managed to siphon off twenty kilos of pure cocaine from those crates, just in case some liability like you messed up my job here. But never mind, life goes on. One door closes and another opens, as they say. And the sight of you bleeding your guts out on the dustsheet meant for Tim will give me happy memories as my wife and I relax in the Spanish sun. You take care now, you fuck."

A scream suddenly shot from Jeff. And when his right leg gave way, he fell back on top of Jimmy.

Jimmy yanked the butcher's knife out of Jeff's calf and pushed the Storeroom Manager off him.

He stabbed again, this time higher up.

Jeff moaned when the blade went into his lower back.

He began dragging himself away from his attacker, across a slippery dust sheet which was now heavily streaked with blood.

An evil smile formed on Jimmy's lips as he watched.

Then he began crawling after the Storeroom Manager; the bloodied knife held in his right hand.

Tears of agony and desperation flowed from Jeff's eyes. He had to get to the other end of his desk if he wanted to live.

Salvation was there in the form of a crowbar. With it he could fend off Jimmy until he died from his stomach wound. Surely to God that wouldn't be long.

But his progress was slow. His clawed hands scooped up the dustsheet, slowing him down.

He stopped, looked back and saw Jimmy coming after him.

Then he saw the knife in his hand.

"Don't, Jimmy: please don't!" he sobbed crawling once more. "Oh God: oh God: please don't."

"What's the matter, Jeff?" Jimmy laughed through gasps of breath. "I want to give you something, you arrogant bastard."

Jeff screamed when something touched his right foot.

He jerked it away, but his left foot was grabbed.

The grip was strong. He couldn't break it.

Suddenly he was sliding backwards.

Terror paralyzed his body. "I don't want to die: I don't want to die."

Jimmy's left hand raised as his right hand held Jeff in a grip like a vice.

For a moment the knife hovered over the centre of Jeff's back.

Then it plunged down and drove deep into his body.

Jeff's eyes bulged when the blade pierced his right lung. His mouth filled with blood, and a gurgling croak left his lips.

Another stab of the knife sent the blade through his liver.

"Hey Jeff," said Jimmy, dropping the knife and reaching for a thick envelope laying on the floor, "you missed one. I'll get it for you."

Jeff managed to roll over on to his back, still conscious enough to want to live.

Jimmy ripped open the envelope and dozens of transparent sachets, each containing a heaped tablespoon of pure cocaine, fell out.

He grabbed a fistful of them and dragged himself nearer to Jeff. "But don't you worry, mate, I have it here now. I wouldn't want you to run short in Spain, you know."

He smiled down at him as he tore open a sachet with his teeth.

Then he held both sides of Jeff's mouth with his left hand. "Open wide, mate."

Jeff clamped his mouth tight shut.

"Naughty," said Jimmy, holding the sachet between his teeth, and squeezing Jeff's nostrils with his right hand.

For ten seconds Jeff resisted an impulse to breathe. Then his mouth opened in a loud gasp and the cocaine poured in.

Coughing and spluttering, Jeff desperately tried to expel the drug from his mouth. But when a second and then a third sachet poured in and the dry, white powder was sucked into his lungs, his struggles began to fade and then the life left him.

"Looks like you were right, Jeff," said Jimmy. "One door did close; for you. But the door that opened was for me."

Jimmy lay on the floor next to Jeff's body for five minutes, trying not to pass out. Then he forced himself to his feet. The blood from the wound on his arm was slowing, but the one to his stomach was bleeding profusely.

How was he still alive? He should be dead. Surely he was going to die at any moment.

Putting such thoughts from his mind, he searched a first aid box and held a piece of padded gauge against the wound with strips of plaster. He felt sick and dizzy, but he had to get away before the police arrived.

Then having put on an overcoat that had been hanging on a hook for at least three years, he left the office. Pain seemed to ooze from every pore in his being as he finally staggered out of the storeroom and headed towards the train station. He dare not risk waiting for a Taxi.

Chapter Thirty Four

The journey home was a test of Jimmy's endurance. People on the train stared curiously at him as he fought to stay conscious. His buttoned coat concealed his wounds, so the passengers were probably trying to work out only if he was ill or drunk. Whichever it was they didn't really want to know beyond simple curiosity. They had enough problems of their own to worry about.

Eventually Jimmy staggered through the door of the maisonette and he slowly climbed the stairs to the bedroom. He was desperate for medical treatment, but he realized that the police would certainly be called if he went to a doctor or a hospital. Both of his wounds seemed to have stopped bleeding and he prayed it meant that the blade of the butcher's knife had missed all the important organs and arteries. But even if, by some incredible luck it had, he knew he was still in serious trouble and could take a turn for the worse at any moment.

Carefully he lowered himself on to the double bed and wished with all his heart that Sally was there beside him.

Then he passed out.

Something was hitting his face, and he could hear the voice of a woman.

The voice sounded desperate.

He opened his eyes.

"What happened to you?" Sally cried. "Did you call an ambulance?"

"No ambulance," Jimmy croaked. His mouth was dry and sticky.

"Don't be so stupid," Sally declared, worried sick. "I have to get you to a hospital straight away."

"I'll be all right, Sal," Jimmy answered, wincing as a spasm of pain tensed his body. "I think the bleeding has stopped."

"But you could be bleeding inside," Sally protested desperately. "You could die; please, darling."

"I don't think so," said Jimmy. "Get me some water will you, Sal. And don't call anyone until you know what happened."

Sally left the bedroom and returned seconds later with a glass of water. She propped her husband's head up and allowed him a couple of sips. She had no idea if it was safe to give someone something to drink with such an injury to their stomach. But it was clear he needed it.

"Thanks, Sal," Jimmy said with a weak smile. "Lager will never taste quite so good after this."

"Please let me phone for an ambulance!" Sally begged. "That wound in your stomach looks really serious."

"I'm ok," said Jimmy. "I just need a few days rest. I was very lucky. The blade seems to have missed all my organs, otherwise I'm sure I would be dead by now."

"You mean someone stabbed you?" Sally's expression revealed her shock. "Who was it?"

"Jeff."

"Jeff! But why?"

Jimmy managed a brief laugh. "Because I'm useless, Sal. But then you already know that, don't you."

"Right, I'm calling a ambulance," said Sally. "You're beginning to sound delirious,"

"No; not delirious, Sal; philosophical," said Jimmy. "You see Jeff was right, I am useless, and I deserve this for all the worry I've caused you. But Jeff was useless as well, and that's why I killed him."

Sally gasped. What Jimmy was saying was too terrible for her to take in. Here she was, playing a dangerous game with Steve Wilson in order to get her husband out of trouble, and all the time he was killing people as if it was a new hobby for him.

Jimmy saw how shocked she was. "Listen, Sal, I had to kill Jeff. You see, another member of staff started getting suspicious about Dennis going missing and he told Jeff. So good old Jeff decided to do him in as well. And he was another of your poor children and you certainly wouldn't have wanted him dead.

Anyway, Jeff lured Tim: that's his name by the way, into his office. I grabbed Tim from behind and Jeff was suppose to stab him. But Tim wasn't very cooperative: I mean, you know what kids are like these days; no respect for their elders. Anyway, Tim struggled so much, Jeff stabbed me in the arm instead. Then Little Tim gave Big Jeff a good hiding and shot out of the storeroom like a politician looking for a vote. Of course Jeff blamed me so he stabbed me in the stomach as a punishment for being useless. I think he thought I'd bleed to death in his office, otherwise he'd have finished me off. But like everything else he's done lately, he got it wrong. So: and you'll like this, Sal, I pulled the knife out of me and stuck it in Jeff. Mind you, I think the irony was lost on him."

Sally sat on the edge of the bed. "You do know the police will be looking for you, don't you?"

"I wouldn't be a bit surprised. Tim may be the world's slowest to do anything, according to Jeff, but even he can't be that bad. After what Tim tells the police, and what they find in Jeff's office, I'll be facing a murder charge. But you know something, Sal, I don't think I care very much anymore. I've had enough. I caused all this and I deserve to pay for it. And I wouldn't be one bit surprised if when the Day of Judgement finally arrives for me, the Devil himself isn't there to say hello, Jimmy, I've been waiting for you."

The phone rang and it made them both jump. Sally answered it with a trembling hand. "Yes?"

"Oh, Sally, it's Mr Harris. Is your husband there?"

"I'm afraid he's ill, Mr Harris," said Sally.

"Again? Oh dear, I do hope it's not serious?"

"Just a touch of flu."

"Then he must have plenty of rest," said Mr Harris. "But I do wish he had told me he finally decided to go home. I've been looking everywhere for him."

"His temperature is up a bit, Mr Harris, and I suppose he became confused."

"Yes, he does seem to react rather strangely to being ill. But never mind. Now you stay at home with him for the next few days until he can fend for himself. I'll explain the situation to Mrs Tobin in the morning."

"Thank you, Mr Harris," said Sally.

"Think nothing of it, Sally. We must look after out future chairman, now mustn't we."

Sally spent the next few minutes seeing to her husband's wounds as best she could. Fortunately the knife had had a narrow blade, and by some miracle no organs or arteries seemed to have been damaged either in Jimmy's stomach or arm. He might recover, but it would probably take a long time.

But Steve Wilson would be expecting her in three days time and she wouldn't be able to make it, not when she had Jimmy to nurse. And would everything change when he found out what happened at the store? Would he accept that Jimmy had no choice but to kill Jeff; that he was acting in self-defence? And if Jimmy was as valuable to his organization as Steve said he was, surely he wouldn't have him killed.

An image of a sailing ship with ripped sails burst into Sally's mind for a moment, but she pushed it away. Now was not the time for doubts: they could end up crippling her plans.

She decided to phone Steve. And when he answered in a friendly voice, she told him that she would see him on the following weekend instead. He wasn't too happy about it, but accepted the change of plan. The next thing she had to do was get Jimmy out of the maisonette before the police called. She phoned her friend Sarah from a telephone box and explained the situation. Sarah told Sally to leave straight away.

It was with the greatest difficulty that Sally managed to get Jimmy to the car, and the exertion opened up his stomach wound once more. Sally dressed it again and set off for Scotland.

Twelve hours later Sally and Jimmy were in Sarah's house. Jimmy was put to bed and made as comfortable as possible. The journey by car had made him worse and he was soon in a very deep sleep from which he looked as if he might never awaken, such was his frightening pallor.

Sarah called in the services of a good friend who was a freshly qualified doctor. And having stitched Jimmy's wounds and left a bottle of antibiotic tablets for Sarah to administer every twelve hours for the next ten days, announced that as far as he could tell, Jimmy would make a full recovery, but he would be bed-ridden for at least three months. Then the doctor left, promising to drop in occasionally to keep an eye on his first private, but non- paying patient.

Sarah smiled at Sally as they both sat at the kitchen table drinking coffee. "You know something, Chuck, you sure have been living an interesting life lately."

"Is that what you think it is?" said Sally with a wry smile. "A top drug dealer wants me to sleep with him: a stranger has made three attempts on my life, and my husband has killed two people. I'd call that a nightmare."

Sarah frowned. "There's been something about that on the news. It seems Mr Harris found Jeff's body, and the police want to question the two of you. They can't find Tim either. The poor kid must be in hiding at a friends house."

"Just like me," said Sally.

"You don't have to worry," said Sarah. "There's nothing to connect you to me. You'll be safe here."

"Jimmy was forced into killing those people," Sally replied. "You do know that, don't you?"

Sarah shrugged. "If you say so, Chuck. But I don't think anyone could make me do a terrible thing like that. Anyway, I invited the two of you here to help, not to pass judgement. Stay as long as you like."

Sally smiled. How good it was to have such a friend.

Sarah, who was the same age, considered herself to be plain looking, but Sally didn't agreed. It was true that her small, brown eyes, bulbous nose and thin mouth robbed her face of any real beauty. However, her rich chestnut hair cut to just below her perfect ears and her slim figure had their own attractions for men. But most of all, it was Sarah's personality that people saw within minutes of meeting her for the first time. For when Sarah smiled, it made those on the receiving end want to smile too. And although she lived alone at the moment, it was purely from choice. Sarah always said, 'Men and tom cats belong outside the house, Chuck. Let them in and they get up to all sorts of mischief, such as leaving the loo seat up and spraying the furniture.

"You know, you've been fantastic support for me lately, Sarah, and I'm really grateful." Sally said after a while.

"I think you better hold off on the gratitude until you've tasted my cooking," said Sarah with a grin. "So, what plans do you have, if any?"

"Jimmy's just messed up my plans, and I haven't had time to make new ones. But one thing's for sure. I have to spend next weekend with Steve Wilson."

Sarah was shocked. "God; you're not still going ahead with that nonsense?"

"I have to. Who knows what he'll do if I back out now."

"But the situation has changed, Chuck. Jimmy has just buggered up Wilson's plans for the Mulville's chain. At this very minute the police are probably swarming all over the store looking for clues. I can't see Wilson forgiving Jimmy, or you, for something like that."

"There's only one way to find out," said Sally. "Can I use your phone?"

"Sure," said Sarah. "But don't tell him where you are. I don't want any more visitors."

Sally dialled Steve's number.

A man answered and put her through.

"Sally; how nice to hear from you again, and so soon," said Steve cheerfully.

"Have you listened to the news this morning?" said Sally cautiously.

"I have indeed."

"And?"

"And what, Sally?"

"And; what are you going to do?"

"What can I do. That part of my business has been destroyed; your husband saw to that. I'm sorry to say."

"He had no choice!" Sally declared. "Jeff attacked him first. Jimmy is with me now. He has a knife wound in his arm and one in his stomach. He could have died."

"Well, I won't be sending him a get-well-soon card, if that's what you're after."

"And I suppose next weekend is off ?"

"You must be joking," came the reply. "Look, Sally, one thing has nothing to do with the other. Ok, so under normal circumstances I would have Jimmy tortured to death for what he's done, but that would be only to set an example to others in my organization who might be watching my every movement: looking for any signs of softness or weakness. And as for the loss of finances, I'll have you know that if The Rich List knew how much I was really worth, it would make Bill Gates himself nervous. No, Sally, this is just a game to me, and like all gamblers you have to accept the losses as well as the gains. Now, once you have spent the weekend with me, we'll be quits. After all, I have already lined up something else to replace Mulville's. So, don't you go worrying about it. I want you fresh, alert and prepared to have a great time when you come here. And don't think I won't try and convince you to repeat the experience: I'm hoping you will enjoy yourself so much that I won't even have to ask. But don't worry, I will accept your final decision. If nothing, I am a man of my word. So, you take good care of that husband of yours and I shall see you next Friday."

There was disbelief on Sally's face when she put the phone down.

"Well; what did he say?" Sarah asked, full of interest. "Should we nail the front door shut and block up the fire-place?"

Sally stared at her friend. "He said that what happened at Mulville's was just the conclusion of a bad investment and he wants me to see him next Friday."

"Really?" said Sarah, just as surprised as Sally. "But are you sure you can trust him?"

"I think so. There was no anger in his voice at all. He hinted that he is one of the richest men in the world and he doesn't need the money from Mulville's. And his home convinces me that it must be true."

"And if you do spend the weekend with him, you and Jimmy can start again somewhere else: is that it?" said Sarah, not entirely convinced.

"That's the deal," said Sally.

Sarah pursed her lips. "Well, considering the mess Jimmy has gotten you both into, I suppose it's the best offer on the table."

Sally's face brightened with hope. "You really think so?"

"Sure. Look, Chuck, I realize that nothing I can say will talk you out of doing this, so I'm not going to try. Now, I know how important it is for married couples to be faithful to one another, but sometimes life derails you, and when it does you have to break the rules to get back on track. And don't forget, Jimmy was the one who started it. If he had told you what was happening when Billy Bennifield first approached him, none of this would have happened. So, if you have to be unfaithful for a very short time to sort out his mess, that's his fault. Now you go and have that weekend with Steve Wilson, if you really think that's the only thing to do, and then you and Jimmy can get on with your lives. And another thing, how about a shot of whisky in that coffee you've been nursing. You're in Bonny Scotland now, you know."

Two days later Sally saw something in The Daily Mirror that stunned her.

"What's the matter, Chuck?" Sarah asked, noticing her friend's anxious expression.

"It's Andy Saunders," Sally whispered. "His body was found floating in the Thames."

"Oh my God!" Sarah exclaimed. "Then it must be true about Steve Wilson. Look, Sally, there's no way now you can see him after this. Obviously Andy Saunders was right about Wilson being called The Sailor because he cuts people loose."

"But it might not have been him," said Sally.

"For Christ sakes, Chuck, who else could it be. Saunders was making plans to get rid of Wilson, but Wilson got rid of him first.

And he'll probably get rid of anyone else connected with Saunders, and that certainly includes you and Jimmy."

Sally was clearly uncertain. "But what if it was someone else? What if someone wanted Andy's position in the organization?"

"Stop kidding yourself!" Sarah snapped. Then her harsh expression softened and she smiled affectionately. "Look, Chuck, I know you were hoping it would be all over once you had spent the weekend with Wilson, but Andy Saunders' death means that your deal with Wilson is off. You go into that house and you won't come out alive."

"I'll just have to risk it," Sally replied. "This could be my only chance to get Jimmy free and I'm not going to throw it away on an assumption. I know Steve likes me a great deal, and if you must know my worst fear is that he will ask me to stay with him in exchange for Jimmy's life. Anyway, maybe he had to kill Saunders. I mean, how else can you get rid of an enemy in that kind of business. Maybe he did it for the same reason Jimmy killed Jeff; not for gain or revenge, but to save his own life. Now, can we please drop the subject. I'm feeling nervous enough as it is."

"Ok, Chuck," said Sarah with a sigh. "But watch yourself with that man: he didn't get to where he is by being forgiving and understanding: ruthlessness and self-interest are more likely to be his main attributes."

The days passed quickly for Sally.

Jimmy's recovery was more or less straight forward except for a slight fever he had on the Saturday. But by Sunday his temperature was back to normal.

Friday finally came.

It was 5:20am and in a few hours she would be on her way to see Steve Wilson. She was filled with apprehension but also determination. This was her only chance to get Jimmy free from the nightmare he had inadvertently plunged them into and she had to take it no matter what the cost. Sarah had tried just once more to talk her out of it, but her friend had finally bowed to the inevitable.

She told Jimmy that she had to spend a few days away sorting out a few problems, and he had reluctantly accepted it. The police were still looking for them and she had pointed out that they were far more likely to be spotted if they were seen together.

She left Sarah's house at 7:30am.

It was going to be a very long drive to Steve Wilson's place, and she didn't want to be late. She had considered driving to London on the Thursday and taking a room for the night, but she wanted to spend every minute with Jimmy. It had been a miracle that he had survived such terrible injuries, but until he was fully recovered she could not afford to take his return to health for granted. She also considered and rejected using the train. She just couldn't bear the company of other passengers.

Sarah had packed a couple of spare trousers and tops for her, and made her promise to phone her regularly; otherwise she would get in touch with the police.

She hoped it wouldn't come to that.

Chapter Thirty Five

Eight hours later, Sally pulled into the gravel drive of the Drug Baron's home.

When she rang the bell, a smiling Steve opened the door.

He kissed her on the cheek and invited her in.

"May I use your bathroom to freshen up?" Sally asked as her coat and bag were taken.

"Up the stairs and second door on the left," Steve replied.

Steve was waiting in the hall when Sally came down the stairs twenty minutes later. She had changed her clothes and looked far less tired than when she first arrived.

"We will have to fend for ourselves," said Steve. "I have given the staff the weekend off. I hope you don't mind?"

"Of course not," said Sally, feeling a twinge of concern.

"Excellent. Now you go on through to the drawing room and pour us both a drink. I'll join you in a moment."

Sally let herself into the drawing room, and on this occasion its beauty was lost on her. She was beginning to feel very nervous about the whole situation. Surely Steve couldn't be as philosophical as he seemed to be over the loss of Mulville's? It would cost him millions of pounds in future profits: could he really put that down to a bad investment as he said he would? Perhaps such losses were minor to him: she hoped so.

She saw a round, silver tray of drinks on the coffee table.

She poured whisky into two glasses, and carrying one with her, made herself comfortable on one of the settees.

A minute later Steve came into the room. And having collected his drink, sat on the settee opposite Sally. There was a relaxed look on his face.

"I suppose you must be feeling nervous?" he said.

"Just a bit," Sally replied, taking a sip of her drink.

"So am I," said Steve. "Ridiculous isn't it; two adults feeling like a couple of teenagers on their first date."

Sally frowned. "I wouldn't exactly call it a date."

Steve's eyes narrowed. "Oh, and what would you call it?"

Sally stared coldly at her host. "What you would call it; a deal."

Steve shrugged. "I suppose it is. But can we make another deal, Sally?"

"If you want."

"I do. And let it be that we both consider this weekend an exciting adventure; an adventure of pleasure and discovery."

"I don't find any pleasure and excitement in being unfaithful," said Sally. "And as for discovery; well, the only discovery I expect to make is how far I am prepared to go to free my husband."

"I think I need another drink after that," said Steve helping himself to more whisky. He was smiling, but now it appeared strained. He returned to his seat. "So how is my lost prospect doing?"

"He's mending slowly, although he still gets tired easily."

Steve nodded. "That's good to hear."

Sally's lips twisted in contempt.

"No, I mean it!" Steve declared. "Believe it or not, Sally, I'd like to see you happy for the rest of your life, and if that means spending your life with Jimmy Mason, much as it may confound me, then that's the way I want it. I have no designs on you beyond this weekend; unless you wish otherwise from me, of course. All I am asking is for you to give me your total commitment for the next couple of days. Then you can begin your new future with your husband."

Sally stared into her glass for a moment, then her jaw tightened with determination. "Did you kill Andy Saunders?" she asked.

"Of course I did," said Steve, staring fixedly at her

Sally couldn't prevent the small gasp of shock that left her lips. "You're not even bothering to deny it?" she said quietly.

"Of course not. You want the truth from me, don't you?"

"Yes," said Sally. "But to admit to murdering someone as casually as if admitting to avoiding paying taxes is; cold."

"Why should I regret killing him," said Steve. "He wasn't family and he certainly wasn't a friend."

"All right. But why did you kill him?"

Steve leaned forwards in his seat. His expression was almost fierce. "I'll tell you why I killed him, Sally," he replied in a even tone. "He was a successful businessman in his own right. That company of his has a turnover of twenty million pounds per annum. And on top of that I was paying him one hundred and fifty thousand pounds a week; that's right, one hundred and fifty thousand, and what does he do; he decides that he isn't being paid enough and so he sets about trying to have me killed so that he could have even more. And, of course, you already know that last part, don't you?"

A gasp of shock left Sally, and she was about to protest, but a raised hand from Steve silenced her.

"Don't bother denying it," he went on; "I had a few bugs put in Andy's office more than a year ago. And I have tapes of everything he talked about in that room. Why do you think those security guards were present when you first arrived? They must have given you one hell of a fright when you saw them. But to your credit you hid it perfectly. Anyway, it's no surprise Saunders got it wrong. Usually I live alone with just Philip and the housekeeper to keep me company. And don't worry, I soon realized that you couldn't go through with it. But Andy was another matter. I brought him into my organization because I knew him to be a very determined and disciplined individual who would let nothing prevent him from achieving his goal. And I was right about him. Under his management my organization doubled its profits. But when his goal changed from managing my business to taking it over, I had to act. He would eventually have found someone else to do the job, and I couldn't have that, now could I?"

"No, I suppose not," Sally admitted. "You must be expecting this sort of thing all the time?"

"Of course," said Steve. "It's been tried before, you know; four times as a matter of fact. And as you can see, I am still here, although those who tried to kill me are long gone."

260

"But why did you wait so long to kill him?" Sally asked.

Steve shrugged. "Nothing I know about in advance frightens me. And I was curious to see how he intended to go about it. Don't forget, I'm a gambler, and surely the game of life and death is the greatest of all."

"And me?" said Sally.

Steve smiled. "You haven't done a single thing wrong, Sally. You were only trying to look out for your husband. I admire loyalty in a woman. Jimmy doesn't deserve you."

Sally's relief was then replaced by concern. "So, who else are you going to get rid of?"

"Aaaa; The Sailor, again," said Steve. "What was it Andy told you; that I would kill all of you to be on the safe side. Well, Andy was wrong. He was the only one who was plotting against me, so I'm going to leave it at that. Anyway, I'm curious. What did you finally do with that gun he gave you?"

"I wrapped the bullets in tissue paper and flushed them down the toilet," Sally replied. "Then I put the gun in an empty corn flakes box and put it in the pedal bin."

Steve laughed. "An ignoble end for a wonderful piece of precision engineering; women!"

"There was nothing noble or wonderful about that gun," Sally replied grim-faced. "It's one purpose was to take human life. Only God has the right to do that."

"I would never have taken you for being the religious type?" said Steve, staring at her with an amused look on his face.

"I'm not. It's just that I believe certain commandments are important whether you believe in God or not."

Steve continued to stare at Sally for a few moments. Then he sat up straight and slapped his knees. "How about something to eat? You must be starving after your long journey?"

Sally's guard went up. "What do you mean, after my long journey?"

"You would hardly have brought clothes to change into as soon as you arrived, unless you were going to drive a long way before hand, now would you?" said Steve.

Sally silently cursed her oversight. But outwardly she appeared calm. "A ham sandwich would be nice," she said with a tiny smile.

Steve stood up. "Fair enough. But tomorrow and Sunday I'm going to take you to the finest restaurant in London: agreed?"

"Agreed," said Sally.

An hour later they had finished their sandwiches. And when Steve suggested they go up to his bedroom, Sally explained that she was very tired after her long drive, and would rather sleep in a room of her own just for that night. Steve reluctantly agreed and said he would prepare one of the spare rooms for her.

When he left the drawing room, Sally reflected on what she was about to do. But there were so many conflicting thoughts galloping through her mind, she suspected that there was little chance of putting them in any kind of order. So, with a sigh of acceptance, she concentrated her efforts on admiring her fabulous surroundings.

"All ready," Steve said walking briskly in twenty minutes later. "But I'm afraid your room hasn't been used for quite some time. I wasn't expecting you to be sleeping alone tonight."

"I'm sorry," said Sally. "I am really tired after all that driving from Manchester. But tomorrow night will be a different matter."

"Then what can I say, but I'll show you to your room," said Steve. "Oh; I have taken your bags up already. And no, I didn't search them for any guns. So if you decide during the night to shoot me, well, all I can say is it serves me right for being so charmed by a beautiful assassin."

Sally followed as Steve led the way up the wide staircase. The landing had a pale blue shag pile carpet, and the walls were painted in cream and had various sporting prints lining them. Some of the prints looked very old and valuable to Sally.

"Here we are," said Steve, stopping at a panelled door that stood ajar. "Now, I have left you a little present on the bed; nothing too extravagant mind you, but I think you will like it. And before you refuse it, I promise that it wasn't bought from the proceeds of ill-gotten gains. It also doesn't commit you to anything. But if you still don't want it, I won't be offended."

"There was no need to buy me anything, but thank you," said Sally, relieved at the thought of sleeping by herself.

Steve kissed her on the left cheek. "You know something, Sally Mason, you deserve only the finest things money can buy. And if you ever get tired of that husband you have lumbered yourself with, then I'll be glad to see that you get them."

"Good night, Steve," Sally said, smiling. Then she entered the room and closed the door.

She looked around her. The room was huge, and against the far wall was a four-poster bed. The ceiling was heavy with plaster work of flowers and Greek vases, and the walnut writing desk situated by one of the two windows was one of the most beautiful pieces of furniture she had ever seen. The marble top dressing table looked old French, and the chair in front of it looked to Sally as if it would be equally well placed in a boudoir.

She then approached the bed.

The bed itself had a dark wood headboard, with elaborately carved vines and birds winding across it. There were pale green pillows and blankets, all edged with gold trim. The thick, duck feather quilt was clearly Chinese with stunning embroidered figures of a Mandarin surrounded by semi-nude figures carrying baskets of flowers.

"Oh my God," Sally couldn't help saying, "how beautiful!"

Then she focused her attention on the package sitting on the middle of the bed.

She sat next to it and picked it up.

It felt light.

The package was obviously a cardboard box of about one cubic foot in size. It was wrapped in shiny red paper with a dark pink ribbon tied in a bow.

Her mind buzzed with excitement as she slowly undid the ribbon.

She knew Steve Wilson; he obviously loved being flamboyant, and there was no way he would present her with anything cheap.

Diamonds in a tiny container, hidden in a large container for fun, came to her; but she tried to tell herself she couldn't accept them if that was what the gift was, and failed.

Finally the ribbon and paper were removed, and she was presented with a plain white box.

She pushed the wrapping paper well away from her and then stared at the box. A fierce and delicious anticipation heightened all the senses in her body and she didn't want to do anything to end it. There were so few moments like this in her life. But curiosity burned inside her just as fiercely.

The thought of pure silk underwear entered her mind for a moment, but she rejected that possibility. Surely Steve wouldn't be so obvious.

Then she took a deep breath.

It was time: the box had to be opened: she could resist no longer.

Lifting the lid and absentmindedly laying it down on the duvet, she looked inside.

She saw dark pink, tissue paper.

She slowly spread the paper, and the content of the box was finally revealed.

A puzzled expression appeared on her face.

She could see at once that it was of a dark material, and coarse, not like silk at all.

Tentatively she reached inside and lifted it out.

At first she thought it was a woollen scarf: but as she manipulated it, the awful truth hit her like a sharp blow across the face.

Her surroundings suddenly shot away from her at frightening speed, leaving her light-headed, with only the object staying in focus.

She screamed; dropped the balaclava and leaped from the bed.

"Surprise, surprise, bitch!" a sneering voice declared.

She spun around in terror.

Wilson was standing in the doorway and the hatred on his face was so terrible, for a split second Sally thought he was wearing a mask.

Wilson then walked into the room and closed the door behind him.

Sally took a few steps backwards, utter disbelief and shock squeezing her throat shut and paralyzing her vocal cords

"So there you stand, you whore!" Wilson growled. "And how I've waited to see you, just as you are; shaking with fear."

Sally's voice trembled when it returned. "I don't understand; what's going on, Steve?"

"Don't you use my first name, you bitch," Wilson roared, "or I'll tear your tongue out with my bare hands!"

The smile that then appeared on Wilson's now ugly face made him even more terrible looking. "You mean a clever bitch like you hasn't figured it out yet. Well, let me clarify the situation. I invited you here to kill you. Is that clear enough for your stupid little brain?"

"But you said you weren't going to hold it against me for what Andy tried to make me do?" Sally protested, trying to control her terror.

"I don't hold that against you," Wilson scoffed. "I tried to kill you before you had anything to do with Saunders. Remember that little accident at the station; the incident at that dive you call a home, and when you were passing that alley? That was me."

"You?" Sally cried in disbelief.

"The one and only," said Wilson, spreading his arms wide.

Confusion mingled with Sally's fear. "But why? What have I done to you?"

"What have you done to me!" Steve roared, and his hands clenched into fists. "I'll tell you what you've done to me, you fucking bitch! You took someone away from me; that's what you did; someone I loved more than any one or any thing in the whole stinking world. And you're going to pay for that."

Sally tried to understand what she was hearing, and watched as tears rolled down Wilson's face.

"But how could I have taken someone away from you?" she pleaded. "I don't know what you're talking about. You must have me mixed up with someone else."

Wilson suddenly marched towards the bed with long strides.

Sally gave a cry and retreated across the room.

Wilson picked up the balaclava from the bed.

He held it against his right cheek and his eyes closed in tenderness.

Then he opened them and glared at Sally.

"Do you know what this is?" he demanded.

"It's the balaclava you wore when you attacked me at home," Sally said in reply; her mind more focused on finding a way to escape the madman Steve Wilson had somehow become.

Fury returned to Wilson's expression. "Not just any balaclava, you stupid bitch. I had this one made from one of his jumpers that he left here. It was his favourite. He said it was only in this house; only in my company that he felt truly happy."

"What do you mean he?" Sally demanded, convinced now that there was some terrible mistake "What has some man you're involved with got to do with - ?"

Suddenly Sally couldn't catch her breath. "Oh my God! No," she gasped.

"That's just about what I said when I heard that you had killed my poor Robert," said Wilson. "He was the most beautiful man in the world and you took him away from me."

Deep down, somewhere beneath Sally's fear and disbelief something ignited, and soon it was a blazing furnace of outrage and injustice.

"He wasn't the most beautiful man in the world!" she screamed. "He was a monster. I spent the last year of our marriage being abused by him, so don't you go on about how wonderful he was."

Wilson's expression softened again and he smiled. "He didn't treat me like that; not a bit of it. He was warm, loving and kind. He put my feelings before his own every time."

"That's a load of crap!" Sally retorted. "He was a selfish, brutal human being who never gave a single thought for anyone but himself; I know; I have the scars if you want to see them."

"That's because you didn't understand him," Wilson replied, still smiling. "He was a tortured soul; trapped by convention into living a lie. That would have had a terrible effect on any man. But on someone as sensitive as Robert, it was devastating. Oh, I told him it didn't matter; that he should ignore what other people might say when they found out about him, but he wasn't strong enough to stand up to them, you see. He wouldn't have been able to hit back at their jibes: he just didn't have it in him."

"He had enough in him to send me to the hospital half a dozen times," Sally spat. "But that's because he was a coward as well as a bullying pig."

A condescending look appeared on Wilson's face. "How could you possibly know what he was. When he was with you he was someone else. All you ever saw was his tormented spirit battling his very soul for control of his true feelings. But I knew those feelings, because he and I were partners once: a long time before he met you. We started our own precious stones dealership in Knightsbridge: splitting the profits right down the middle. And we were good together, in any way that you could imagine. But Robert was very troubled by his homosexuality. He had kept it from me for nearly twelve years, before getting drunk one day and revealing his feelings for me. But even then he wouldn't give in to the way he really was, and begged me not to tell anyone. And all because a friend of his told him once that all such people should be rounded up and castrated. Shortly after his confession to me, he dissolved our partnership. All he was concerned with was appearing to be conventional. So he met you, and despite my protests he married you. But he never loved you. There was only one love in his life and that was me. He could never separate himself from that fact. And so for the last fifteen months of his sham marriage to you he used to spend a few glorious hours a week with me; here in this beautiful house."

"So that's where he used to be," said Sally. "I thought he was working late."

Wilson shook his head. "There was never any working late; only quality time with me. You were just a shield against the snide remarks he feared so much. But I knew that some day he would come here and never leave. He was suffering being married to you; it couldn't have gone on much longer."

"*He* was suffering!" Sally spat in outrage. "You must be joking."

"Yes!" Wilson shouted, his anger returning. "He was suffering the torment of spending his nights with someone he hated and detested the sight of. And to think he bought that house just so as he could find some woman to set up home with; so that his so-called friends could say, good old Robert, settling down with a wife like the rest of us normal, macho men. Well, he wasn't settled; he was miserable, and then you killed him; took away any chance I had of making him see sense. Oh, it took me a long while to recover enough to make the effort to track you down after you murdered him and sold his house, you thieving bitch. But I found you. And now I'm going to make you pay for what you did to Robert and me."

"You're crazy!" Sally declared. "Robert wasn't gay. If you knew the way he treated me in bed you'd realize that whatever kind of relationship he had with you, it couldn't have been a sexual one, whatever the two of you got up to!"

The ugliness returned to Wilson's face. "Liar!" he screamed. "You rotten, fucking liar."

"I'm telling you the truth," Sally screamed back. "And if you don't believe me, ask the doctors in the hospital. They warned me that whoever had caused some of my injuries was probably mentally disturbed; a potential rapist and a danger to all women."

"Liar. All lies!"

"Ask them. They'll tell you about your so-called lover. If anything he wanted women too much; in his own sick and perverted way, of course."

"You lying bitch!"

"Look, Steve," said Sally in a calmer voice, deciding on a change of tactics, "before we go any further with this madness, just tell me something will you? First of all you tried to kill me three times and then you invited me to your home: we even went out to dinner. It doesn't make any sense to me."

Some of the rage left Wilson.

His shoulders straightened and there was a smug air about him. "Yes: I suppose you should know how I manipulated you so successfully these past weeks. And yes, I did try and kill you three times. Of course normally I would have sent a professional to do the job, but I hated you more than anyone else in the world and so I had to be present at your death. I had to witness your suffering and your terror as the life left you. I wanted to feel the touch of your body as I strangled the life from it. But you have; or at least had a charmed life and you survived my clumsy attempts to achieve justice for Robert. However, just in time I realized that I was making a terrible mistake trying to make your death a swift affair when I could instead have it drawn out as you deserve; extracting every single ounce of agony you are capable of giving. And so I came up with a plan to build up your hopes of getting your fool of a husband free from my clutches, and then dashing those hopes for a future with him as viciously as you dashed mine with Robert. And now just to add a little more spice to my revenge I want you to know that when I have finished with you I'm going to hunt down your husband and put him to death just as painfully as I shall you in a few moments. So, does that answer your question?"

"You know I have left a detailed account of your drugs business at Mulville's, with a friend," said Sally. "So, if anything happens to me, you'll end up in prison for the rest of your life. And the last I heard the prison service doesn't supply chandeliers or butlers called Francis. You'll be just another drug dealer locked up in a tiny cell where he belongs."

A contemptuous laugh burst out from Steve. "You think you're very clever, don't you. Well, for your information all you have is the ravings of a woman who killed her former husband, and then, along with her second husband, involved herself with a drug gang before killing them also; along with an eighteen year old innocent. And then having tried to murder a second teenager, you both disappeared from the scene, leaving behind only anecdotal evidence of my involvement, simply in revenge for my rejection of your sexual advances."

"That's what you think," Sally replied, trying to hide her desperation. "But George is still alive, and I'll bet anything he'll tell the police the truth to get a lighter sentence."

"Not at all," said Steve clearly unfazed, "because George, just like Andy and young Dennis, was stabbed to death with an eight inch butcher's knife. So you see, Sally my love, in reality you have nothing to prevent me from killing you, which I am about to do now with the greatest of pleasure."

Suddenly Sally flew towards the door.

Wilson lunged at her as she passed him.

He grabbed her arm and swung her around.

She screamed when she was thrown across the room.

Her momentum sent her crashing into the dressing table.

She rebounded and fell to the floor in a daze.

Wilson rushed at her; dragged her to her feet and punched her in the stomach. Then he back-handed her again and again across the face. Her head rocked back and forth as each blow smashed into her.

Blood poured from her nose and mouth.

Her mind reeled in agony; her senses lost all coordination as the pounding against her face continued. Then she was tumbling towards blackness.

Wilson shook her. "Wake up, slag!" he screamed.

Then he shook her again. "Open your eyes, you fucking bitch."

Through blurred vision Sally saw a face of unadulterated hatred glaring back at her.

She tried to pull away.

He hit her again, this time with his fist.

The blow caught her on the chin.

Her legs buckled and she dropped to the carpet in a sitting position.

He kneed her in the face and she was thrown on to her back.

He stood over her, gloating at her suffering. Then he moved away, but he was back in seconds; the balaclava covering his face.

He dropped down astride her and his fingers slid round her throat.

Her mouth opened as he began to squeeze; cutting of her air.

A searing agony burst in her deprived lungs and she pounded at his face with her fists.

He ignored the blows, but relaxed his grip.

Oxygen poured into her lungs through hoarse coughing, and she stopped fighting back.

"Fun, isn't it," said Wilson. "And I wonder how many times someone can almost suffocate to death before finally dying. Let's find out, shall we."

Suddenly the pressure was around her throat again, and Sally renewed her resistance; pounding at his face.

This time Wilson cursed and grabbed her right hand. And ignoring the blows from her left fist, pushed it down on the carpet and knelt on it.

Seconds later both hands were secured.

For a moment, Wilson, breathing hard from the exertion, simply stared at his victim. Then he leaned down so that his covered face was only inches from hers.

"Now then, Sally," he growled. "I think it only fitting that your last breath should wash over something that was Robert's, don't you. So let's get your death over with and then I can go looking for your husband; not forgetting your parents, of course: abroad, aren't they."

Again Wilson's fingers tightened around her throat and the agony in her lungs returned.

Sally struggled with all the strength she had left.

But it was hopeless.

She was going to die at the hands of an insane killer and she was helpless to prevent it.

Wilson laughed with glee.

How good it felt to feel her body thrash beneath him.

How good to feel her filthy flesh beneath his fingers.

How good to at long last experience the revenge he craved.

Suddenly there was the sound of glass breaking, followed by a thud.

Wilson stared in confusion as a small rock rolled across the carpet in front of him.

He looked at the window behind the dressing table.

One of the panes had a large hole in it.

He climbed off Sally and approaching the window, looked down onto the drive.

It was dark out, but the external house lights were on.

The drive was empty.

He cursed, and throwing a quick glance at his semi-conscious victim, left the room. He locked the door behind him and then quickly made his way downstairs to the kitchen.

Picking up a large, stainless steel meat cleaver he went out on to the drive.

Having searched the front, he slowly made his way around to the back of the house where five acres of garden lay shrouded in darkness.

In the bedroom, oxygen began to revive Sally.

Slowly she got to her feet.

The effort sent agony tearing through her body, but she fought against it.

If she wanted to live she must get out of the house. But the stairs would be a mountain to descend and the front door seemed a mile away. How could she manage them?

Her face was on fire with pain and her throat felt like there was a spike stuck in it. She coughed to clear it, but the spike stayed.

Then the bedroom door slowly opened.

A scream welled up inside her, but shock dissolved it away.

"Sarah!" she gasped through battered lips.

Sarah rushed to her side. "We have to get out of here, Chuck. Can you walk; please say you can?"

Sally nodded. "My car keys; in my bag by the bed," she said, finding it difficult to speak.

But a quick search by Sarah proved futile. "Bastard," she growled, "he must have taken them."

Sarah then pulled Sally's right arm across her shoulders and together they stumbled towards the open door.

As they passed through, Sarah locked the door behind her and put the key in her pocket. "With a bit of luck he'll think he had the key with him," she said with a grin. "It just might buy us a few extra minutes."

With some difficulty, Sarah half carried her friend down the winding stairs.

"My bag!" Sally cried when it slipped from her grasp and dropped over the banister.

There was a loud crash when it hit the floor.

"Sorry, Chuck; have to leave it," said Sarah, "We've got a bit of a walk ahead of us. I couldn't risk bringing my car too near the house, so I left it outside the entrance. Thing is, I also left my own bag and mobile on the passengers seat, fool that I am. But don't you worry; we'll make it, and have that bastard locked up where he belongs."

"But my mobile is in my bag," Sally protested.

"Doubt it will still be working," said Sarah. "Can't spare the time to check. Wilson is probably on his way back by now."

Chapter Thirty Six

A cool breeze was blowing as Sally and Sarah left the house and set off along the winding drive, which was over four hundred metres in length: twisting and winding to allow maximum visual impact of the garden to visitors as they approached the house. However, to the fleeing women it was anything but a feature of beauty; more a passage through hell that had to be negotiated if they wanted to live. For at the end of it lay a main road and safety.

But when Sarah heard running feet behind her she quickly guided Sally into the bushes that lined the drive, and waited.

She cursed softly to herself.

She had hoped Wilson would spend a longer time searching the grounds. Now he was already back in the house. But would he be fooled by the missing key and spend time looking for it?

The two women then moved back on to the drive and set off at a stumbling run.

This tactic carried more risk, but they could make better time.

Suddenly Sally cried out and fell, dragging Sarah down with her.

Sarah jumped to her feet and pulled at Sally's arm. "Get up, Chuck: we have to keep going!"

"I can't, I can't!" Sally sobbed, her whole body limp with pain and exhaustion.

"Yes you can, Look; I think I can see the gates," Sarah lied. "Just one more big effort and we'll be safe."

"I tell you I can't!" Sally exclaimed through sobs, jerking her arm out of Sarah's grip.

Fury took hold of Sarah and she grabbed hold of her friend's arm again. "Get on your feet, damn you! I drove all this way to save you from your own stupidity. So get on your feet before I put the boot in as well. And don't think I won't do it, because I will. Now, get up, you fucking, lazy cow."

Sarah's harsh words cut through Sally's despair and she struggled to rise.

"That's it, Chuck; that's it: good girl," said Sarah, helping her.

But just as Sally managed to stand, they heard a scream of rage and frustration from the house.

Seconds later the sound of running feet was back.

"Oh shit; he's coming!" Sarah hissed.

Once more she took her friend into the bushes.

The footsteps grew quickly louder.

"Not a sound, Chuck," Sarah warned.

Then she saw Wilson run past their position.

She listened.

The footsteps began to fade, then stopped suddenly.

Sarah realized Wilson was probably looking around where he had stopped.

Now the footsteps were coming back; but slower. She could imagine him looking about, staring into the shrubbery, and behind the mature trees at the edge of the drive.

She retreated with Sally deeper into the bushes.

She held her breath as a shadowy figure passed slowly by; stopped; then came back. She could just about see his face through the leaves; sweat-covered and strained with a mixture of rage; desperation, and insanity.

Then Wilson ran in the direction of the road again.

Sarah struggled with her thoughts, trying to decide on the safest course of action. The only way off the property, as far as she knew, was along the drive and through the gates, because high railings separated the gardens from the outside world. And whereas she thought she could just about manage to climb over the railings if she had to, there was no way Sally would be able to in her condition. But how else could she reach the road?

The gravel was noisy under foot, but the front garden was extensively planted with shrubs and trees, and they made their own kind of noise when brushed against. Neither option offered much hope.

Then she decided to opt for the bushes. But she must wait for Wilson to return towards the house, or he might lay in ambush near the gates.

And when Wilson ran past them once more, Sarah waited for the footsteps to fade into silence before making her move.

"Ready to go, Chuck?" she said to Sally in a hushed voice.

Sally pulled herself free of Sarah's support.

She squared her shoulders and smiled. "As I'll ever be, Chuck."

"That's my girl," said Sarah in admiration. "We'll get out of this jungle yet. But keep it quiet: that bastard knows we must still be in the grounds"

Sarah then moved off slowly.

Sally followed, fighting her suffering.

Although her strength was returning slowly, the fire on her face continued to burn with full intensity. But that didn't matter now; only the dead never felt pain; it was sometimes the price of being alive.

As they moved through the vegetation, Sarah wondered what Wilson was doing. Had he gone back into the house to phone for help in catching them, or was he searching the garden? She needed to know.

Then the faint sound of leaves being brushed aside somewhere behind her answered her question.

She stopped.

"What's the matter?" Sally asked.

"Schhh!" Sarah hissed. "I think he's coming this way."

A sob of terror burst from Sally, but she suppressed a second with her fist.

"Get down," Sarah warned.

The two women crouched low with their backs to a giant holly bush.

The sound of vegetation being brushed grew louder and louder.

Suddenly, just twenty metres from their position, Wilson came into view between two rhododendrons.

They could only just make him out.

He stopped and peered around him.

The sky was filled with large, dark, rain-laden clouds, hiding a full moon. But there were gaps between the clouds and occasionally the garden filled with a soft glow. And then as the moon revealed itself in a blaze of unwanted light, Sally and Sarah retreated under the holly bush.

Needle-like thorns pierced their flesh but they ignored their torment.

The large meat cleaver in Wilson's hand glittered momentarily in the moonlight, and Sarah suppressed a gasp of horror. Whatever she had thought might happen if Wilson caught up with them, being hacked to death had not crossed her mind. It would be a terrible way to die.

Suddenly Wilson ran forwards in a crouching, almost primitive posture, and disappeared.

Sarah could hear his passage through the shrubbery.

Then there was silence.

"Let's get going, Chuck," she said after a few moments. "But no noise whatever you do. I can't tell where that maniac is."

Together, Sarah and Sally left their position and crept towards what they believed to be the way out. They avoided crossing patches of open ground, keeping to the cover provided by the numerous ornamental shrubs the garden contained.

Time passed and still there was no sign of the railings that bordered the property.

Sally sensed her friend's confusion. "Shouldn't we be there by now?" she asked.

"I can't understand it," said Sarah. "I was sure we were going the right way, but I think I've seen that tree over there, before. We must be going in circles."

"Oh my God; we're lost!" Sally cried, her voice rising.

"Stop that!" Sarah ordered. "We're not lost. I just need to recalculate where we are; that's all."

Even in the poor light, the terror in Sally's eyes was visible. "He's going to find me. I'm going to die, Sarah."

Sarah held Sally's shoulders in a strong grip. "Like hell you are! Even if I have to stay behind and confront that maniac by myself, you're getting out of this alive; understand?"

Sally simply stared back.

Sarah shook her. "I said; do you understand?"

Sally nodded.

"Good girl. Now, this must be one hell of a big garden, but it's still only a garden and sooner or later we're going to come across those gates. And all we have to do is stay hidden until then; ok?"

Again Sally nodded.

"Right then, let's get moving. It's getting near my bedtime, and I'm a right old grump next morning if I don't have a good night's kip."

Five minutes later Sarah spotted a large structure ahead. "Damn, where did that bloody thing come from?"

"You mean the greenhouse?" said Sally, confused by her friend's reaction.

"Yes, the greenhouse," Sarah growled. "It means we're behind the house instead of in front of it. Mind you, I might be able to find something in there to defend ourselves with. I'd like nothing better than to run that bastard through with any kind of fork."

Before Sally could protest, Sarah led the way to the fifty foot long Victorian greenhouse that had clearly seen better days. Many of the panes were cracked or broken, and the obvious, prolific wood rot that was destroying the ornate frame was a testimony to the structure's terminal decline.

With reckless regard for her safety, Sarah pulled open a creaking door and entered.

Sally followed.

Long rows of rotten shelving and stands were the only contents to be seen, except for a galvanized bucket lying on its side on the leaf-strewn, tiled floor.

"At least we won't go thirsty if we have to stay here until Christmas, Chuck," Sarah quipped, moving slowly past the bucket.

Suddenly she dragged Sally under one of the benches.

"Wilson!" she hissed. "Quiet."

Trying to hear above the loud pounding of her heart, Sally listened for the sound of approaching footsteps.

Only thin wisps of cloud were covering the moon, and Sally felt as exposed in the soft light as she had anywhere in the garden.

Then there was a sound above their position.

A shadow appeared on the other side of the greenhouse.

The shadow moved slowly left and right, like a Praying Mantis judging the distance to its unsuspecting prey. And a soft squeak of flesh on glass confirmed that Wilson was peering through.

Sally held her breath.

If he decided to come in and search, they would both die.

She stared at Sarah, and the fear in the woman's eyes almost panicked her. 'Dear God,' she prayed, 'don't let Sarah become as terrified as me or we will never get out of this terrible place.'

Then the shadow was gone.

Sarah put a finger to her lips to indicate silence.

This gesture and the disappearance of the shadow eased Sally's fear a little. Thank, God, Sarah was still in control.

For a further five minutes, the women stayed where they were, just in case Wilson was still watching.

And then it was time to go.

But as they left the greenhouse, Sally caught her left foot on a root and fell to the ground with a grunt.

Sarah dropped beside her. "Are you hurt?" she whispered.

Grimacing in pain, Sally reached for her ankle. "I don't know," she gasped. "Help me up."

Praying that Wilson wasn't rushing to the spot at that very moment, Sarah resisted a maddening impulse to drag Sally to her feet, instead supporting her weight as she attempted the task herself.

"It's not too bad," said Sally, standing once more. "Just slightly strained. I think I can walk by myself."

"All right," said Sarah reluctantly, "but if you need a rest before we get out of here, let me know. We will have to run for it once we're through the gates. My car is parked down the road a little."

Crouching as she moved through the grounds once more, Sarah led Sally to what she hoped would be the front of the property, and she silently berated herself.

How could she have got it so wrong. Yes, the house must sit on four or five acres, but even so, she usually had an instinctive sense of direction. Perhaps it was their situation that was confusing her, and the thought of having to rely on sheer luck to find the front gates was a trial she decided not to share with her fragile companion. She also decided to say nothing about seeming to pass every tree on the grounds at least three times.

Then the glow of street lights beckoned and her heart quickened in anticipation. "At last!" she declared.

She led Sally towards them, only a slight limp slowing the pace.

Soon metal railings came into view, but the street beyond looked wrong; it was too narrow.

An awful truth hit Sarah with stunning force. They were still in the wrong section of the garden.

She decided to keep this to herself.

"Listen, Chuck," she said to Sally who was clearly relieved by being at the railings. "The gates are very near here, but I'm not sure which way to go, so I'm going to go right. If I don't find them in three minutes, I'll come back and we'll try the other way together."

Sally's eyes were wide with terror. "You're not leaving me here on my own!"

"I'm sorry, but I have to, love," said Sarah, smiling to reassure her friend. "I can go much faster without you. Don't you see, you have to rest that ankle, and I have to find the exit. But don't worry, I'll be back for you one way or another. Now you listen out for Wilson and hide in that bush there if you hear him coming. He'll be the one moving about and making noise, not me, so you'll hear him first. And as long as you keep quiet he won't find you in this light. So chin up, Chuck, I won't be long."

Sarah didn't wait for an answer, and quietly slipped away.

Sally looked about her.

She felt so vulnerable and alone. Never in her whole life could she ever have imagined that a garden in a huge city could be such a lonely and terrifying place. Every bush could be concealing the deranged killer who was hunting her. Every movement of a leaf could mean that he was approaching.

She shivered in the cool night air; her thin clothing doing little to retain her body warmth.

A rustle to her right drew her instant attention.

"Sarah?" she whispered as loud as she dare.

There was no reply.

Instinctively she backed against the railings, desperately craving the false security offered by the street lights. But the chill contact of the metal against her body made her flinch and she moved away.

A change in the level of light caused her to look up at the sky. High winds were driving the clouds across it, revealing and then concealing the moon in a frightening game of confusion.

Something touched her left ankle.

She squealed and pulled away.

The hedgehog raised it's snout; wondering where it's new discovery had gone. Then it scuttled away in search of worms, slugs and beetles.

Sally let out a sigh of relief and returned to her watch for danger.

'Sarah; where are you?' she begged in her mind.

Then there was another rustle, but this time it was no caress of the breeze. This noise had strength behind it; but she couldn't tell which direction it came from.

Panic spurted up inside her and she felt sick.

She was desperate to run: but which way?

She might run straight into Wilson!

But if she stayed where she was; out in the open and exposed, he might creep up on her. He might be doing it now, keeping under cover until he was close enough to grab her.

Suddenly even bushes too small to conceal a grown man became a source of terror. And as powerful instincts finally overwhelmed the caution of her mind she took to her heels; desperately trying not to scream at the top of her voice.

Unthinking, she dashed across a patch of open ground and thought she could hear running feet behind her.

Desperate to look back but terrified by what she might see, she ran on, and straight into thick vegetation.

Spiky leaves stabbed at her flesh and she tried to push them away from her. But the leaves seemed to fight back; getting stronger and more determined. And somewhere in the recesses of the part of her mind not yet taken over by panic she realized that she was trying to pass through the heart of a mature holly bush.

She stopped fighting and backed out, her body covered in dozens of tiny puncture wounds.

The panic subsided and she looked about her once more.

She spotted a tall, bushy shrub nearby that didn't appear to be a spiky holly. She walked to it and pushed herself in between it's long, thin branches: a warm embrace of safety.

A cautious sigh of relief left her.

Then she sat on the soft earth to wait.

The minutes passed, or were they hours; Sally didn't know. She wasn't wearing a watch, and the experience of being attacked had wiped out her sense of time.

Then she saw something glittering; just ten metres in front of her.

She stared at it in fascination.

It seemed to be winking at her.

She almost laughed.

Then the glittering was gone.

But when a large shadow passed very close to where the glittering had been, she backed further into the bush, suppressing a cry of panic.

For a few minutes there was nothing but her anxiety and the gentle touch of the leaves as she adjusted her position.

Suddenly a dry twig snapped nearby.

She held her breath and listened.

There was only the soft sound of a breeze

Then she could hear the slow but heavy breathing of another living being.

Fear froze her mind, but her body began to shake.

Someone was standing very close to her position.

Was it Sarah or Wilson; she had to find out, but at what cost? If she called out she would give away her position. Was it worth the risk? Surely Sarah was looking for her by now, and probably fearful of calling out herself in anything above a strong whisper.

She listened intently for the whisper but she couldn't hear anything only that slow, regular breathing in; pause; out; pause; in; pause; out - an unnaturally long silence between each breath: either the breathing of a listening hunter or a listening friend. How could she tell which?

Indecision raged inside her; what to do, what to do?

Maybe she should risk calling first?

Sarah might be too frightened to speak and was at this very moment desperately waiting for a sign she was still alive. It was probably Sarah. After all, Wilson couldn't afford to just stand about when for all he knew she had escaped and the police were already on their way. And the unknown person breathing was standing still, of that she was certain.

Then she made up her mind.

"Sarah?" she whispered. "Is that you, Sarah?"

The breathing stopped.

She listened for a moment, then whispered again; a little louder this time. "Sarah?"

A soft chuckle drove the realization of her mistake through her heart like a spike.

"I knew you were in there somewhere, bitch."

The voice was Wilson's, but changed by being laced with insanity. "And now that I have an idea where, we can have a bit of fun, can't we."

Sally suppressed a scream when she heard the branches to her immediate right moving.

"Not in here?" said the voice. "Well then, what about; here?"

Sally's gasped when a hand hovered over her head; the fingers twitching, spider-like.

'Run! Run! Run!' her instincts screamed.

"Naughty, Sally," said Wilson, and the hand withdrew. "All I want to do is cut you up a little and you keep hiding from me. But I think I know where you are now, little girl. And; what's this;

I can see you, sitting on the ground like a little frightened rabbit Do you believe I can see you, Sally, my love? Can you see me? Maybe you can't see me; reaching in for you? Are you ready, because my hand is coming closer and closer."

Sally pressed her body back against the trunk of the bush. It felt as hard as the wall of a building

Her heart pounded in her chest, and her breath wheezed through her damaged throat. Waves of panic wound her body tighter than twisted cables - trying to send her dashing out into the open with its awesome power.

She knew she had trapped herself.

There was no way out of the bush but forwards.

Then she decided to obey her instincts; to make a run for it.

Gathering herself like a one hundred metre sprinter, she made ready. If she was fast enough, she might take Wilson by surprise; give herself a head start.

But a tall, dark shape appearing directly in front of her cancelled her dash for safety.

"Got you!"

The shape rushed at her.

She screamed.

Her hair was grabbed.

She screamed again and struggled, but irresistible strength began to drag her from her sanctuary.

"Out; out!" Wilson barked.

The grip on her hair forced her to obey.

Then she was standing face to face with him.

Wilson's evil-looking, sweat-covered face glared at her with insane eyes.

"Don't hurt me, please!" she sobbed.

"I'm going to do more than just hurt you!" Wilson spat. "See this."

Sally stared at his right hand and almost passed out when she saw the huge, meat-cleaver in it. "Oh, no - no! You can't, Steve, you can't."

"There isn't anything I wouldn't do to you for what you did to me and Robert, you fucking bitch."

Sally looked wildly about her as Wilson then raised the cleaver high. "Sarah; Sarah!" she screamed.

Wilson lowered the cleaver. "Wondering where your friend is?" he sneered. "Well; how can I put this in a delicate fashion. She's over there by the pond and she's over there by the statue and over there on the drive. Because you see, Sally, it all depends on which part of her you're wondering about. But never mind, you won't care for long."

A sob of grief left Sally's lips, and suddenly she wasn't afraid any more. Sarah was dead; she had sacrificed her life trying to save her. Her husband had killed two people and was being hunted by the police and they both would almost certainly be implicated in the deaths of Andy Saunders and George. Their happiness was gone forever, so what was the point of living any longer.

Wilson, now with his left hand holding Sally by the right wrist, and the cleaver held in his right hand, saw the fear leave his captive.

He became infuriated. "What's this!" he roared. "You think you won't suffer because you've given up, you bitch. Well, you can still suffer pain. So let's see how you feel after I do this to you."

The cleaver was raised high once more.

Sally closed her eyes and prepared herself.

A terrible, prolonged, almost inhuman scream tore apart the silence of the garden.

Wilson's head spun round.

A figure was flying at him.

He let go of Sally and turned to meet it.

The figure crashed into him.

Claws raked his face and he fell back against Sally; lost his balance and tumbled to the ground.

The figure crashed down on top of him.

The cleaver slipped out of his grasp.

His face was clawed again.

Strips of skin and flesh were torn away.

He grabbed desperately at the fury that threatened to overwhelm him with raw power, and caught hold of its two arms.

He twisted the arms violently and the weight was gone from him, but a head-butt in the face made him let go.

"Run, Sally!" Sarah shouted.

Suddenly the two women were tearing across the garden.

A chance to live drove the weariness from Sally and she kept up with her friend.

"Where are we going?" she asked, when Sarah finally slowed the pace.

"Just anywhere, for now," came the curt reply. "I couldn't find those damn gates. Now, let's get going."

They ran on for a while longer. Then Sarah called a halt.

Crouching down amongst a huge clump of Dogwoods, they caught their breaths.

Sally stared at her friend.

She hardly recognized the harsh-looking face that portrayed fear but also determination.

"You ok, Chuck," said Sarah, wiping a small patch of blood from her forehead and examining her red-stained fingers.

"You're hurt?" said Sally in alarm.

"Naaa; it's that bastard's blood," Sarah replied, wiping her fingers on a few leaves.

"He said he had killed you," said Sally, tears welling up in her eyes.

Sarah grunted with contempt. "He was probably trying to extract every bit of suffering from you he could. I don't know what you did to him. Chuck, but you sure pissed him off."

Wilson running across their vision silenced Sally's reply.

"Christ; doesn't that crazy bastard ever give up," Sarah went on when Wilson disappeared. "He's more persistent than a bloody tomcat during the mating season."

"What are we going to do?" said Sally. "You won't be able to catch him off guard again."

"Too right there, Chuck," said Sarah grinning. "Fun while it lasted, though. And he's not so pretty now, is he. Anyway, better get going, I suppose."

"But which way?" Sally protested.

"Take your pick," Sarah answered. "One way is as good as another in this crazy place."

But as Sarah stood up, she immediately dropped down again.

"What's the matter?" said Sally.

"Schhh!" Sarah's finger was at her lips.

Sally then heard footsteps approaching.

Both women settled lower into the shrubs.

Then the footsteps moved away, and they relaxed.

A couple of minutes later a terrible squeal of protesting metal assaulted the silence of the garden.

"What's that?" Sally cried, looking wildly about her.

"Damn him and his cleverness," said Sarah. "He's closing the gates by hand instead of returning to the control switch in the house. He'll be listening out for that racket now; damn him."

"What are we going to do?" Sally begged. "We're trapped."

"But we're not dead yet," said Sarah. "For now we better just concentrate on keeping away from him."

"But we can't do that forever," said Sally. "Sooner or later we will make a mistake."

Then she winced.

Sarah frowned. "Your ankle playing up?"

Sally massaged it. "It's just a bit swollen."

"Then you better rest it for a while. But be ready to run if I give the word."

Sally nodded.

For a few moments the two women sat in silence, each giving in to their thoughts.

Suddenly there was a soft thud.

Sarah's right hand shot across Sally's mouth, cutting of her response.

There was another thud; this time further away.

"What's that noise?" Sally asked in a whisper, when Sarah let go.

"I don't know," said Sarah, listening as the thuds continued.

Then the answer came to her.

"He's throwing rocks; trying to flush us out," Sarah whispered. "He must be getting really desperate."

The sound of something falling through branches in the distance confirmed Sarah's interpretation.

She grimaced. "Don't worry, Chuck. With a bit of luck he'll give up and go back to the house. I don't know about him but I would sell my soul for a glass of water right now."

Another crash of vegetation to their right proclaimed that their attacker was still searching for them.

"That will only tire him out quicker," said Sarah. "All we have to do is outlast him."

"Come out, you bitches!" Wilson's voice shouted. "Come out or I'll burn every bit of vegetation in this garden until I find you."

"Not a chance," Sarah said hurriedly when she saw panic rise in Sally's eyes. "He won't risk leaving the front of the garden uncovered.

But when something flew into the thin branches above Sally's head and then dropped on to her back, a piercing shriek shot from her.

"Shit; time to go!" Sarah ordered.

And as they bolted from concealment, Wilson was already running towards them, an inhuman smile of glee on his face.

"This way, Chuck!"

Sarah grabbed Sally's hand and they headed away from the approaching Drug Baron.

Sally struggled to keep up.

Her lungs felt raw, and a throbbing ache invaded her ankle.

She knew the madman was close behind, and catching up.

His footsteps were getting louder.

She could hear his grunting efforts and imagined she could feel the cold touch of the meat cleaver against her back.

"Run faster," Sarah ordered.

On and on they ran: ploughing through bushes, with no idea if the next one would be the one to bring them down.

Trees and bushes flew by as they tried to increase the distance between themselves and Wilson. But it was clear that he was constantly gaining on them.

"It's no good, Sarah!" Sally cried.

"Yes it is; just keep running."

"I can't!"

"Don't you fucking dare give up now!" Sarah threatened through her gasps. "I'd rather kill you myself than that bastard get you."

But when Sally suddenly stumbled and fell," Sarah cursed and stopped.

She helped her up. "Head for the house and phone the police," she ordered.

Instantly, Sally ran on; the lights from the house visible through the trees. And she begged God for her friend's life.

A roar of utter hatred blasted out of Wilson as he bore down on Sarah.

She stood her ground as, cleaver held high, he came at her.

She threw herself aside when the blade swung towards her head.

Then to her horror, Wilson continued on after Sally.

"No!" she screamed, taking off after him.

But it soon became clear he was faster. He would reach Sally before she got to the house.

Continuing to give chase, she desperately scanned the ground for a weapon. Then she spotted a circle of small, smooth rocks.

She stopped, grabbed one of the rocks and threw it with all her strength at the receding figure of Wilson.

He stumbled when the missile hit him square on the back.

For a single moment she thought he would go down, with something inside him damaged.

But her hopes vanished when he recovered his balance and turned in her direction.

"Want some more, you bastard!" Sarah snapped. "Then come and get me, you ugly piece of shit."

Wilson raised the cleaver and took a single step towards her.

Then he stopped and turned away.

"How's your face, Stevie," Sarah cooed contemptuously. "I enjoyed ripping half of it off, but I'll probably be picking bits of your rotten skin out from under my fingernails for the next few months."

Sarah saw Wilson's body stiffen. Then suddenly he was running for the house again.

Cursing, Sarah ran after him.

But when he reached the house, Sarah, just ten metres behind, was puzzled to see him run past the open front door and on to the end of the building.

Her mind reeled with confusion. Surely Sally had gone inside to use the phone? Or had she, for some inexplicable reason, decided to go round the back?

Undecided whether or not to follow Wilson, Sarah stood by the doorway to think.

Then she made up her mind.

As soon as she entered the house, she risked calling out. "Sally?"

"Up here, Sarah," came the faint reply.

Taking the stairs two steps at a time, Sarah soon joined Sally on the landing.

They moved further along, then stopped.

"Did you phone the police?" Sarah demanded.

A puzzled expression appeared on Sally's face. "I started to, but the line went dead as I was dialling, for some reason."

"So that's why he made straight for the end of the building; to cut the outside telephone cables," Sarah growled. "There are probably a dozen or more rooms with phones in a house like this. He wouldn't have been able to search them all in time."

"Then he knows I came in here," said Sally, her panic returning.

"Keep an eye out for him," Sarah ordered and she rushed towards one of the far bedrooms.

And as she came back two minutes later, Sally saw Wilson coming slowly in through the front door. He looked weary, and his face was smeared with blood.

"This way," Sarah whispered, and Sally followed through the door just behind.

Holding it an inch ajar, Sarah peered out towards the top of the stairs.

She suppressed a gasp when the top of Wilson's head appeared.

Then she gently closed the door and turned to Sally. "No noise now, Chuck. He has two rooms to check before this one. I hope to God my timing is right."

"Timing for what?" said Sally.

"Schhh!" Sarah hissed when the sound of footsteps from the landing reached them.

Listening intently both women heard Wilson searching first one room, then the second. And he made little attempts at stealth since they heard a great deal of crashing about.

Suddenly a terrible desire to make a run for the stairs overtook Sally.

She reached for the door handle, but a strong hand grabbed hers.

Sally winced at the pressure.

"Keep calm," Sarah warned.

But when it became clear that Wilson was approaching their hiding place, Sally began to struggle, trying to free herself from her friend's restraining hold.

Silently, Sarah used her superior strength to resist Sally's efforts.

Then there was a distance noise, and Wilson shot past their room and along the landing.

Instantly, Sarah released Sally. And opening the door she poked her head out.

Then she looked at Sally. "Quick, Chuck; time to go," she ordered.

Together the too women left the room and quickly made their way down the stairs.

And as they left the house roars of anger followed them.

Once more they were making their way through the shrubbery.

"Oh God, what are we doing out here again," Sally moaned. "We can't keep on like this, Sarah. I would rather try reasoning with him than spending any more time in this terrible garden. I'm exhausted."

"I'm not giving up," Sarah stated, leading the way around a Japanese Maple.

"Then you keep looking for the gates," Sally offered. "I'll confront Wilson and keep him occupied. Maybe you could get back with the police in time."

"No!" Sarah snapped. "We're both getting out of this; understand?"

Sally reached for her friends right shoulder.

Sarah stopped and turned.

"Listen," said Sally, "I know how you feel, but I'm too tired to go on with this. You don't understand why he hates me so much, but I do. And I think I can use it against him, at least for a little while. I know I can get him to talk about it. And I can tell him you decided to lay low in the garden until daylight. He might believe that."

Sarah's expression was hard; almost fierce. "No. I came here to stop you doing something stupid, but I was too late. Well, this time you're going to listen to me."

"But it's my life and my decision," Sally declared.

"That's where you're bloody wrong!" Sarah hissed. "Now, you have two choices, Chuck. You can do as you're told, or, so help me, I'll lay you out and carry you: which is it going to be?"

For a few moments Sally search her friend's eyes for sincerity. She saw it. Then she nodded.

"Good," Sarah grunted. "Now let's find those bloody gates."

Five minutes later, Sarah stopped by a mature Ash.

There was a strange expression on her face.

"What's the matter?" Sally asked, looking fearfully around.

"No wonder we have been wandering around this bloody place for ages!" Sarah spat. "The grounds at the front of the house have been planted exactly the same as the back; every shrub; every tree, and even their positions duplicated.

"But why would anyone do that?" Sally asked.

Sarah shrugged. "Probably some Ying and Yang rubbish. Who knows and who cares. What is important is that I found out. Now I can find the way out."

But seconds later the running figure of Wilson sent them scurrying for cover, down behind a patch of Dogwood.

"That bastard is really beginning to get on my tits, now," Sarah said when he disappeared from sight.

"Maybe he'll give up," Sally offered.

"Lunatics don't have the sense to give up, Chuck. They have to be stopped. Now, stay here."

"Where are you going!" Sally cried in alarm, as Sarah stood up.

"I just thought of something," said Sarah hurriedly. "I'll be back in a sec. But don't move whatever you do. I need to know exactly where you are when I come back."

"But what if you don't come back?" Sally protested.

"I will, Chuck; don't you worry," said Sarah, grinning,

"But if you don't. How long should I wait?"

"Count to five hundred," said Sarah. "Then do what you think best."

"Let me come with you?" Sally begged, the thought of being by herself, terrifying.

"Sorry, Chuck; you'll only slow me down with that ankle of yours."

Then she set off in a crouching run, leaving a bewildered and very frightened Sally alone with her thoughts.

Chapter Thirty Seven

Steve Wilson prowled his extensively planted garden like a leopard patrolling its territory.

His senses of sight and hearing were tuned to the slightest sounds of footsteps and rustling vegetation. He was desperate to find Sally Cooper; not because he feared she would run to the police if she escaped: that prospect held no concern for him now, but to satisfy an overpowering desire for revenge. He hated the woman so much that he could actually taste it when he spoke her name. She had to die no matter what the cost, and he would willingly burn his mansion to the ground with all its treasures in it, to achieve that.

The bitch was still on the grounds; of that he was certain. For in his cleverness he had created a few small mounds of gravel across the entrance, and so far they had not been disturbed.

The top of the railings surrounding his property were unusually sharp, and he doubted very much anyone could scale them without some form of thick padding. And since the women didn't have any padding, they would be left with no option but to try to escape through the gates.

He was confident of catching them eventually. It was only a matter of time before the cleaver in his hand was coated with the blood of the bitch who had killed Robert, and her friend.

At the thought of this stranger to him, the fingers of his left hand gently probed his ruined face. Never in his life had he experienced such rage and fury from another human being, and it shocked him, most of all because it was easily a match for his own. He would have to be very careful of Sally Cooper's protecter.

The sky was still playing games with the light as Wilson continued his search. One second the grounds were in almost total darkness; then they would be illuminated by a pearl-coloured glow that had an incandescent quality about it.

Wilson loved these conditions, for they were conditions suitable for hunting: revealing one moment, concealing the next. And in his heart he realized that never again would he experience such a night.

It was as Wilson walked past a bed of stately hollyhocks that something caught his eye.

He froze.

Someone was moving past a small group of young Lime trees.

He shielded his eyes from the moon's glare, and suddenly his heart pounded in his chest with excitement: Sally Cooper!

He dropped low to the ground.

At last he had her; but there must be no more rescues; no more escapes. Her debt to him was far too long overdue. It was time she paid it.

He watched as Sally slowly passed one tree after another. He could tell she was confused and frightened, for she occasionally stopped and looked about her; even giving little starts of alarm, though there was no one nearby to harm her - except for him.

"Poor, frightened little girl," Wilson whispered to himself. "Are you all alone. Have you lost your friend."

Then, to Wilson's delight, he saw Sally change direction, and begin walking directly towards him.

His excitement grew. Justice was clearly on his side.

He crouched lower, his fingers tightening and loosening around the handle of the cleaver.

Nearer and nearer came Sally, despite her fear and caution, walking across open ground.

And Wilson waited for her; his body trembling in anticipation. But he must time his attack perfectly: too soon and she would run, and he had had enough of the chase. He needed to see the life leaving her body; that need could be denied no longer.

Then it was time.

But just fifteen metres from the Hollyock patch, Sally stopped.

Did she sense his presence?

Were long dormant instincts awakened; heightening primitive senses?

Wilson licked his lips and held his breath.

Sally took another couple of steps, then stopped again, her hands held away from her body, and her eyes peering into the gloom.

Wilson shot from his position.

Sally screamed and turned to run; but it was too late.

Wilson raised the cleaver as he reached her.

Suddenly something slammed against the back of his head.

He grunted, and dropped to the ground.

"Got ya, you fucking, bastard!"

Sarah stood over the prone body of Wilson, a spade handle, minus its blade, held in her right hand. "Never even entered your arrogant head that we might set you up; did it, you murdering scumbag."

Then she raised the handle to strike again.

"Sarah - don't!" Sally begged.

Sarah glared at Sally. "We have to finish him. He'll only come after you again when he wakes up."

"Please, Sarah, I don't want you killing someone for me. I don't want any more deaths on my conscience"

"Sod your fucking conscience," Sarah growled. "This bastard put us both through hell, and that's where I'm going to send him."

"We can go straight to the police:" Sally said hurriedly, "explain everything to them. If you want to you can tie him up until the police arrive. He couldn't have expected it to end like this, and I'm sure there must be some incriminating evidence still in his house no matter how careful he was."

Frustrated, Sarah kicked Wilson in the stomach. "I'd rather finish the bastard and have done with it. But if that's how you feel, then, ok, it's your show, Chuck. Now, you go back to the house and look for something to tie him up with. If you can't find any string or tape, clingfilm will do so long as there's a roll of it."

The prospect of being alone alarmed Sally and it showed on her face.

"I have to stay here in case he comes round, Chuck, and give him another cavewoman's love-tap, or six," Sarah explained in a gentle tone and smiling. "Now, go on; you'll be ok,"

A powerful kick suddenly whipped Sarah's legs from under her.

She hit the ground with a jarring thud.

Wilson climbed to his feet.

He dragged Sarah back up by the wrists.

She spat in his face before shouting at Sally to run.

Wilson shook her violently and her head snapped back and forth. "Quite the wildcat, aren't you. But you have just earned yourself the death I promised the other whore."

He then released his right hand, and making a fist, jabbed it straight into Sarah's face.

Her head snapped backwards and blood spurted from her nose.

"Fucking bitch!" Wilson growled, punching her again.

Then three more punches followed and Sarah's legs buckled.

And when she went down, he kicked her in the stomach, doubling her up.

"Slag," he muttered, staring down at her. "Interfering slag. This is what -"

Wilson's words were cut short at the same instant that there was a dull thud.

He slowly turned to see Sally staring at him with a strange look on her face.

Then he reached behind his back; felt the cleaver and pulled it out.

Holding it in front of his face, he stared at the small, red stain of blood on the tip of the blade.

"You fucking bitch!" he grinned. "You have about as much strength as a three year old."

Then he raised the weapon,

Suddenly his hair was grabbed from behind and the cleaver was pulled from his grasp.

Instantly he jabbed his right elbow backwards and felt it drive into soft tissue.

Sarah collapsed in agony.

Wilson turned and placed his foot on Sarah's throat.

"I laughed when I stuck the carving knife in him!" Sally declared.

Wilson stared at her, his foot still on Sarah.

"That's right," Sally went on. "I didn't have to stab him a second time, but I wanted to. And do you know why, Steve, because he was conscious; pleading for me not to kill him. And I enjoyed that. I enjoyed listening to his begging. But then I got bored and finished him off like you do some rabid dog."

The expression on Wilson's face was so terrible as Sally's words tore at his insides, that he no longer seemed human.

He took his foot of Sarah's throat and turned his body to face Sally.

And as a roar of pure hatred shot from his mouth, Sally suddenly flew at him, her fingers curved into claws.

But Wilson was fast.

He grabbed her by the throat, with both hands, to keep her nails from his face.

"Not this time," he laughed.

Then he squeezed.

Sally tried to pull away from him, but his fingers were like iron.

Once again she found herself struggling to breathe.

His strength was terrible; squeezing the life out of her.

Her flaying fists plummeted uselessly inches from his face.

His long and powerful arms kept her helpless.

Her legs give way but his crushing hands followed her down; easing her slowly to her death.

A cry of rage from behind startled him.

He let go, and turned, just as something came towards his head.

He raised his right arm defensively.

The cleaver sliced through his shirt and deep into his flesh.

He screamed and moved backwards; tripping over Sally, but recovering his balance.

Sarah, her face covered in blood, followed, the cleaver held ready to strike again.

Wilson saw the spade-handle on the ground and grabbed for it.

Sarah swung the cleaver.

The blade caught him across the chest, just as he picked it up. It fell from his grasp.

A huge, red stain discoloured the front of his white shirt.

Desperately he tried for the cleaver, but the blade cut open the palm of his right hand.

He screamed again and retreated. "Please - don't!"

But Sarah was in a killing frenzy now, advancing and swinging the cleaver before her in a deadly arc. Her expression was no longer human, displaying only the primitive: the heart of a savage beast: incapable of mercy.

Blood poured from gaping wounds in Wilson's hands and arms as he staggered away from his attacker.

A blow took the flesh from his forehead and another sliced through his right ear.

Still screaming he turned to run.

But Sarah was ready.

Roaring her hatred she brought the blade down on his back again and again; chopping through bone, flesh and sinew with the power of a butcher's arm.

Wilson gave one last gurgling cry, then fell forward, hitting the grass-covered ground with a soft thud.

"Get up from that, you fucking bastard!" Sarah panted breathlessly, her eyes glowing as she stood over the body. "Get up from that."

For a few moments the two women stared silently at Wilson's motionless form.

Then Sarah placed the cleaver on the ground, and using a tuft of grass, wiped the handle clean. Then she stared at the body again and spat blood from her damaged mouth, on it.

"You mess with my friends, you bastard, you mess with me," she said in a low voice; her rage reluctantly beginning to ebb.

She approached Sally who was transfixed by the body. "You ok, Chuck?"

Sally nodded.

"Glad to hear it," said Sarah. "And you did good. He would have finished me if you hadn't done what you did."

Sally continued staring.

"Right then, let's get away from this place before I throw up," Sarah ordered. "The bastard caught me a few good ones, but not good enough. I never did stay down for long, even when some bloody great bully at school was trying to punch my lights out. Mind you, I'll need a visit to the dentist: a couple of my front teeth are loose. And I think he broke my nose as well. Mind you, the doctors can probably do a better job on it than nature did: they definitely can't do any worse."

"Thanks for helping me," said Sally, finally able to look away from Wilson.

Sarah grinned. "Think nothing of it, Chuck. Us girls can give as good as we get when we're pushed too far, and we have to stick together against the bastards of this world, you know."

Sarah then searched Wilson's pockets and found the key's to Sally's car. But when they returned to the house for Sally's things, they discovered Wilson had removed the spark-leads from the engine.

Side by side the two women made their way along the drive, towards the gates. "You do realize that you and Jimmy will have to go into hiding?" said Sarah.

"Yes, I know," Sally sighed.

"Well, don't you worry about it, Chuck. The two of you can stay with me for as long as you like. And as to the future, that won't be a problem. A friend of mine can provide you with new identities. He does this kind of work for people in the Witness Protection Programme, so the two of you won't have any problems getting new identities. Rob and me used to live together until I threw him out. But he'll do anything for me because he's been pestering me for years to take him back. And you know something, Chuck, I have been getting a bit lonely these past few months and this would be a good opportunity to do something about it. And since all your calls to me have been from a kiosk, there's no way I'll get a serious visit from the police."

"So why did you follow me down here?" Sally asked.

Sarah smiled. "If you think I was going to stand by and let my best friend walk into danger like that, then you sure don't know me, Chuck. I was against you going to stay with Wilson, in the first place. But hey, as my grandmother used to say, 'A friend who thinks she's a parent to her friend doesn't stay a friend for long,' so I had to accept that it was your decision to make. But an hour after you left my place it was on the news that someone called William Bennifield died with his family in a house fire last night and that an employee of Mulville's was found dead in his bath. I realized then that Andy Saunders had been right about Wilson. And I knew it would be a waste of time phoning you. You were hell bent on going through with that weekend. So I had no choice but to follow you down here. Good job too. Anyway, I hung around outside the house. I saw the bedroom light go on. I heard a scream but then I heard you and Wilson talking. I couldn't hear what was being said, but when the talking turned to more screaming and there was some crashing about, I knew it was time to act. So, I found a rock small enough to throw and flung it through the window. I prayed to God it wouldn't hit you. Wilson left the front door open when he came out to investigate, and the key in the bedroom door; luckily for us. And the rest, as they say, is history."

"But how did you manage to distract him on the landing?" Sally inquired.

Sarah gave a proud swing of her head. "I guessed all the bedrooms must have on suite bathrooms in a mansion like that, and I was right. Luckily I managed to find a large glass bottle of bath crystals, and I hung it from the shower head so that it would make a bit of noise when it dropped on to the ceramic base."

"But what did you tie it with and what did you use as a timer?" Sally asked incredulously.

"Why, nothing more than good old loo paper, and a bit of ingenuity, of course, my dear Watson," Sarah quipped, smiling with pride. "You see, I carefully tied one end of the paper around the bottle and hung it from the shower head. Then I tied the other end of the length of paper to one of the sink taps, leaving a few inches to hang down into the basin as a wick."

Sally smiled also. "Then you put the plug in the basin, and turned on the other tap so that the basin filled slowly. And when the wick soaked up the water as far as the knot around the tap, the knot lost its strength and the bottle dropped."

"Elementary, my dear Watson," Sarah replied. "And now I remember why I chose you as my associate. Anyway, what was it all about? Didn't Wilson trust you to keep your mouth shut about his business, or something?"

"It wasn't that," said Sally, her expression serious. "He and Robert were lovers and he wanted revenge on me for killing him."

Sarah stopped dead in astonishment. "What? You mean your Robert was -"

"It's a long story," said Sally.

"Oh good," said Sarah, walking beside Sally once more. "But wait until we get home, will you, Chuck, because I like nothing better than a mug of cocoa in front of a coal fire, and a good old chin-wag with my very best friend."

THE END

Lightning Source UK Ltd.
Milton Keynes UK
13 June 2010

155422UK00001B/51/P